Events Leading to the Battle of Shiloh

February 4, 1862: General Ulysses S. Grant (US) begins operations ~~~ ˙ ˙ the river forts Henry, on the Tennessee River ~~ ˙ ˙ junction between the Tennessee and Cur

February 4, 1862: Admiral Foote (US) beg ~~~ e to Fort Henry on the Tennessee River.

February 6, 1862: General Ulysses S. Grant (US) captures Fort Henry on the Tennessee River without firing a shot.

February 12–16, 1862: General Ulysses S. Grant (US) begins a siege of Fort Donelson on the Tennessee River.

February 13, 1862: General John B. Floyd (CS) assumes command at Fort Donelson.

February 14, 1862: General P. G. T. Beauregard (CS) begins to concentrate all available Confederate forces in his department at Corinth, Mississippi.

February 15, 1862: General John B. Floyd (CS) orders a breakout of Fort Donelson, which fails; General Nathan B. Forrest (CS) marches out of Fort Donelson under cover of night rather than surrender with his brigade of cavalry.

February 16, 1862: General John B. Floyd (CS) turns command of Fort Donelson over to General Gideon Pillow (CS) and slips away; Pillow surrenders Fort Donelson to General Ulysses S. Grant (US).

February 23, 1862: General Albert S. Johnston (CS) assumes immediate command of the Confederate Department of the West.

February 23–25, 1862: Nashville, Tennessee, is evacuated by the Confederates and occupied by General Don C. Buell's (US) Army of the Ohio.

March 5, 1862: General Henry W. Halleck (US) relieves General Ulysses S. Grant (US) of command of the expedition into Tennessee, putting General Charles F. Smith (US) in command.

March 5, 1862: General Braxton Bragg's (CS) forces begin entering Corinth, Mississippi. He begins organizing his own forces, plus newly arriving regiments, into brigades and divisions.

March 6, 1862: General P.G.T. Beauregard (CS) officially assumes command of all Confederate troops in Corinth, Mississippi.

March 14–17, 1862: Tennessee Expeditionary Corps (soon to be christened the Army of the Tennessee, General C.F. Smith (US) commanding) expedition from Savannah, Tennessee, to Yellow Creek, Mississippi, and occupation of Pittsburg Landing, Tennessee.

March 14, 1862: General Don C. Buell's (US) Army of the Ohio ordered to cooperate in conjunction with C. F. Smith's (US) expedition encamped at Pittsburg Landing on the Tennessee River.

March 15, 1862: General P. G. T. Beauregard (CS) reports to General Albert S. Johnston (US) that he has concentrated 44,000 men of all arms at Corinth, Mississippi.

March 17, 1862: General Ulysses S. Grant (US) is ordered to Pittsburg Landing to take command of forces consolidating there under C. F. Smith (US).

March 18, 1862: General Don C. Buell's (US) Army of the Ohio reports three divisions at Columbia, Tennessee, 100 miles from Pittsburg Landing, Tennessee, and slowed by heavy rains, high water, and bridge repair.

March 22, 1862: General Albert S. Johnston's (CS) Confederate force from Bowling Green, Kentucky, arrives at Corinth, Mississippi. Johnston assumes command of the Army of Mississippi (CS).

March 28, 1862: General Don C. Buell's (US) Army of the Ohio's 6th Division is ordered to resume marching toward Pittsburg Landing, Tennessee.

March 29, 1862: The Confederate armies of Kentucky and Mississippi are consolidated under the latter designation, General Albert S. Johnston (CS) commanding and General P. G. T. Beauregard (CS) second in command. Generals Leonidas Polk, Braxton Bragg, James Hardie, and George Crittenden are assigned to the First, Second, Third, and Reserve Corps, respectively.

April 3, 1862: The Confederate Army of Mississippi marches out of Corinth, Mississippi, after dark, six hours later than intended.

April 4, 1862: General Leonidas Polk's (CS) Corps encamps for the night 10 miles from Corinth, Mississippi, owing to incessant rain, narrow roads, and inexperience of the troops.

April 4, 1862: Skirmish between cavalry advance of General Braxton Bragg's (CS) Corps and Union patrol, close by the Union camp at Pittsburg Landing, Tennessee.

April 4, 1862: The day of General Albert S. Johnston's (CS) intended attack on the Union camp, General Braxton Bragg's (CS) Corps is still marching on Corinth Road. General Albert S. Johnston holds a council of war and postpones attack by 48 hours to April 6.

April 5, 1862: General Nelson's (US) division, Army of the Ohio, arrives at Savannah, Tennessee, at General Ulysses S. Grant's (US) HQ; his division is a day's march away.

April 6, 1862: General Albert S. Johnston's (CS) Army of the Mississippi's corps moves out in the early morning hours and attacks General Ulysses S. Grant's (US) encampment. The battle of Shiloh begins.

Cover photo:
Byrne's Mississippi Battery marker (Ruggles' Battery, facing the Hornet's Nest) Shiloh National Battlefield Park, Hardin County, TN

ISBN 978-1453857946

LCCN: 2011908311

Background and Acknowledgements

In the fall of 1987, I was home on leave from Army basic training for two weeks. Armed with a stack of books and nothing to do but eat and sleep, I was taken by the idea of writing a story about one of the most interesting Civil War battles, Shiloh. I had visited the battlefield when very young and, as the years passed, studied it whenever I could. Armed with a stack of notebooks and a pen, I began to write a story that I would never finish. The story described various aspects of the battle, with my friends as the main characters.

Those notebooks, with their college-ruled lines now faded as they collect dust in my bookshelves, provided the notes to rewrite this novel. I began to reformulate the story in early spring of 2000, taking a cast of tens and turning it into a cast of four. For the next seven years, I wrote in my spare time, on trips, on weekends, and in coffee houses. This story, based on the original manuscript, is the result of extensive research and planning.

I'd like to thank David Megill, a friend now for these last twenty-three years, my pastor and mentor, and my first editor. His short story, written with his friends as characters, was the inspiration for my own first attempt.

I'd next like to thank the instructor from the lower-level creative writing course I took in 1992. She graciously agreed to suffer through that long and unfinished work and give me her opinions, the best of which was ". . . way too many characters." I have lost her name and regret that I cannot give her recognition.

To my pards James Hall and Ward Yarbrough of the 23rd New York of the Albuquerque contingent of that Arizona-based reenacting unit, I owe a debt for educating me on soldier life in the Civil War. To my pards in the Army of the Pacific, a hardcore re-enacting battalion, and Dom DalBello for making my days as an infantryman memorable and for their pursuit of grasping those "magical moments" out in the field, I am grateful for many memories of camp fires, sleeping on arms, camp guard, and picket duty.

Thank you to my wife, who encouraged me to start writing again. My wife read my early edits and never sugar-coated the critique. Thank you for being my partner in this endeavor.

To the owner and chief editor of Precise Edit, David Bowman, a long-time friend and character in that first draft, thank you for agreeing to edit and proof the final version. David and his team used their skills to smooth out the rough edges of the story and bring out its strengths. It is their spit and polish that you now hold in your hands.

To my cover artist, Anna Dykeman of Anna Dykeman Creative Services, I give my thanks for the cover design and for helping me navigate the world of copyright law and keeping me on the right track.

I wrote this novel first as a gift to my friends and later as a means to educate others on the Civil War, bringing details of a soldier's life and experiences out of personal memoirs and historical monographs and into the universal medium of story.

Phillip M. Bryant, Albuquerque New Mexico October, 2010

Cast of Primary Characters

Union Army

Army of the Ohio, 24th Ohio, Nelson's Division, Ammen's Brigade

    Pvt. Philip Pearson: A Methodist minister turned infantryman

    Pvt. Theo "Mule" Mueller: A Catholic Dutchman

    Pvt. Samuel "Sammy" Henson: A farm boy born of New England stock

    Pvt. Johnny Henderson: another of Philip's pards

    5th Sgt. Harper: A former member of one of Philip's Methodist societies

Army of the Tennessee, 25th Missouri, Prentiss' Division, Peabody's Brigade

    Pvt. Robert Mitchell: An American raised within the strongly German population in St. Louis, Missouri

    Pvt. "Hube" Huebner: A young, simple lad of German stock

    Pvt. "Hilde" Hildebrand: A Swede with military experience from his native land

    Pvt. "Gus" Gustavson: A first-generation German immigrant

Confederate Army

Army of Mississippi, Polk's Battery, Polk's Corps, Bushrod R. Johnson's Brigade

    Cpt. Michael Grierson: A volunteer with the 5th Texas Artillery, later an officer in Polk's Tennessee Battery.

    1st Sgt. Mahoney: Michael's subordinate and confidant

    Cpt. Marshall T. Polk: A veteran of the early Indian Wars in the West

6th Mississippi, Hardee's Corps, Cheatham's Brigade

    Pvt. Stephen Murdock: A young boy turned man at the outbreak of the war

    Pvt. William "Willie" Hawkins: Stephen's pard and best friend.

Chapter One

Michael reached into his jacket pocket for his rag and dabbed his forehead and face. The early morning rains had cooled the long columns of marching soldiers for a time, but the temperature rose quickly again. A rhythmic cacophony surrounded him as his artillery battery rolled slowly through the drying mud. The creak of the wooden caissons, the tink of metal against metal, the heavy fall of hooves into the soft road, and noises of conversations lulled him. He needed a distraction from the aches and pains caused by too many hours in the saddle. Being in an artillery battery afforded him accommodations that the luckless infantry could only wish for, a ride. They wouldn't envy us so much, he thought, if they knew how uncomfortable it is to ride in a saddle for nine hours.

Michael stood up in the stirrups to stretch his legs. Just ahead of him were his number two gun, "St. Peter," and its half-asleep gunners riding on its caisson. Jones and Harper stared blankly back at Michael. Their heads nodded as the caisson dipped and rose with each undulation in the road. The heavy brass Napoleon had seen action in the invasion of Mexico with Winfield Scott's army. It had stood sentinel at the San Antonio depot in Texas until "liberated" by secessionist volunteers after the Federal garrisons withdrew. Now it was on its way to engage the Federal forces encamped at Pittsburg Landing, Tennessee.

The heady days of secession were over, and the delusion of a short war was shattered after the battle of Manassas in Virginia and a bloody skirmish in Springfield, Missouri.

Though both engagements ended with victories for the fledgling Confederacy, the early twin victories did not bring the fruit anticipated: international recognition to keep trade alive with Europe. Instead, they steeled the North's resolve to re-unite the Union.

Southern strategists had hoped to quickly tire the North of the effort by fending off any incursions into its territory. Lincoln quickly called for 100,000 more volunteers to replace the 90-day men whose enlistments began to end even before the two armies met at Manassas. These new volunteers were to serve for three years or for the duration of the war. With this call, Jefferson Davis, newly elected President of the Confederate States of America, was forced to fashion a new war direction if the Confederacy was to survive. Victory would have to come by more than just a defensive policy. He made a similar call for volunteers from the Confederate "White House" for three-year volunteers. Like their opposite numbers from the northern states, volunteer regiments were sworn into the Confederate service and marched off to training camps after they were up to strength.

The men who would eventually become the 20th Texas Light Artillery mustered in Austin, Texas, amid much fanfare and attention from the local citizenry. Speeches by the mayor, prominent politicians, and others filled the men of the new regiment with pride and determination to throw the invaders back from the sacred soil of Virginia. Volunteers and private citizens alike dined on sumptuous dinners in open air parks, and ladies visited the encampment on the lawn of the state capital, laden with baskets full of sweets and food.

To some of the men, this was a cornucopia. Texas was mostly frontier settlements, farming, and ranching. From the surrounding counties came men and boys whose knowledge of weaponry and small arms was as great as their knowledge of grammar was poor. Ranchers' sons and wealthy politicians volunteered along with city clerks and criminals. Although Texas was far removed from the theaters of the war, Texans had always answered the call to arms. Most families had relatives who had fought with the republic army against the Mexicans, had fought Santa Ana in the revolt, and had fought him again in the U.S. army as volunteers.

As a frontier state where most men served compulsory militia duties in the presence of an outlaw breed spawned by open spaces and anonymity, most families took it for granted that conflict was always a step away. The vaunted Texas Rangers operated alongside locally organized posses to rein in the lawless or to campaign against the still unconquered Apache in the New Mexico territory. From this mix of patriots, villains, and rough-cut citizenry, the 20th Texas Light Artillery was formed.

They also had a willingness to throw in their lot with Jefferson Davis's cause. Texans, as a whole, owned few slaves, and its cotton economy was still young compared to the Virginian tobacco or Georgian and Carolinian cotton. Most men and boys knew nothing of the refinements of the infamous southern society that would produce such future leaders as Robert Lee, Thomas Jackson, Pierre Gustav Toutant Beauregard, and George Pickett. These men, born of influential plantation aristocracy, would have been derided as rich dandies by the rough-cut Texans.

In spite of their frontier ways, the Texans did possess a militaristic history and a desire to be free. The other commonality was the theory of continual westward expansion of "that peculiar institution." Southern political thought preached that if the agrarian society was to survive, it would need to add new westward territories to the slave-holding fold. This doctrine would bring about the first foreboding of coming conflict after the Mexican–American war.

Even before the guns fell silent around Mexico City, southern politicians were lobbying to create territories that would provide new cotton-producing lands. They were motivated not just by economic doctrine but also by political interest, for the South needed representation in Congress to counter the growing abolitionist influence from northern politicians. More slave states would mean more representation for the southern way of life. Southern politicians cared little that most of the territory gained in the war with Mexico was of little use to the cotton producers.

The land in the first cotton-producing states had begun to play out as early as the 1830s. Landowners were pulling up roots and moving westward as fast as the government evicted the Indians. Even before Texas won its independence, slave holders began trickling into the territory, ignoring their Mexican landlord's prohibition against slave holding. With slaves came rich and influential men with a taste for the good things that money brought. But for every successful plantation owner and cotton producer came thousands of would-be scions of fortune.

Michael's father, Finneaus, was one such influence seeker. Michael's early recollections of childhood were of constant motion as Finneaus moved his family from one place to the next to build his personal fortune. Though not a slave owner himself, Finneaus wanted what, at that time, was the American dream. Immigrating to South Carolina as a boy from Ireland prior to its great potato famine, he quickly entered the struggle to make it in the burrows of Charleston, South Carolina, by the only means he had: his unconquerable desire to rise above his own common birth. By the time Michael was born in 1840, Finneaus had gone from bright-eyed store clerk to would-be tobacco producer to merchant.

The journey took the family from Charleston, where Finneaus had married an Irish immigrant named Melissa Iverson, the daughter of an influential family who operated a shipping business with several ships and a dry goods store. Finneaus made his start working for Melissa's father as a clerk in the store and eventually made his way onto the bottom rung of Charleston's genteel society. Armed with a nice dowry and an unquenchable desire to make a fortune, Finneaus and Melissa struck off westward. Then, using his shipping family contacts, Finneaus bought a stake in the tobacco trade. As new arable land opened up in the 1820s in Georgia and Alabama, he was able to purchase land and begin his dream. Melissa gave birth to a son, Andrew, in 1821, then to a daughter, Michelle, in 1822.

Farming tobacco was intensive labor. The plants needed constant vigilance and care. This need for workers gave birth to the slave trade in the early 1700s as indentured servitude gave way to shanghaied Negroes whose labor was both permanent and excessive. Finneaus had the capital neither to buy a slave nor to hire help. After five years of struggle, he decided that he would make his money not by growing tobacco but by selling it. Armed again with money made from selling the farm, he packed up the family, now with four youngsters—Emma born in 1828 and Paul in 1831—and moved westward to Mississippi.

The two parts of the country were striving to meet in the middle, with the founding of St. Louis in 1820, which grew from a remote shipping waypoint on the Missouri River to a booming trade port. Finneaus set up shop along its waterway. Settling in Natchez, Mississippi, he transported interior tobacco downriver to New Orleans, the gateway for water-born transport from the Deep South to the East. By 1839, Natchez would grow to be a city instead of just a merchant port on the last leg of the river journey from St. Louis to New Orleans.

It was here that Melissa bore him two more children, Eunice in 1837 and Katherine in 1838. Eunice, Katherine, and Melissa succumbed to an outbreak of measles in 1838, a not uncommon happenstance. This left Finneaus with Emma and Paul, both in their early teens, and his two eldest sons. As was also common for a man of means or, in Finneaus's case, a man of would-be means, to take care of the younger children he married Paula Ecklandburg, the daughter of a prominent German merchant family in Natchez. Paula, Michael's mother, was twenty-two when Finneaus married her, and she would bring him another four children in the years that followed Michael's birth in 1840.

Keeping his merchant business going in Natchez consumed Finneaus for the next five years, as the trade boomed then busted. Michael remembered his easy-going childhood in Natchez, playing with his younger siblings, Gertrude, born in 1841, Stephen, born in 1843, and Eva, born in 1844. Paula was a doting mother. She chose to raise her own children despite being a woman of means and preferred to spend hours with them rather than enjoying a life of limited luxury. Michael grew up with the odor of the river and the smell of dry goods from the warehouse. Emma, a comely lass of 16 when Michael was born, attended school in Charleston where she stayed with her grandparents, about whom she knew little until Finneaus sent her there in 1840. Paul, thirteen years old in 1844, when he wasn't in school, looked after Michael as they wandered the wharf and shop areas or when they strayed too far from Paula's watch. Paul, being the only male child still at home and the closest thing Michael would have to an older brother, was expected to take care of him despite the difference in parentage. Michael's oldest brother, Andrew, was twenty-three by that time and worked for his father most of the day. Michelle, back from boarding school in St. Louis, helped Paula mind the younger children who were still at home.

Michael had little to occupy his time at the tender age of five, other than exploring with his older brother Paul, playing with Gertie and Stephen, or forcing Michelle to chase him around the neighborhood. His earliest remembrances were of watching the paddle steamers and smaller steam craft moving up and down the Mississippi, spilling forth their loads of goods onto the docks. He watched blacks and poor whites moving bags of beans, piles of tobacco, or rolls of cotton from the ships into wagons or directly into the warehouses. His first contact with slavery was watching the wharf hands laboring under the watchful eyes of the foreman. Even at five, he recognized that they were different from himself. He could come and go as he pleased; they couldn't. They were marched to the wharf in a gang and marched back at the end of the day. He was too young to dwell on the inequalities of their disposition. Andrew told him they had to work there. He tried to explain slavery to him as best as he understood it.

"Think of it as a punishment. They are being punished for being niggers," Paul said.

Michael related to punishment. Sometimes Paula or Michelle would rein in his adventures and make him stay at home. Now, as he thought about it, he realized that life for the blacks was much like the life of soldiers.

*****

Michael was far removed from those days of freedom in Natchez. The musty, damp morning gave way to welcome sunshine as breaks in the trees afforded patches of sunlight, allowing him to soak up the heat. The roads were still muddy, and the regular sucking sounds made by horses' hooves and water-logged brogans on the feet of the infantry added to the sounds of thousands of men on the move.

So far, Tennessee proved most undesirable, as it seemed to Michael to have rained every day for the past two months. If it wasn't raining, it was oppressing them with the humid heat of early spring.

Their tenure in the state was made more difficult by constant retreats and bad news. Since the year before, Confederate fortunes had waned in the west after a promising beginning. Union armies had maneuvered Albert Sidney Johnston's forces farther south as, one by one, key forts along the Tennessee River fell. Grant's army had not been idle in the winter months of 1861 and 1862, taking Fort Donelson late in the campaigning season. His army now rested on the banks of the Tennessee River at Pittsburg Landing and at an additional camp five miles downriver at Crump's Landing and at Savannah, where Grant had his headquarters.

Confederate General Albert Sidney Johnston had not been idle either, putting together troops from around the various command departments in the region until he enjoyed a numerical superiority to Grant. Regiments from Arkansas, from Kentucky, from Missouri, and from his own retreating forces from Bowling Green, Kentucky marched to Corinth, Mississippi, and became the Confederate Army of Mississippi. If Johnston could bring these forces together in time, he could surprise the Yankees and save Tennessee once again.

Confederate forces were pushed out of Missouri the year before, and Johnston was given command of the Trans Mississippi West. The string of reversals convinced Confederate President Jefferson Davis that the disparate Confederate forces in the trans-Mississippi west needed a firm hand and Johnston was given command of the department. A glimmer of hope reinvigorated the Confederates to regain what was lost. But before Johnston could make a positive impact upon the strategic situation, the Confederates lost two key forts, Henry and Donelson, which controlled the Missouri and Tennessee rivers.

Michael was not privy to the grand strategic designs of Johnston and his staff, but the rank and file knew that a battle was brewing and that they were going to "surprise the Yanks in their beds" on the morrow. The Texans were up before dawn and on the move all day. The troops had been told to observe strict noise discipline, but with thousands of men, some were bound to have lapses in judgment.

As the rain gave way to clear skies, many infantryman decided it would be a good idea to test their powder. The sight and sound of men discharging their muskets made the march seem like a holiday parade or celebration. Michael had to laugh as he watched staff officers riding to and fro along the columns yelling at the tops of their lungs for the men to "stop that infernal noise!" As soon as an officer got the men in line at one point, firing erupted farther ahead or behind, causing another paroxysm of rage and cursing from the staff. Despite the racket, they had not seen any enemy.

The Texans considered themselves luckier than most artillery regiments when they marched off to the war, resplendent with their six twelve-pound Napoleon cannon. With its ability to send a twelve-pound, solid shot 1,800 yards, the Napoleon was a prize. They came compliments of the United States government, collected from several outposts manned by U.S. army units throughout Texas before the war. Being well-supplied with the Napoleons made them the mainstay of the divisional artillery, or so they thought.

When they had arrived in Corinth with the rest of the forces from Arkansas, they were shocked to find themselves reassigned. They were placed under the command of Captain Marshall T. Polk and were to support the movements of the newly formed 2nd Brigade under Bushrod R. Johnson. With the reorganization Johnston initiated came the second shock. The 20th Texas Light Artillery lost its designation. In line with the Confederate artillery's penchant for referring to batteries by their commanders, they became known as Polk's battery. The original battery was broken up, and the Napoleons were farmed out to other organizations. Two sections of the 20th were then combined with a battery from Tennessee, Polk's own command. Though initially this hurt the Texans' pride, they soon got on with the business of making war and drilling under the watchful eye of Captain Polk.

*****

Squinting wearily as the sun found a hole in the cloud cover and bathed the soldiers in warmth and brightness, Michael stared up the road at the long and seemingly endless column trudging forward. Somewhere up that same road lay the enemy camp at Pittsburg Landing. He thought to himself, *Do they already know of our approach? Had they heard all this ruckus? Will we carry the day?* Surprise was essential.

The Union army settled into camp at Pittsburg Landing to await the arrival of several of its disparate parts before moving on Corinth, Mississippi, and completing the cleansing of Tennessee of Rebel presence. Rumor had it that another army was moving slowly from Kentucky to merge with the force at the Landing. They needed more speed, but so far as he could see, speed was only a dream as the near constant rain turned the Tennessee roads into mush and slowed the march to a crawl. He looked toward the sun burning away the clouds. Maybe it was a good omen.

A voice called to him, "Captain Grierson."

"Sir?" Michael shook himself from his reverie as Captain Marshall Polk moved his horse alongside.

"When we get to Michie's Tavern, move the battery off the road somewhere and bed for the night," Polk told him. "We're to wait for Bragg's Corps to move past us before moving on again into line of battle. Maintain strict noise discipline, no fires, and have the men ready to move at 0200."

"Yes, sir." Michael said curtly. "Should I have the men brew something at the first opportunity, then?"

"With the pace we are keeping, I doubt they will get the chance, but you may try."

"I'll tell Mahoney to have the men ready for march at 0200 tomorrow." Just before Polk could leave, Michael asked him in a whisper, "Hey, Marsh, do you think we're gonna pull this off? What's the latest talk at headquarters?"

Polk looked in the direction the column was moving. "Well, I can't see how the Yanks don't know something is up with all the noise an army this size makes. Michie's is supposed to be two miles or so from our form-up point, and from there it's only three more miles to the enemy encampment. It's kind of eerie, ya' know," Marshall Polk said. He took off his hat and scratched his head, revealing greasy, sweat-matted auburn hair. "I'd almost rather that the enemy knew we were here."

"What?" Michael said loudly, looking at Marshall. In a quieter tone, he asked, "What are you meaning?"

"It's the tension. Every noise, every idiot infantryman what decides to test his wet powder or carry on as he'd just seen the paymaster means the tension gets rougher. You know this whole thing is bent on surprise." Polk waved his hand to indicate the men marching forward. "Well, if we know that they know we are here, then all we have to do is make up our minds to attack or go home. But as it is, we creep forward, not knowin' if the slightest rustle of the leaves is going to bring a heap of cavalry upon us or if we're going to march into an open field to find the whole enemy host arrayed for battle." He paused for a moment and examined the pommel of this saddle. "I'd rather we knew what we were getting into than have this game of cat and mouse."

"So you don't think this'll work?" Michael broke in.

"I hope for all these boys it works, or many of them will have been sacrificed for naught."

Michael pursed his lips and thought that all war is a gamble, just like business. Father gambled plenty, and lost plenty, and the kids either paid the price or enjoyed the benefits.

The two of them rode in silence. Michael wasn't sure what to make of these revelations from Marshall. Their relationship had been strained by the inevitable politics of military officers vying for commands and position. When the Texans marched to Louisiana and thence to Arkansas to link up with General Ben McColluch's forces, he had been in command of the men. Voted captain, Michael was honored to lead "these fine young examples of Texan manhood." Like the other officers, he didn't have any clue about how to lead a unit, especially one of artillery. His training consisted of some manuals found in the abandoned armory in Austin. Michael and the other officers tried their hands at drilling the men in the rudiments of artillery maneuvers. Comical at times, suicidal at others, Michael soon recognized that he hadn't the faintest idea how to form these rugged individualists into a cohesive unit.

The march to Louisiana was a trial in and of itself, with many of the men acting as if they were on posse. The lack of command experience was buttressed soon after their rendezvous at Camp Pendleton in Louisiana, where they were introduced to Captain Marshall T. Polk, a grizzled old Indian fighter and former U.S. Army lieutenant stationed in California. Polk had resigned his commission after Ft. Sumter fell and accompanied several other southern officers, including Albert Sidney Johnston, from California to offer their services to the Confederacy. Polk had his hands full, not only with the Texans but also with other artillery units that marched into camp throughout the quiet months leading up to the battles of Bull Run in Virginia and Wilson's Creek in Missouri.

Polk took a heavy hand to the volunteers with a relish and instituted a strict schedule of duties that initially chaffed the Texans. The men were accustomed to lolling around camp tending to their horses. Polk put a stop to the holiday atmosphere, and soon the Texans got a taste of real army life with guard duty, stable duty, drill, drill, and more drill.

Michael thought it was time well spent. After being removed from his position as commander to commanding just a section of the battery, the tarnish to his honor and pride had taken a while to heal. For some, this was affront enough to resign one's commission and travel back home. But from his father Michael had learned well-placed pride and an honor not too easily bruised. Michael had seen his father alternately succeed and fail in one effort after another but still rise up for the next challenge. So he took the downgrading of his position with a grain of salt.

Michael was given the second slot of command. He no longer minded not being the commander, though at times he missed being in the know. The officers themselves had to endure such a tough regimen of classes in maneuver, command, and parade that many soon longed for the days back in Austin. They had to learn how to identify terrain features useable for artillery for greatest effect. They worked the guns themselves to learn setting fields of fire, utilizing the various types of ammunition, and when to use them. They learned to recognize positions that would limit their fields of fire or allow the enemy to bottle them up. The hardest part for some was the mathematics and engineering needed to use artillery effectively. They were given what seemed to Michael like four years of West Point classroom learning in a couple of weeks. The hardest part of this training was doing it, as Michael would muse and commiserate with his fellow officer classmates.

While at Camp Pendelton and being whipped into artillerists, the war went on without them and caused no letup in grumbling from men and officers alike. They celebrated with General Price's victory over Nathanial Lyon at Wilson's Creek and with Joseph E. Johnston and P.G.T. Beauregard's victory over McDowell at Manassas Junction, and they worried that the war would be won without them. With concern, they followed Price and McCulloch's army as it invaded northern Missouri, and then was maneuvered into Arkansas where it was defeated at Pea Ridge, and they heard rumors of a Union invasion of Virginia.

By the time Polk was satisfied he had whipped the volunteers into soldiers, it was 1862. Grant had already reduced Fort Henry via river gunboats and captured Ft. Donelson and moved his army into winter encampment at Pittsburg Landing. The loss of Ft. Donelson cut off access and control of the Tennessee River and made supplying Confederate forces in Tennessee impossible. As Johnston hurried to cobble together a force large enough to challenge Grant, the tide was turning against the Confederacy in the west.

Chapter Two

"Sir, the battery has formed for review," First Sergeant Mahoney said to Michael and returned his salute.

The wind whipped Mahoney's greatcoat collar as he stood in front of the assembled battery in formation by section. Not one to be trifled with but conscious of his duty and position, Mahoney stared icily at Polk, cursing him for tearing him from his slightly warmer hut. Behind them were the battery's cannon with caissons in the rear. A fortnight had passed since their arrival at Corinth, Mississippi, and they were undergoing yet another inspection by that "dammed old fart Polk," as the popular quip went.

There had been little joy or celebration this Christmas. The cramped quarters, drill, duty, and military life left little room for holiday celebrations.

Michael swiveled on his heel to face Polk. He saluted and declared, "Sir, the battery is formed."

"Very well, Captain. You may proceed," Polk replied and returned the salute.

Michael turned to face Mahoney and the rest of the battery. He took a deep breath and shouted, "Battery, atten–shun! First Sergeant, review the battery." Mahoney began to pace the line of men. Michael walked with him to the first section and thence to the cannon.

After an hour of shivering in the cold, they were back in the semi-comfort of their huts. The hut that the men crouched in was eight feet by three feet, and was mostly bunks propped against the log walls. Tent canvas served as a roof with a pork barrel for a chimney; any remaining space was clogged with the occupants' personal effects. Light from several candles lit the interior, and to open the flap for the door was to invite the biting wind. Those gathered in the hut were men Michael had known since before the war.

"Damned old fart Polk," Mahoney gripped. "Did you see any other fool unit or battery out there today? No you didn't 'cause they all had the sense that God granted a mule to stay indoors."

"All except us'ns of Polk's Battery," replied Private Jones. "Cap'n, can't you talk some sense into Old Fart about this business of drill in this kind of weather?"

Michael gave him a sympathetic look. "You know I can't do that."

"Did you see the papers?" Corporal Harper asked Mahoney.

Mahoney picked up a copy from the table at the back of the hut. "Unconditional Surrender: Grant Takes Fort Donelson," Mahoney read dryly. "20,000 troops walked off into captivity, led by that coward, Pillow."

"What's this?" Jones asked. He rubbed his hands together and grimaced. "I still can't feel my fingers!"

"Yeah," Harper added. "Tennessee is now in Union hands, too. Here, sir, read for yourself."

Harper handed the copy of the *Corinth Courier* to Michael. There, emblazoned in the banner headline, was more bad news for the cause. What was left of Confederate troops in Tennessee streamed into Corinth, Mississippi. The only good news was the escape of most of the cavalry forces under Nathan Bedford Forrest.

Michael glanced at the stories. "He refused to surrender. Forrest escaped and is heading here," Michael said as he read.

"How long has it been since we've heard any good news?" Jones asked. "Isn't there anything good happening for us?"

"Having Johnston with us is a start," Michael replied. "He'll whip Grant when the time is right. These things take time. Just do your job as you've been trained, and fight for what you believe, and we'll prevail."

His companions stared openly at him, and he felt his face heat up. He wasn't accustomed to making inspirational speeches. "Well, anyway, something's gonna happen in the spring, just you watch." At that they fell silent, each to his own thoughts.

Michael watched as Jones busied himself with his bunk and reverently laid out a well-worn book and papers. Michael looked over at Smith quizzically.

"Vespers," Smith said.

"You don't think I'm going outside in this weather, do you?" Jones said to them.

Mahoney stood and stepped to the door flap. "Well, I need to see that the fatigue details are going."

"You do this every day?" Michael asked Jones.

"Yes, every day. If I didn't have my faith, all I would have is this," he said and motioned to his torso. "This body's fragile, and in these times ya need something more than yer body to keep ya going. So I pray an' recite my Scriptures. It reminds me that they's a God an' Christ died fer me."

"Well, I don't think much on that."

"Maybe ya oughten ta. You're not going to live forever, Sir," Jones said.

"Maybe I will sometime when I feel the need. Put in a good word for me, ok?"

Michael exited the hut. As the flap swung back behind him, the icy wind lashed at Michael's face. He curled the collar of his great coat snugly about his neck and headed toward his own hut.

*****

The sun warmed Michael as he remembered that cold day in Corinth. Riding next to him was Marshall Polk.

"This is a welcome change to those freezing days in Corinth, eh, Captain?" Michael asked.

"Yeah, it is," Marshall Polk replied.

Polk hadn't said a word since revealing his thoughts about the coming battle. Michael had not known what to say to him, or how to react to the sudden and strange familiarity. Michael turned his gaze toward Jones and Smith riding on the caisson in front of them. Smith was now asleep with his head bobbing. Now and again he woke abruptly, only to doze off once more. Jones was dreamily staring off into the distance.

"Well, Grierson," Polk said, "I gotta report to General Cheatham. Make sure you see to our dispositions. I don't know when I'll be back. Oh, also make sure that each section has ammo before the trains get all jammed in the rear." Polk spurred his horse, broke out of the column and moved on ahead.

Michael moved his horse out of the column as well and waited to the side until abreast of Mahoney, who was riding at the rear of the column.

"First Sergeant, we're going to stop for the night at Michie's Crossroads. 'Old Fart' wants us to form in columns of sections and be ready to move by 0200. No fires and strict noise discipline enforced. Make sure section leaders inventory their ordinance."

"Yes, sir," Mahoney nodded.

"I know the boys aren't going to be happy about no coffee, so if you can find a covered spot, build one fire for coffee and keep it small. If you're caught, tell them you were acting on my orders," Michael said.

"Sure, sir, no problem. I'll take care of the boys," Mahoney replied with a slight grin.

"Good man," Michael said.

He gave a tug on the reins and moved out along the column once more. Most of the men were either half-awake or dozing with heads hung low in blissful slumber. The weary march continued as the sun began its arc toward the west and bathed the scenery with rich orange and red hues. The road was drying in places now, making it more bearable by the absence of choking dust.

It was almost dusk when the column of troops in front of the battery peeled off to the right and left of a fork in the road. Michael thought they must be at Michie's. He picked up his pace and rode to the front caisson of the battery.

"I'm going to ride ahead and show you where to move off to," he told the soldiers on the caisson. Michael nudged his horse and trotted along the outside of the column of infantry. The foot soldiers were becoming more animated now that a stop was in the making. He could hear quiet whispers among the men as he passed by.

Michael came to the already-choked crossroads and looked on in awe as other units of the corps marched by. He saw Bankhead's Battery drawing up in the corner of an adjacent field. Next to them was as good as a place as any. It would also give his men a chance to visit with comrades. He waited for the battery to draw up.

The infantry brigade of B. R. Johnson moved off the road, his men marching mechanically in exhaustion and forming into columns of battalions to lie down on arms. No one was pitching camp. Everyone knew that they were near their enemy.

"Move off to the left of Bankhead over there," Michael said and pointed to the lead caisson. By now it was becoming harder to make out individual faces in the dark as caissons and men moved past him. Thousands of figures were milling about the fields on either side. Here and there a fire was flickering despite orders to the contrary.

It was April 3rd, just a day away from the planned start of the attack.

With the battery situated and parked, the men began to gather in groups around the guns as only pards can do. They chatted softly as they ate a cold meal from their haversacks. Michael made his way over to a group of officers gathered between the two batteries. On the few occasions he had tried to get chummy with the common soldiers, he had been greeted with wariness and not a little suspicion. Here he was greeted by several familiar faces. A flask quickly made the rounds, and each man took a tug from it as they discussed the coming attack. There was no fear here, only expectation and nervousness.

Gathered around a lantern, they chowed down on hard tack and bacon supplied by the mess sergeants. The bacon was cold and greasy, but no one cared. The light shining eerily from the ground cast odd shadows upon the dirty faces. Far from the Victorian ideals of genteel officering, the officers made the best of the situation, suffering the same privations as their men.

"Too much infernal noise. The Yanks will know we are close," said one.

"Naw, I've heard that not a single vedette or picket has been encountered up front. They don't know we're even here," said another.

"We are going to be too late, ole Buell will be joined up with Grant by the time we're ready."

"Buell will take a month of Sundays to get to Grant. I heard tell he was still at Bowling Green, Kentucky."

"I don't know. The sooner we get to our attack point the better I'll feel. I'm tired of thinking I see a Yank behind every tree or bush."

The flask passed around one more time, and then one by one the officers left to attend to other responsibilities. Michael made his way back to his own section, finding Jones, Harper, First Sergeant Mahoney, and a few others brewing up coffee for the battery in a big pot. Mahoney scrounged an empty pork barrel to place over the fire to hide the light and had drilled a few holes toward the bottom to allow air in. The pot was suspended above it.

"We'll douse it quickly, once the brew is done," Mahoney said to reassure Michael. Michael nodded his approval. Other groups of men loitered nearby or stood around the contraption to hide any light that might shine through, eagerly waiting with their cups.

"Don't mess with a man's coffee," Mahoney said to no one in particular.

"Just make sure I get some, ok?" Michael asked him with a smile.

"I'll get your cup and bring you some myself."

"Good man," Michael said and patted Mahoney on the shoulder.

He made his way over to his horse to retrieve his haversack. "Hey, boy, how ya' doin'?" He stroked Charger's nose and scratched behind the ears of the spotted brown and white sorrel. Charger had been a gift from his father and had made the long trek from Texas with him. Though long in the saddle on this march, Charger didn't look as worn as Michael felt.

With a pat on Charger's neck, Michael told him, "We'll get ya' some fodder soon, boy."

He pulled his pipe from his haversack and leaned against his saddle while he filled it. Ghostly apparitions of men moved about him. Glancing to his left toward the road, he couldn't see them, but he could hear the troops and wagons moving down it in a constant stream.

Michael didn't know it, but the columns of Braxton Bragg's Corps had been tramping behind the divisions and brigades of Polk's Corps. Not until 2 p.m. of April 5th, the planned day of attack, would Bragg's men pass by and allow Polk to take the road again. Michael also didn't know that yet another delay would frustrate Johnston's plans.

*****

Two miles away, Private Stephen Murdock and the 6th Regiment were getting ready for an uncomfortable night. Talk among the men was of the prospect of a battle on the morrow. Forbidden to light a fire, and thus deprived of another hot meal and coffee, most men lay down and drifted off to a fitful sleep. Some whispered among themselves in twos and threes of the prospect of a battle on the morrow.

The East Mississippi Greys, men who volunteered from Scott County, Mississippi, a year ago, formed Company C of the 6th Regiment, joining companies with such names as "Rankin Rough & Readies," "Quitman Southrons," and "The Rockport Steel Blades." Sporting their brightly colored battle shirts made for them by the womenfolk of Carthage, the East Mississippi Greys marched into Jackson, Mississippi, to be mustered into service. Though they appreciated the gesture of the women, most of the men had begun to look bedraggled after a month of camp life with its fatigue, work and other duties.

Weary from the day-long exertions, Stephen stretched out on his blanket. His head was propped up on his arm as he talked with one of his Comrades in Battle resting next to him, Private William Hawkins.

"Remember when we got to Jackson? How eager we were for war? How nice we looked in our red cotton battle shirts and blue trousers?" Stephen asked.

"Yeah, those were the days. We had food to eat, and the womenfolk couldn't do enough for us." William rubbed his eyes and glanced around at the rest of the company. "Now we're all that's left; the 40 of us."

"We don't look too 'grey' now, do we?" Stephen returned, examining his dirty wool shell jacket and brown trousers.

"Unh, no, we don't," William said and grinned.

Stephen sighed and shifted. After another few moments of silence, he closed his eyes. "Remember that nonsense speech Governor Pettus gave as we stood around the capital building in the freezing cold? It seemed inspiring at the time, but now it just rings hollow."

"Yep, that do seem like a lifetime ago, don't it? We sure do look smaller than we did that day in Jackson." William frowned and shook his head. "And we were afraid the war was gonna pass us by, and like a bunch of fools we wanted to get into the thick of it. To see the elephant, not show the white feather, and bring honor to the 'Great State of Mississippi.' Well, we are in the thick of it now."

"We've waited, marched, drilled, gone hungry, and been cold and wet, and we are on the edge of battle now," Stephen said. "But now that the moment is here, I don't feel like I thought I would." He rolled over on to his back, stretching. "A fight is a-comin' in the morning, but I don't feel all that great about it. I don't know. It's like waiting for something to arrive or a day to come, but once it comes, it's a letdown. The waiting seems to be more exciting than the event."

William lay back and crossed his arms behind him. "A fight is comin', fer sure. The army don't gather like this unless we're a-aimin' to hit the Yanks." William stared off into the waning light toward the line of march. "You think they know that we're here? Been weird, no sign of pickets, no firin' like usual when we're this close."

"Don't know, but it is curious that we hain't seen any Yanks or at least cavalry if we're this close. Maybe ole Johnston has pulled it off. Maybe we'll drive the Yanks into the river and reclaim Tennessee," Stephen replied.

"Mayhaps," William agreed. "Or they'll be waitin' fer us as we come through them trees," William retorted and exhaled slowly.

They were quiet for a moment until William continued, "Either way, bullets is gonna be flyin' thick, and we're gonna be a might smaller once it's over."

Stephen thought a moment. "Who's gonna get shot tomorrow? Who's gonna die? Who's gonna lose a limb? "Gets me to wonderin' about stuff I'd rather not wonder about, you know? I don't want to be wonderin' about it when the stuff starts to fly."

"Gotta think about it sometime," William said. "We're not long for this life. Birth and death are set fer all of us. What we do in the middle is up to us, but we can't add or subtract from that last date."

Stephen turned and faced William. "You believe in fate? Like bein' able to change that date based on what you do? Seems hard to believe that you can't change that last date. It doesn't seem fair or somethin'."

"Naw, I don't believe in fate." William explained. "Good Book says 'It is appointed for a man to die once, then face the judgment.' We choose what we do in this life. Then we're judged on that after our life."

Stephen closed his eyes and lay in silence. He thought of his youth and of church services with his family on Sunday mornings and remembered how his only thoughts were of playing with his pals after the service instead of the message emanating from the pulpit. His earliest memories of church were of chaffing in the nice clothes he had to wear each Sunday and trying to sit still in the pew, and the stern looks of his mother if he should forget the taboo of not swinging his feet back and forth. When he was older, his motivation for attending was to meet girls from the surrounding families or to demonstrate his prowess in the games he and the other boys would play after service.

The churches in Carthage were the social centers for their parishioners. The Presbyterian Church in Carthage was the scene of weddings, funerals, meals, and games in Stephen's memory, but rarely was it a place of spiritual enlightenment. Having grown up in a family who prayed before every meal and punished for the blasphemy of taking the Lord's name in vain, religion was something to be lived around and accepted as part of life instead of practiced with any deliberation. Good people went to Heaven, bad people went to Hell, and the parishioners of the Presbyterian church of Carthage were good people.

Thoughts of Heaven and Hell weren't foreign to Stephen. Before the East Mississippi Greys left for Jackson in January, they were treated to fantastic feasts at each church and inspired by each minister to achieve feats of heavenly glory. Imbued with the knowledge of the righteousness of their cause and indignation at the federal government, the young and old men of Carthage marched out of the city toward adventure. The adventure was soon upon them, as the rigors of military life dulled their enthusiasm. Inadequate clothing, food, and armament plagued the 6th Mississippi as officers and men struggled to learn soldiering together. Most officers elected at the company level were hardly more suited to being officers than their men were to being soldiers.

Fitted out with 1,002 officers and men when the regiment was christened the 6th Regiment of Mississippi Volunteer Infantry, the attrition from sickness, accident, and officer resignation commenced rapidly. Stephen thought back to that day in Jackson, picturing the regiment standing resplendent in its new uniforms before the governor's review stand. How smart and large the regiment looked then.

Stephen sat up and dropped his arms into his lap. In the near darkness, he surveyed the camp to his right and left. He compared what he saw before him with what he saw in his mind's eye of that day. It looked as if someone had taken a cleaver and cut the regiment in half. Cleburne's brigade was stretched out alongside the 6th. The 23rd Tennessee made up the right flank of the brigade, with the 6th next in line, followed by the 5th Tennessee. Just as men within a company become accustomed to the touch of elbows from comrades, just so with the placement of regiments within a brigade line of battle.

Regiments take on the character of their members and, at times, that can become an odd assortment of superstition and behavior. Knowing that other regiments that have stood the tests of combat were on either side of one's own builds a sense of security. Looking at the sad remnants of the 23rd and 5th Tennessee, Stephen thought back to the experiences from the brigades' Kentucky sojourn several months ago. There they had first tasted combat with minié balls whizzing overhead, the exhilaration and rush, and the deadly roulette of opposing lines of infantry pouring lead into each other.

By all counts, the brigade had seen its baptism of fire in Kentucky as it occasionally brushed with Federal cavalry and infantry in Johnston's retreat from Bowling Green, Kentucky. The whittling away of manpower continued as each meeting brought its wounds and death and as comrades vanished. This was the first time Cleburne's brigade had been on the cusp of such a momentous gathering of force occasioned by this march.

Stephen turned to William. "Ya' know, I just was thinkin' that what we saw in Kentucky ain't gonna hold nuthin' on what's gonna happen tomorrow. We didn't have a fraction of the army there that we have here now."

"Yeah, best not to think on it too much," William replied. "Thinking on it only makes ya' worry too much about it. It's like them fellers what say they git premonitions of their own death and sure enough get killed. Maybe if you don't think about it, you won't get the premonition, and then maybe you won't fulfill it."

"Well, I still don't reckon that's the case, though I have wondered what it is that makes a man feel he's gonna die at a particular time. Nothin' in the Good Book speaks on it."

"I reckon many a fellow's feelin' that premonition now," William said.

Stephen looked up at the overcast night sky. "Well, I know what we're about to start feelin'." The rain that had relented to allow the army to march on hardening roads was about to revisit misery on the gathering Confederates yet again.

"Another sleepless night with no fire to warm yourself by," William said sullenly. "Fer all this misery the Almighty is a-visitin' on us, He'd better bestow victory on us to reward us fer all the trouble."

"Be nice to be back home again, huh?" Stephen replied and lay back down on his back. "Back home, dry, well fed, and comfortable."

"Aw, you know that comfort is only fer officers and folks who is rich and important!" William jibed and threw his hat over Stephen's face.

"Hey, git that smelly thing off me!" Stephen threw the hat back at William.

Several hundred yards behind them, the army continued to gather as the brigades of Bragg's Corps sorted themselves out and filed off the road and into their jump-off formations. The muffled tramp of feet droned on and on. Several hundred yards in front of the 15th Arkansas's skirmish line, a row of paper cartridge remains lay fluttering in the wind. Earlier in the morning of the 4th, a Federal cavalry patrol moved on Michie's Crossroads and encountered the advance of Bragg's Corps. After a brief engagement, the cavalry was driven fleeing from the field into the woods, losing several men as prisoners. Worry about discovery spread, for the presence of so much infantry would surely belie the intentions of General Johnston—yet, inexplicably, the Federals didn't react.

Chapter Three

"Company, attention to roll call!" First Sergeant Hammel called out. Just minutes after waking up and crawling out of their Sibley tents, a row of men stood comatose in front of him. Reveille sounded, followed by a postlude chorus of hacking and coughing as thousands of men woke up and began the daily routine. The famous army cough was the true sound of the start of the army day.

The 25th Missouri shook itself to life as the companies formed in their respective streets for the morning sick and roll call. The soaking rain from the early morning hung heavily on the acres of tent canvas. Another day of drill and duty awaited Grant's army on the banks of the Tennessee River.

The spring chill still clung to the thick, musty air. Humidity from the rains caused the men's breath to billow out in cloudy exhalations. The sun slowly poked its beams over the eastern horizon, turning the clouds pinkish. Smoke from company cook fires wafted lazily into the air, and the smell of brewing coffee greeted the men's nostrils. Robert Mitchell stood in his place in the formation as Hammel called down his list. It was a place he had stood countless mornings.

"Dismissed!" shouted Hammel, and the company formation dissolved as the men broke ranks. Robert rubbed the dried matter from the corners of his eyes and coughed before stuffing his hands into his pockets and walking back to his tent to retrieve his washcloth and soap. Ducking under the flap and stepping over bed rolls littering the floor of the circular tent, he tended to his own bed materials. The Sibley was a tent large enough to sleep fifteen to twenty men arrayed like the spokes of a wheel around the central pole and stove. Robert's bed consisted of his rubberized gum blanket for a ground sheet, his blanket, and his overcoat. His knapsack sat at the end, along with his leather accouterments, or traps, as they were called.

He rolled his gum and blanket together and tied them to the top of his knapsack. He found his soap and cloth after rummaging through one of the compartments. By now, the tent began to fill with its other occupants going about similar activities.

"*Ach!* Another day of drill!" complained Hildebrande when he entered with Gustavson.

"Drill is drill; something *ve* has to do," Gustavson chided.

"Oh, *der Alte Hasse*, the old hand Gustav is going to teach us the importance of drill!" Hildebrande said and smirked.

"Ach, visdom is vasted on *die Jungen*." Gustavson waved his hand at Hildebrande , a man only five years his junior, and rolled his bed.

Robert ducked out of the tent and headed for the sinks. The stench of urine and dung affronted his nostrils long before he came in sight of the common refuse pit. Quickly taking care of his business and a brief wash from the water barrel, he made his way to the company cook fire where he found an open spot among the men. Sullen, half-asleep faces stared into the fire and awaited the completion of the coffee. The coffee boiler suspended above the fire steamed slightly, circled by men with their mugs held out like patients waiting for their quinine dose.

Robert watched as the flames flickered upward. One man sat cross-legged opposite him and poked at the coals with a stick, while others just stood comatose.

"Isn't that thing boiling yet?" the company cook asked.

Silent nods answered him.

"Well, have a go at it. You waitin' fer me to pour it for ya?"

One by one the mugs were filled with steamy liquid. Once-vacuous faces showed signs of life.

Robert slowly stirred a chunk of hard tack in his coffee and nibbled on the corners. Hildebrande and Gustavson eagerly consumed their crackers and coffee, engaging in a lively debate about who made better women, Tennessee or Missouri. Robert listened in amusement as Hildebrande got the worst of the argument.

"Light marching order for drill," First Sergeant Hammel muttered when he walked past the fire watchers.

Robert reached for his time piece and noted how much time he had remaining before formation. He worked on his hardtack, gnawing at the end softened by soaking in coffee.

"Feels like it going to be another hot one, *ja?*" Hildebrande asked. Beads of sweat glistened on his forehead as he gulped his coffee.

The air was thick with the aroma of cantonment, the gathering of thousands in a long-term camp. Fires billowed at the ends of company streets, and the living dead gathered around them, waiting for the coffee to re-awaken their stiff bodies. In quiet comradeship soldiers gathered, watching flames lick the air and avoiding serpentine smoke trails. This was the part of army life Robert loved—the silent togetherness. Soon, though, the relaxation would be broken by the exertion of drill. But for now, it was peaceful.

The other characters of the camp, personalities that could be found around any fire, were busy with their peculiar pursuits. Robert was solidly in the camp of the fire watchers whose only enjoyment in the morning was to crawl out of blankets and seek the flames like insects sought light. Little conversation occurred, merely the uttering of some baleful line or exclamation followed by grunts and nods of agreement. Occasionally, the company wag, those men gifted with a sense of occasional comic brilliance, became inspired and started up a tale or waxed philosophic on favorite topics. Otherwise, it was each man to his own thoughts.

Then there would be the dutiful. Always in motion, always cleaning or prepping something or attending to their hygiene, these men were as lively when they awoke as they were before they slept. They were always the first to be in formation, always the first to have their traps prepared, and always ready fifteen minutes before they were needed. They rolled their blankets and stowed their personal items before taking any coffee or breakfast, ensuring that their equipment was ready. Theirs was a cheerful countenance around the fire once the morning chores were completed, adding an edge to any conversation or offending the ear with inane talk. They were conservatively scattered about by chance amid the company camps and were always to be relied upon in a crisis.

Last of all, and to the relief of all, were the company *Jonahs*—a term as mysterious as referring to one's mess mates as "pards." All agreed that the biblical Jonah played no small part in describing the hapless, clumsy individuals that inhabited every camp and wrought destruction upon many a fire. They were neither hated for their obtuse nature nor loved for their innocent carelessness. They were the ones whose intelligence was enough to allow them to pass muster and sign their own names but not enough to keep from making nuisances of themselves. They were the dread of the first sergeants and the bane of their mess mates.

Robert pulled his attention away from the mesmerizing dance of the flames to catch sight of private Huebner making his way toward them. Instinctively, he reached for his coffee mug and scooted back a foot from the fire. One by one, the others performed similar acts of coffee preservation as their company Jonah innocently stumbled to a halt.

As if by cue, and as a direct refutation of the old adage that smoke follows beauty, the waft of smoke drifted in Huebner's direction, causing those standing next to him to clear a path. Choked by the smoke but committed to pouring from the coffee dangling over the flame, Huebner closed his eyes and held his breath. Teetering back and forth with his cheeks puffed out, aim hampered by tightly closed eyes, he poured most of the precious liquid onto the fire. With a billow and a hiss, a white cloud issued forth, causing a fine layer of ash to spread over everyone slow enough not to retreat before disaster struck. Withstanding the chorus of curses, he attempted to gauge the weight of his mucket to know when to stop pouring until his need for breath competed with his desire to get a full dose of "pick-me-up". Finally, unable to hold his breath longer and having gotten enough into his mucket to satiate his desire, Huebner unsteadily backed away, still clenching his eyes tightly shut and gasping for air. A path had been cleared of obstacles by alert pards so as to minimize Huebner's chances of making the simple chore of coffee any more event-filled. Once he was clear of the smoke trail and able to breathe normally, he opened his eyes, made a smile of triumph at having beaten the smoke, and took a gulp.

Robert's coffee and clothes were covered with a fine layer of ash. The fire, or what was left of it, continued to billow thick white smoke. He used a piece of hard tack to work the ash out of his mucket and continued to sip as if nothing had occurred. Used to the daily fumbling of their Jonah, his pards resumed their own breakfasts.

"Huebner! You goober-brained *Dunkopf!*" Hildebrande shouted. *"Ach, meine Kaffe ist fertig!"* He upended his cup, dumping the ashen liquid to the ground. Following a quick glare in Huebner's direction, he snatched up his haversack and turned quickly toward the Sibley tent, cursing to himself.

With the fire prematurely extinguished, the fire watchers slowly dispersed to attend to their traps. The Nervous Nellies had already put their traps on and were huddled in small groups in front of the company street in anticipation of morning formation. Hoisting himself up, Robert felt his knees creak and blood rush back into his feet.

Huebner stood where he had backed up from the smoke, with a piece of hardtack in his mouth and coffee still steaming in his other hand. An expression of blissful ignorance contorted his face as he mechanically chewed the cracker. Robert felt sorry for the waif, but at the same time felt a revulsion that told him the man was a menace. What was worse, Huebner was part of his Comrades in Battle, along with Hildebrande and Gustavson. Together, they made the four-man team who marched and fought next to one another in formation.

Robert walked slowly past Huebner. Huebner smiled at him as he passed, an idiotic grimace marred by chunks of hardtack and glistening moisture. Robert stared straight ahead of him and passed Huebner, hoping that Huebner wouldn't take eye contact as an invitation to follow. When he ducked into the Sibley, he gathered his traps and exited quickly, escaping the quickly warming and stuffy atmosphere of the tent. Huebner was still in the same spot, totally lost in his breakfast.

Robert brushed the grass from his sack coat and donned it, proceeding to sling his cartridge box and haversack before securing his belt about his waist and adding his canteen. Robert's haversack held everything that he might need during the day. It held his daily rations, his pipe and tobacco, his plate and fork, and anything else he considered indispensable. His mucket, that fire-blackened tin cup, dangled from the strap of the haversack. Fully accoutered now, he reluctantly walked behind Huebner.

"Hube, get your traps, or you're going to be late for formation."

Huebner turned and smiled at him. "*Ja*, get traps, right, get traps." Huebner started to run for the Sibley but sloshed coffee from his mucket down his hand and kerseys. Trying to maintain his pace, yet holding his upper body motionless while cradling the coffee, only made him start and stop in comic fashion, neither hurrying his pace nor holding coffee in the cup. Robert watched him disappear into the Sibley and waited. The company street began to fill with privates completing their kit and lining up in order. Robert glanced back at the Sibley, noting the absence of his erstwhile charge.

"Hube!" he shouted toward the tent, "double quick!"

Huebner burst from the tent, cradling his traps and coffee with his sack coat flapping from behind and only secured by one arm. Hurrying, he tripped and sprawled upon the grass, his coffee and armload of leathers spilling outward, his mucket coming to rest at Robert's feet. Robert glared in Huebner's direction and bent down to pick up the mucket. Huebner managed to push himself up from his prone position and sheepishly grinned at Robert.

"I fell," he said. He tried to scramble for his equipment on all fours but became caught in the haversack strap coiled about his legs.

"Hube! Hube! Stop, just stop, will you? Here, just stop, and I'll untangle you." Huebner lay on his belly and tried to reach his mucket that was half an arm length away while Robert unwound the haversack strap from his legs. Finally freed, Huebner stood and finished putting on his sack coat and equipment as Robert handed it to him.

"C'mon, Hube, they're waiting!"

Robert took Huebner's arm and hustled over to the company formation, where he shoved him into his spot. Gustavson rolled his eyes and shook his head. Hammel looked at his time piece and then at the company lined up in front of him.

"In one rank, count twos!" Hammel's command echoed off the wall of neatly ordered Sibley tents that demarked D Company's street. The ordered routine of army life marched on. Robert scarce could remember a moment without it.

He had lived a childhood mixed between the decidedly unique American culture and that of the German enclaves of St. Louis—dual tongued and European. His father was a merchant and community figure whose father before him moved the family to the bustling trade town connecting the East with the West along the Santa Fe Trail. The elder Mitchell chose early on to cultivate his business and social ties to the growing population of Dutchman. The term was a misnomer and accidental mangling of the German tongue from *Deutsch* to Dutch.

This decision to associate with the growing community of German ex-patriots afforded Robert a unique childhood. His father, Edward Mitchell, saw within the small but fiercely independent community an opportunity to expand his own business interests into Europe and avail himself of the industrious nature of these new "Americans." Many who crossed the Atlantic to touch down in the New World were fresh from the violence of the constant in-fighting of the confederation of German states. The states of Saxony and Thuringia fought to free themselves of Prussian domination; the failure to do so brought to America's shores an influx of the disaffected, well-to-do, and ex-military men. They migrated to the interior to St. Louis and brought with them a culture and a business sense that intrigued the elder Mitchell.

Robert's father enrolled him in a parochial school run by the Lutheran Brotherhood, which ex-patriot German businessmen and clergy formed to care for the spiritual and cultural needs of St. Louis's burgeoning German population. Here, Robert found himself immersed in the foreign culture of its German charges. Although English was the principal language taught, German was still the unofficial language used by both students and teachers.

Purposefully exposing his children to German culture, the elder Mitchell hoped to pass on his own business efforts and alliances to his sons once he was too old to maintain the imports and shipping empire he hoped to build. Going so far as to instruct them to speak German whenever possible at home and at the dinner table, Robert's father gave him a childhood with the same mixture of American ideals and German culture that had gained him entrance to one of the German societies as an associate member. The societies became an extension of the public life the members did not have in the old country, eventually coming to control the political and social life of the neighborhoods. Shaped after the Turnverein Society started in Berlin in 1840, the Turners provided both a gymnastic education and sport and an intellectual grounding from the old country. Chess clubs, debate clubs, rifle teams, and political networking allowed the Mitchells to solidify business and social ties that would otherwise have been denied them.

Given such a childhood, Robert felt at home amid his fellow European soldiers in the 25th Missouri. Swedes, Irish, Germans, Norwegians, and the smattering of other ethnicities made up the companies of the 25th and created a multiplicity of languages that could be heard round the camp fires. Robert's own company had a highly Germanic flavor, as many of its members were fellow Turners from townships surrounding St. Louis. It was Turner militia companies, hastily formed by Major Nathanial Lyon, that confronted pro-secessionist companies composed largely of Irish ex-patriots for control of St. Louis in the early days of the conflict. Bloody confrontations ensued as agents of the federal government and the Confederacy wrestled for ownership of Missouri.

Of his pards and messmates, Hildebrande was a fellow Turner and had worked as a foreman for his father at the Maple Street warehouse. Gustavson was a burley Swede whose rough voice and booming laughter always announced his presence nearby. Then there was the hapless Huebner, a youth from St. Louis whose father escaped from Saxony. After the 25th was mustered into Federal service, these men became Robert's constant companions, placed together by luck.

Early in the siege of Fort Donelson, his close childhood friend, Gunther Hauser, took a minié ball to the leg while in the rifle pits and had been sent to the hospital steamer, Princeton. Gunther's regiment, belonging to W. H. L. Wallace's division, weathered the bitter Tennessee winter by besieging Fort Donelson while the 13th Missouri cooled their heels on garrison duty before being reorganized and filled out with recruits as the 25th Missouri. Robert and his comrades were saved the embarrassment of being made prisoners when the old 13th Missouri surrendered to Major General Price's Confederates along with the other regiments garrisoning Lexington, Missouri. Colonel Everette Peabody was made prisoner himself and soon exchanged. It was Peabody who had conducted several recruitment rallies in St. Louis and convinced Robert of the need to volunteer.

Anxious that he should soon join his friend, Robert was saddened to receive a final letter from Gunther describing the amputation and hope of eventual release and discharge, but nothing further. Robert learned from his mother months later that Gunther had succumbed to diarrhea before his release. The news caused him much grief. A devoted Lutheran, Gunther would chide Robert that his Methodism wasn't good enough to get him into God's good graces; he needed the original Protestant faith and message to truly please the Lord. This often caused Robert to worry about grace and works and about which philosophy was right. The elder Mitchell, though desirous of absorbing as much German culture as possible, could not be driven to abandon his Wesleyan upbringing.

The counting finished, Hammel conferred with Captain Schmitz. Robert shifted his weight from one leg to another, weary of inactivity. From the corner of his eye he caught sight of Huebner chewing on his tongue, a constant action the boy engaged in when either bored or busy. His forage cap sat high upon his forehead, and his brownish hair dangled lazily under the bill. Shifting his own traps about his sack coat slightly, Robert released a long sigh and waited for the next command.

*****

"Rest!" echoed the command of Colonel Jones.

With relief, Philip staggered down the embankment and found a shady spot to relieve his shoulders from the weight of the knapsack. He unbuttoned his sack coat and shifted the haversack and canteen strap higher on his chest, exposing his sweat-soaked shirt to the open, cooling breeze. Plopping down heavily next to him, Sam Henderson let out a groan and allowed himself to slide comfortably down the embankment. In front of them, Theo Mueller eagerly stripped down of everything but his kersey blue trousers and undershirt with a look of ecstasy upon his face.

Company officers conferred in the middle of the road while the men of the 24th Ohio made for whatever shade and comfort could be found along the lane. Philip was content to leave his traps on so he would not have to bother with them when the call came to form up. Theo Mueller sat down, leaned his back against the other side of the embankment, and smiled at Philip.

"You be much cooler if you take that stuff off," Theo told Philip.

"I be much fine, thank you," Philip grinned.

"You two don't know what you missing," Theo persisted.

"We're conserving our energy for the march by not putting our traps on and off at every stop," Sam said after he wiped his brow.

"We catch up to Grant. Then we whip some *Secesh, ja?*" Theo blurted. "Secesh" was their term for the secessionists.

"We never catch up to Grant. Even if he does stay still at Pittsburg Landing, we're going to be marching until we're all old and gray, always marching and marching and marching," Philip said and closed his eyes. "Our lot in this war is to fight it with our feet stomping on all of the Secesh lice."

"How long we been on the move?" Sammy asked.

"Since sun up," Theo replied.

"No, on this march from Nashville," Sammy asked again, with a glare at Theo.

"Ten of the longest days of my life," Philip moaned.

"Liked the roads better in Kentucky. Softer," Sammy said as he wiggled his toes within his brogans.

"Roads not different! Same dusty, rock-filled, ill-cared-for southern roads," Theo complained.

"No, there's something different about these Tennessee roads, softer somehow. You notice how the dust is slightly different in color, a lighter brown than the dust in Kentucky. I think they are softer," Sammy said.

"You gettin' sun madness. Nothing different 'bout these roads," Theo said.

"Parson, you think these roads are different, right?"

Philip, jarred from his reverie, sputtered, "Huh? What roads?"

"Sammy thinks the roads in Tennessee is different than the roads in Kentucky. Tell him he's got sunstroke." Theo stretched his legs and released a satisfied sigh.

"Is that the only thing you two can argue about? I hadn't noticed the difference. Maybe it's softer. I don't know, hadn't given it no mind," Philip replied, entwining his fingers into the straps of his knapsack.

"You believe what you want to, but I notice the difference all the same. My feet don't hurt as much as they did in Kentucky," Sammy retorted.

"Ground is softer in Tennessee. You better answer next sick call. You going to keel over with the stroke," Theo said.

Not to be outdone, Sammy shot back with "Hush up, you Dutch skulker."

"Backwoods hillbilly."

"Hessian papist."

"Protestant heathen."

"Papal emissary of Beelzebub!"

That last one made Theo's face turn red. He looked over to Philip. "What you got to say, Rev? You think that the Pope, the one descended from Saint Peter himself, the man who knew Christ, be of the devil as our bumpkin here says?" He sneered at Sammy. Philip hated it when Theo or anyone referred to him as The Reverend. Turning to look at Theo, he shook his head and said, "No comment."

Theo and Sammy's argument turned to Luther's Protestant revolution. He tuned them out. Reminded of his father's chosen profession and the hard life that came with it, Philip tried to think about something else. He tried to resume his daydream of walking the other way from the town meeting that led to his volunteering. Now, all he could think about was his father. Charles had spent countless hours traveling from one church to the next, often dragging Philip and his younger brother along with him. Most of the church buildings were as old as the small communities that they served, with dark and cold wooden benches. Recollections of dank odors of mildew and rotting churches filled with the solemn parishioners reminded him why he had volunteered. The desire to escape his father and the expectation that he, too, would become a minister of God's Word had brought him to the meeting that day in Waynesville, Ohio. As a good, proper young itinerant minister, Philip learned the art of impression. He kept an impression of himself before the prying eyes of busy-bodies and stern gazes of adults to be separate from the cavorting gangs of youths and children that swarmed the church grounds after each service. Never far from his father's reach, Philip did not experience much of the farmer or merchant family childhood like his peers. Living out of a wagon coach for days at a time as they traveled along the banks of the Big and Little Miami Rivers, whose courses emptied into the greater Ohio River, they crossed in and out of the counties that made up his father's circuit. Methodist societies and classes dotted crossroad villages and farming communities between the two Miami River valleys.

At the age of twenty five, he consented to take on a few of the communities to shepherd the flock. He found the work agreeable at first and brought his own brand of the Good Book and teaching to his circuit. Young and often in over his head, he began to feel the itch to do something else after the novelty wore off. He was well regarded in each class and society, but he felt that but for the labors of his father he would be little revered. His father was the more eloquent teacher, but Philip could write. To compensate, he began writing out his sermons and committing them to memory. This worked well when he remembered his lines; often he would break his oratory in mid-thought, leaving his listeners acutely aware of his predicament. He would panic when that happened, nervously shuffling the pages on his podium in a vain attempt to remind himself of the next part of his oration. Rather than hiding his subterfuge, he would begin again, under the concept that the need to impart God's wisdom was more important than hiding behind a façade.

The monotony of the circuit began to wear upon him; his restlessness was heightened by the disturbing news from the southern churches. Talk of secession should the "Black Republicans" come to power reached his ears in the run-up to the 1860 elections. The balance between slave and free states and territories was a decades-old topic. Secession, however, was a decidedly new and unthinkable one. Moreover, many in his circuit migrated and still had relations in Kentucky and Virginia; even as late as a generation prior, people with a decidedly southern flavor and sympathy were opening up the rich farmland in the river valleys. Although none brought slaves with them, they were uneasy with the abolitionist platform of the Republicans. The time of the campaign and vote was tense. Each visit to his societies was progressively more distressing with talk of dividing of the country. Many parishioners after vespers voiced support for the southern complaint that northern interests were wielding a heavy hand on their southern brethren, both financially and morally. When asked what the good Lord would say in those troubled times, Philip was unable to reconcile his own feelings from those of the movement.

Even the Methodist leadership could not answer that question with a unified voice. Word coming from the national assemblies was of bitter recriminations and debate as to the propriety of slavery and the clergy's response based on biblical teachings. At times, in the debate chambers, a southern apologist would harangue his listeners with biblical proofs of God's ordination of slavery, only to be replaced at the podium by a northern speaker who would use the same scripture to prove the opposite. Without a solid foundation to deal with the worried looks of his parishioners, Philip attempted to reason his own way through.

Then the unthinkable occurred. The Republicans were swept into the White House and both houses of Congress. South Carolina's secession began the feared break-up of the country; one state after another followed her lead. Divided in loyalty by family ties to the states seceding, but contemptuous of the secession ordinances, the residents of the Ohio River valleys girded themselves for what was to come. Overnight, Methodists as a movement became sectional, though little divided them relationally. His parishioners whole-heartedly supported the federal government, and overnight the debates over God's ordination of slavery ended.

The question of war had not manifested itself after the election, although both politicians and traveling orators fanned the patriotic fervor. In his own heart, Philip began to see a way that he could quietly slip away from the pressure he felt in tending to the spiritual needs of his circuit and not disappoint his father too terribly. He was torn by his desire to see the life through but relieve the burden of responsibility. Then, in 1861, the brazen acts of the Confederates in Charleston Harbor released a national tension that had peaked with the election of Abraham Lincoln. Faces that day were grim with the talk of war, and southern recalcitrance became indignity. Faint stirrings of his own patriotism were realized that day in Waynesville at a war rally. He would volunteer, not as a regimental chaplain, but as a foot soldier and join the familiar faces he found in the crowd from his own circuit.

Relieved at the release from his ministerial burdens and the chance to relinquish his collar, before the events of the Harper affair forced the Bishop's hand, he bade farewell to his parents and joined with his fellow volunteers in Waynesville, Ohio. They traveled to Columbus by rail for muster into Federal service. The life of patriotism was as hard as he had imagined it would be, but he was no longer responsible for people, their well-being, or their spiritual education. In that regard, army life was a relief.

In no time at all, the men in the company began calling him "reverend." Philip was not quick to act the part, wishing to be left alone, but the needs of familiar faces prevented him from distancing himself from his old responsibility. Resigned that he could not escape his former calling, he saw to the spiritual needs of anyone who inquired; after all, even Jonah was compelled to bring God's warning of repentance to the Ninehvites. Being called "Rev" had its advantages, as he would discover. Men would confide in him just about anything, which kept him in the know about everything. However, he soon found this to be a double-edged sword, creating both instant companions and instant enemies. Most were not malicious in their dislike, and no hostility directed at his person. There were just those from whom he knew association would not be reciprocated. A few men, such as Second Sergeant Harper, who was from a family in his circuit, could not restrain their feelings of disdain even before things turned ugly between him and this family.

As second sergeant, Harper was often put in charge of fatigue details, which the squads rotated now and again in their duties. Normally, this meant seeing to various and sundry details about the encampment or march. Invariably, Philip would find himself and his pards detailed under Harper's watchful eye for company cook fires, cleaning up around the sinks—a particularly disagreeable task, especially after a few days of the normal deposits of human waste--picket duty—or preparing the officers' tents. Harper referred to Philip as "the good minister" and took every opportunity to heap abuse or criticism upon whatever Philip was assigned to perform. Never knowing when he might be under Harper's heel again, Philip struggled with his own resentment toward those injustices. At times, he could not curb his own tongue and would fling barbs of his own Harper's way until the two men would barely be on civil terms, even for soldiers. The days of the march had been somewhat pleasant for Philip because he and Harper had not crossed paths.

"Mule, where's the big bugs?" Johnny Henson asked Theo from under the bill of his forage cap. Johnny made up the fourth of Philip's pards and old acquaintances from the Ohio River Valley Methodist Societies.

Philip perked up at the question and opened his eyes. "Oh, Johnny, when'd you sit down?"

"While you was sawing logs not just ten minutes ago," Johnny replied.

"Yeah, Mule, what's happenin' on the road?" Philip asked.

"You's going to have to find yourselves another spy. I'm tiring of this officer watching," Theo griped as he stood and peered down the road. Once the officers began to gather and move about, the order to fall in would soon follow. "Relax, *meine kinder*, them bugs is nowhere to be seen."

"Well, I see the good reverend is busy workin' on his back like any shiftless man of the Good Book," a voice above them stated. Harper stood off the road embankment above Philip and the others with a smirk creasing the corners of his mouth. The soft earth began to trickle down the slope and onto Philip's neck and shirt. Rising quickly and wiping the dirt off of his neck, Philip retorted, "I'll be sure to request of the good Lord a nice case of the Kentucky quick step for the rest of your movement. Should complement the diarrhea of your mouth, Sergeant."

"You do that, Rev," Harper said with a smile and turned away. When he was out of earshot, "Rear rank, skulker," Philip hissed. Johnny piped up. "I seen Harper pretending to take care of the ammunition at Nashville, hanging back with the other riff-raff while we formed line. He always makes sure he is in charge of some important rear guard action, like guarding the knapsacks or equipment when danger is in the air."

"How you think he got second sergeant?" Theo asked. "He didn't get it whipping Secesh. He got it with that bragging mouth of his."

Sammy frowned at them. "Bah! The time will come, and one day he will be seen for what he is. Once we face the Secesh again, then we'll see that white feather he's been a-hidin'. He'll turn and run first sign of trouble. Just you watch and see if he doesn't." Theo got up and stretched. He looked down the road and then pointed. "I see movement on the road, pards. Looks like the rest is over." The men groaned. Philip sighed as he struggled to sit upright against the knapsack's pull.

Chapter Four

"Up, up! Company B is ordered to stand to arms. C'mon, up, up."

The voice of First Sergeant Hammel sounded into the tent as an unwelcome messenger of bad news. Robert rubbed his eyes and allowed them to adjust to the darkened tent. The fog of deep sleep melted away slowly, bringing with it the realization he had not been long in slumber; something odd was up.

"Up, up! Get your traps and fall into the company street with arms. Light marching order. Get off your arses and get moving!"

"What's going on?" Huebner asked.

"Get up and get you traps, *Dunkopf*. Get ready for *Marsch*," Hildebrande snapped.

"March? In this dark?"

"*Ja*. Get up."

"Get dressed, Hube," Robert said as he buttoned his sack coat and felt around for the rest of his leathers. "We got to form up on the company street. Light marching order, Hube. Just grab your leathers and haversack. Don't need your knapsack."

Huebner made a whining noise. "Isn't today Saturday?"

"*Ja*, what does it matter, *Kind*? Rouse!" Gustavson tersely ordered.

"I thought Hauptmann Schmitz give us morning off from drill."

"Hube, just get ready for a march, all right?" Robert said, exasperated.

The Sibley began to empty rapidly as others finished dressing and stepped out. Robert stepped over the bedrolls of his tent mates and ducked out into the open air. It was dark, chilly, damp, and uninviting. The company area was alive with noise and muffled conversations and, except for the darkness, would have seemed like a typical morning. At the head of the company street roared a fire, its light illuminating a crowd of orange-faced watchers.

Robert squeezed his way into the circle and welcomed the warmth on his face and legs. The essential gallon of coffee was boiling, and he could detect just the slightest wisp of steam rising out of its vent. Like vagabonds or street urchins, the men held their muckets, awaiting the generosity of the company cook.

Hours could be spent just staring into the flames. At this hour, there was little talk. Even the company wags were content to just watch the flames and rub the sleep out of their eyes.

A familiar face poked itself into the light of the fire. "Form up on the street in thirty minutes." The face disappeared just as quickly as it had appeared.

"What time is it?" a voice broke the silence.

A figure in the circle produced a time piece. "Two in the morning."

Like a solitary rain drop that announces the coming storm, those first words broke the quiet at the fireside.

"Patrol?"

"Dunno."

"That's why we have pickets."

"They've got us and D and E Companies rousted. What else could it be?"

"Maybe we're increasing the pickets."

"Maybe ol' Colonel Peabody has finally gone mad. He's sendin' us chasin' Rebel ghosts again."

"Maybe so, but he could've picked a better hour to do it."

"He's probably still in his tent countin' Rebs in his sleep."

"Naw. Saw him not more than ten minutes ago talkin' to Colonel Van Horn, and he looked his normal agitated self."

"He's still gone mad, seein' Rebs behind every bush and tree for weeks."

"No matter how mad he may be, *vir sind die Soldaten* up in *die Morgen*."

"Isn't it boiling yet?"

"No."

"*Vo ist das Kind* Huebner?" Hildebrande asked.

"Probably still in the Sibley," Gustavson stonily answered.

"Needs to get his arse in shape."

"Uh oh, here he comes."

Huebner's cheery early morning expression appeared between Hildebrande and Gustavson.

"Alvays just in time for *die Kaffe*," Gustavson groused.

"*Wird der Kaffee gebrüht?*" Huebner asked.

"*Nein, Kaffe nicht gebrüht,*" replied Hildebrande.

"We ought to try it anyway. Hammel's going to be showin' up any second to call formation," another man said.

"*Ja,* no more wasting time. Let's get it before it's too late," Hildebrande agreed and bent over to lift the boiler from its hook above the fire.

As the pitcher was delicately tipped to pour its contents into the crowding muckets, Hildebrande and Gustavson kept Huebner at bay until all had been served, allowing the others to enjoy a full un-spoilt cup. The circle instinctively widened as Huebner bent down to fill his mucket but lost his balance, pouring a healthy portion of the liquid into the fire, raising yet another cloud of ash. The lid over the pitcher protected its contents, and everyone else was far enough away to be immune from the fallout.

Robert held the mucket to his lips and blew across its surface. It was hot enough to enjoy, but the rim of his steel mucket was too hot to put his lips to yet, allowing only quick sips. He let the aroma sink into his consciousness. The early morning wake-up was unusual, but not so much so as to cause alarm. He was used to being rudely shaken awake occasionally, as when on picket duty he would have to spell the previous watch for a few hours, and he usually drew the worst time of the night, between one and three a.m. At least he was enjoying a fire and a hot cup, two things denied while on picket. In the last two weeks, his regiment and the others of the brigade had been ordered to patrol the woods in front. Only the evening before, two other companies had been formed for an early morning march with no results.

The cold, damp air was filled with the noise of clanking equipment and the crackling of the fire. Even the insects were smart enough to be resting at this hour. The darkness cloaked the forest, which sat only a few hundred rods from the edge of the camp. Somewhere out there, the company pickets were posted, and Robert wondered if they were going to join them or push on ahead into the unknown.

As the coffee enlivened them, the men began to move about with more alacrity. Groups of men formed, and conversation became lively. Robert moved over to where Gustavson and Hildebrande stood. The flicker of the fire danced shadows about their faces.

"Probably just another fool's errand," Robert said.

"*Ja*, it's just our turn. A and C had their turn *die andere Morgen*," Hildebrande replied.

"Here comes Hammel." Robert quickly took another draught of his mucket in anticipation of having to dump the remainder. He spied Huebner happily munching on a hard tack and cuddling his mucket to his chest. A quiet expression lit his face as he stared mesmerized by the flames.

A shout interrupted their reverie. "B Company! Form up on the street!"

With one last gulp of coffee, Robert up-ended his mucket and secured it to his haversack. He walked over to Huebner and shook his shoulder vigorously. "Hube, we gotta form up. Dump that and get moving."

Robert turned and took a few steps in the direction of the company street, but not hearing foot falls behind him, he stopped and turned. Huebner was still transfixed by the fire. "Hube! C'mon." Robert walked back to his erstwhile companion and grabbed the sleeve of his sack coat and dragged him away.

"Time to form?" Huebner asked.

"Yeah, time to form."

*****

They made their way down the goat track that stood for a road. The early morning dew and rain of the day before left his brogans soaking wet, and his toes squished about in wet woolen socks. Robert's company was third in line of the column. All he could see in the front was a line of heads and rifles. The still, dark forest put Robert on edge. They had marched silently, not by order but just by the thought of not being caught unawares after leaving the picket post half an hour before. The blackness made it exceedingly difficult to see but a few feet in any direction, and the general downward slope of the track forced him to control his stride lest he blunder into the back of the man in front. The lead company was extended in a skirmish line and as flankers, spread out at five pace intervals in front and on flanks parallel to the march column. Despite the chill, Robert was sweating as the tension built.

He could see his pards well enough in the darkness to see they, too, were uneasy. Every shadow they passed, each odd grouping of trees or bushes, looked like bandits ready to attack. Each sound or break of a twig sent shivers down him as they waited on another halt. Peering into the thickness of the woods to the side of the trail, he saw numerous ghostly apparitions flitting from shadow to shadow, blending in with the trunks and shrubs. Sudden movement in the distance would form silhouettes and then morph into something different as he stared. He imagined an army of ghouls moving about, only to freeze at the right moment just as his gaze fell upon them.

"Forward, march," Captain Schmitz said softly.

The silence was broken again by the shuffling of several hundred foot falls upon the track. Resuming the march allowed Robert to relax once again. He concentrated on keeping the pace, which was preferable to imagining Rebels lurking in each change of shadow.

Without warning, the report of a musket rang out. Robert jumped at the sudden sound breaking the relative quiet. A string of individual shots followed from the skirmish line ahead. In between he could make out the fire of pistols and the pounding of hooves.

"Halt! Halt!"

Like an accordion, the company columns compressed at the suddenness of the command. Cursing rang out when men blundered into the backs of their fellows. They heard wild and irregular firing ahead in the distance. For brief moments, the horizon was lit up as a musket discharged. Robert craned his neck to make out what was going on in the distance.

Captain Schmitz returned to the company and loudly ordered, "By the right oblique, forward march!"

Sluggishly, the men stumbled forward off the rough trail and into the underbrush. From Major Powell, the command rang out, "By company into line, form battalion!" With unsure footing stumbling on numerous obstacles in the dark, the marching column changed into a double rank front. Robert kept his arm in touch with the man next to him. Others were similarly groping along.

The next command heightened the tension. "At the double quick, forward march!" Captain Schmitz shouted as the column broke into a labored trot through the thickets and toward the next company forming in front. Robert struggled to keep his balance. Every man grabbed the one ahead of him to follow the pell-mell race to form a line of files.

Each company found its place in the line for battle. All were breathing heavily and struggling to maintain balance in the midst of the rising tempo of musketry to their front. Officers moved about nervously, animated by the adrenaline that came with the nearness of action.

"Forward, march!" commanded Major Powell, and the battalion lurched forward. Company officers and file closers in the rear kept up a constant stream of commands and admonitions to keep the pace, keep the guide to the right, keep their resolve. With a full view now of what lay ahead, Robert kept his attention glued to what might appear in front of them. To his relief, the trees gave way to the solid blue of an opening in the forest. He made out the bobbing heads of the skirmish line through the intervening trees. Beyond the skirmishers, he saw moving forms in the distance, and a fence line leaped into view.

Glancing to his left and right, he made out the weary faces of his pards. Gustavson was on his right, and Hildebrande and Huebner were directly behind him. The firing was still sporadic from both the skirmishers and the invisible enemy cavalry.

Like the opening of a door releasing one from cramped confines, they stepped out from the forest and stood in front of a fence. Before them, in the dim blue of morning, they could see an open field and the dim outlines of the Fraley farm upon a slight rise three hundred yards from where the men of the 25th and 21st Missouri of Peabody's brigade broke into view. Darting to and fro between the buildings and the opposing skirmish lines, the heads of the enemy could be seen appearing then disappearing in the field opposite. In the darkness, a small ditch could be made out that cut across the length of the field and separated the two skirmish lines. The skirmish line of the enemy held a position slightly elevated from theirs, and minié balls whizzed uncomfortably near.

"Halt! Dress your line. Dress on the colors!" shouted Captain Schmitz.

A sudden shifting of bodies ensued as the men dressed right and each one in turn pressured the man next to him to move to the right. Near the fence line the ground was uneven, and the act of moving to the right in the dark was unnerving. The morning dew made the field slippery, causing more than one man to stumble and draw a string of cursing from the file closers.

The level of fire had not increased beyond the *pop, pop, pop* of the cavalry opposing them. Feeling confident that only a few volleys would be needed, the Federals stood confidently stolid. Robert looked down the line of men that seemed to disappear into the blackness. There was a confidence to be felt in numbers. A volley, a move forward, and another volley should scatter the cavalry and put them to flight.

"Ready!"

The shifting into the position of ready and the half cock of hammers echoed about the fence line. Robert felt his heartbeat quicken with excitement as the execution of incessant drilling was put to the test. The supreme test of mettle and bravery, honor, and devotion to cause was about to be displayed. Company officers and first sergeants kept a steady stream of chatter from behind.

"Aim low."

"Send them sons of perdition straight to Hell."

"Aim for the discharges."

"Aim!"

Four hundred muskets leveled upon the enemy, and four hundred hammers locked into firing position. Robert stood with his rifle to his shoulder. Huebner's musket bounced unsteadily upon Robert's cocked right arm, Gustavson's on his left, forming a solid phalanx of iron that would in seconds be sent down the field into the enemy cavalry.

"Fire!"

As if by one action, a solid crack of sound exploded around them and briefly obscured their front in a cloud of smoke. A chorus of *hurrahs* erupted from the Federal line, celebrating the solidness of the volley. Hours of drill and discipline displayed in singular action swelled Robert and his pards with pride.

"Load and come to the ready!"

The smoke began to clear. They could see their enemy out in their front and around the farm buildings. The command to move forward was given, and Robert clambered over the rail fence and grabbed Huebner's rifle so he could climb over as well. Dressing their lines once more, the command to forward march was shouted amid the increasing fire from the Confederates. Ineffectual skirmishing by both sides caused little damage in the darkness. The line was halted again at a ditch in the field. From here, the farm buildings and beyond could be seen more clearly. The field was wide and long and rimmed by forest. The enemy fire became more focused, and they could hear the uncomfortable *zip* of lead.

"Ready!"

Robert brought his rifle to the ready position and cocked the hammer to safe. *This time, we should do some damage,* he thought. He could see another tree line in the distance behind the farm houses. The clearing looked to be a mile in width but only half that in length, creating a pocket of tillable land in the intervening space. He noticed movement behind the houses, looking much like something solid and long creeping forward. The movement extended far beyond the right and left of the battalion. When he realized what it was, his heart skipped a beat. Others began to see it as well, growing quiet as they did. Following gasps of realization, four hundred Federals held their breaths as they stood exposed in the open field. They stood transfixed, watching the wave of movement wash toward them in the darkness. Robert felt a tremble in his gut.

*****

Stephen followed the step, step, step of the pace set by the tramping of thousands of footfalls upon the uneven ground. The movement made so much noise that he wondered how the enemy could fail to hear the elephantine throng lumbering forward. Shouted commands and admonitions competed with the clanking of tin cups, heavy foot falls, and the rustling of undergrowth and bushes. The sound invigorated him, the sound of an immense and irresistible fighting machine moving forward to crush anything that lay in its path.

He stumbled forward in exhaustion. The previous day saw his regiment laying upon its arms or hastily forming line of battle when one false alarm after another brought everyone to his feet and ready to move forward. The strain had become unbearable. They knew they were in a difficult position should they be discovered prematurely. The well-laid trap became more and more a risk as anxiety gave way to carelessness; any noise, no matter how soft, was enough to cause a man to freeze and look in the direction of the enemy camp.

They had gone without coffee and palatable food for three days. Awakened now by the commencement of the attack, Stephen's senses were fully engaged. The touch of elbows while evading trees and obstacles kept his attention riveted upon the guide file. Like a giant accordion, the formation ebbed and flowed, morphing into a snaking movement until it resembled a wave more than a straight line, drawing commands and curses from company officers. The formation extended in both directions as far as he could see.

The division formed before the tree line of the forest that separated them from the enemy camps and the enemy soldiers who had confidently entered it twenty minutes ago. The strain of struggling through the thickets was unnerving. They were more than a little relieved when the forest suddenly opened up to a vista of cleared fields and farm buildings.

Sudden sounds of musketry surprised him. The noise of their movement through the trees had drowned out the sounds of the skirmish occurring around the farm buildings. The shock widened their eyes; quizzical looks passed from man to man. So close had the enemy been to their step-off point that Stephen's heart stopped; their preparations for the grand attack in secret coming to naught. Yet there was the enemy giving fight to the advance skirmish lines. The dim light and distance obscured what was going on to their right, save for the muzzle flashes. A farm was situated on an elevation, and its now-barren field extended downward. The uncomfortable prospect of advancing over the open space in the face of a well-hidden enemy in the tree line fell heavily upon him. If the enemy were there in force, the attack might fail before it had even started.

As if to punctuate his fears, the sudden crack of a volley thundered and echoed out to the right in the darkness. The advance had taken him to a position 200 yards to the right of the farm buildings, and he saw the 15th Arkansas skirmishers keeping a steady pace out front. The cheering from the enemy line confirmed his fears, and the hitherto steady move forward faltered a step.

"Forward! Forward!" shouted Colonel Thornton as he wheeled his horse about.

Stephen glanced over at William, who returned his worried expression.

"I thought we was to surprise 'em. Sounds like they is waitin' fer us!" William shouted over the din.

"I guess we'll just see what's on the other side of these buildings," Stephen shouted back.

"By the right flank, by column of companies, forward march!"

The firing to their right increased in volume, making the absence of any hint of the enemy in their front more unnerving. Stephen could only see the brief flashes of light from the discharge of the guns.

"You see anything ahead?" Stephen shouted.

"Too dark still," William answered.

The movement hardly skipped a beat despite the racket.

"I don't hear any cannon fire. This ain't their main line!" William shouted.

Stephen could make out the blurry and dark line of the enemy between volleys in the middle of the field on their right. From behind them came the booming report of a battery of cannon as the guns fired one by one. Still, the darkness could yet be concealing disaster, and Stephen withheld his elation until he could see the enemy's backs. The scene was lit for seconds at a time by cannon fire, flashing the skirmish line in their front. It also illuminated the opposing enemy line.

They heard another boom, and a flash lit the darkness, this time from the Federal line. Somewhere, hidden by the darkness of the pre-dawn morning, off to his right, men were locked in deadly combat.

"Halt," called Colonel Thornton. The advance stopped dead in its tracks.

"What's goin' on?" Willie asked.

"Don' know," Stephen answered.

A staff officer rode up and conferred with Thornton for a few moments before galloping off again into the blackness.

"Wood's brigade is engaging the enemy," Stephen heard the man say to

Thornton. "A general halt of the line to keep alignment has been ordered by Colonel Cleburne."

The 15th Arkansas skirmishers went to one knee seventy-five yards in front, and the breaking of the eastern skyline illuminated the scene. They spied a small line of the enemy three hundred yards away, standing forlorn and pitiful on the edge of the field now dominated by Hardee's entire corps as it marched through the trees and into the open field.

From his vantage point, Stephen could see a depression cutting down the length of the field. Just in front of it, the enemy's formation confronted Wood's skirmish line and regiments as they advanced. Stephen knew the halt would be short, for they overlapped the enemy line and could easily brush it away.

*****

"Load and come to the ready!" went the call, taken up by the company officers and bellowed in voices made urgent by the multitude of the host approaching.

Robert roughly guessed their number in the still poor visibility. He could hear them, however. Thousands of footfalls upon the ground and a rustling of undergrowth surrounding this little force standing like a lone island of sand before the breaking of a mighty tidal wave. The dark line steadily approached and loomed larger with each step forward.

"Fire by files! Ready! Aim! Fire!"

From the right-most company, the ripple of fire moved down the line. One man from the front rank and the man directly behind him in the rear rank took aim and discharged their weapons. Robert nervously waited his turn and watched the slow but continuous discharge follow each front and rear man in turn. The pull of the trigger and jerk of the discharge rocked his weapon upward, and he mechanically let it slide down his hand and into place between his feet. Without thinking he reached into his cartridge pouch for the next round. The irregular discharge of weapons filled the air with an unceasing urgency.

"Keep up your fire! Quickly, quickly!"

"Steady, boys, steady! Load and fire!"

Robert squinted as Huebner's musket leveled over his shoulder and discharged a flash that temporarily blinded; a spark from the cap flashed too close to his cheek.

"Mein Gott!"

In the gradual lightening of the eastern skyline, objects became more discernible, and the enormity of what was approaching became evident. The march of humanity seemed to be bursting forth from the trees all around them, extended from horizon to horizon.

"We're in trouble!"

"Keep up your fire! For God's sake, load and fire!"

"We can't stay here!"

"*Ich habe geschoßen!*" a voice croaked behind Robert, "I am hit," followed by something heavy falling upon his back. Catching his balance upon his musket, he stumbled forward as the body of Hildebrande crumpled to the ground. Huebner paused lifting his weapon to his shoulder and gawked at the body.

"*Schieß, Huebner! Zünd Ihr Gewehr an!* Fire, Huebner! Fire your weapon!" Gustavson shouted at Huebner angrily while he ripped open a cartridge.

"*Ja, ja, ich zünd mein Gewehr an.*"

Robert inched back into the formation as best as he could and straddled Hildebrande's body. He accidentally dropped the butt of the musket heavily on Hildebrande's back. "Sorry, pard," he muttered. The noise was deafening, a constant roar of musketry and cannon thundering from the advancing lines of the enemy. Far to the right, another enemy brigade moved across the field and overlapped their position. The enemy in their front was advancing its colors.

The voice of Captain Schmitz shouted from behind them. "Listen for the next order! We're about to move. Listen for the major's command!"

"Battalion! About face! At the double quick, march! Back to the fence line!"

Quickly turning as well as he could with Hildebrande's body between his feet, Robert put his back to the enemy and gladly moved off at a trot until they came back to the fence. Tense moments passed as they climbed back over and tried to untangle themselves to reform behind it. There wasn't much to protect them from the hail of minié balls that continued to whiz all around. The occasional sound of splintering wood did give some comfort. Robert made out the prostrate forms that once marked the spot of their former line. The woods behind them bled a trail of wounded men struggling to find a safe place to rest or limping back in the direction they had come.

Like a mist, the discharge from their weapons hung low upon the ground, forming a murkiness through which little could be discerned. Then, from the haze, the color guard of the enemy burst through, followed closely by his double lines.

"Ready! Aim! Fire!"

The command barely reached his ears before Robert and the others discharged their weapons simultaneously. The bravado they had voiced upon the first such accomplishment was absent, and they scarcely noticed its perfection. Pre-occupied with survival, each man did his best to suppress the urge to turn and run. To run and seek shelter when the body was still whole and healthy was to abandon one's pards to the enemy.

The moments passed with excruciating slowness, counted only by the rapidity of the loading and firing of weapons. Robert thrust his hand into his cartridge pouch only to discover that the top tins were empty. Now came the awkward attempt to retrieve the wrapped package of ten paper cartridges and caps from his lower tin while balancing his weapon between his legs, a difficult maneuver in the close confines of the formation. Ripping open the package sent the paper cartridges fumbling about in his shaky hands, with a few dropping to the ground out of sight.

"Ten paces, backward march!"

Startled by the command, Robert chanced to look up. The enemy was steadily marching toward them. He felt a tug on his belt that drew him backward, and he quickly grabbed his weapon and tried to hold on to the loose cartridges, tin, and package of caps in his other hand. Hurrying to put the cartridges into the open top tin and empty the caps into his cap pouch, Robert heard something that made his heart freeze. They were deep into the trees once again when he looked up. The brightening skyline from the split rail fence they just vacated suddenly became dark as the enemy stopped extending far to the right and left.

"Fire!"

The fence, the enemy, and the light of the morning were engulfed in smoke and the booming of the volley. Robert didn't know how close they were. The thickets, and his attempts to replenish his cartridge tin, had occupied his attention until that moment. On the heels of the volley, he heard the sound of minié balls striking trees and bodies. As if the ground had suddenly been pulled out from underneath them, men who had been standing erect the moment before were now tumbling to the ground. Stunned, Robert suddenly found himself in the open and alone. The comfort of pards to the right, left, and rear was absent. At his feet lay the crumpled and writhing bodies of the men. A banshee-like yelling emanated from the enemy at the destruction wrought by their volley.

"To the rear, march, to the rear, march!"

Robert stood motionless and watched his remaining comrades turn and move farther into the woods. A few of the men who had been felled by the volley began to stagger to their feet and move to the rear.

"*Hilf mich! Kameraden! Hilf mich!*"

In the tangle of arms, legs, and torsos prostrate before him, Robert recognized Huebner and Gustavson. Huebner was struggling to crawl from underneath the body of someone Robert didn't recognize in the dark, and Gustavson was cradling his arm and watching the others move away. Robert grabbed Huebner's outstretched hand and yanked him to his feet.

"Grab Gustavson and run!" Robert shouted into Huebner's ear and then turned to help another soldier to his feet. The enemy was climbing the fence and reforming on the other side.

"Go!" he shouted and tripped over the pile of bodies in his way. The rest of the company was rapidly disappearing from view. The fear of being separated and captured pushed him and his comrades to make haste in their departure. The sounds of musketry ceased, replaced by the sounds of thousands of footfalls heralding the approach of something large and horrible.

Breathless and fatigued, the small party rejoined their company and fell in as the battalion continued the march. The intervening trees between the foes provided a small amount of protection, and the fear of being shot in the back abated. The enormity of what they had witnessed and what it meant for the whole army began to dawn on each one. They had been caught unawares. Had it not been for the early morning foray, the outcome might have been worse. Worry and doubt creased the face of each silently marching man. Even while casting furtive glances to the rear, they maintained a brisk pace.

Dawn finally brightened the eastern horizon and revealed the casualties as familiar faces went missing. The company felt smaller. The reassurance of pards was gone, their places taken by strangers. The wood was no place to fight, and Robert longed to be free of its presence. Reaching their own picket line, the battalion shook itself out, absorbed the picket companies they met, and continued the march back from whence they had come.

Chapter Five

Stephen looked about uneasily. The brigade halted beyond the fence line to straighten out the formations, and the wait was insufferable. No one expected to meet any resistance so soon after stepping off. Instead of victory, he saw concern and worry on every face. At any moment, the enemy might burst into view and unleash upon them death from every quarter. The grand army entered the thickets, but his feeling of invincibility dissipated in the blindness. The enemy dead and wounded lay scattered about. In the morning's first light, he could see the faces of the dead. They held every form of expression. He felt a twinge of guilt and pity, and he had to shake off the shivers. He was a patriot fighting a patriot's war against the hated despots. Yet, in the presence of death, they were men and not so much his enemies.

The battalion was strung out in a ragged line where they halted after climbing over the rail fence. Officers rode up and down the formations to untangle the companies and regiments and restore order. A few feet ahead lay several blue forms. Stephen studied them curiously. They were normal men in abnormal positions of rest upon the ground. One man, in particular, lay upon his back with his body perpendicular to Stephen. He had fallen and struggled for a time with his wounds. His sack coat and trousers had been opened as if he were searching for something. His accouterments lay splayed about him. Perhaps he had been struggling to relieve himself of them. His chest and stomach were stained crimson, his hands clutching at his clothing as if still in great pain.

A few men in the formation joked and taunted the corpses, but quietly. Stephen could countenance the sight and even the morality of viewing the enemy as more monster than man, but disrespect toward the dead was more than he could fathom.

*****

Thoughts of home displaced images of the dead. In his mind, he wasn't in a line of battle surrounded by comrades but at the dinner table surrounded by family. A battle of a different sort was being waged between his father and a scruffy, fat boarder. Stephen's father considered that the dinner table was his place to instruct his children, the art of debate as the principal subject.

"Stephen, Esther, Sarah, Paul, my good wife, Elizabeth, honored guest in our home, let us give thanks to the Lord of Hosts for this provender."

John Murdoch waited and watched before he bowed his head to ensure compliance from all at the table. Little Paul fidgeted in his chair until a glare from his father ensured his compliance in closing his eyes and folding his hands in prayerful fashion.

"Oh Lord, we thank Thee for Thy wonderful provision and protection over this humble deacon's family, and we seek Thy wisdom and knowledge so as to live a pleasing life in Thy sight. Oh Lord, we thank Thee for the sacrifice of Thy Son that we might approach Thee with confidence and grace. I pray, oh Lord, for protection over our good guest, Mr. Hastings, as he continues his travels and thank Thee for allowing us the privilege of sharing in our bounty. We ask Thee, oh Lord, to protect the poor and humble patriots who face perdition's destruction every day in Missouri against the evil and sin-filled abolitionist ruffians, those so called *Kansan Jayhawkers* who prey upon the innocent and shed blood without mercy. We ask, oh Lord, that Thou bring them to justice that they may receive within themselves the due penalty of their violence."

A sudden clank of metal against ceramic stalled the prayer. Mr. Murdoch looked up to find the perpetrator. All of the children were statuesque with their eyes cast downward and closed, hands folded. Clearing his throat, Mr. Murdoch continued. "Dear Lord, use this bounty to strengthen our resolve to serve Thee with all of our hearts, souls, minds, and bodies. We ask Thee, in Thy Son's holy Name. Amen."

The silence was broken with the sounds of dishes moving and diners eating. Stephen sat closest to Mr. Hastings and the other siblings in order of age down the length of the table. Mr. Hastings held the seat of second honor at the table's head and opposite Mr. Murdoch. Seats along the other side of the table were empty that night, Mr. Hastings being the only boarder. Stephen, seventeen, was not yet able to participate in the evening conversations, nineteen being the age his father deemed as necessary for such supper activity. The children ate and listened as Mr. Murdoch opened the evening's "teaching," as he called it, while the children and boarders were his captive congregation for that hour and a half each night. Stephen's mother ate silently. Teaching time was the sole domain of "Pappaw" and his captive dinner guests—and of little interest to her.

"What say you, Mr. Hastings," Mr. Murdoch began, "regarding where we ended last evening's conversation about your views of the freedom of salvation versus the elect?"

Mr. Hastings cleared his throat, perhaps wondering if he should have sought lodging elsewhere. "I see you are prepared with more of your great store of opinion and knowledge on this particular topic, Mr. Murdoch, judging by the ravenous glint in your eyes over the prospect of trouncing me once more," replied of Mr. Hastings.

"Oh, come now, Mr. Hastings. You portray me in such a poor light. But I must confess to you that I have indeed been looking forward to the continuance of our debate, as you have so astutely observed. Perchance, do I appear that eager for the challenge?"

"Oh, yes, you do indeed look rather eager, and prepared, I might add, to continue our conversation that I scarce dare to think I would indeed come out on top."

Stephen ate slowly, listening intently as Mr. Hastings and his father exchanged a few more customary pleasantries. He could tell by the flash of fire in his father's eyes that he had indeed been preparing for this evening's contest. He also noted the overly polite and austere language his father used. Being a plain man of simple means and simpler parentage, he spoke now in language more befitting a scholar or orator than a cobbler or a deacon in a small Presbyterian church.

"I believe," Mr. Hastings finally said, "that you, sir, have the first point to be laid down, considering that I ended last evening's debate."

"Oh, you are the honored guest in my home. How could I take such an honor to myself regardless of where we ended on the evening last? You have the honor of beginning."

"This I could not do, for the rules are very stringent on this point that you should begin with an opening statement of some sort. I would not be able to sleep tonight knowing that I had taken a continuance of the remaining points," Mr. Hastings replied and smiled affably.

Stephen watched as his father squirmed slightly and a hard look creased the corners of his mouth. Stephen knew that his father was only prepared to rebut Mr. Hastings's first challenge before launching into his teaching. He must have forgotten who ended last night. Now he was interested in what would happen. His father hated to be bested at anything and would be a bear to deal with the rest of the evening. Despite what the consequences might bring for him and his siblings, Stephen waited impatiently for his father to relent and try to recover his grand strategy. Seated next to him was Paul, who was two years younger than Stephen but old enough to appreciate what was happening. Paul lightly kicked Stephen in the shin and continued to eat as if nothing was out of the ordinary. Stephen grinned slightly in return and stirred the food on his plate, his appetite forgotten.

Mr. Murdoch fumbled about his plate in a veiled attempt to forestall the ruining of his grand strategy. Concern for fair play and owning up to consequences, favorite topics of instruction to his children, did not come into play at times like this. Although he would end the evening's teaching with as much grace as he could muster, his father would have the last word.

"I'll grant you that the Holy Writ says for it is by grace that thou hast been redeemed and this not of anything that comes from the self. I do not deny that grace plays a part in our relationship with the Father. But ..."

Hastings interrupted him. "Now, Mr. Murdoch, did you not just moments before concede that you were unable to give answer to my point that if grace be not a free offering that we would be compelled to eschew the cross and make a righteousness of our own?"

"Well, yes, I did, but you see..."

"Mr. Murdoch, is this the example you would give to your progeny, that to not humbly admit to one's own shortfalls merely refutes the same message you have most eloquently but ineffectually offered up this same evening?"

"Yes, I see and concede once again that I have no answer worthy of offering to your last statement and cannot refute it without bringing upon myself more condemnation than I already am deserving of in my words of the last few moments."

"Come now, Mr. Murdoch, for it is not condemnation that I seek, only acknowledgement that the truth of Scripture is unassailable on this point of grace. I take neither praise nor accolades upon myself on this point, although I gladly accept your concession, as it means some small vindication of my own words. But only as they compare to the truth of the Holy Word."

Stephen looked from Mr. Hastings to his father and back again, studying their features and trying to divine what was going on behind each countenance. It was one of the few times he saw his father admit to a defeat in debate at his own table. A week later, following retribution and tightened discipline, he hoped to never see it again.

*****

Stephen's thoughts returned to the present, and he noted the similarity to the corpse in front of him to that of Mr. Hastings. He longed for the comforts of that innocent time with his family. He was now a man facing alone the consequences of his decisions. The death and dismemberment around him was one such consequence of the decision to go to war. Amid the continued joking, William stood in silence, unable to find a distraction from the carnage he saw.

"Forward, march!" came the command, and the regiment stepped off. Stephen tried to step over the corpse but kicked its hand heavily. The unwelcome thud against his brogan caused more shivers racing along his spine. The trail the Federals took was littered with weapons and accouterments and more dead. It was a relief to him to be moving again despite the dangers that lurked just over the barely visible, forested horizon.

*****

Stephen couldn't help but contrast this day's experiences, and the tension he and every member of his battalion still felt, with the innocent pleasure of just the day before.

The morning before, William had waked him with the toe of his boot. Feeling tight and sore, Stephen reluctantly rolled over and felt the wetness of the dew.

"Up, Stephen. We're standing to," William called to him.

"Unh, did you sleep at all?"

"No, we threw out a skirmish line, and I got tagged along with half the company. We went into the wood line and stayed awake the rest of the time," William rubbed his bloodshot eyes. He was bigger than Stephen and slightly older. Stephen had known him in Carthage, and the two had been fond friends as long as either could remember. "Why didn't you wake me?" Stephen said and sat up.

"They had plenty of us who were still awake. 'Sides, it weren't nothin' but a different place to lie awake."

"Any sign of the enemy?"

"Naw, though I did hear the lieutenant sayin' something about how they's supposed to be a council of war last night 'tween the big bugs. Somethin' 'bout whether we should all go back to Corinth, seein' as we was supposed to attack the Feds this mornin'. I suppose they chose to stay, seein' as we still here."

Stephen looked toward the road they had marched down the day before. It was still filled with the wagons, cannon, and infantry of Braxton Bragg's corps.

"I suppose we're still waitin' on Bragg to come up?" Stephen asked.

"He's been comin' up all night long," William replied.

"With all the racket they made last night, it's a wonder the Feds ain't attacked us by now."

"Yeah, we'll stay or go back as long as we do somethin' here soon. I'm mighty tired of this waitin'," William said.

Sergeant Thompson strode up to William and asked them, "You two birds got water?"

"No."

"C'mon. Collect canteens from your squad and go down the pike back to that stream near that farm called Michie's and hurry back," Sergeant Thompson ordered.

Loaded down with ten canteens each, they made their way out of the camp.

"I'll bet this pike has been filled ever since we marched off of it yesterday," Stephen said.

"My word, you ever see so many men afore?" William wondered.

"No, and this line goes all the way down the pike as far as I can see," Stephen said as they walked along the edge of the road.

There was a well-worn trail through the grass to the stream bed, blazed by countless other soldiers seeking water. The trail dipped suddenly, and the sounds of the stream competed with the sounds of the marching on the road. A long line of half-wet men met them coming back up from the banks. They had had to wade out into the deep portion to avoid the muddied water caused by too much traffic. Arriving at the water's edge, Stephen could see hundreds of men moving about the banks and in the water.

"Think it's cold?" Stephen asked William.

"Cold or not, you want to drink muddy water?"

All in all, it had been a good day.

*****

They were making slow progress through the woods, and he was already panting heavily with exertion. The welcome sight of a lightening in the horizon invigorated their steps. The skirmishers of the 15th Arkansas came to life. The *pop, pop, pop* of their weapons firing sounded through the trees. The line of regiments came into a long field. The enemy, posted dead center, stood defiantly. Wood's and Cleburne's brigades extended down the length of the field. Stephen could see their desperation.

The Rebel yell swept down the battle line as the regiments stepped out of the trees. The solitary Union battle line did not extend much down the length of the field, and only fifty yards separated the two forces. It was an unequal contest, but the Federals stood their ground defiantly. Then, as the 6th Mississippi swept forward, the Federals executed an about face and rapidly quit the field, melting into the tree line. With a yell, the brigades marched forward convinced, now more than ever, of their invincibility.

Soon the signs of a hasty departure marked the location of the vacated Federal picket line. The enemy camps were close. Another tree line and thicket greeted them. Keeping alignment in the confined space was difficult. Ahead, another opening presented itself, and Stephen's heart leapt.

Their exit from the forest was as welcome as a long draught of water after a long march. He could see another thin line of trees in their front, plus a wide, swampy, lowland patch from which drifted a small stream. The swamp was causing the rest of the divisional battalions to move obliquely farther to the left. Tell-tale puffs of smoke from the thin line of trees appeared at irregular intervals but played upon them without effect. Their own skirmish line entered the swamp, struggling to find good footing. The swamp wasn't so deep that the skirmishers couldn't walk forward without sinking. However, the prospect of being caught unable to maneuver or move quickly caused Stephen anxiety. The tree line concealed what was behind it, though the presence of the enemy skirmish line at least revealed that they were close.

From far off to the left, Stephen could hear a low rumbling. Like the sound of a heavy barrel rolling toward them on a wooden floor, the noise grew in intensity until it was clear that the battle had been joined. They stepped off toward the swamp and ignored the cold water up to their shins. The rumbling of battle coursed to their right, and unseen combatants faced off on other parts of the field. Surrounded now by the cacophony of battle, Stephen was swept up in the emotion of attack, thoughts of what might happen forgotten. The exhilaration of being part of a grand host, the largest assembled in the west to date, and the feeling that certain victory was assured propelled Stephen and his comrades through the soggy ground. He forgot his earlier trepidation of the surprise encounter at the farm house, longing to finally close with the enemy and display a feat of honor that only a Mississippian could possess.

Rising, rising, rising was the terrible sound of death and destruction all about them. Their own skirmishers steadily pushed through the muck and reached the tree line, disappearing into it. In front of Stephen, sitting in the water and nursing a shoulder wound, sat a skirmisher. His face was creased with pain and weariness, his clothes were soaked with brackish water, and his rifle was resting upon his good shoulder. A lone Federal forage cap lay a few feet from him, its crown lying upside down, its owner nowhere to be seen. Further on in the wood line, half submerged in the backwater, lay a Federal skirmisher with only his waist and legs visible. Stephen drew nearer and saw that the man's arms and head were under water. A pool of red spread upon the surface of the water. Stephen had to step lightly so as not to kick the man as he marched past.

Stephen leaned forward to catch William's attention. "We're doin' it! We're whoopin' 'em!"

The skirmishers made a ragged chorus of hoots and hollers when they finally entered the tree line and found drier ground and surer footing. Ahead, he caught short glimpses of the enemy skirmishers ascending a long steep hill. At its crest stood an enemy camp. The sight of the enemy's tent line brought another chorus of yips and yells from the whole of the brigade. The moment of truth was near.

After what seemed an intolerable pause and reshuffling of the brigade regiments in line of attack, the moment arrived.

"Forward, march!"

At the command came the emanation meant to strike fear into any Federals for miles, the queer, high-pitched yipping that was the trademark battle cry of the Confederate fighting man. The trees resounded with the yell. The three regiments tapped for the attack stepped off proudly. They cleared the trees that had hitherto shielded not only them but the enemy, as well. Stepping into the open, they beheld a sight that might have dampened the spirits of lesser individuals. Arrayed before them on the top of the steep hill was a long unbroken line of blue.

Shouting and yelling, Stephen girded himself once more for what he hoped would be another short succession of volleys followed by their triumphant entrance into the enemy's camp. With their color guard stolidly marching ten paces in front and leading them ever upward, all sense of danger and foreboding was drowned out in the rush of movement.

The long blue line erupted in a cloud of rushing smoke. The crack of the report engulfed their yelling and caused Stephen's heart to skip. The zinging of lead filled the air and stung the ground, sending chips of sod flying into the air and bodies crumbling earthward.

For an almost imperceptible instant, the Rebel yell was hushed, replaced by the gasps and groans of the inflicted. As if the air had been sucked from their lungs, they ceased their cry. Men gasped at the suddenness of the enemy's destructive fire. The vacuum was soon filled by the guttural and manly *huzzah* from the Federal line atop the hill. Without order, the movement forward halted. Stephen scarcely perceived that he and his pards were no longer moving at all. He, himself, was riveted by the sight of the man lying at his feet. Known to him only as Ox, the man was hardly to be recognized without the top of his head.

"Forward, forward!" rang the voice of Colonel Thornton from astride his horse at the rear of the regimental line. "Forward, march!"

Reinvigorated, the regiment and cry resumed with a greater intensity. The cry steadied Stephen's mind, and the fear that had spiked in the instant when Ox fell was forgotten. The hill was steeper than it had appeared from its base. The effort to keep up the pace told upon his legs. They were close enough now to see individual faces in the enemy formation, faces that didn't look much different from their own, faces with names and histories and families and hopes for survival. In these faces, too, were fear and that particular look of men in a desperate situation.

"At the double quick, march!"

They gave one last shout and jogged forward. Stephen brought his weapon to the position of port arms and braced himself for the clash.

The long line of blue vanished once again in a cloud of sulfur and smoke. In that instant, the words of his father echoed in Stephen's mind.

"I looked, and there before me was a pale horse! Its rider was named Death, and Hades was following close behind him."

Chapter Six

A breathless rider flagged Michael down while he and the battery moved toward the sounds of fighting.

"Captain Grierson?"

"Yes?" Michael said as he pulled Charger to a stop.

"Sir, Captain Polk sends his compliments! He wishes to direct you to place your battery east of the Shiloh Road on that hill there," the courier shouted above the din, "where that Yankee camp is."

Giving a hurried salute, the young lieutenant wheeled his steed and raced off toward the fighting.

"Sergeant, head to that hillock to the right of the Shiloh Road and go into battery," Michael shouted to one of his section sergeants. Charger danced nervously to and fro, forcing Michael to keep turning him in the direction the battery was heading. The divisions belonging to Corps Commander Leonidas Polk, the fighting Episcopal bishop, were arrayed in line of battle and advancing upon the string of enemy camps rumored to be that of William T. Sherman's division. Motioning to Sergeant Gibson to follow, Michael spurred Charger forward in the direction the courier had taken.

The battery raced by with urgency and a rumble that made him swell with pride. An artillery battery at full gallop is a frightening sight to behold. The seeming ease of the movement, combining alacrity and grace, belied the danger of such recklessness. They followed the sounds of battle unengaged all morning until finally being called upon to practice their deadly art. At the base of their camps to the right, the enemy established an unbroken line of resistance, repulsing the first attempts to push them out. Two Federal batteries played havoc upon the infantry as solid and case shot landed amid General Polk's advancing lines. Three of their own batteries were trying to support the advance but were taking the worst of the punishment. Wrecked caissons and gun carriages pointed in haphazard directions. A small creek running east separated the two forces, the enemy gathering on the high ground in their front.

Michael watched First Sergeant Mahoney direct the placement of each of his three guns. Even as the first gun swung into position, solid shot rained down about the battery. Leaden balls screeched to earth, many rebounding dangerously into the air. Michael turned in the direction the shot came from.

In the distance, far behind the enemy line upon a hill, stood a Federal battery that he missed in his quick survey of the field. This put his battery in a direct line with that of the enemy, but on a lower elevation, making return fire more difficult.

"Tarnation," Michael muttered and spurred Charger forward. His guns, now in battery and gunners taking positions, had yet to fire when a case shot came hissing and bounding up the hill. Striking sixty feet in front of the battery, it bounded into the rear caisson and horse pickets. Michael watched in horror as the shot came down. It missed a caisson by a few feet but caught one of the men in the back, breaking him in half and slicing into the hind quarters of a horse. The explosion a few seconds later lifted another three horses into the air, causing the rest to stampede.

"Mother Mary!" Michael shouted as he drew up to the rear of the battery and quickly dismounted. He handed Charger's reins to a private. "Private, see to the horses with every available man!"

Tarnation, he thought again. *Even if I wanted to leave now, I couldn't until those horses are secured.* Despite the fire they were taking, the men stood to their posts.

"Mahoney! Direct fire on those sons of Hades there! We have to support the attack and ignore the counter battery fire we're taking!"

General Cheatham's brigades moved forward once again toward the enemy's line; the long lines of butternut and brown uniforms snaked toward their target. Mahoney directed each gun's target and gave the order to fire. Guns one and two, St. Peter and St. Paul, spoke in succession, the concussion of their report causing a shockwave to raise a cloud of dust from the ground and Michael's clothes to vibrate. Down the Shiloh Road, another artillery unit roared up the hill and prepared to go into battery next to them. The gun crews stood to their duty and fired case shot into the Federal defense line, one from St. Paul cutting obliquely felled a whole company of infantry before disappearing into the camp and knocking down several Sibley tents.

Michael's job was done. He was forced to watch his men take to their work. The battery coming up next to them swung into position but not before a solid shot dismounted a carriage. An entire crew was killed while rolling the piece into position. Body parts and splintered wood lay strewn around the piece. The men of that battery took little notice. Their four remaining guns went into position and started firing.

There was a rhythm to the crews' work. The six-man crews stood around their pieces and performed a role that kept the gun in play. With each pull of the lanyard, the guns rocked violently backward and were quickly rolled back into position. The barrels needed cooling and were swabbed before powder could be re-introduced, lest a remaining spark ignite and take the gun out. Targets were determined and fuses on case shot timed. Then powder was added, followed by the round rammed down the barrel. Finally, the lanyard with its percussive fuse was placed into the touch hole, and the gun was again ready to fire. The ammo bearers ran back and forth from the line of caissons to the gun after each report. If even one of these men should become incapacitated, the smooth working of the crew would slow and its efficiency would decline.

So far, the crews were full, and the work was heated. Polk's regiments began to falter in the face of the Federal defense. The additional batteries did not make much of a difference to the infantry struggling to find a weak spot. The regiments in front of their battery regrouped and moved forward once more. They bled a constant stream of dead and wounded behind them.

Michael ran over to St. Peter's crew sergeant. "Fire on that line in front with solid shot!" Moving from gun to gun he repeated the order. Working the guns quickly, the crews sent shell after shell into the Federals. Michael watched as their shots created havoc in the enemy line. His heart leapt as he watched the Federal line begin to disintegrate, as a trickle at first, then as a steady stream. Then, as if on cue, the enemy regiments retreated for the rear.

The once-solid line of blue stretching across the open valley melted. The enemy moved in a mob, skittering through the camps and away from the advance of General Polk's victorious legions. The sight brought forth a cheering and jeering from Polk's infantry as they advanced through the abandoned tents and reaped a crop of wounded and prisoners. Terrified Federals surrendered as fast as they could be caught.

"Stand down! Stand down!" Michael shouted. He motioned Sergeant Mahoney over to him and shouted in his ear, "Limber up and get ready to move forward."

Despite the breaking of the enemy's lines, the racket of battle did not abate nor did the fire from the enemy batteries. While St. Peter was being swung around and the caisson brought up, a solid shot landed near the gun. It rebounded into the crew's swabber. The boy's leg was torn off at the knee. Those standing near were splattered with blood and dirt. The crew stepped over him to finish the work of securing the gun to the caisson.

Michael studied the boy with pity, knowing he would bleed to death before anything could be done. What was worse than leaving him there, though, was being down half a team of draft horses to pull the guns, which left nothing free to take the wounded to the rear.

"Lieutenant," Michael called out, "take the section off this infernal hill and onto the pike. Go through the camp there and unlimber on the elevation to the left of that command tent." With a quick salute in return, the bookish man trotted off.

Michael ran over to where Charger was, still held by the private. "Private, find Captain Polk and tell him I have moved my section down the Shiloh Road in support of B. R. Johnson's brigade."

Michael mounted and followed the battery as it descended the hillock to the road below. The sides of the road were rapidly filling with a stream of wounded and prisoners. The prisoners looked beaten and shocked. They slogged by him with downcast faces and vacant eyes. Many were nursing flowing wounds. Though a few of the enemy were lively enough to chatter with one another, overall they did not seem fearsome to Michael. Only minutes before, both captor and captured had cursed and poured fire into one another. Now, the scene was different, and camaraderie existed where none had been before.

Michael had heard stories of illicit consorting between enemy picket lines where tobacco, newspapers, coffee, and anything of scarce value was to be had. He wondered if he was seeing this first hand as the battery made its way past the throng. Picket duty was performed by the infantry brigades, and his artillerymen had no such experience.

The approach to the former lines and area of the hardest fighting was littered with corpses and discarded equipment. Far from being peaceful looking, the fields surrounding the enemy's encampments were literally crawling. Hundreds from both sides were moving along the ground or staggering about as if having imbibed too much drink. Faces blackened with powder and bodies reddened with blood moved to and fro, looking for comfort and water. Comrades, some wounded themselves, moved about with these crawling wretches, giving what aid they could. There were so many lying on the ground that Michael wondered who was still standing and fighting. Friend and foe lay intermixed where the waves of attack had washed into the walls of defense, and, in places, the bodies were stacked several layers thick. He remembered his own men left on the hill, the dead and the wounded; each of these had once been a man who had been known and loved.

First Sergeant Mahoney's horse sidled up to Charger, and the two men rode in silence for a moment. "Brisk work," Mahoney said.

"Indeed," Michael muttered.

"We're pushin' 'em. I heard that we are moving forward all along the line, 'cept to the right. Cleburne is stuck in front of some swamp."

"Shouldn't matter as we push forward. The enemy'll have to fall back," Michael replied.

"You hungry? Seems to be plenty of vittles in these camps. How 'bout I send someone to gather some hot food? Probably be last chance fer anythin' hot," Mahoney said when they rode into an encampment. Fires still smoldered in company streets, and coffee still steamed. Food, fresh and in various states of preparation, lay scattered about. Stragglers from Polk's corps rifled the tents for plunder.

The passage of time struck Michael as oddly motionless. How much time had elapsed since they first limbered up in the darkness of early morning?

Save for the passage of the sun in the sky, Michael had little to tell him how much time had passed. Still feeling the energy of excitement, Michael had to think a moment to realize he was famished and that the morning was turning hot.

Michael shifted in his saddle to look at Mahoney. "Better send Chapman and Scott, but tell 'em to be quick about it."

"Yes, sir," Mahoney said. "The battery's unlimberin' over there in that clearing. A few Fed batteries is playing upon the right of Clark's division, but we got a good enfilade fire on their flank. Them trees in front will mask us from any Fed batteries in front of Polk's advance."

"Good. Get them going as soon as they are able."

Mahoney pointed toward a horse and rider advancing in their direction. "Uh oh, looks like a messenger comin' our way."

Michael and Mahoney reined to a stop, and the messenger brought his steed to a quick halt.

"Sir, General Cheatham's compliments. He wishes you to position your battery so as to support his advance, and you are to detach from B. R. Johnson's brigade to support Stephens's brigade. Follow me. I will direct you to the position chosen by the general." At that the rider spurred his horse and made his way through the encampment.

"Forget the food, Mahoney. Get the battery limbered up and ride in that direction."

Michael spurred Charger to catch up with the courier. Everywhere was a sea of white and green from the Federal camps sprawled between overlapping tree lines like rough, foam-capped water. All about him was movement, and he had to rein in several times to avoid groups of prisoners and troops moving across his path. Catching up with the courier, he stopped and surveyed the surrounding ground.

"See there, Captain?" the messenger asked. "General Cheatham wishes for you to engage those enemy batteries on that high ground to the south of the Hamburg-Purdy Road. His direction is to take those positions to the south of that little hill in the center of their lines and continue marching up the Shiloh Road. You will move with his advance." His instructions delivered, the courier quickly turned and galloped off to the rear.

Michael pulled his glasses out of their pouch and focused on the enemy artillery. Two batteries of what he could make out as six-pound Napoleons, formed in line of battle off of the Corinth Road, were shelling Cheatham's brigades. The enemy infantry, positioned upon a slight rise several hundred feet in their front, formed a continuous line that ran down the rise and across both the Hamburg-Purdy and Corinth Roads. Taking cover in the tree line just below the hill upon which he stood, the infantry of B. R. Johnson's and Stephen's brigades were showered with explosive charges that burst in the tree tops. Only two hundred yards of open ground separated them from the enemy guns.

A low rumbling and creaking sound rolled up the hill from teams pounding up the slope and swinging the cannon into play. Mahoney's horse came trotting up beside Michael and reined to a halt.

Michael shouted to him, "Silence those guns up there on that hill to the left of the Purdy Road."

Mahoney scrambled toward the three remaining guns to pass the orders on to each crew. Working feverishly, the men brought the weapons into ready positions. Michael dismounted and moved to the center of his gun line and studied the enemy through his glasses again.

"Five second fuse, ten degree elevation, Sergeant!" Michael shouted to the gun sergeant of St. Paul. "Fire for range!"

The guns spoke, and Michael waited for the shells to detonate. The gun crews would make adjustments as each shell landed before locking the elevation and firing for all they could humanly manage. Geysers of earth erupted behind and in front of the enemy position.

"Sir, if General Stephens don't move soon, we're gonna be eatin' lead from those guns up there," Mahoney shouted to Michael.

Below, still in the tree line, the Confederate infantry mingled and showed little evidence of moving forward. As Michael watched, four guns of one of the enemy batteries changed position to front him.

"Quickly, work that range. It's gonna get hot quick," Michael shouted.

As if to punctuate his command, a shell came screeching overhead and hit the earth at the bottom the hill before exploding. More shells came singing over in quick succession, all landing behind them.

Three quick reports and shells began exploding around the enemy guns. Michael's guns began to speak as rapidly as the crews could work. The incoming rounds began landing closer; the enemy was finding its range. The hill shook with the concussion of the reports and the landing of shot. Above the din, Col. Stephen's troops shouted with enthusiasm while marching out of the woods and onto the plain. Michael saw three of the enemy guns change front once again to fire on Stephen's men. His own guns kept up the fire, and he watched a trio of shells dismount a carriage and silence one of the guns firing on the Confederate infantry. A ragged and short lived cheer arose from St. Peter's crew before an enemy case shot plowed a furrow into the earth twenty feet from the gun, erupting in a shower of dirt clods. Shielding his eyes, Michael recovered his hand to see Mahoney raging up and down the gun line, hatless and covered in dirt. Suppressing a smile, Michael dusted himself off and motioned to one of his lieutenants.

"Take the extra caisson to the rear and find the supply trains. Get as much case shot as you can! Take the crew from St. James with you," Michael shouted in the man's ear.

A thunderous volley added to the near constant booming of cannon, signifying that the infantry had engaged. The lines were engulfed in smoke. The crackle of rifles grew as the firing rolled down the opposing lines. Michael felt a tap on his shoulder.

"Grierson! I've brought the other section up on Cheatham's orders," shouted Captain Marshall Polk. Four more guns with their crews rolled up the hill and unlimbered alongside their comrades. "Hope your Texans are up to the task, or shall we show 'em how Tennesseans parley with the enemy?" shouted Polk with a grin.

"With my compliments, sir, Texas is ready to join Tennessee in sending them a-runnin'," Michael said and bowed with mock deference. "We've been playin' on those Fed guns up there." Michael gestured toward the cannon with a sweep of his hand. "We could use more help. They're sweeping the lines and ignoring us. We did unseat one gun."

"All right, we'll get four guns on the enemy batteries, and the rest will fire on the enemy infantry," Captain Polk ordered.

"Yes, sir," Michael said.

He turned and ran over to Mahoney. Once Mahoney heard Polk's orders, he ran from crew chief to crew chief to get each in compliance. Michael regretted his commander's arrival and the sudden loss of initiative and freedom. Polk, in the West Point graduating class of 1859, ranked and had seniority over Michael. Although Polk never lorded his rank over others, Michael still resented having his command of the battery superseded. He stood behind the guns of his section while the crews worked and occasionally shifted the fire to a different target. For the most part, he felt ancillary to the fighting, particularly when Captain Polk sent him directives for new targets.

The area separating the two opposing lines of infantry was choked with smoke. Michael could make out little through the swirling haze. The enemy shifted troops from spot to spot. Reinforcements marched down the Hamburg-Purdy Road, and more batteries lumbered into defensive positions. Both infantry lines bled a trail of wounded that led to the rear. Singly or in pairs, the shattered men ambled along as well as they could manage. The wood line where the division had formed filled with the injured and faint of heart.

Lifting his glasses once more, Michael slowly panned the length of the enemy formation. The ragged line of blue forms stood obstinately in the face of General Cheatham's advance. To his left, B. R. Johnson's brigade surged forward, only to halt then rush head-long back from whence they came. He saw little movement from the enemy toward the rear. The crash of musketry bore upon his ears, as did each concussive report of a cannon. From his vantage point, the enemy seemed like faceless forms that gaggled into groups to form a solid light and dark blue mass. Sometimes, this mass would disintegrate into little patches of color, only to re-form into a solid wall. The enemy guns, served by enemy soldiers intent upon visiting death and destruction on him, were but distant objects needing to be silenced in any way possible. Occasionally he would witness the detonation of a shell near a gun crew and watch its men duck or fall to the ground. Though he felt nothing for their plight, he recognized the terror they must feel.

"Captain, direct all your fire on that battery there." Captain Polk pointed at the enemy artillery upon the hill to his right. "It's propping up their line. We silence it, the enemy infantry'll run."

Michael passed the order on and watched as a mass of General Cheatham's brigades marched toward the enemy-held hill overlooking the Purdy Road. A thin line of enemy infantry arrayed itself below a five-gun battery. The ground leading up to the position was quickly dotted with still forms, and the intervening space was swept with lead. Soon, the hill top was peppered with explosive and solid shot. A large explosion, lit with flame and flying debris, announced the destruction of a caisson. The Confederate infantry surged forward, their colors streaming ahead, then disappearing into the enemy line. A cheer arose from the gun crews as the enemy retreated through their own guns, followed closely by General Cheatham's men. The enemy's guns were taken in a wild rush for the summit with Confederates reforming at its top.

Though the guns now sat silent, Michael hardly noticed. The enemy line began breaking apart. Blue forms marched or ran pell-mell to the rear. The enemy artillery, just as quickly, limbered up and rode off if they could. Everywhere, the Confederate line moved forward to the high ground surrounding the Hamburg-Purdy Road and leaving Michael without targets. Enjoying the respite, his crews sat by their guns in exhaustion. What had been a sea of blue only minutes before now seemed devoid of that formidable wall of defense. Cheatham had taken the Purdy Road defensive line of General Sherman.

"The boys did fine work," Polk said. Michael hadn't noticed his arrival.

"Yes, Captain, they did," Michael replied.

"We'll wait here for a spell. No sense in moving forward until we're called for," Polk said and wiped his brow with his shirt sleeve. "See to your section. Might be the only time to eat and brew coffee today."

"Sir," Michael said with a nod. He walked wearily to where Mahoney was chatting with one of the gun crews. "Mahoney, get the boys on eatin' and brewin' coffee as they can after securing the guns." He turned to Sergeant Pope. "Ol' St. James did good work today, gave the heathen a taste of the Good Word," he said and patted the still-hot gun barrel.

"St. James always giveth the wicked a grounding in the gospel of lead," Sergeant Pope replied with a grin.

Michael turned and walked back to the center of the hill, and Mahoney followed at his side.

Walking with Michael, Mahoney said, "We seem to be pushin' them everywhere, although I'd say it was hotter on that hill back at the Shiloh Road." Mahoney scratched his chin and ran his hand over his stubbly cheeks.

"Yes, we may just do what Johnston hoped to do, drive the Feds into the river," Michael replied.

"Cheatham's division took a pounding, though. It'll be awhile afore they move forward again," Mahoney said, staring out over the hill and into the quickly dissipating smoke.

"He'll be moving forward soon. He'll have to in order to keep the enemy from forming another line."

"With what? The division is all in disarray. Most of that movement atop the ridge there is fugitives and wounded. I'll wager this division ain't movin' for another hour."

The field that witnessed the contest of arms was now being picked over by souvenir hunters and men looking for friends or relatives among the dead and wounded. The Purdy Roadway filled with the walking wounded, most making their way back toward the camps they had passed through earlier. The less fortunate made themselves as comfortable as they could where they lay, and some were carried to the cover of trees by comrades.

"Makes you wonder, don' it?" Mahoney asked after a moment of silence.

"Wonder what?" Michael asked.

"Wonder if the good Lord really meant for an end such as this. None of us really thought that we'd come to our end as an old man in bed. Least not me. How many came to their end with the scream of a minié ball in their ears or the screams of the wounded before they died?" They looked over the field of fallen men. "Just makes me think is all."

Michael nodded in reply.

Mahoney continued in a rush. "I don't believe in premonitions or dreams or such tellin' me somethin'. I don't think much on it while we're workin' the guns an' watchin' the enemy fall. Just lookin' out afterward causes me to stop and think about what we just done." Mahoney fidgeted with his hat, rolling it over and over in his fingers. His pale blue eyes studied something out in the distance.

"I often wonder, Sergeant," Michael said after a moment, "if any of us will face this ever after and find any favor. Will both sides stand at those gates and find succor? Are any of us really on the side of the God Almighty?"

"I don't know," Mahoney said. "Don't think side has anythin' to do with it. Was always told it was the soul that mattered."

"Surely God must answer someone's prayers? We both can't pray for victory and both be answered on equal terms. How can a supposed righteous man in the blue uniform be as right in his cause as a southern patriot in seeking freedom from his oppressor?" Michael asked.

"I don't suppose them sees it the same way. Take these Tennessee boys we's with under Polk there," Mahoney said and motioned with a nod of his head in Captain Polk's direction. "I heard tell from a few of them that the Yankees have raised several infantry regiments and three batteries of artillery from Tennessee on this very field. Now, these fellers is fightin' fer some reason. Our boys is fightin' these invaders, but them other boys is bein' moved by some other hand. Maybe they pray to the same God as we do, but what other righteous cause can a feller have than the defense of his own home?"

"It would be grand to see this contest of arms be the divine appointment of victory and eventual peace, a peace that leaves us be as we see fit," Michael said. "But I don't think God takes any mind to this contest in the least. Otherwise, He would be torn between both sides as righteous men, or men who perceive their own righteousness, call upon His divine intervention for their own victory." Michael sighed deeply. "No, I suspect He has washed His hands of this matter altogether."

"I sincerely hope not, sir. For what else would sustain us? Just look at the number of this enemy host that has set upon a sister state in our beloved country. They's like them great locusts that we see in Texas in the summertime, almost as uncountable. I hope you are wrong, Captain. We need something else besides audacity and this splendid attack to force the government of these Black Republicans to leave us be."

Michael nodded at the truth of that comment. Mahoney continued, "Perhaps it is men more believing than I who will bring about this divine intervention you speak of, Captain. I suspect that if it were left to my prayers, we would be in a world of difficulties now. Maybe it will be these very prayers that will bring about the intervention of the Almighty from His perch up there."

Michael looked into the cloudless, blue sky. "Who knows? Perhaps it was these prayers that have brought Him down here today to poke about our affairs and allow us to rout the enemy upon this field. Maybe it is no mere coincidence that this place be called Shiloh and that it be a Sunday. Maybe this will be the place of our eventual peace. That is what Shiloh means, isn't it, that road down yonder?"

"I reckon it does. Don't seem like a place of peace today. I've heard tell that Stonewall Jackson prefers to do battle on the Lord's day. Maybe it weren't by mere weather that we was delayed in attacking until today. Ain't no more righteous man in our whole cause as Jackson. Maybe Gen'l Johnston took a page from his book."

Michael chuckled. Who did know about these things? "Lord's Day or no, ain't one day that is any more special than the next. If God really does smile upon our cause and give us the providential victory, it's because He chose to and not because Gen'l Jackson happens to be on our side or not. He could just as soon decide that the Yankees should win this battle or this whole war, despite all that we do," Michael said sternly.

"Well, Captain, they ain't winnin' it now, and barring some miracle of the good Lord's hand, they won't be a winnin' it later neither."

"Better watch what you say there, Sergeant." Michael looked hard at Mahoney, as if he had cursed them both. "We don't want a bad omen now that we are on God's good side."

"Captain, fer a man who don't side by no principle of religion or faith, you sure are quick to knock on wood," Mahoney exclaimed with a glint of surprise in his eyes.

"Why tempt whatever force is out there that can control the fortunes of this day?"

"You surprise me, Captain," Mahoney said. "That's all I mean."

"What might surprise you more is that I don't even believe that, or at least make myself believe in much of anything but what I can see and understand with minimal attention. I imagine my mother shrinking back in horror to hear me talk so." Michael smiled at the thought and imagined the scolding.

"Mother would have knocked me into the nether world for so much as uttering His Name in vain, in pain or not!" Mahoney chortled. "You, sir, would not have lived to see the next day, declaring what you have just done."

"I jest mostly, Sergeant. I reckon most of us have to possess some measure of faith to be here on this field at all, a faith beyond what we can understand, for we've seen what a lack of faith will do to a man once fear and terror has seized his limbs. I reckon I'm not the heathen I pretend to be," Michael admitted.

"Don't take me for the righteous man you are makin' me out to be."

"Oh, I'd as soon listen to some Shaker tell me about the stillness of the Holy Spirit than believe you was a saint," Michael said with a grin.

The sound of heavy hoof-falls quieted their conversation. They turned and watched a courier pound up the hill and dismount in front of Captain Polk.

"Looks like our respite just ended," Mahoney said gravely.

"I'd better head over there and get our instructions." Michael stood, brushed the seat of his trousers and straightened his tunic before heading over to meet with Polk.

"Grierson," Polk said when he arrived, "Cheatham's movin' forward down the Hamburg-Purdy Road and then off down this cart trail here. You'll support his 2nd Brigade once again, and I'll take the other section in support of Stephen's brigade. If these maps are accurate, we're going to be losing the high ground as we move forward, so be ready to unlimber on the fly. I suspect you'll have to get in close to provide any support."

"Sir," Michael said curtly and saluted.

Making his way back to Mahoney, he passed on the order to get the men ready to move. With luck, Michael mused, they wouldn't have to get in tight with the infantry too often. Braving random case shot was one thing, but braving infantry fire was another.

"Sir, section ready to move!" called Mahoney.

"Section, by column right, forward march!"

The three-gun carriages and caissons peeled off one by one and entered the road at an even trot. Creaks and groans from the riggings and wheels sounded loudly amid the clopping of the teams. The drivers sat atop the right-most horses of each carriage, with the remaining crewman atop the rear caisson seats. The officers and gun chiefs rode their own steeds. Together, they formed a long column that stretched back to the hill they had just vacated. In the distance, sounds of fighting rumbled persistently.

The short journey over the Purdy Road into the small valley was speckled with discarded Federal equipment and the corpses of both sides. The captured Federal cannon had been removed, although their last position was still marked by broken gun carriages and the scars left by the ferocity of the fighting. Lonely and rifled bodies sprawled about the slopes of the opposite hills near the road. Michael thought of the few he had left behind earlier that morning, now left to bleed and die alone in the trodden grass. The same was true, he saw, among the enemy. The section passed the grisly remains of the enemy gun crews in silence, each man thinking of his own safety and hope-filled journey home.

Chapter Seven

Stephen balanced himself upon his wobbly legs. Bent over and panting heavily, he fought for a full intake of air. Stern calls from company officers and groans of the wounded filled the swampy lowland they sheltered under.

The hoarse voice of Colonel Thornton called out again and again to the men of the 6th Mississippi to "rally on the colors, rally on the colors, boys, rally!"

Twice they formed and moved up the hill at the enemy line, and twice they were forced to retreat to the shelter of the trees. The way leading up to the crest of the hill was covered with dead and wounded, and little time was given to aid their suffering. A constant artillery fire swept the length of the hill from an unseen enemy battery, and the enemy at the top showed no sign of defeat. Little semblance of company command remained; each man fell in as he found a space and a familiar face to stand with. Stephen lost sight of Willie Hawkins.

Colonel Thornton appeared in front of their thinned ranks. His left arm hung limply and dripped blood down his trouser leg. A bandage rested cockeyed upon his crown; a splotch of red marked where the minié ball had relieved him of his hat and part of his scalp.

"Mississippians!" Thornton shouted. "This hill will be taken!" Ragged and hoarse shouts of agreement sprang from the parched throats of those still able to stand. "Men of the 6th, you are alone, and the enemy is above you. Show these Tennesseans of the 23rd Regiment what mettle Mississippi is made of!"

The effort of exhorting the men was too much for him. Thornton doubled over and wobbled painfully to the ground. The survivors of the 6th Mississippi would go it alone. The 23rd Tennessee was still trying to sort themselves out after suffering numerous casualties, and they showed little sign of rallying.

With that, Captain Harper of Stephen's company sprang forward with drawn sword. "Battalion, forward march!"

Back through the trees and into the sunlight Stephen marched. They stepped over the fallen as if they were mere rocks in the way. His heart leapt once they emerged from the trees. The crest looked devoid of the enemy. Keeping a steady pace, they strained once more up the steep slope. At every step, they encountered a body. Staring eyes looked up into the blue sky of morning. Others grasped at invisible objects in front of them with a frozen attitude of desperation, and still others quivered uncontrollably, clutching at gushing wounds that colored the once-green hill with a reddish hue.

Up and up they marched with only the distant sounds of battle and their own foot falls to greet their ears. The artillery that had swept that slope was also silent. Stephen hoped the enemy had retired and that it would soon be done.

Encouraged by the silence and seeing their objective so near to being taken, the men of the regiment gave a prolonged yell. Movement above the crest caught Stephen's attention first, and then, suddenly, the enemy ranks sprang up from the ground as solid as before. For what appeared to be a slow movement of time, the combatants eyed one another in surprise.

"Halt!" shouted Captain Harper. "Ready! Aim! Fire!"

Stephen pulled the trigger, and the weapon leapt from his shoulder, the smoke of the discharge clouding everything. He could hear the calls of the enemy officers and the shrieks of their wounded. Another sudden concussion rang in his ears when the enemy poured a volley into the 6th.

"Load and come to the ready! Load and come to the ready!" The commands from both sides were audible to all as both regiments hurried to load and be ready. A distant yelling behind Stephen told him the Tennesseans behind the tree line were rallying and ascending the hill.

"Fire!" rang the command, and another burst of thunder issued from their weapons, followed by another reply from the enemy. In that moment, the ground around him was littered with wounded.

"Load and fire at will! Load and fire at will!" rang the call.

Stephen dropped his musket and hurriedly fumbled for a cartridge. Both lines came to life with the popping of musketry in an ever-increasing crescendo. Another thunderous volley added to the staccato. The Tennesseans halted next to the remnants of the 6th. They readied their weapons and poured fire into the enemy. The assault visibly staggering them, another chorus of the shrill yipping and yelling from the Rebel line added to the tumult.

"Load and come to the ready! Load and come to the ready!" the command was given again and passed down the line. "Forward march! Forward march!"

Lurching forward, the two regiments stepped off while the enemy hurried to load and fire as fast as they could. Every foot fall brought another body tumbling to the earth.

Men to either side of Stephen went down. He felt exposed and alone before others covered down to close the holes in the line. The space separating the foes seemed to be an interminable distance that would never be closed. Stephen kept his pace and watched the enemy fill the space separating them with lead.

"At the double quick, march!" Their cries and yells increased, and the regiments broke into a trot. Stephen joined the yelling and forgot for the moment that life and death were determined by the random shot of a musket; he was caught up in the thrill of shared heroism and devotion.

"The bayonet, give them the bayonet, the bayonet, boys, the bayonet!" Captain Harper's exhortation rang over the tumult, and the 6th Mississippi lurched up to the crest of the hill and sprang upon the waiting enemy. The clash of opposing sides produced the ring of metal upon metal and the thud of wood meeting flesh. *Hurrahs*, yells, screams, and curses sprang from hundreds of throats. Stephen only saw the flash of colors around him. Friend and foe intermixed and fought with their hands. Thrust met parry, club met block, steel met soft, yielding flesh, and fist met face. Each man fought whoever was within arm's reach and with whatever he had at his disposal.

At Stephen's feet lay the broken and stumbling of both sides. The urge to run overtook him. He shoved a man in blue aside with his rifle and made his way through the melee to the edge of the hill. As if by queer instinct, the remnants of both the 6th Mississippi and the 23rd Tennessee were making their way back down the hill. Stephen broke free of the throng and raced down the hill, leaping over the prostrate, not stopping until he was safely within the shade of the trees. He found a dry spot by a thin tree and sat wearily. Familiar faces were missing, the faces that told him he was in the company of friends and comrades. The faces he did see were scarred by fatigue and horror.

The long hillside before him was covered with so many bodies that little of the grass was visible. Breathing heavily, he rested his head upon the smooth bark of the tree and closed his eyes. Images of the charge and fighting were etched upon his vision. Exhausted, Stephen wept.

*****

"Run! Run for it! Save yourselves! Run for God's sake, run!"

Through the camp, Robert dragged Huebner along with him. Everywhere men in blue could be seen running wildly to the rear through the camp and beyond it. Robert didn't know where he was heading. He only knew that the enemy was already breaking through. Regiment upon regiment broke and ran. Bursting out of their own camp, he saw thousands of men in blue running. The men of his own regiment streamed past him. Huebner was standing stock still in the tide of men.

"Run, Hube! C'mon," he shouted into Huebner's frightened face.

"I tired, Robert!" Huebner complained.

"C'mon, Hube, you want to get captured?" Robert yelled. He grabbed Huebner's arm and started to run once again. He was astounded at the number of men he could see running for the rear. "We're whipped, Hube. God, we're whipped!" Huebner tripped, but Robert pulled him up without slowing.

"Where we goin'?" Huebner asked.

"Anywhere but here!" Robert snapped and kept hold of Huebner's coat sleeve.

Since the fight earlier in the morning and the retreat through the trees, his company had been either in motion or fighting continuously for the last five hours. By the time they arrived back at their camp on the hill, the company was exhausted and begrimed with powder. Only a short respite was enjoyed before they were formed upon the crest of the hill to face the oncoming enemy once more. Shock of the sudden reversal after what felt like a successful stand was only now becoming clear to him. Word spread quickly through the ranks that the enemy had broken through the other regiments of Peabody's brigade. Those camps were a mere tens of yards to the right of the 25th Missouri's. The thought of being caught in a vise and captured was more compelling than all of the officers' threats, insults, and cajoling. The regiment dissolved into a fleeing mass. Indeed, as Robert and Huebner made their way through the trees and beyond, Robert turned and saw the irregular colors of the enemy making their way through the camps of the 21st Missouri and the 16th Wisconsin. Those two regiments were running ahead of him. Their colors stopped for moments at a time as an officer rallied the fugitives surging past, attempting to make a stand, only to have the panicked men peel off moments later.

"Where we goin'?" Huebner whined.

"Just run!" Sternness and aggravation tinged Robert's voice, but Huebner began to run again. The woods soon gave way. Fugitives ahead of them made their way in the open in small groups or singly.

"I need stop, Robert," Huebner pleaded and slowed down his pace.

"Hube, c'mon. If we walk, we'll get caught," Robert reasoned in return.

"*Ich bin fertig ausgeführt*. I finished running," Huebner snapped. Pulling his arm from Robert's grasp, he collapsed upon the ground, heaving.

"*Nein, Komm schön, Hube. Komm schön!* I don't care if you're finished running!" Robert stopped, grabbed Huebner's collar, and heaved. Huebner didn't budge. He sat breathing heavily and refused to be hoisted. "Aw, c'mon, Hube! We can't stay here. We'll walk for a while, all right? C'mon, Hube." Robert tried to coax him into forward movement.

"*Kein Betrieb*," Huebner said, panting defiantly, but he slowly stood.

"No running, Hube, not for a while. But we gotta walk." Robert took a tentative step forward and looked back at Huebner to see if he was going to comply. Red-faced, Huebner started forward. Both men walked in silence toward the road that bisected the open space and led toward Pittsburg Landing. They had marched down that road after disembarking from the steamers that carried the brigade. The throngs of men in blue were making for the same road, as if drawn by the force of gravity. Robert set a brisk pace. He kept a vigilant eye behind them lest a line of butternut burst into view. Huebner matched his pace in silence. Striking the road, they saw it was clogged with men and animals. An overturned gun caisson and carriage lay abandoned off to the side. The horses, still in their traces, struggled to free themselves. A supply wagon was also overturned and abandoned by its teamster. Its contents spilled haphazardly along the roadside. They passed several groups of wounded slowly and painfully moving. Robert saw the pain, confusion, and terror in their eyes. He understood that look. He had had the same experiences. The approach of horses caused both men to stop and turn suddenly. A courier galloped recklessly down the road, ignoring all who were foolish enough to remain in the way. Another courier sped past along with an onrush of frightened men who brushed by with little regard for propriety. Most were weaponless and were shedding equipment as they went. The road soon looked like a quartermaster's store upset by a tornado.

Both men were carried along with the current and were running with no regard for Huebner's entreaties to slow down. A regiment coming down the eastern Corinth Road from the landing was disrupted by the riot of fleeing men despite the cursing of the officers trying to slow the panic and stop their own men from joining the rout. Calls of "Save yourselves," "We're all whipped," and "There's death down that road," rang out from the panicked men to anyone moving toward the fighting. A mixture of uniforms bespoke the mixing of regiments and the states that produced and clothed them. Frock coats, Ohio Volunteer Militia shell jackets, sack coats, forage caps, and officers' kepis, with their distinctive gold braids, could all be seen in the crowd of bobbing heads. In the midst of the mob, he lost hold of Huebner's arm, and they were separated.

Robert was comforted when he realized that the sounds of battle were fading. Soon, the tree-covered road opened to a wide, grassy plain, and the landing came into view. It was awash in soldiers milling about haphazardly. The mass of men surrounding Robert made straight for the level river bank. Robert couldn't guess at how many men were already there. Along the slope and stretching one hundred yards down the muddy bank, thousands of demoralized Union soldiers gathered. A gun boat lay in anchor mid river and intermittently fired shells inland. Some men flung themselves into the river to swim to the gun boat or to the opposite shore, a distance of roughly one hundred yards, only to be dragged down stream by the current and into oblivion. A few around him babbled incoherently with wild and dangerous expressions. Robert shoved his way through the bodies to look for Huebner. There were so many men crammed into that small space that Robert had to grab men by the shoulders and forcibly turn them to see their faces. Occasionally, he would encounter annoyance, but mostly he saw fright and fatigue. Most seemed like him, lost and alone and wandering aimlessly about.

Fist fights broke out as one man would decide he wanted the muddy spot occupied by another. Because few men knew one another, the fighting would carry on until one of the fighters was senseless or dead. Everyone else just wanted to escape the brawl.

Robert came across many officers who shared the same look of despair. He lost count of how many men he accosted in his quest. How much time had passed or where he was made little impression upon him until the shoulders he grasped revealed familiar features.

"Robert!" Huebner cried and grasped tightly onto Robert's arms.

"Hube!" Robert replied with equal enthusiasm.

Huebner started laughing for joy, jumping up and down like a little boy. "Robert, *mein Kamerad!* Robert, *du bist hier!*" Huebner released Robert's arms and wrapped him in a bear hug.

"*Ja*, Hube. I'm here. I'm here," Robert replied and tried to squirm out of the vise grip Huebner had him in.

"Robert, *komme. Komme*," Huebner shouted and grabbed Robert's arm. He began dragging him through the crowd and up from the river bank about fifty yards to the Pittsburg Road. The grassy expanse was filled with men relaxing, sitting, standing, or lying. The aroma of thousands of pipes filled the air with a panoply of aromatic flavors. There was more room than by the river bank, but they had to step carefully around the seated and standing figures. They had nearly reached the roadside when Robert saw a cluster of familiar forms. "*Sehe, unsre Kameraden.*"

Seated upon the ground near a copse of trees were twenty men of the 25th whom Robert recognized easily enough. To his surprise, Gustavson was there and two other privates from his company. They celebrated a cheerful reunion, laughing with relief. Robert sat down next to Gustavson, and Huebner sat next to him. The initial excitement of reuniting wore off quickly. They stared into one another's faces. A pall of depression hung heavily about the group, and the vacant expressions of his pards reflected his own feeling of failure. Defeat is not easily shaken. It follows an individual and an army the rest of their days. The fear that overtook him and the suddenness of their flight were memories he wished to blot out. He remembered the bravado of taking the oath, the triumphant march out of St. Louis for the grand adventure, and the taste of contributing to the cause of saving the Union. Would they now be unable to march back home when the world heard of their cowardice? More than the shame of faltering, he and his pards, and, from the looks of it, the whole army, had shown the white feather in ignominy.

There was little comfort in the company of cowards. He was not relieved by the knowledge that he wasn't alone in failure. Gustavson's voice broke into his thoughts.

"Know what happen to rest of *Kompanie?*"

"I seen Hammel fall," Huebner said.

"I don't remember much, only men turning and running. I didn't see Hammel after the Rebs charged into us. I didn't see much of anyone," Robert said.

"I seen Hammel fall," Huebner repeated.

"*Ja*, I just turned *und* run, too," Gustavson said. He scratched his head, looking confused. "No care 'bout Rebs or officers, just run. Dem Rebs no quit now. Dem Rebs kept comin' up hill, and no matter how many we kill, dem just keep comin'."

"Hammel fell in front of me. I seen him."

"I've seen other regiments break and run," Robert said. They turned to focus on him. "I've ridiculed them. I've scorned them. I've felt superior to them. We stood this morning in that field though. I felt the fear for the first time when we seen them just appear out of the darkness all around us." Robert fiddled absently with the grass blades at his feet.

"Hammel stare at me from the ground the whole time."

Robert turned toward Huebner. Huebner was looking from man to man, watching for any reaction. "Did you see him fall, Robert? Did you see him?"

"No, Hube, I didn't," Robert whispered.

"When Hammel fall, he knock *meine Gewehr* from me. I stood a long time looking at him. *Mit alle herum kämpfen*, fighting all around me." Huebner's eyes grew wide; his voice cracked. "But I keep looking at him look at me."

"Not your fault, Hube," Robert said in even tone. "We all panicked."

"No panic. Just face staring at me. I couldn't *not* stare back," Huebner pleaded.

"Stop vorryin' about it, *Junge*," Gustavson said to console him. "*Ve* all seen tings ve'd sooner forget."

"*Nein*, no scared, no freeze. Him just starin' at me whole time we was fighting. I closed my eyes and still saw Hammel stare back. I don't want to see Hammel no more!" Huebner sat hard on the ground. He dropped his head between his knees. He began to rock and shake. They looked at him, then one another, silently agreeing to let Huebner work it out the best he could. They all had images they would rather forget.

He felt a nudge from Huebner's foot. Robert looked down into Huebner's vacant eyes.

"What we do now? What about regiment?" Huebner asked.

The rumbling of battle, continuous and muffled, still echoed about them. "As long as it sounds like this, *ve* ok. If it gets nearer, *ve*'ll have to stand or surrender," Gustavson replied.

"From the sounds of it, there must be some part of the army still under arms," a voice behind Robert added. It was Private Piper from Company D, someone Robert recognized but didn't know well.

"What does it matter?" another voice chimed in. "Look around you.

We're licked but good."

"Must be parts of several divisions here wandering about. The whole left flank of the army is here," Robert stated.

"Can't be every division. Dere's a-fightin' *shtill*," said Piper.

"What does it matter? You saw 'em comin' this mornin'. We'll be prisoners afore the day is done!"

"*Auslieferung? Mutter und Vater würden beschämt sein,*" Huebner whimpered.

"*Halt die Schnauze,* Huebner!" Gustavson snapped back.

"*Ich bin beschämt. Wir sind alle Fahnenflüchtiger!*" Huebner cried.

"*Halt dich!*" Gustavson shouted.

"Hube! Hube, quiet, pard, quiet down." Robert grabbed Huebner by the shoulders and stared into his eyes. "You're alive, you hear me? *Du bist lebendig. Wir verließen nicht.* We didn't desert. We were licked. *"*

"*Wir haben verlassen. Verlassen. Ich habe* shamed *das* regiment. *Wir haben verlassen. Verlassen.*" Huebner began to sob quietly.

"We all shamed the regiment, Hube." Robert pulled Huebner's head to his shoulder and held him for a moment until the sobs passed. With his eyes, he dared anyone to say anything. Robert saw the same feelings of shame and defeat upon their begrimed faces. They were simply too proud to get it out of their systems. Pity and understanding echoed from each man in their little circle.

*****

Stephen stood in a company-sized formation with men he hardly knew. The pitiful remnants of the regiment had been gathered together by Captain Harper. They stood within the tree lines from whence they had sallied forth into the enemy guns atop the hill. Formed into companies by such leadership as each boasted, they barely counted the size of one large company. The Tennesseans had also regrouped and were forming in a march column to rejoin the rest of Cleburne's division, whose advance took them far beyond the obstinate hill and its now-absent defenders.Stephen held his rifle loosely at his side, its butt resting against his shoe. He felt the sorrow of the losses heavy upon his heart. Fifteen men answered to role for Stephen's company, which was called by the fourth corporal. The one hundred and twenty-five men who answered to their names looked haggard and dispirited. Early that morning, the regiment had marched to the sound of the drum with four hundred and twenty-five men answering the morning call. Emptiness filled the eyes of the men around him, and the bewilderment of the engagement hung heavily upon his mind. Upon the hillside, medical orderlies picked through the jumble of corpses for those yet alive. William lay somewhere upon the hill or within the enemy camp where they had first penetrated. Captain Harper took the report from Second Lieutenant Preston and gave the command to stand at ease.

"Men of Mississippi," Harper shouted, "by virtue of your valor and your steadfastness, you have compelled the enemy to retire from this hill. Our ranks were torn and serried by the enemy's fire, but you stood to your duty and carried our banner forward and into the enemy ranks. The name of the 6th Mississippi regiment of volunteers has been emblazoned with the glory of our cause and the dedication of your mettle. If it were not for the desperation of our efforts here, I would turn you about and march you back from whence we came this morning. But I fear that every musket will be needed before the day is over, and your valor may yet be needed upon this field." Harper saluted the men, and they weakly responded with the same. "Company commanders; see to your men's needs. We will march in ten minutes."

Stephen's heart sank. He could hear the sudden release of despair from the rest of the company at the word "march." No question of valor or bravery would keep these men from standing to their duty, but upon this field and on this day, they were spent. They wanted nothing but to see to their pards and to rest. The fourth corporal gathered the small group about him, checked their ammunition pouches, and bore the brunt of their collective disgust. Stephen looked back at the forlorn hill and wished to drop his weapon and search for William. The wounded were being carried slowly up the hill and into the enemy camp. The 23rd Tennessee was right-faced and began marching up the hill behind the 6th. Snaking their way around the hillside to avoid the ground they had charged over, both regiments came up to the top and filed through the camp silently. The Yankee dead were still lying where they had fallen. They filled the tents with their own wounded. A scant hour before, the camp and hill were covered in smoke and filled with the sounds of battle. The eerie peacefulness of it gave Stephen the shivers. Everywhere was movement and carnage. The path of retreat was clearly marked by clothing and equipment. As they exited the camp, the corpses of the enemy became fewer. He no longer thought anything about them. Seeing one was like seeing a bush or a stump. He didn't feel hate or curiosity; he felt nothing at all.

They entered another dark wood and slowed to avoid getting tangled in the dead leaves, twigs, and bushes. Stephen soon felt the remaining energy sapped from his legs. The sounds of the crunching feet became lost in the sounds of furious cannonade and volley firing ahead. The men surrounding him were quiet, neither excited nor fearful. The thinning of the trees ahead and the growing brightness of daylight led them out once more into a great grassy plain. A scattering of their own dead and wounded brought them once again into the battle zone. Ahead of the two regiments stood a long line of butternut separated by another line of blue. The road that twisted beyond the Federal line was the focus. Batteries from both sides belched fire at quick intervals, and the Federal line was engulfed in smoke. Down the road, coming from the enemy's lines, poured a stream of blue columns to buttress their stand. Stephen shuddered as he envisioned what was to come.

Chapter Eight

Reveille shook Philip from his slumber in the morning chill. Huddling his arms to his chest, he lay motionless. Grunts, groans, and coughs multiplied as his comrades awoke to the fading darkness of early morning. The crackling of cook fires and smell of char replaced the former quiet of the morning fields. Resigned to being awake, Philip rubbed his eyes and sat up in his bed roll. Pushing his night cap back from his eyes and forehead, he sat for a few moments more as the clouds of sleep slowly lifted. The flickering fires cast momentary flashes of orange and red upon the tree line a few rods away, making the figures in the distance look like demons.

Philip curled his legs Indian style and drew the blanket up to his chest. Next to him, Sammy crawled out of his blanket and stood, his face drawn and eyes mere slivers behind squinted eye lids. To his left, Mule lay motionless and huddled under his blanket.

"Mule, wake up," Sammy croaked softly.

Philip stared at the heap for a moment and marveled at Mule's ability to sleep through the growing clamor.

"Mule, get up," Sammy repeated louder. "Philip, nudge him."

Philip turned to the Mule's form and said, "Hey, Mule. Up."

"You know that never works. Ya' gotta nudge 'em," Johnny said as he sat up in his bed roll next to Mule.

"C'mon, Mule. Reveille, wake up. Time to get up, Mule." Philip shook what he thought was a shoulder, and a grunt sounded from the lump of blanket.

Mule suddenly swept the blanket off and sat up with a dumbfounded expression painted on his features. "Mornin' already?"

"Better get moving. We probably got an hour afore we got to form," Sammy said while he stretched and sat down to pull his brogans on.

"Who's makin' *Kaffe*?" Mule grunted and ran his thick stubby fingers through a matted lump of hair.

"It's Philip's turn for mess. Better get him a-goin'," Johnny said. He brought out his tin cup.

"*Ja, Kaffe.*" Mule thrust his cup into Philip's face, shaking it.

"Ok, I'm going." Philip grabbed the cup and let it drop on the ground as he struggled out of the blanket and to his feet. "Give me the cups."

Johnny's cup landed by Philip's foot. Quickly slipping his brogans on, he made his way to the company cook fire and filled the cups with water. Philip dug through his haversack to retrieve a muslin bag and loosed the string enough to form a spout. After sprinkling the crushed coffee beans onto the surface of each cup, he set them in a row around the coals. The fire pit was ringed with cups and soldiers chatting. Philip settled down at the fire's edge and nibbled on a brick of hardtack. Staring into the fire, he imagined they were Perdition's flames, and the suddenness of the thought caused him to wonder at the irony of using them to heat the coffee.

On occasion, he had tried to teach a lesson on Hell, of its flames, pain, and thirst. Those were his worst sermons, for he lacked the oratory passion to make Hell seem like Hell and not some fantastic place of the imagination. The dance of the flames also brought to his mind thoughts of war and the fires of passion that had burned in the early days. Each flame flickered for a moment, and then shrank back into the coals, only to birth another.

The parishioners in his circuit had little interest in Hell and Satan or anything else that had to do with the mysteries of the spiritual realms. He couldn't help but teach on those topics, regardless. He knew that if he did not ponder their effects, he, too, would become complacent in his faith.

The growing sectional conflict brought out questions of war and what was the pious, spiritual response. These were questions that he could not answer even for himself. Instead, he taught respect for authority as given by God and prayed for wisdom. Leaving this all behind was a relief, for he no longer needed wrestle with answers that met ecclesiastical requirements. The flames consumed him as they did the wood that slowly disintegrated into glowing coals of red and white. In the same way, flames consumed the nation and families that composed his circuit. Their hearts burned with indignation at the affronts caused by the Rebel states and against the administration for its excesses in wielding power. Few, if any, that he was specifically aware of, worried about the darkies or even mentioned the issue in conversation. His own thoughts were just as vague, and he had given little thought about it until the regiment encountered the first sad columns of contrabands in Kentucky. Seeing only ignorant and pathetic forms under ill-fitting clothing, Philip tried to move himself to the righteous indignation he thought he should feel.

He pitied their plight and the sometimes dumb and numb expressions of the oppressed. Yet, he also saw smiles and expectation in them, a reverie in camp and a willingness to show graciousness for any small kindness shown them. They carried their world upon their backs and followed the army, hoping for protection and salvation. Often, they were turned back and looked upon as a nuisance. Starving and penniless, the runaways and liberated slaves presented a reality that shook Philip to the core. For good or for ill, the status of the black man was in the balance, and no one realized that more than the slave himself.

The eastern horizon brightened slowly and cast its lightening shades of blue westward. Slowly the surface of the cups stirred with bubbles rising to the surface. Soon, they were ready to drink. Deftly pulling each one from the coals, he set them down on the fire's edge and doused the surface with cold water to settle the coffee grounds to the bottom.

"Ah, coffee," Sammy walked to the fire and said. He bent down to grasp his cup.

"Are we ready?" Philip asked.

"Yeah, I rolled your blanket and put it on your straps. You just need to pack your things into the sack. Your traps are set by the pack."

Johnny grunted as he set himself next to Philip and grabbed his cup. "You got any more apricots?"

Philip dug into his haversack and tossed Johnny the bag. Mule was the last to join them, and soon each was cooling the surface of his cup and chewing hardtack. Philip handed around a bag of cooked salt pork he had prepared the evening before. The strips were greasy and chewy but would suffice for a little intake of meat until they could cook again that evening.

His mess duties finished, Philip grabbed his cup and went back to his pack. Sammy had rolled his blanket up, and it fit onto the top of his pack properly. He always had trouble getting it rolled right himself. After exchanging his night cap for his forage cap, he grabbed his Testament and quickly thumbed the pages to the book of Isaiah. He hadn't read much in that book before the war, nor had he taught on it. Reading it now gave him comfort as he compared Judah and her call to repentance with the rebellion. Who was the guilty party? Who was the faithless? He had no idea, only a faint hope that the North was not.

*****

Daybreak revealed the weary regiments gathered once again upon the road to Savannah where they waited impatiently for the commencement of the march. Some commotion was occurring at the head of the column after a halt was ordered twenty minutes earlier. Philip rested his hands on the barrel of his musket and leaned forward to release the pressure on his shoulders from the pack. He had barely gotten his marching legs when the halt came.

"D'you hear that?" Mule asked.

"What?" Philip answered.

Mule stood straight and motionless as if all of his faculties were bent upon hearing something of great distance. "That."

"Don't know what you're hearin', Mule. I don't hear nuthin'," Johnny muttered from the rank behind.

"No, I can hear a rumble," Mule said.

"I wasn't aware mules had good hearin'," Johnny teased him.

"No! There's somethin' happ'n' down this road. I hear booming!"

"Could explain why we stopped," Philip said.

"Not s'posed to be any Secesh where we's headed," said Johnny.

"Secesh or no," Mule said, "I hear a battle where we's headed."

Philip stood up straight to adjust the weight of his knapsack. "We're supposed to meet up with Grant. Maybe he's been attacked." He listened for a moment, but didn't hear anything out of the ordinary. "Can you see anything happenin' up there, Mule?"

"Naw, I just see heads. I don't see any of the big bugs."

A soft breeze blew through the ranks of the dusty blue column of men who stood four abreast. Philip strained to hear anything that would indicate something amiss but could only hear whispered conversations and coughs.

"Mebbe we're bein' countermarched. Think the Rebs got in behind us somewheres?" Philip asked his pards.

"Secesh in Corinth," Johnny said. "Unless Forrest's troopers are on a raid, there ain't a Reb in Tennessee or Kentucky. Don't see where we'd be marched back to."

"They must be ahead of us," Mule reasoned. He craned his neck to look down the length of the lane.

"They ain't ahead of us. They ain't even in Tennessee!" protested Johnny.

"You kin thinks what you want, Johnny. I know what I heard." Mule huffed and glared straight ahead.

They heard the sound of approaching hooves, and all eyes strained to see a group of horsemen riding down the length of the column and past them. Another group of riders appeared and halted at the head of the brigade column. Urgency animated the riders' movements, and the looks of worry and stress creased the faces of the officers returning to their commands.

Philip watched the officers and said, "We gonna know soon enough, I reckon." He dug the straps of the knapsack off his shoulders, realizing that its weight felt more cumbersome this morning than usual.

Colonel Jones dismounted and ordered the bugler to sound Officers Call. Soon a gaggle of gold braids and shoulder straps were gathered around the colonel at the head of the regiment. Distant bugle calls and a rise of dust ahead signaled the resumption of the march. The officers' meeting broke quickly. Whispers and comments rose from the men speculating on the purpose of the meeting. The regiment's adjutant scurried along the road, and company commanders began shouting orders to the company sergeants.

Without word, news, or explanation, the regiment was ordered forward, and the march resumed with a quickened step. What had promised to be another day of marching had become a movement of urgent anticipation and mystery. That something was up was clear to all. Grim-faced officers marched or rode silently. Along the road, orderlies and messengers galloped to and fro between clusters of officers poring over maps. The ranks marched ahead silently.

An hour passed without a halt, and Philip began to look for indications that one would soon be called. Sweat trickled down his temples. With each step, the shock ran up his heels to his ankles. Each jolt rattled the weight of the knapsack, causing it to dig deeply into his shoulders.

A moist wind blew in their faces and rustled the trees along the roadside, carrying with it a sound of dread. Like a distant storm upon the horizon whose darkened clouds foretell a tempest's approach, the bursts of breeze brought the rumbling of cannon for the briefest instant. Philip glanced at Mule occasionally to confirm or deny what his own ears heard. Mule appeared lost in his own concerns and trudged step by step without expression. The couriers continued their frantic movements, tracing the sides of the dirt track in frightening succession with communications and counter-replies between unseen commanders.

Philip watched them ride with interest. Each coming and going seemed to represent a staccato conversation of some import. He could not divine their content or intent, but he imagined the seriousness of the communiqué. Such activity was normal along a march as brigades and divisions kept tabs upon one another, but the frequency and urgency was something he had not seen before. Nor had he found himself marching into the unknown with the intervening distance carrying with it a portent of battle upon a fickle wind. He tried to count the suddenness of each echo to discern its distance or its origin, to no avail.

The march had carried them eight miles closer to their end goal of Savannah, and yet the pace had not slackened. A sudden gust of warm wind accosted his face and with it another sound of rumbling and something else. Philip glanced about and noted the interest and concern; even Mule had taken note and snapped out of his torpor. The sound in that gust wasn't just the low rumbling of a far off cannonade. It was something less mechanical, more human. It came and went with the gust. Philip couldn't characterize it easily. It was death and life; it was war.

It was becoming clear that Mule had heard something long before anyone, and that something terrible was occurring down this road. Grant was attacking or being attacked. The distance was still great that separated the combatants and the marchers upon the Savannah Road. Philip felt himself lean in to each step. Each one brought help and aid to Grant in whatever fashion it was needed that much sooner. He could sense the same from the ranks of his company, an energy that propelled them beyond the distraction of fatigue. Something was happening up the road, and each man wanted to know what it was. They were no longer propelled by green ambition for glory. Nor were they veteran enough to shy from closing the gap between themselves and battle. All knew intuitively that their rifles were in need or that the tide could turn with their presence upon the field. Stepping lively, the regiments forced their march to hasten.

"It has to be," Philip gasped.

"What?" Johnny called from behind.

"Mule heard it a few hours ago. You can hear it now on the wind." Sweat streaked down Philip's temples and ran down his cheeks. He could feel the sweat running down his legs and soaking through his shirt.

"You can see it in their eyes." Mule added, as another courier sped past.

"How many miles?" Philip asked and sucked in a breath of air to fight being winded.

"Don' know," Mule replied. "Ten?"

Philip looked up into the muggy haze to espy the sun. It was riding high but not yet at its apex.

"Should almost be to Savannah," Johnny said between gulps of air.

"You been watchin' the messages back and forth?" Philip asked.

"Yeah, never seen that much traffic afore. A battle to be sure up the river," Johnny said.

"How'd you hear that, Mule? Back there, how'd you hear it?" Philip asked.

"Don' know. Just did."

"You ever hear stuff like that before?" Johnny broke in and asked.

"No."

"Why now?"

"Don' know. I jes' heard it. Like a low rumble of cannon way far off."

"You heard it way before I did," Philip said. "Did you hear the other thing in that last gust?"

"What other thing?" Johnny asked.

"Yeah," Mule replied.

"I don' know, like screeching or screaming or shouting," Philip said.

"Yeah, shouting's what it sounded like," Mule agreed.

"All I heard was the rumble," said Johnny.

"It was human, but not. Like it was haunting the rumbling." Philip wiped his brow with his neckerchief.

"You ain't talkin' about ghosts, is ya'?" asked Johnny.

"No, nothin' like that. It was like the noise of the elephant or battle, but not just the firing and all. It was human, but inhuman."

"You aren't makin' sense," Johnny scolded him.

"He's right," said Mule. "That's what it sounded like."

"It's what I always imagined the furies sounded like from Greek myths. That sort of hollow tumult." Philip conjured his image of the mythical creatures that could flit about like humming birds and peck their prey mercilessly. What he heard, though, sounded like a host of furies all screeching at once.

"More like the roar of the fires of hell," added Mule.

"That sounds more reasonable," Johnny said.

"That may be closer to the truth than we want to know," Philip said with unease.

*****

"Stack arms!"

Philip "threaded the needle" by sliding his bayonet through the interlocking ones of the men in front of him. Then the number two man swung Philip's musket around to form the sturdy teepee-shaped rifle stack. Once the weapons were stacked, a long bristling line of gleaming metal stood in front of the formation. The command for rest was given, and Philip trudged over to the shady side of the farm's outbuildings and collapsed upon the ground. A provost guard stood by the farm's well and ordered the clamor for refreshment by turns. Tearing at his sack coat, he unbuttoned it to allow his soaked undershirt to breathe. The straps of his knapsack no longer hung heavily upon his shoulders, and the other straps could be loosened. Lifting off his forage cap, he felt the cool rush of air relieve his sweaty scalp.

The shady spot soon teemed with sprawling figures until a man couldn't shift position without disturbing the one next to him.

"Can we brew?" Johnny asked his pards.

"Don't know. I think we only have time to fill canteens before we resume," Mule answered.

"Mule's turn for that," Philip said. He struggled to get the sling of his canteen over his neck and passed it to Mule. "Sorry, Mule. You'll be standing awhile." The line at the well was long and full of tired soldiers. Mule hoisted himself off the ground with a groan and collected the canteens. The afternoon sun bore down upon the men hapless enough to be stuck standing or lying underneath its merciless rays.

They reached the town of Savannah after another five hours of march. On the way, they had passed Grant's headquarters, a stately manor with the typical southern penchant for Greek columns and wide porticos. Another gaggle of gold braids and shoulder straps was gathered about the steps, and a picket line of horses stood off to the side in wait for the next rider to mount. A troop of cavalry had made its camp on the other side of the houses. They could see its men scurrying about their own horses and tending to their equipment. They looked dusty but otherwise well-rested and fit.

Philip looked at his own begrimed and haggard comrades and marveled at the difference. He had chortled as they passed, "Hey, mister, where's your mule?" to the wearied chuckles of those near him. Nobody really knew what it meant or exactly where the phrase originated, only that it was a popular rib against the cavalry.

One of the troopers retorted, "We ride our dumb animals. Looks like they's ridden you pretty good."

Enlivened a touch by the prospect of a brief respite, Johnny added, "Ever hear tell why you never did seed a dead cavalryman? It's 'cause they always beat ya' to the rear!"

"Ever know why you always see dead infantrymen?" came the reply, "Because they too dumb to get out of the way!"

Cheered by the brief repartee, they marched a little easier until the near constant rumbling in the distance, clearly audible now, reminded them of the danger ahead.

Philip listened to the rumble. They had seen the paddlewheel gun boat, *Tyler,* at the loading docks as they passed through town and now could clearly hear its fire amid the other sounds. It was firing every fifteen minutes by his count and must have been lobbing huge shells. Each report was loud and drawn as if thunder suddenly cracked. They also saw several other boats of low draft docked and taking on supplies or soldiers. The town thronged with men in blue, and the procession along the road was as continuous as the roar in the distance.

"We gonna get to ride the steamers?" Sammy asked.

"That'd be nice. Give these feet a rest for a spell," Philip said with a sigh.

"Ha!" said Johnny. "Have we ever ridden anything but our own feet?"

"Ridin's fer paper-collar soldiers like them troopers we passed." Sammy said.

"Paper collar or no, I could use a transport about now." Philip answered.

"Looky there," Sammy said. A line of ambulances and wagons tottered down the road toward the docks. "That's somethin' a man don't wanna see afore headin' down this here road."

"I'll march. Them's for band box shoulder straps an' the dyin'," Johnny said glumly. "You'll see every one of them later carryin' one officer each, drunk and feignin' injury."

Second Sergeant Harper passed them and interrupted. "I'll bet the good Reverend would gladly have exchanged his holier-than-thou collar for a paper one any day, seein' as he always liked lookin' the dandy."

Johnny snapped back at him. "Nobody talkin' ta you, Sergeant."

"You hear that sound, Harper?" Philip called to him. "It's the sound of the flames of Hell and your brother callin' you home!" Philip could see he struck a sore spot, and he worked it. "You're just as evil and hard-hearted as he was and twice as deserving of perdition's flames!"

"Watch yourself, Reverend, or it'll be me givin' your eulogy befittin' a dead dog! You'll be beatin' the Secesh to Hell's gates. Beelzebub hisself will roll out the welcome mat for another of Methodism's servants!"

"You wish," Sammy shouted at him. "We'll just have to see who greets who in Hell first, you nasty piece of rat filth!"

Philip put his hand on Sammy's shoulder. "Shut up, Sammy. Don't pay the mean-hearted beggar any more mind. He's heard his true father callin' him home, and he's just scared." Philip stared hard at Harper. "I do hope it is I who can send you to him with proper words so your brother can feel rightly reunited with his kin. I told the truth then, and I'd tell the truth again. Only this time I won't mince my words with pleasantries and empty platitudes as I did for Robert, your fornicating, gambling, liar of a half-wit brother whose only mistake was to be smarter than yourself by dying first!"

There was an awkward silence while Harper and Philip brooded upon their hasty words and Philip's comrades looked upon him with puzzled expressions. Philip explained, loudly enough for Harper to hear him, "I had the good pleasure of having the Harper family in one of my smaller societies that I was blessed to give spiritual comfort to upon occasion. It was one of my poorer societies, in both value and understanding, requiring much of my energies. It seems that the Harper progeny had not taken well to their studies of Scripture nor of their letters. They were the scourge of the county and subject of whispering behind closed doors.

"It seems," Philip continued, "that one day Robert Harper, the youngest of five, found himself at the business end of a rifle and his hands upon the sullied breasts of ole man Puget's homely but buxom wife. He was duly shot by Mr. Puget and drug out into the lane to die. Bein' the notorious scalawag that he was, nary even the most pious Good Samaritan would stoop to dirty their hands upon his dyin' body. It was I who picked up the sufferin' soul and took his absolutions and confessions of guilt, and I tried to make his last moments upon this earth comfortable. He remained un-absolved to the end, refusin' to recognize God or his Savior, and he died in his guilt. Even the family of this upstanding model of humanity refused to give their own aid as he lay dyin'."

Harper's face turned bright red, and he shouted in Philip's face, "What you did at the funeral was not right, you messenger of Satan! You knew mother didn't know what kind of life he lived, and yet you still stood there like a judge and passed the sentence of Hell upon him for all to hear! You knew what to do, and you didn't do it!" He shook with rage, and spittle flew from his mouth. "I don't care what you thought of me or my brother or what you knew to be fact or rumor! You had no right to tell your version of piety before a gathered crowd! My mother's ill health and death are on your hands, you son of Satan!"

"It was a slip, but no less believed and known to all!" Philip shouted back. "If I erred in anything it was to allow that wretch to be buried in God's name to begin with. If I would have allowed it, you Harpers would have run your business out of the meeting house in open view of all."

Harper's fists came up. "Don't you say another word, Reverend, unless you…"

"Fall in! Get your traps back on, fall in!" rang the first sergeant's voice.

Philip's heart beat in his chest, angered and shamed for his outburst. Falling in line in front of the stacks of muskets, he took his place in the rear rank. An officer gave the command to take arms. In an instant, the orderly rows of stacks disappeared, and the weapons returned to their owners. With the command to right face, the formations moved into march column of fours. In the sudden hush once the men were in place, they could hear the sound of continuing battle ahead.

"Men of Ohio!" shouted Colonel Jones, "a great battle is being fought up this road. General Grant is hard-pressed by an obstinate enemy who believes by pure guile they can defeat the arms of our great cause. We will be force-marched upon this road for the hour is grave. We march to the cause! To the cause!"

A chorus of "To the cause" rang out from the regiment, and Jones gave the command to forward march. Stepping off, the fifers played "John Brown's Body," and all voices joined in with hearty accord.

John Brown's body lies a-moldering in the grave.
John Brown's body lies a-moldering in the grave.
John Brown's body lies a-moldering in the grave,
But his soul goes marching on.
Glory, glory, Hallelujah!
Glory, glory, Hallelujah!
Glory, glory, Hallelujah!
His soul goes marching on.

Chapter Nine

Michael lazed upon the pommel of his saddle, watching a long line of Federal prisoners move down the Corinth Road. Dispirited and exhausted, the prisoners trudged along unaware of the beauty of the afternoon. Fires still burned in the underbrush along the road, and smoke billowed from the wood line where the division of Federal General Prentiss made its last stand. Thousands of men in blue streamed out of the trees in silent dejection. The guns were finally stilled, and the men in each battery collapsed at their posts. More guns than Michael had ever seen in battle, of every caliber, were hub to hub as the artillery arm of the army flexed its muscle in one accord.

The nest of Yankee holdouts was vanquished in violence, and other than the noise farther to the right, the stillness on this part of the field was welcome. The battery strained every muscle and collective will since the opening shots. Michael felt the same numbness he saw in the faces of their captives. Victory can be as exhausting as defeat, he thought. The haggard appearance of his own men made him thankful for the respite, though every sudden crash and burst of noisy battle ahead made him wish to be a part of the final victory.

Infantry regiments sorted themselves out and began filing down the Eastern Corinth Road toward a new battle line. They left behind the guns and rear chaos of fugitives, couriers, staff officers, and prisoners. The wounded and winded lay where they fell, making it hard to distinguish who was hurt from who was too enfeebled by the heat and fatigue to move on. Scavengers wandered among the dead, rifling through haversacks and coats and stealing anything of value. Every dead and wounded Federal soldier had been stripped of his shoes.

A lawless element accompanied any command. Generally, it was motivated by the desire to possess a Yankee souvenir or a replacement article of clothing. A watch, smoke pipe, Testament, or gold rings were things that Michael could not countenance. It was desecrating the dead. So far, his men were refraining, or at least the presence of the command structure was keeping them honest. Those robbing the dead were loners, separated from their own units and free to do as they pleased.

"You'd think them stragglers would have some sense of decency, even if they is the enemy they's robbin'," Mahoney said.

"I suppose that's why this army has men like you and I, Mahoney. Someone's got to keep the men in line," Michael replied.

"Even when we's not 'round to watch 'em, not very Christian-like to rob the dead."

"What about war is Christian-like?" Michael pondered aloud.

"Well, them fellers out there strippin' them Yanks certainly ain't doin' it for God or country but out of greed an' avarice. The act of war may not be Christian-like, but we didn't ask for war but for independence," Mahoney replied.

"Never considered this no crusade. Just a fight to survive." Michael watched a looter dragging something heavy through the brush. "Maybe war jus' brings out the worst in us."

"No argument there, but it also brings out the best in a man. What is it the Good Book says? No greater love can a man have than this, that he give up his life for his friends. Love, love of country and one's pards, that be a good thing," said Mahoney. He, too, stood silent and watched the spectacle. "Still, someone should put a stop to what they's doing."

"Suppose that's what the provost is for, but it's a big area," Michael said and straightened in the saddle, "and these thieves would just go and do it somewheres else. That's why we need to keep a tight rein on our own men."

"They's not all robbin'. They's some out there bringin' water to the enemy wounded, see?" Mahoney pointed to a figure in the distance going from spot to spot.

"That man's got the idea of Christian charity, all right, I suppose."

"Don't take church goin' to have that kind of charity, jus' a sense of right, wrong, and honor. That be someone who loves what is right."

"They would seem to be character qualities anyone can have regardless of claiming a faith. There is a sense of honor inherent in the officer corps, for example, though I can't say who is or isn't someone I'd call a Christian," Michael stated.

"They's a difference between a society of gentlemen an' Christian charity, though I'd say that the code of conduct for officers wasn't developed by men of faith."

"If that be truth, it would seem a disconnect betwixt peace, war, and faith. Ol' Stonewall Jackson's reputed to be a man of faith and Christian principles yet be a man of war," Michael said. "They say Johnston be the same."

Mahoney thought about that idea for a moment. "No disconnect that I can tell. War be the basest of humankind in response to pressure and strife. It trains a man in killin' and to do it without remorse or feelin'. A man needs a faith to buttress times of war, and war brings a man closer to his Creator than any other happenstance. War is just as Christian as peace is."

"I'd much prefer peace. Safer that way," Michael said with a chuckle. "Although I suppose the good Lord did say sumthin' 'bout not bringin' an olive branch but a sword and dividin' family from family in the end times."

"Don't know that the verse is one of war or not, but of realism in dealin' with anythin' contrary to the faith, but I suppose it might also describe a time of strife such as this."

Michael laughed suddenly. "I'll bet we sound like a seminary class at the moment. Queer place for holdin' such a discussion, no?"

"It is on such a field that it is most appropriate, fer many a man has faced his mortality this morn in both honor and dishonor." Mahoney motioned with a sweep of the gauntlets in his hand at the scavengers in front of them. "Maybe they's angry at some slight by them Yanks, or maybe they's jus' angry and resorted to thievin' to settle they's souls. Who knows what evil can come out of a man? You and I, we don't pull the lanyard in hate or anger. We do it out of honor and dedication to our cause, and we'd punish any of our command for pilfering the dead, even if they were Yanks. 'Vengeance is mine,' says the Lord, and we don't 'venge. We fight with honor. That's the difference between a Christian act and a devilish one."

Michael shook his head and said, "I would surely wish pain and trouble upon any of the enemy what caused me any personal pain or loss, for sure. Only my rank and my own sense of honor would prevent me from such desecration, not God."

"I think you be closer to God than you think, sir. For it ain't an absence of hate that makes a man think twice before striking back or planning revenge but the presence of the Almighty in him that restrains the passions of a man." With that, Mahoney looked at Michael with the fatherly glance Michael had grown to enjoy from his older subordinate.

"You keep that talk up, we gonna have to pitch a tent here and turn our seminary into a meetin' tent," Michael laughed.

"I think we got a fight to win firstly," Mahoney returned the grin. "Sir, if I may, I'm of the mind to scatter that lot of grave robbers and give them the flat of my sword for they's impudence." He stood straight and saluted.

"You have my leave, certainly, First Sergeant." Michael returned the lazy salute tendered by his subordinate and watched Mahoney spur his horse forward to a trot. Was this an act of Christian charity or military honor that drove Mahoney to put the lash to the carrion scavengers? Michael didn't know which, or if they were even separate, for military honor and guidance seemed to owe much to what he could only label as Christian or gentlemanly honor. Yet the two together upon the field of battle presented him a conflict of their own. Love for his fellow man and death to him who stands in opposition did not mesh with Michael. How could he love and kill in the same spirit of charity? It was not out of any specific deploring that he beheld any man in blue, but for the cause for which he stood.

The sun bore down upon the combatants, and the heat sapped their energy. Like the spring in a watch, the army of men, animals, steel, powder, and lead had sprung and recoiled and sprung again as the fight progressed. At this time of elated victory over the invading foe, Michael sensed the weariness around him in the men's lethargic lounging upon the grass and search for shade. They gathered as families of gun crews. They were men of different births but bonded by their common brotherhood of membership in the battery. With familiarity not seen even among brothers, they lay upon one another and caught whatever rest they could. Michael saw it in the lines of infantry brigades marching down the road. The army was spent, and yet the fight continued—the enemy fighting for survival and the Confederates for victory.

Michael watched Mahoney herd and scatter the dozen or so thieves in the distance, and he began to get restless, even though he knew every one of the gun crews needed rest. It was inaction in the midst of battle and a straining to be a part of it that tried his patience. The act of limbering, unlimbering, and bringing the guns on line, and the working of each and every load meant constant motion and strain on the nerves. Looking at his men, he knew the battery would be slow in responding should the order come to limber up. There was only so much a man could be asked to do in a single day.

Often the target of both infantry and opposing artillery, the bombardment arm killed from a distance. Yet they were prized possessions from an impetuous charge of the bayonet, or they were jeered by their enemies when disabled by well-aimed salvos. It took a special courage to march forward and face the enemy. It took something else to be the magnet of all of his fury once unlimbered upon the field. For once today, they were not the targets of either artillery or infantry, and the respite was most welcome.

"Splendid work," came the voice of Captain Polk, causing Michael to startle.

"Yes, it was," Michael replied.

"Is that your man out there?"

"Yes, that's Mahoney."

Polk frowned at the thieves Mahoney was chasing. "Scalawags. I'd turn the battery on them if I could get away with it," Polk sneered. "Every army has its skulkers."

"They'll scatter and come back later once we're gone," Michael replied. Without taking his eyes from Mahoney, he asked, "Fight's still going, but I've not seen any movement from any of these batteries since the surrender. We in reserve?"

"Don't know. Half the corps artillery was gathered to this spot for reducing that nest o' Yanks an hour ago, but it don't sound like they's any less for guns up yonder," Polk replied.

"They's gettin' close to the river," Michael added. "You can hear them gunboats booming now and again."

"Yup, mighty close. Heard tell Johnston was wounded a bit ago leadin' an attack on an orchard down that-away." Polk pointed across the road. Michael couldn't see any orchards, only the long tree line formerly occupied by the enemy stretching across the road and on down toward the river.

"Johnston was jus' wounded?" Michael asked, surprised.

"Don't know that either. Just heard it is all. We thought we was doing capital work on this day only to hear of that. Dead or not, it don't spell anything but problems if it be true. Like changin' yer lead horses mid fording a stream. Can't be nuthin' but trouble for our enterprise on this field," Polk said.

"Good God," Michael exclaimed.

"Them batteries what took off a bit ago did so on they's own, but I'm inclined to let the men rest a spell more." Polk stopped and thought for a second or two. "Still, that would explain the lull we's havin' and, unfortunately, that of the enemy beyond them trees, as well. All that noise is comin' from Bragg's Corps on the right."

"If this be true, it does not bode well for the success of our arms today," Michael said with a frown. The lack of coordinated movement and energy exhibited upon that part of the field indicated that Johnston was no longer driving the attack. The intervening confusion and lack of coordination would soon tell upon their army.

"That will remain to be seen, Captain. If you're a prayin' man, you might start, for if we lose this opportunity to destroy this army of invaders, we'll have lost any prospect of retaining Tennessee for our cause of arms."

"Can't say as I am," Michael replied sheepishly, "but I would agree that some praying couldn't hurt."

"We've cut the enemy down by a good third at least with that crowd what surrendered awhile ago. If we can't capitalize on that and seal this victory now, perhaps the Almighty was against us all along," Polk surmised.

With Polk's candid summation ringing in his ears he said, "Who can say what the fates will bring? We still have many more hours of daylight to finish this thing."

"That's true," Polk said. "This will be a shame if, after all this effort and loss, we throw it away on the chance that Johnston is un-horsed in the midst of the climax. We're in possession of the enemy's lower camps and pushing him into the river, but for all of this to hinge upon one man and control of the effort, it will be as nothing if not finished before sundown."

Michael faced Polk directly. "Marshall, if called upon, the men will stand to their pieces as they did this morning under shot and shell." He was proud of his Texans, and he hid his own doubt to praise them.

"That is a given, Michael. Your Texans are always reliable in a fight and have yet to dishonor their flag. I fear if something is not got up soon, what they will be called upon to do may be in vain."

With that, Polk turned his steed to the side and spurred it away from Michael, leaving him with the words echoing in his mind.

Mahoney trotted back from his errand with a gaggle of miscreants cajoled at pistol point and divested of their spoils.

When Mahoney reached Michael, he asked, "Sir, if I may take my leave to deliver these rapscallions to the division provost?" The dozen or so fugitives looked downcast and ashamed. Michael doubted they felt any true repentance.

"Carry on, First Sergeant. Hurry back. We may be ordered forward soon," Michael replied.

"March, you band of fools," Mahoney ordered, and the men started forward past the line of guns.

The men being herded by Mahoney were a rough-looking lot and from as many different commands. Yet there were healthy-looking men, too, moving about to bring water to the enemy wounded and to give a hand in making for the aid stations. They were not looting but aiding an enemy. How could these two extremes co-exist in such an army? Though some were rogues and others were angels, most men were those who stood to their positions in obedience to the call of arms, not shirking the honor of falling in with their cohorts.

"Section Sergeants," Michael called out, "get your sections limbered up. I want a column to the right of the road ready to march."

The men had rested for half an hour by his recollection, and the inactivity would not last before some staff officer noted the current state of their unemployment. A battlefield is a site of horrors and depravity, as well as bravery and honor. The dead rent apart by the work of his own guns lay along the sunken road ahead and over the field of retreat. Heads, arms, legs, entrails, and cast-off equipment littered the way. Moments of supreme sacrifice for one's cause were evidenced by broken bodies of the enemy on the field and by the victors laying on the ground in exhausted revelry.

Michael hated passing over ground where he knew he'd caused the enemy to leave their dead men, horses, and broken gun carriages. To see up close the damage done with such clarity was often enough to make him sorry for the poor fellows left mangled in the aftermath. And yet, he'd had to do just that several times this day, often occupying the ground that had been held by the enemy batteries he'd shelled or the lines of infantry he'd bombarded. The infantry dead were the most pitiable. In close formation, a bounding shot would bowl through whole ranks and leave human remains scattered in every direction.

Once this morn, after being ordered forward, the battery unlimbered on a rise formerly occupied by an enemy battery and line of infantry. Michael directed the battery's fire upon this height for a time to silence the enemy guns whose own work was slowing General Polk's advance. From the distance, Michael observed the enemy working his guns and receiving fire in return without hesitation. Only upon arriving at that locale did they witness their own destructive efforts. A ruined caisson and broken, twelve-pound, smoothbore cannon shattered by a bounding shot now sat silent and abandoned. He had noted a deep furrow in front of the cannon where the solid shot struck the earth and ricocheted into the gun, knocking it from its axle and splintering its left wheel. The gun's commander had been eviscerated, a sergeant whose body now lay prostrate at its tail.

The men cheered when, from the distance of a hundred yards, the shot disabled the gun. Yet the enemy kept up their fire upon the line of Confederate infantry, not slowed by the tragedy. The loader, his station by the right wheel, had been struck full in the chest with the shot passing through his body cavity, severing arms and head from his lower torso. He left only that evidence to remind one that a human once stood on that very spot.

It was not good to fight upon soiled ground. It affected the men, just as it affected Michael, to bear witness to their own destructive deeds. Michael tried to pull the gun line farther from the slope of the hill, but the ground slid down the opposite side too steeply to work the guns, and they were forced to bear the indecency of fighting upon blood-consecrated ground. Michael had never been so glad to surrender the high ground, even in ignominy, when the converging fire of several enemy batteries caused the death of one of his own and wounded three others. It was not a hard decision to limber up and re-position, even if it meant a tactical retreat to preserve his strength.

The enemy's fire upon them was severe from the moment they unlimbered to the time they galloped off the slope. It was Gunner Jones from Michael's third section who carefully moved the enemy gun sergeant splayed behind the ruined gun and covered the body with his own blanket. There was little time for such activities in the midst of hot action with solid shot bounding around them. Jones casually did his errand, and then returned to his own gun as if he'd been ordered to treat the Yankee corpse with such kindness and humanity. Michael, though preoccupied with the action of the battery, could not help but watch Jones and feel a sense of pride in the honorable act. Even the lower ranks understood and recognized a noble enemy.

Would the enemy treat one of his own, or even him, in a similar manner? The thought of an honorable enemy seemed like a contradiction to him. An honorable death for the rough-cut Texans was in facing one's adversary, not found face down in attitude of retreat. The dead men of that opposing battery served their task well and fell victim to the skill of his own gunners by no fault of their own. Jones's singular act would more than likely be the gentlest treatment the man's corpse would find. After the field was rightly won by their arms, others would come behind and pitch the remains into a common grave with a marker reading "ten Yankees." If lucky, the burial parties would get to the job before the dead putrefied

During the lull, St. Peter's crew buried Private Nelson, who had been killed by shrapnel during their trying fifteen minutes on that deadly ridge. His body had lain upon the gun's caisson and was interred at the foot of his gun with the whole battery taking part in the quick but solemn ceremony. Michael stood back so the men could run the particulars out of reverence for the man's pards. His lieutenant said a few words on behalf of the section crew.

Soon, the battery was drawn up on marching column, per Michael's instructions, with the men sitting listlessly upon their stations. They drooped with heat and exhaustion. When and if the call came, they would be ready to move, but Michael hoped it would not come soon. The battery had given yeomen service since first light and deserved a break.

One by one, the batteries began to limber up and trot off. Michael knew their rest was about to end. Some of them headed toward the rear, and others across the field to the Corinth Road, and then along it toward the fighting. There were three sections of a battery of guns settling ready to march. By whose order would the call come? From Captain Polk? Or from some staff officer hell-bent on solving a problem and grabbing the first guns he saw?

Captain Polk trotted up, and the battery perked a bit at his approach, knowing that whatever the outcome, they would be moving with a wry eye upon what direction that entailed. After a few hurried words with Michael, and a nod of agreement, Polk galloped off in the direction of the fighting. Michael turned Charger and trotted down the rise to the battery drawn up by the roadside. He motioned Mahoney to come stand by him. It was always better to have one's first sergeant around to exercise control over the men when delivering bad news.

He faced the men and shouted, "To the right by sections, march!" For a moment, no one moved. Then, without complaint, the limbered sections filed down the Corinth Road.

*****

Aboard a paddle steamer anchored past Pittsburg Landing, the 24th Ohio's companies crowded the upper decks, staring at the pandemonium on the opposite shoreline. Philip and Mule leaned on the railing and watched in awe. Over the trees that lined the shore they could see a cloud of haze marking the place where the fighting was fiercest.

"We seen some sights in West Virginia in the rear of a battle, but nothin' like this," Mule said.

"If we didn't hear the firing, it wouldn't be a stretch to question what was left on the firing line. There's thousands of men milling about on the shore!" Philip answered.

Exclamations of surprise and curses were heaped upon the cowards. The boats anchored away from the shoreline to avoid the crazed and fear-stricken mob attempting to board the steamers arriving with Buell's forces. Life boats and anything that could float were being used to ferry the companies ashore twenty men at a time. Philip and the others waited impatiently for their turn.

Whenever one of the smaller boats pulled to the landing, the men aboard had to fight their way through panicked men attempting to climb aboard. Philip watched as several men launched themselves into the water to follow an empty life boat. One by one they disappeared below the surface. Those on the shore line waved and screamed at the boats but cared little for anyone drowning in the water. Philip's pards had no pity either; disdain for the mob ran high.

Philip, watching the spectacle, said to Mule, "They're mad with fear. What must be happening over there is unbelievable."

"I think I even see officers among that rabble," Mule said.

A loud report shook the water's surface as the gunboat *Tyler* let loose with its large 32-pound rifled gun. The gunboat shook and swayed slightly as the huge gun recoiled. At long intervals, this gun and a 20-pound Parrot rifle fired at the battle lines advancing toward the shoreline. Farther up the river, the gunboat *Lexington* fired into the Rebel rear areas, hoping to cause havoc.

Philip shook his head and asked, "What are we rushing into? What is there left to save but that cowardly lot at the landing?"

"They must be some need for us. The enemy ain't at the landing yet."

"But will there be anything to save once we all get ashore?" Philip asked. He watched the boats slowly make their way back.

They turned at the sound of a sudden splash and crashing in the trees behind the Lexington. A group of horsemen appeared on the opposite bank, and with them two cannon were sending solid shot at the transports. They didn't have the range yet but soon would.

"Jesus Christ!" someone shouted as the shower of water drenched all unlucky enough to be near the geyser. "Oh, sorry, Rev," the man stammered.

"My exact thoughts," Philip said in return. "Jesus Christ, protect your own."

The man looked at Philip and smiled.

The gunboat *Tyler* turned in the water to bring her port side cannon to play upon the Rebel guns. They were not too far away from the landing, only a few thousand yards by Philip's guess.

Mule made a whooshing sound. "Well, we either gonna die over there or get drowned here on this boat."

A puff of smoke marked the firing of another shot from the Rebel guns that crashed into the trees behind them. Philip watched the gunners on the *Tyler* prepare a response from their cannon. The sailors worked mechanically, and every movement was practiced and precise. Soon, the *Tyler* was exchanging shot for shot with the cannon on the shore line, and the Rebel gunners turned their attention to the *Tyler* with little effect. The *Tyler's* crew peppered the shore with fire until the Rebel guns limbered up and beat a hasty retreat, to wild cheers from the 24th Ohio.

A sudden increase in noise drew their attention back to the shore line at what all guessed was the active line of defense. Yells and musketry sounds mingled and reminded all that desperate work was being done a short distance away.

Chapter Ten

Back across the river, past throngs of uniformed men drained of courage and cowering beneath the rising river bank, Robert Mitchell sat with his pards of the 25th Missouri Volunteers. With their fight behind them and their regiment scattered to the winds, they whiled away the time in the shade. There was a comfort here—to not be the lone coward but be amid an army of cowards.

Robert knew it wasn't mere cowardice that kept these men and him there. It was the lack of the power of one's pards to keep a man in line. One fought with one's family at his side; if that family were beaten or scattered, the fortitude to fight was gone, as well.

"Hube," Robert said to Huebner, *"du bist nicht ein Fahnenflüchtiger. Das Regiment würde beendet.* None of us deserted. The regiment was destroyed."

Huebner had quieted somewhat but still carried a look of disgrace upon his face. Robert tried to get through to him that he was not the disgrace he felt himself to be. He knew that this boy, barely a man, should not have volunteered. Yet despite his mental deficiencies, he had managed to survive this far.

"*Ja,*" replied Huebner.

Gustavson poked Huebner in the ribs and said to him, "We all *kaput. Das Kämpfen* get closer, *ja?*"

The racket crept closer, and the stream of fugitives increased from a trickle to a flood. Wounded men, some helped by three or four others, were brought to the landing. Regiments from the line came to replenish ammunition, some resting near the sea of fugitives to heap scorn upon them. Occasionally, an officer or two, looking to fill out their regiments, would gather what skulkers with weapons were within reach, but even threats and blows with the flat of their sabers did little good, and the men scattered at first opportunity.

Robert's group ignored the attempts and the scorn, but he knew it wasn't right to sit there while the battle went poorly for their banner. The first transports arrived off of the landing about mid-afternoon, and a stir swept the cowards closest to the water. The first reinforcements began to gather inland from the overcrowded landing area. Others trickled in from smaller boats in a clearing to the left of the landing. Roberts's group had chosen shade away from the mass but still near enough to have its protection. The trickle marched past them in small squad formations lead by corporals and sergeants. To a man, they were wide eyed and rattled, and they huddled close together.

Calls of "You'll be whipped sure" and "the Devil's down the way awaitin' fer ya' " followed these newcomers. Several fist fights broke out as reinforcements clawed their way to their compatriots forming just beyond the cowards. Robert watched them closely, for aside from the milling masses and the sounds of impending battle drawing nigh, the newcomers were the freshest game to be gawked at.

Gustavson motioned to the passing group of newcomers. "Lambs to the slaughter, *ja?*"

"They doing th' right thing," Huebner said.

"Ach, vas is right? To be alive *und* breathing or *märz zur Schlacht und zum Würfel?"* Gustavson replied. "I choose *der* breathing *und* alive part."

Huebner gave him a sharp look and said, "Rebels still out there. Reason we volunteered still out there. What difference?"

Robert looked at Huebner in surprise. This lad of barely twenty years was speaking with authority and passion about something. It was odd to see this in him, the boy whom he allowed to constantly follow him around because he felt some small responsibility.

Gustavson snorted. "Difference be that *ve* done seen *der* elephant and give our share." The men in hearing ranged nodded their agreement.

"Gus is right," Robert interrupted. "The regiment did its share this morning and got broke for it. For all we know, we's the only ones left either alive or captured. It's time for others to give their share."

Before someone could counter that statement, Robert added, "Those still fighting are fighting under control of their officers and men they respect and know. What are we but some twenty-odd survivors of the Hell we witnessed this morning? From the patrol to the camp, we stood and died and were overrun. What more can a man do?"

The question was barely off his lips when it struck Robert that there was more to be given and that Huebner was driving for that very thing as well.

"Because *der* Christ no gives up in his cause, *und* we no give up on our cause," Huebner protested. *"Vater marschierte mit der* Regent of Saxony against *der* Holy Roman Emperor *und* did it for same cause of Christ. *Vater* expect same out of me. *Der Krieg* of rebellion no different."

Robert saw the fire in Huebner's eyes and wondered what lion had been awoken in him. Robert didn't know how he felt about it himself. He certainly wasn't there for any principles of religion. Growing up Lutheran himself, he knew what Huebner was talking about. In the old country, where the German principalities still warred with one another over alliances, both religious and political, men still marched against each other in small wars of conquest. He did his duty and served it well before the regiment broke under the pressure of the enemy.

"No fight for a Pope or some Lutheran Bishop!" Gustavson told Huebner. "You serve for yourself. *Ve* volunteered to put down *der* rebellion, not to die for some lost cause."

"*Nein, kämpfe Ich für* cause, for *der* country's call like our *Vaters marschiert mit* kings against each other. *Vater* served *und märz* as we now *märz mit der* Federal government." Huebner stared at each man and fidgeted with the blades of grass between his legs.

Robert put his hand on Huebner's shoulder and looked in his eyes. With a quiet voice, he said, "Hube, Gus is right. There's a line between foolhardiness and devotion to duty. We stood the test this morning and suffered for it. Hilde is gone for that duty. You saw him fall. I don't see what else can be done that hasn't been paid for."

"More, we need to do more. *Ich* need do more than just sit," Huebner said. "We could join back into *die Schlacht*, get back into the fight."

"Go back? *Sie krank im Kopf?* Your head on right? We were there and survived. What more can a *Soldat* ask for?" Gustavson protested.

"What is it that would satisfy your desires, Hube?" Robert asked him, still holding the boy by the shoulders. "How long we been comrades in battle? We've been comrades in battle since we mustered in St. Louis and I've never known you to speak out on anything. Why now?"

Huebner fidgeted with a stick and looked from man to man. Robert wondered what was going on in that mind, which always seemed to be muddled and unable to cope with the simplest of duties, like falling in for morning roll call. *Hube's just a simpleton,* he thought, someone touched by a different spirit needing to be looked after with a gentle but cautious hand.

"Because, like St. Paul, Christ's blood compels me. Because *Ich* feel *shamt* that I not give my all for the cause for which *Ich* volunteered. Because bring not shame *und* disgrace to *mein Vater. Meine Bruder, Karl, marz mit der* 2nd Missouri *und* died at Wilson's Creek. I am only one left to *meine Mutter und Vater, und Ich bin kein Fahnenflüchtiger. Ich bin ein Soldat.* I am soldier *mit* Christ *und* cause and will not be captured or desert." With that, Huebner, visibly nervous, stood and gathered his traps, donning each item without looking at the men's surprised expressions.

Robert was dumbstruck. Cause and Christ? The words were not foreign to any of them, but the voice and the orator were. In spite of the serious turn of their conversation, Robert nearly laughed as Huebner got tangled in his traps. He stood and took Huebner's canteen from around the boy's neck.

"Here, lemme help you, Hube." He removed Huebner's haversack. The boy *cum* patriot and zealous "*Soldat*" for Christ had forgotten to don his sack coat first before adding his leathers.

Huebner smiled at Robert and something of the innocent Jonah reappeared. Robert handed him his sack coat and traps one by one. The awkward child and boy was still there, and Robert was relieved.

Once his traps were straight, Huebner picked up his musket and stood in front of the group.

"*Ich* join those men there. I not sit moment longer knowing I could add musket to the defense," Huebner told them. Without further demonstration, he turned on his heels and made his way to the regiment gathering in the distance.

Robert watched Huebner go, undecided what he should do but feeling the need not to let Huebner go the distance alone. Without a word, and to his own surprise, he gathered his traps and followed Huebner's trail. It didn't make sense, but he couldn't leave his young charge to do it alone.

"Hube, wait!" Robert shouted while holding the various straps and his weapon in both hands.

Huebner stopped and looked back. When he saw what Robert was doing, he smiled broadly. "Robert! You come with me?"

"I can't let anything happen to our company Jonah. Where else would we find one?" Robert made an unconvincing titter that grated on his own ears.

Huebner closed the distance to Robert in two strides and engulfed him in a bear hug.

"Hey, lemme get these things on first," Robert said with a grunt in Huebner's embrace.

"Robert, you not going to let me go alone!" Huebner beamed.

"No, pard, I couldn't let you go alone. Now, help me get these things on," Robert said. He tried to move his arms from Hube's hug, which was holding them firmly to his sides.

Huebner released Robert, grabbed the traps from Robert's hands, and let his own musket clatter to the ground.

Robert gave Huebner a slight push backward. "Hube, letting go of me was help enough," Robert said and laid his equipment upon the ground.

"Need some help?" a voice behind Robert asked.

Robert turned to find Gustavson standing behind him. Other men of their company began to trickle into line until the whole crowd was standing around Robert and Huebner. Startled by their sudden appearance, Huebner danced with delight.

"You come, too?" Huebner said.

"Not let our pards go off alone," Gustavson said with the agreement of the rest.

Robert hung his last trap over his shoulder and looked about him. "Well," he said, "we'd better go find some officer to offer our services to." The men around him gave a hearty, though nervous, cheer.

Despite the teeming humanity all about, it was easy to be ignored, especially if someone looked like a cowardly skulker in the sea of skulkers. But they all still had their essentials for fighting. As they meandered up to the gathering regiment, they were eyed closely by those lounging by their stacks of arms. The men lying on the ground were fresh and much animated in conversation, looking quite different than the small group standing now in front of them.

Robert found the company first sergeant and asked him where his commander was. The sergeant, eyeing him closely, pointed to a group of officers gathered in the distance with an unconcerned nod of his head and turned his back on the group. There was distrust in his eyes.

"We've got to go over there," Robert said to his pards.

The men of this regiment didn't look any different from Robert's save for their choice of headgear. They wore army hats, with several already slouching well from service. They stood out with their forage caps, and that alone was enough to draw more attention to them. A captain stopped their progress with a wave of his hand.

"What business do you have?" he asked. The man was sweating profusely in the heat, but his uniform was clean. Following the familiar officers' prerogative of adding flair to their uniforms, his high-cut shell jacket and rows of brass buttons were decorated with a red sash and saber. As in most western commands, the dainty officer's dress often found in the eastern armies was dispensed with as immaterial. Though plain in dress, the officer stood out in his attire.

Robert stood straight and formal and looked the captain in the eye. "Sir, my pards and I wish to offer our services. Our regiment met the enemy in force this morning out on a reconnaissance and fought them up to our encampment where the rest of the 25th Missouri Volunteers is either now dead on the field or captured. We who are left wish to give our aid."

The captain inspected each man briefly before turning around and rejoining the conference behind him. Robert looked at the others with him and shrugged, as if to say, "Perhaps our services are not wanted." They stood and waited.

The captain returned after a few minutes of conversation and addressed Robert.

"You men all have weapons?" he asked and received affirmative nods in response. "Go fall in with the leftmost company, that man there." The captain nodded toward a bearded fellow, whose only symbol of command was the red sash and sword he wore over a plain sack coat. Robert turned back to the captain, who continued, "He's the captain of Company K. Go on over there to his company and rest. We'll be moving as soon as the other companies form up."

"You men!" a voice from the crowd of officers rang out. "What command you with?"

"25th Missouri Volunteers, Union, Sir," Robert shouted back.

"You been in many engagements?" the officer inquired and stepped forward.

"Yes, some of us. Brigaded with Colonel Peabody of Prentiss's division," Robert answered.

The captain spoke up. "This is Colonel Ammen, 10th Brigade, Nelson's division."

"Well," Colonel Ammen said, "these men behind you, the 36th Indiana and my old command, have yet to see the elephant but have seen hard marching through swamps and mud to get here. They are good men. Your muskets will steady the line." Robert glanced quickly at Huebner, then at Gustavson. Ammen continued, "I worry their enthusiasm will melt at the first fire, and this is a desperate time. You men are a godsend. God speed."

Colonel Ammen turned his back to them and returned to the group he had been conversing with, a group, Robert noted, that also contained several generals.

Robert turned to his pards. After that "bucking up" speech from the colonel, he could not hide his worry about what they were getting into. It was enough to attach themselves to a foreign command, but another thing to do so with a green regiment.

The sudden report of several cannon in simultaneous discharge rent the air, causing everyone to start despite the near constant rattle of musketry that became something easily ignored after a time. The companies of the 36th rose to their feet and became animated by the noisy exchange. Robert and the others made their way to the far left company and took station at the end of the line. They exchanged nervous *hullos* with the Indiana men closest to them, and the company first sergeant came up to them, a stern and worried look upon his face.

"What you men doing here?"

"Your captain told us to form up *vis* your *Männer*," Gustavson replied and eyed the man coldly.

"He did, did he? For what purpose?" the first sergeant replied.

"Because *der Männer* 36th *isht* green, *und der Männer* 25th Missouri not. *Ve* show *der* first sergeant *der* elephant *und* hold his hand."

A crowd appeared around the first sergeant. Robert wished he could shut Gustavson up, but the exchange had already gone too far.

"We came to offer our services," Robert quickly interrupted. "Our regiment was broken this morning at the battle's start, and we're what's left, First Sergeant. Your captain directed us over here to fall in with your company."

There was something in the look of a seasoned soldier that was apparent, even in Huebner, that distinguished him from a green one—something in the way he carried himself and how his uniforms fit said he had seen the elephant before. Although the Indiana men looked the worse for wear after their march, they still had the look of unseasoned troops.

The first sergeant grunted and asked, "That so?"

"We've been in two different engagements now, and I think we can help bolster your company, First Sergeant," Robert added.

"So, you part of them skulkers behind us then? Company K don't need yer he'p. I'm gonna keep my eye on you all the same. You ran once, you'll run again."

"*Ach, Dunkopf!*" shouted Gustavson. His face was fiery red, his fists clenched. "*Das* sergeant first man to run *hatte er gewesen mit* -- had he been with -- the 25th this *Morgen; der* Rebels thick as *der* lice in *meine* sack coat. Charged us *fünfmal*, five times up *der* hill *und* no stop until 25th broken. Many good *Männer* go down. *Das Sargent* should be grateful we *Männer seid mit seiner Kompanie.*"

Huebner tugged on Robert's sleeve and asked quietly, "They dun' want us?"

"Seems so, *Junge*," Gustavson replied, and he spat on the ground.

Robert gave the first sergeant a hard stare. In a quiet tone he asked, "Are you going to turn down twenty more muskets willing to fight for the honor of the 36th Indiana?"

"No, I'm not. I have no choice about that, it seems. At least as long as those muskets stay in line and mind my orders."

Captain Armstrong jogged up to the company, barking orders as he came.

"First Sergeant, re-line the company and get these other men integrated quick. We march to the sound of the guns!"

With the newcomers, the company had to be re-aligned, and, by necessity, pards would be split up. The first sergeant ordered the company to line up by height, then to count by twos. One became accustomed to the man to the right and the left and those behind when formed in a line of battle or when marching. These also became one's Comrades in Arms when formed for skirmish duty, and, with that familiarity, any sudden change was unsettling to even the most seasoned of troops.

A chorus of groans and grumbles followed, making it uncomfortable for all involved. Huebner, Gustavson, and the late Hildebrande had formed Roberts' Comrades in Arms in the old regiment, but even they would be separated from Robert. Gustavson was a few men down from Robert in the first row, but Huebner's position in the new rank was farther separated. Robert saw the disappointment in Huebner's eyes and tried to look aloof in his new surroundings.

The men of the company eyed each of the newcomers suspiciously. Yet there was a hint of expectation and watchfulness from the others toward him, something of the older and more experienced brother amid his younger siblings or an older student in the presence of under-classmen. They were the strangers, but they were strangers who had seen the elephant, and that alone made them enviable to the newcomers to battle.

A group of mounted officers galloped up to the officer conference in front of the regiment, and Robert recognized General Grant among them.

The man to Robert's right commented, "Looks like we 'bout to move."

"Gen'l Grant up there," Robert added.

"That's Grant?" the man to Robert's left asked.

"So I'm told. Only seen him from afar mostly," Robert said.

Grant was dressed in a plain, mud-spattered frock coat and a plain felt slouch hat. He wore no decoration save for the officer's bars declaring his rank of major general. He was followed by two aides on horseback and was gesturing toward the loudest of the fighting in the distance. Robert needed little imagination to figure out they were about to double quick into that maelstrom.

Faced to the right and formed into marching column, the 36th marched off the field and onto the Shiloh Road. They moved in the general direction that Robert and his pards had raced away from earlier in the day. Leaving behind the landing, they reentered the rear area of the fighting. They passed scores of wounded men making their way toward the safety the regiment just left. Desperate work was ahead.

The road sloped downward. The high ground bristled with cannon, as batteries from the morning's fight collected themselves for a desperate last stand. Though Robert had heard the fighting all day, it always seemed far enough away to be out of mind. Now, as they reentered this zone of combat, the reminders of the morning came back, along with the fear that accompanied those sights and sounds. Broken men and equipment lay all about the road, and rivulets of fresh blood flowed upon the dirt.

A courier galloped up from the direction of the firing. He motioned toward the fighting, and another regiment marched out of the trees bearing its wounded. The regiment's colonel ran to the front of the column, waving his sword.

"Halt!" the colonel commanded.

The company's first sergeant turned to growl at the men. "Company K, this is it. Steady yourselves. I'm watchin' you Missouri men, fer the first one ta run will get a minié ball in the back from me." A few of the men tittered nervously.

"And one from me, Sergeant," Gustavson snapped in return, "when you show *der* white feather *und* run."

"Use the fear, boys," Robert called out. Thrust into the presence of green soldiers, he could not help but play the experienced veteran, though his experiences palled in comparison to some others in his own regiment. "Use the fear to make you stand instead of run. Load times nine like Hell itself is after you."

"Quiet in the ranks!" the first sergeant shouted.

The colonel glanced over the men with narrow eyes before giving the order. "Forward, march!"

The 36th Indiana marched off of the road and into a field. The late afternoon sun was washing the trees with a yellowish fire. The low-hanging smoke wafted in ribbons from of the discharge of thousands of muskets and cannon. There was mean work being done ahead of them.

The regiment shifted from marching columns to columns of companies, and each company moved from marching four abreast to company lines of battle in two ranks. They would fight and die in this formation. The unfamiliar touch of new comrades reminded Robert of the morning's combat and losses, a lonely feeling he pushed from his mind.

Again the report of guns in succession rocked the ground. These were no ordinary guns but heavy-caliber cannon. The men stirred with excitement. Most were eager to get on with it, and the company front bowed and ebbed as the nervousness animated the marching rhythm too fast or too slow, eliciting shouts and curses to guide right. They heard the Rebel yell.

"Dat's jus' them Secesh wailin'. You'll be hearin' more of that soon enough, *Mann*," Gustavson told the soldier to his right.

"We've only ever heard about it," the man next to Robert said.

The first sergeant half turned to bellow at the men, "Quiet in the ranks!"

"They only do that when they gets their blood up, which is all the time," Robert said and cracked a wan smile.

"By the right of companies, into line at the double quick," yelled the regimental adjutant. "March!"

A scramble ensued as the column of companies split into a regimental line of battle. Company K, being at the tail of the column, had to swing in an arch to reach its place on the left of the regimental battle line, and the men were winded by the time they reached it. Captain Armstrong reformed the company line in accordance with the rest of the regiment. The noise of battle was loud and continuous. Looking through the trees ahead, they could see crews frantically working a line of cannon. It was here that they were being formed to support. The energy in the air and the movement of the men belied the dread they felt. Each loud discharge made the green soldiers of the 36th Indiana jump, and the men around Robert looked to one another for any clue as to how to react. Robert could not help but notice the many eyes that were upon him.

"Forward, march!" the colonel ordered, and the regiment surged into the trees.

Leaves and twigs fell on them, and the zipping of flying lead caused a jittery reaction from the green Indiana men. Though his own heart raced and his stomach churned, Robert and his other pards remained calm. He knew the queer feeling of being under fire for the first time. He also knew that fear caught on like wild fire once exhibited by one person. Each man felt the fear but tried to appear courageous before his pards. The first person to crack and run made it all the easier for the rest to do the same.

The 36th cleared the trees and entered an open field to the right of the gun line. They discovered they were the only regiment in line to support the guns. A line of dead and broken men lay before them. Several hundred men in uniform, not including the crews of the guns, lurked in the trees. None but the 36th stood between the enemy gathering in the distance and the only embarkation point for several miles at the landing.

The regiment marched obliquely to position itself between the gunners and the enemy forming to their front. Several hundred yards of open field separated the foes. The regiment was large, larger than any active campaign unit on the field and, but for the single color displayed in the middle by the color company, could have been mistaken for a brigade of regiments. To Robert's estimate, Company K held seventy men, and the other companies in line seemed to have full compliments of NCOs and officers. They would need their muskets in this supreme moment of testing.

The regiment halted, and Captain Armstrong ran down the front, evening out the line in accordance with the company to the left, and then took his station at the left of the company front. In their excitement to move out from the assembly point, the regiment had not loaded weapons. Robert wondered if anyone was going to realize this in time, as the movement in the distance looked like another push up to the guns. He felt the nakedness that comes from not having another unit to anchor their right flank; there was nothing to stop a Rebel rush from rolling up the whole regiment into flight.

The gun line behind the regiment kept up its rapid fire, causing many in the rear to glance nervously over their shoulders. Were the guns elevated enough to clear their heads? Why were they taking the chance and firing over them?

Robert knew what they were thinking and called back, "They're shelling the wood line over our heads. They know what they're doing."

"Load and come to the ready!" Captain Armstrong shouted, having finally realized the error of putting the 36th in harm's way unloaded. Eight hundred ramrods clanked against cold steel to push charges home, followed by stiff attention as each man brought his musket to his side, clasping the trigger guard between thumb and forefinger and allowing the barrel to rest upon the shoulder. Soon the elephant of battle would make its terrible appearance upon the field.

"You *Männer* want to see *das* elephant? *Das* elephant wants to see you, too," Gustavson shouted.

Robert gave Gustavson a fast glace and then turned to the men around him. "Just load and fire. Ignore the zip of the minié balls past your ears. Just load and fire." He paused and then added, "Load quickly."

The distant battle line of the enemy lurched forward, unevenly interspersed with seven stands of colors. The line was clearly wider than the 36th's. If not checked, the enemy would pour flank fire into the exposed right and left of the regiment. Robert's feeling of nakedness intensified.

With flapping red and white banners and a chorus of Rebel yells, the enemy legion stepped toward the piteous few that stood for Grant's last bastion of defense. The Rebels would certainly take advantage of the 36th's unsupported stance in the field, bereft of supporting regiments on its right and left and with the prized guns at its back.

"K Company, right backward half wheel, march!" Captain Armstrong commanded. The company pivoted on the last man of Company K that connected it with Company B, like a door upon a hinge, in a maneuver called "refusing the line."

The Rebel line halted a scant few rods from the 36th Indiana and dressed its lines in a formality that sent chills down Robert's back. The crowd of butternut and gray did not appear any less tired than when they had assailed the 25th Missouri's camp earlier in the morning.

"Ready! Aim!" came the staccato call of the company commanders as the regiment readied itself to deliver a wall of lead into the enemy and receive same. Eight hundred hammers clicked from half cock to full, and eight hundred muskets leveled upon the enemy. The gentlemanly silence preceding unrestrained violence descended upon the field.

The Rebel line stood as if in mirror image to them, both sides with leveled rifles awaiting the command to fire. Holding his rifle level, Robert felt a quivering in his arms and the fatigue from the morning's exertions. The wait seemed to be hours.

"Fire!"

Robert's regiment loosed a ragged volley on the enemy, who immediately replied in turn. Men dropped. A contest of wills ensued with the opposing sides loading, firing, and waiting for the other to flinch. The Rebels on the flank advanced a few paces then halted, closing the distance. Another volley, and a few more rifles clattered to earth. The ground at Robert's feet was littered with the paper remnants of cartridges he fed into his barrel. A few of the cannon turned to meet the challenge posed by the Rebels. They arched solid shot over the heads of the company, but each shot went long, falling harmlessly behind the Rebel line. Robert felt the panic growing in the men around him. They fumbled with their weapons with panic-stricken fingers and eyed each other in despair.

"Load and fire, load and fire!" Robert yelled.

The man to his left crumpled to the ground, holding his bowels and screaming. Robert looked quickly for his other pards and spied Huebner loading but standing by himself, the men having been hit or gone to the rear with no one covering down to fill the holes.

"Hube, cover down! Hube!" Robert called out.

Alerted to Huebner's plight by Robert's shout, Gustavson grabbed Huebner by the shoulder and dragged him down to the next man in line. Huebner gave him a toothy grin in response.

In spite of their thinning ranks, the enemy advanced again upon them, defying Company K's return fire and the oblique fire from Company B that cut across Company K's front. The Rebels sensed victory within grasp. Robert wondered if they would attempt to rush his line.

More men were going down with each passing moment, and those left standing were bleeding from flesh wounds. Few men stood unscratched. Minié balls whizzed and zipped like hornets. Many a hat or piece of equipment was clipped off.

The other enemy regiments fronting the 36th were holding steady and delivering steady blows as if planted solidly in the ground. In the face of the advancing enemy, the Indiana men began to shrink backward. No order to move was given save for the natural instinct to avoid something terrible. Robert realized he was standing alone, the men to either side having moved backward a few feet. In a moment, though, Gustavson, Huebner, and the other men of the 25th Missouri were around him, pouring their fire into the advancing enemy. The haze of gun powder was so thick they could barely make out individual faces.

"Get back into line! Form on me, on me!" yelled Captain Armstrong as he rushed up to the front of the line waving his sword. The enemy halted once more. Their chance had come to roll up the 36th from the flank. The first sergeant struggled to move the panicky men of Company K back into their spots.

"*Ve kaput!*" Gustavson shouted in Robert's ear over Captain Armstrong's bellows to "Make your stand!"

The holes were plugged in time for another volley to pour into the company from the enemy. Gustavson pitched forward, as if diving to the ground, and shrieks of surprise emanated from those struck. The Rebels let out another cry of their own and surged forward with bayonets charged.

Some Indiana men either stood with their Missouri comrades or scampered off. Those who remained either were too stupid with fear or were dead.

The Rebel line crashed into Company K—it was every man for himself. The eyes of the attackers, now clearly seen, met with those of the defenders, and in the close quarters, they fought with rifle butts, bayonets, and fists.

Robert hadn't the time to see if Gustavson was injured or dead, or time to look upon any of his pards. His attention was upon fending off the large Rebel thrusting his bayonet at him. The man was clothed in a mish-mash of colors: gray pants, butternut coat, brown derby style hat, and mud. A fierce fire burned in his eyes, along with fear, both emotions Robert knew his own eyes revealed. The man screamed obscenities at him as the two tried to relieve the other of life. Without warning, the Rebel charge melted away as the enemy retreated to a safer distance.

Those few moments of contact had been enough to leave many wounded. Captain Armstrong lay upon the ground, shot in the shoulder. A few Confederates surrendered and were lead to the rear, as well as a few Indiana and Missouri men, hauled off with the retreating Rebels. The number of Robert's pards was cut down to fifteen, not including two others no longer moving. The Rebels as a whole withdrew, leaving the 36th Indiana scarred but not licked.

Another regiment appeared and moved down to support their right flank, and a ragged cheer rose from the 36th. With the fight now ended, the men relaxed and tried to reform their scattered ranks. The edginess of the company was settled by the first sergeant taking the men through the manual of arms several times. The piles of humanity were left where they lay, as were a scattering of wounded enemy. The 36th had met the elephant and was still standing in its wake.

The regiment made a collective sigh of relief. The Indiana men seemed to stand a little taller, carrying themselves like veterans, and they exchanged sheepish grins. They were quietly and simply elated to be alive. Their numbers swelled as those who had left the field in fear or to help a wounded comrade rejoined their companies. Everyone looked nicked in some fashion, and those who lay upon the ground behind them managed to crawl away or stand, leaving only Gustavson's body where it fell. The other four of Robert's pards regained their feet and rejoined the ranks, completing their group once again.

Just out of artillery range, the enemy reformed lines to make another go of it. But for all of the madness, danger, and the sudden rush of the enemy upon them, Gustavson died alone. The presence of the enemy in their front prohibited them from doing anything for the body, despite their wish to take care of his remains.

The Rebels let out another yell and advanced back across the field already dotted with their dead, drawing the attention of all back to the business at hand. As the sun's last rays lit the scene on the day's grotesque play, the actors went about the business of destruction.

Chapter Eleven

"By company into line," Colonel Jones shouted hoarsely, "double quick, march!"

"It looks bad, real bad," Johnny said with a huff, and they scrambled out of column formation to form company front.

Sergeant Harper nodded to Philip. "You'll meet yer God now, Rev!"

"And you'll meet your god," Philip replied, "pitch fork, fire, and all!" He gasped for air through the smoke hovering on the field.

Dusk was settling upon the fields, but the battle did not abate. The trip across the river and through the throngs of men crowding the bank had been enough trial without having to face the enemy. A breathless courier directed the 24th Ohio away from the landing and off to the right toward a wood where they were informed the enemy was thick as fleas. Fires burned in the pale of evening. The smell of gunpowder and the smoke created a frightening pallor.

Mule stared wide eyed. "They gonna march us into that? If the enemy's in there, we ain't gonna see 'em."

The wood line was dark and appeared to be solid, perhaps hiding the enemy they sought.

Colonel Jones shouted again. "Forward, march!"

"That answer your question?" Sammy said with a bitter laugh.

"Well, if we're lucky, we'll have missed most of this, though I suspect we'll be in the thick of it on the morrow," Philip said. The men around him looked toward the woods blankly.

A few forlorn, supine forms lay in the field spread out before the wood line. Other than the noise of battle to the left, there was little else to foretell of any danger. The regiment entered the wood and into a claustrophobic, eerie silence. They could hear many staccato footfalls crashing through dead twigs and leaves, but they saw nothing. It was almost pitch black, and but for a pale blue hue that shone through the wood's canopy, no other light existed. The men made enough noise of their own that they soon gave up listening for the enemy.

"You get the feeling we could just be walkin' into the muzzles of an enemy line and wouldn't know it till they fired?" Mule asked Philip.

Curses rang out as men tripped in the undergrowth and were in turn cursed by company officers for clumsiness. Trying to keep in formation was impossible. Men found themselves far behind or ahead of their fellows, despite company officers screaming themselves hoarse.

If not for the deadly seriousness of the task, the scene might have been comical. Philip's company was splintered into several groups who groped around in the near darkness looking for the others. The full strength of the company line was hidden. The men wished only to be out of the evil place.

"Pearson!" shouted Mule.

"Push on, cover to the right, keep your intervals!"

"I can't see a blasted thing. Why're we here?"

"Cursed stump. Ow!"

"Over here!"

The voice of an invisible officer called out, "Quiet in the ranks!"

Mule took Philip by the arm and whispered, "I think the rest of the company is over this way."

"Which way? I can't see them."

"To the left."

Sammy caught up with Mule and Philip and asked, "Whose bad idea was this?"

The scramble continued for interminable minutes as the scattered elements and squads pushed on. Philip and his fellows saw a break in the gloom to the right and angled toward it. Eventually exiting the wood, they found themselves in another field, whose crop of death begged for a shroud such as they just left. As men stumbled into the field, the regiment gathered its lost sheep. They found no enemy standing, only his dead and dying. Forms were discernible in the clouded evening, and equipment was strewn about.

There was much covering down and pushing as newcomers regained their places. Finally out of the Hell of the wood, everyone strained to see into the darkness for the next hellish encounter.

"Fall in at attention," barked Sergeant Harper from behind the formation.

The push to get onto the field in the long march, then the excitement as they came ashore, made the end anti-climactic. Though no man yearned for the thunder of the guns, the hurried formation and chaotic tramp through the darkness only to arrive at this battle-scarred field was a disappointment.

"Why we always rushed to some place just ta stand around?" Sammy asked in a quiet voice.

"Just lucky, I guess," Philip replied.

"At ease," Colonel Jones commanded.

The men relaxed and could move about more freely as long as they kept their right foot in place so that they wouldn't break the formation. Many men leaned upon their muskets, and a hundred hushed conversations began.

Mule crouched down in his position and looked up at his pards. "I take it we here for a while."

"Seems that way," Johnny answered.

"Rebs musta' retired. The skirmishers is all quiet up front," Sammy said and shifted uneasily.

"What you think, Rev? God's work tomorrow?" Johnny asked.

"Wouldn't hardly call it God's work. I suppose if God should bless this Union, though, bringing the rebellion to an end would be His work. One might suppose its execution be more devilish than holy."

For several minutes, they were quiet, each lost in his own thoughts, and for some, in his own doubts.

Mule finally broke the reverie. "The enemy who opposes us might be thinking the same thing about now, flushed with today's successes and all." He looked sideways at Philip, and Philip returned his glance.

"I know of some good Methodist preachers down south who would say they's rebellion has God's blessin'."

Sammy leaned over his musket and asked, "Them Rebs we took in Nashville said some strange things about this war, didn't they?"

"They seemed to not understand what they was fighting for, like the question of slavery was some foreign concept to them," Johnny replied.

"The secession was about their rights to leave the Union, not about slavery," Philip explained.

"Maybe so," Johnny said with emphasis, "but slavery was behind it."

"They didn't think they were fightin' fer their darkies," Philip answered him. "It don't have anything to do with the darkies. It has all to do with the Union."

"It's what we volunteered for, preservin' the Union, that is," Sammy said, a little louder than expected.

Johnny straightened abruptly, hands on hips. "And put an end to slavery. You have to see that slavery will end if we are victorious."

Though his sympathies lay with the righteousness of the spiritual cause they all had answered, Philip could not but wonder about his pard's comments and insistence on the slavery issue. It had always been an issue for as long as he could remember in his life. His spiritual duty as a minister of God's grace and John Wesley's tradition of Methodism taught him to oppose slavery as a mockery of what God intended for His creation. Slavery was something that happened out of reach and always down south. Now the war brought them deeper south than he had ever cared to go. The ragged appearance of the Negroes he had seen through Kentucky and Tennessee did not increase his compassion toward their plight or passion against slavery.

But Johnny's parents, and even he himself, adhered to abolitionist beliefs that ran deep in the New England states. Johnny saw the conflict differently than others. His family had immigrated to Ohio's open land from hardy New

England stock and brought with them New England attitudes about life and social justice, though many of his neighbors were of southern stock. Even so, few refused to volunteer for cause and country when war came.

In this dark night, under the gathering clouds, the rapt debate over cause and reason flourished from these ordinary soldiers with no stake but their lives.

Sammy turned to face Johnny. "You seen 'em. You seen them Secesh banners gather for the attack and the way they fight. Tell me they doin' it ta keep the darkies in chains." More than a few men turned to face him. "That lot what charged us at Nashville and into our volleys weren't doin' it fer darkies. They did it fer the right to sever the Union because of they's darkies."

"Sure," Johnny replied, "for their right to keep 'em."

Sammy's face reddened, and his hands clenched. "It ain't the same at all. Not a man here would go and kill or be killed fer that race of slaves. I'm no lover of them slavers, but I'm not of the mind ta go and get myself rent apart by no grape and canister just to loose upon our land a greater evil. Them people will have ta be educated and eased into polite society afore they be any good."

"You ain't concerned none about them slaves?" Johnny asked. "They gotta be freed!"

"I ain't saying that at all," Sammy snapped back. "I jus' don't see makin' the entire war out of them slaves. You've seen them poor wretches along our march. I ain't arguin' that they shouldn't be free or shoulda not been slaves ta begin with. But them rabid abolitionists would have us doin' more if they had they's way."

"It be the slaves what brought us to this," Johnny argued, his voice rising. "and led to rebellion fer the right to keep 'em. That can't be covered over. Round about, we's fighting for their freedom and the reunification of the Union." The two men stared at each other, both ready to fight.

Seeing the potential confrontation, Philip interrupted the two men. "Both a' you, simmer down. Whatever it is, we can agree that it is a great evil, this war. The times of greatest strife in the lives of God's chosen race were in times of disobedience and war, and would not be much of a stretch to imagine this war bein' punishment fer the evil of slavery upon this otherwise blessed land."

"You preachin' again, Rev?" The voice of Sergeant Harper disturbed their discussion.

Philip glared at the sergeant. "Yes, was just getting to the part about who will inherit the kingdom of Heaven. Neither liars, murderers, fornicators or their fornicating, lying, cheating, good-for-nothing brothers shall inherit the kingdom of God."

"You jus' don't know when to quit, you self-righteous filth! Yer daddy would at least had the good graces ta not disparage the dead nor deny them proper ceremony. But you ain't your daddy, is you?"

"No, I ain't," Philip shot back. "The good Reverend might have conducted your wretched kin to the ground with a mighty fine speech, quelling even the most righteous breast of tribulation, but I wouldn't and still won't. If you fall on this field, I will personally send your soul to the waiting arms of Beelzebub himself and your kin."

"And if you should fall, I will see to it your bones be picked clean by these southern hogs what roam about in the dark woods."

Philip crossed his arms over his chest and cocked his head. "And what if both of us should tumble? Do we continue this feud in the afterlife, hurling barbs at one another from the separating space of Heaven and Hell? If both of us should fall, then perhaps that is the only respite from this desecration. Do we have a pact, Harper? We both should fall?"

"I ain't makin' no pact with you or your God fer my life. I'll let the gods of war pick and choose the time of my passing, but I'm waiting to see the wild pigs tearing at your carcass!" Harper turned on his heels and marched away.

"Rev?" Sammy asked Philip. "How long you gonna keep this up with him?"

Watching Harper stride away, Philip answered, "As long as he does. I know I fall far short of that Christian charity that I am supposed to show even my enemy, but I won't be faulted for not burying that cheat's brother."

"Whatever happened to forgive and forget?" Johnny asked.

Philip exhaled slowly. "It died along with any shred of decency a body might hold onto in the face of reprisal years ago with the shedding of my collar."

"I can see why Harper has something against you, but what is your issue with him?" Sammy asked.

"He and his family forced me out of the pulpit, pretending to be pious and God fearing. They took their case to the bishop, and I was given a choice of resign or be stripped of my collar for refusing to bury the worst man in the valley." Philip sighed loudly. "I suppose I should be grateful to them as I was never cut of the same cloth and collar as my father in respects to piety and preaching ability."

"I can see as where that might make a man kinda' mad."

"I suppose I never forgave them for the personal insult." Philip grew silent and stared into the dark ground.

"I dun' have much in the way of thoughts fer them neither," Johnny said, "but seems that carrying on like this after this long can't be good, given circumstances."

"Ain't there somethin' in the Lord's Prayer 'bout that?" Mule chimed in.

"What that?" Sammy asked.

"Forgive us our trespasses as we forgive them what trespasses against us," Mule responded.

"Yeah, it do say that, Mule," Philip answered. "But sometimes it's another thing puttin' it into practice."

"How hard can it be?" Mule asked him.

"Hard enough, Mule. Hard enough."

*****

Across the way, far into the rear of the Confederate army, Stephen Murdock looked across the wounded laid out around the Shiloh Church, searching for Willy Hawkins. Willy hadn't responded to roll after the Federal camp was taken, and the regiment had moved off before Stephen could pick through the dead and dying on the hill slope. The 6th Mississippi was but a shell of its former glory. Fortunately, they had not been called upon to give more blood this day and had spent several uncomfortable hours resting just behind the firing line. As the fight kept getting farther from them, every face mirrored the relief. They lazed about in formation in the boiling sun until an officer on General Cleburne's staff rode up and directed the regiment to counter-march back down the Shiloh road.

The 6th marched not only to the rear of the fighting but also to the very rear echelons of the army, back to their starting point. They passed the evidence of a great host having trod through the woods for the attack. They saw the acres of wagons and supply trains gathered around Michie's Crossroads and the bustle of hundreds of uniformed men. There, dispirited and exhausted, the survivors attempted to find rest in the growing heat of the forenoon.

Stephen collapsed after shedding his traps. He lay motionless for a time, too morose and spent to engage in chat. Few in the 6th felt like talking. Three hundred names were absent from the roll, including the commanding officer and second in command. Few were left even to make a respectable company. Fewer still were the messmates and pards whom Stephen had grown to know as his family.

Their brief moment of heroism and fury were followed by a calming of emotions and time for introspection. Four hundred men answered the call that morning to march forward, only to leave the greater portion dead and maimed upon the slopes of that rise. For some few hours, Stephen knew not how many, he drifted in and out of a fitful sleep upon the grass. The 6th Mississippi was on its own recognizance, and not even a fatigue detail was demanded of it. Having borne the battle, and bravely so, the regiment was left alone.

Near evening, weary of the idleness, he sought permission to search for Willie. Stephen shouldered his water bottle, and started out on his solitary mission. What had the sacrifice wrought? Had it brought victory? What of the rest of the divisions and corps?

All about him was confusion. The injured lay wherever a building and water was to be had. The field hospitals were easy to spot. He only had to spot the wounded gathered for the surgeon's saws, but no one knew where Hardee's dressing stations were located. Pitiful-looking men sprawled about any shack that would house the quick, painful surgery. Rows of blanket-covered forms attested to those who were now beyond care. Stephen's eyes fell upon gruesome wounds oozing blood and staining the once-green grass.

Others, like him, milled about free from wound or disability. Some sat by comrades; others moved from form to form, offering water or encouragement. Regimental chaplains administered last rites or absolutions, depending on the faith of the stricken, and surgeons' assistants hurried to and fro dressing wounds. Stephen steeled himself, retraced their steps of that morning and spied familiar landmarks. The farmstead where they first met the enemy was silent now. The wood line where the enemy broke and fled was peaceful. In the wood lay yet the still forms of what used to be men. Stephen took in these fell scenes in silence.

The light was fading as he crossed the marsh and the late scene of their desperate charges up the hill. Enemy dead still dotted the hilltop, but the Confederate dead and maimed had already been taken away. Stephen stood alone amid the dead. To the left, right, and ahead, he looked into the cold, open eyes of the fallen enemy, and some small pity heaved in his heart. They had been stripped clean of anything of value. None wore shoes. Some had been relieved of their trousers and lay in shameful exposure in their under drawers. It was too much to understand. Stephen turned and quickly strode back to, and through, the camp. He was reliably informed by a wounded corporal where Hardee had his field hospital, and he caught a rumor that a church lay ahead.

The darkness helped cover the day's sinful work. The Federal camps were occupied now by the victorious conquerors and appeared as if they had never been abandoned. Fires flickered everywhere, and the sounds of murmuring mingled with the rustling of leaves. Only the solitary booming of several large caliber guns broke what might have been a normal night in the vicinity of a large, armed host. The calm betrayed any tenseness, any grief, as if the battle of the morning had been imagined. Those soldiers yet unscathed walked to and fro, riders trotted upon the roads, and the army did what it always did at nighttime.

Stephen's feet hurt. Despite a long rest, his limbs still felt heavy. The light of several fires drew his attention away from his aches to an illuminated building. It was the church. Surrounding it was a mass of humanity prostrated by battle. In the dark, only forms could be discerned moving about the flickering shadows among the crop of furrowed wounded. The fields surrounding the church were filled with wounded, and the task of finding one specific face struck Stephen as ludicrous. Each face would have to be gazed upon to find the one he sought.

Stephen sniffed the air. Dampness mixed with blood and decay offended his senses. As if it wasn't enough to endure shot, shell, and maiming in battle, the heavens added their own form of misery: rain. His heart felt for those sufferers upon the ground, but he had seen enough suffering to build up a callous. He had seen men withered away by disease, and still others die outright before him from sudden and violent deaths. A soldier could surrender to the agony of such sights and desert, he could be discharged for wounds, or he could divorce himself of compassion altogether. Stephen had grown an age since the morning, and his heart felt nothing for the suffering of those hundreds. He only had one objective at the moment and a hope against hope of finding Willie in the dark, rainy night.

*****

The Indiana regiment, after making its stand by the guns as twilight descended upon the field, stood for a time in battle line before moving off farther to the right to be joined by the rest of their brigade. Not far from the Shiloh churchyard where Stephen started his search for his pard, Robert, Hube, and a few of the other survivors from the 25th Missouri walked through the trees on an errand of their own. The group hurried through the darkness to find their late battle line.

"Thish vay," Piper said and gestured.

"It's too dark, and I'm cold," Huebner whimpered.

"We don't have much time before they miss us," Robert said tersely.

The group, five of them, each shouldering a shovel borrowed from the entrenching supplies of their adopted company, wandered about the large field where they thought Gustavson had fallen.

"You sure it was here?" another of the group asked.

"I think so," Robert called back.

"I think *ve vere closher* to *die* trees," Piper said.

The enemy had retreated from the field, leaving their dead and wounded behind, and the field was dotted with still forms. The darkness made it impossible to see in any direction without a lamp, and they had no other illumination. One merely stumbled over something and inspected it for Union blue. The ground was littered with equipment and soggy paper from the thousands of paper cartridges opened and discarded where the combatants stood, but that was of little help when the clutter that usually discerned a battle line was just a mix of random garbage upon the ground.

"We should have done it right away," a man named Henderson said.

"That first sergeant would have shot one of us for sure," Robert told him. "We just need to keep heading toward the river. We'll see him."

"*Ve* be lucky to make it back to *der Kompanie*," Piper said.

"Doesn't matter," Robert snapped. "We couldn't bury Hilde, but we're going to bury Gustavson before those infernal hogs get to him!"

Huebner stopped and leaned on his shovel. "Can't we stop? I'm tired."

Without looking back, Piper hissed, "Hube, get moving *und* look for Gustavson."

A sudden flopping sound reached Robert's ears, and he turned in time to see Huebner hit the ground hard.

"Hube, ya' need to get those feet straightened out. Ya' know, one in front of the other?" He backtracked to where Huebner lay.

"Tripped over something," Huebner said. He rolled onto his hands and knees and gasped when he saw whom he had tripped over.

Robert froze. He knelt down next to Huebner. Crumpled upon the ground where Huebner had fallen was Gustavson.

"Shhh," Robert whispered. "Hube, found him! We found Gus."

Huebner sat trembling. "Tripped *ich über.* . . ."

Robert put his hand on Huebner's shoulder. "Shh. No harm done, Hube. Forget about it. I won't tell anyone." The others gathered around. Each man stared at the corpse who had been their companion since the company had mustered in St. Louis a few months before. Gustavson and Hildebrande had been with the 13th Missouri when Colonel Peabody surrendered the command after Lexington, Missouri, was captured by the Confederate General Price. He had borne the marches and the bitter early engagements at the beginning of the war in Missouri. He had stood with them before the battle that morning, only to fall at last light. None of them knew what to do next, nor had they planned any ceremony for burial. It was raining, and they were five men gathered around a fallen comrade. Thoughts of their own comfort had taken second place to the proper treatment of their pard in his passing.

"Let's carry him over there by those trees. Seems wrong to bury him here in the open," Henderson said.

"Let's get his traps off," Robert said, "and cover him with the blanket."

Huebner looked at the cold body as the others discussed how to disposition the burial. Robert sensed the youth was about to lose it again, just as he had that morning.

"Hube, go pick a spot over by those trees while we get ready to carry him over," Robert said.

"Huh?"

"Go pick a spot to bury Gus," Robert repeated.

"Oh. *Ja, gut*," Huebner responded, slowly gaining his feet.

"So, we just dig a hole and put him in it?" Henderson asked.

Piper nodded. "*Ja.* Carve his name and date on *der* tree."

The others commenced to removing the traps from Gustavson's body. Soon, Gustavson lay in state with the wool blanket for a shroud. The body had begun to stiffen, and righting him took no little effort.

"Come, I find perfect spot," Huebner yelled from the darkness.

"*Shtay z'ere,*" Piper yelled back.

"Well, let's try to carry him best we can," Robert said. The men looked at the shrouded form and hesitated, unable to figure how to carry their pard in the most appropriate manner.

"Let's do it," Henderson said. "I don't think there is any way to do it with the dignity we seek. We just gonna have to pick him up by the shoulders and legs. Someone get the middle. Maybe wrap him in the blanket. Might help."

"We'll come back for the shovels," Robert said. After the effort to wrap and transport the corpse of their friend, they rested at the foot of a great oak that Huebner had selected. The tree's limbs and overgrowth sheltered them from the rain, and they agreed that the spot was the most appropriate for a burial plot, given the circumstances. Soon, they had excavated a hole large enough to accommodate Gustavson and placed the body lovingly within. After Piper finished chiseling the name, regiment, and date upon the tree, the five miserable-looking men stood around the grave.

"What we say?" Huebner asked.

"We said it by what we did," Henderson replied.

"What about Hilde?" Huebner asked.

"Tomorrow," Robert replied. "Maybe tomorrow."

No one wanted to cast the moment with anything trite or irreverent. They had laid a friend to rest upon the field in which his life had been purchased for their cause. Anything to be said would not begin to describe their sorrow or their relief at the act thus accomplished. They were dripping wet and fatigued. There was no time to don mourning cloth or to observe more than a moment of silence. They knew there was still more war to make upon the enemy and more work to be done. One by one, they peeled off into the field in the direction whence they had come.

"C'mon, Hube, time to go back," Robert said when only he and Huebner remained.

"You think Gus *mit Jesus?*" Huebner asked.

"Sure, Hube, Gus is with Jesus now." The thought suddenly troubled Robert. Amid the struggle and the call of the long roll and the thunder of the guns, he had forgotten the soldiers' one companion: death. A soldier only has death to look forward to, and if not death, then a life of maimed existence. But with death comes the question that man will ever ask of himself: What fate awaits his passing?

"*Ja*, he *mit* Jesus now," Huebner said. He managed a weak smile.

Robert looked at Huebner's boyish face and felt a chill run down his back at the surety of those words. There was something dead serious in Huebner's tone, just as it was earlier when he trotted off toward their adopted regiment. It was the tone of conviction.

"Let's get going, Hube. Gus is resting proper now." Robert said.

"*Ja. Gute Nacht*, Gus," Huebner said. He turned from the grave, and the two men walked into the gloom.

Chapter Twelve

The rain was chilly and fell in a continuous drizzle. It wasn't enough to soak a man but was enough to keep him damp and uncomfortable. Those who had them donned their gum blankets or wrapped their woolen blankets about their shoulders. They stood in groups to share the misery of a rainy night without shelter. Rest was the hardest thing to find, despite the mutual exhaustion, and the drizzle was annoying enough to keep the hardest sleepers awake. Those men who had been enterprising enough to scavenge the Federal's camp had found a supply of ponchos. The captured vulcanized canvas ponchos kept the upper torso dry but did nothing for the legs and feet. Michael convinced Mahoney to turn a blind eye to the pilfering; at least they were pilfering the spoils of the enemy and not his dead. Behind where the battery had taken station was a Federal camp with tents and food and equipment just begging to be "liberated," as one private commented.

Indeed, all sorts of equipment were available if one looked hard enough in the darkness. Also to be found were wounded of both sides seeking shelter. To some, including Michael's men, those wounded hampered any scavenging. Out of respect, Michael's men left those tents alone, though others of their kind were not so polite.

Michael sat leaning against a tree and huddled under a captured gum blanket one of his men had given him. There were the day's reports to send up the chain of command, and the gum blanket helped keep the drizzle from falling upon the pages of his notebook as he penciled in the returns. The battery had expended twenty-five cases of grape shot and seventy-five of solid, or round, shot. Three men were carried from the field injured, and two had been killed outright. Ten horses were disabled. The caissons were replenished from stores twice, and the battery moved and fought with the progress of the infantry and covered territory won through hard fighting.

All of these things were described in the return. The numbers were necessary, but they did not belie the memory of their consequences. Union men had been maimed and killed by the expenditures. But a report was not time to wax philosophic about war or those enemy soldiers rent by his fire. They would become expenditures upon the enemy battery's returns and reduced to a solitary column of dead and missing. Later, they would become part of the greater numbers to be calculated at brigade, division, corps, and, finally, army level. In the end, the returns would be someone's success or failure by ground won or lost by rod.

Fires flickered where the enterprise of men kept them lit in the wetness, and men gathered around them to stare into the flickering dance. Looking up, Michael saw his guns covered in canvas to keep the fittings dry and oiled and the large tampions stuffed into the barrels to keep the moisture out. The men of the battery lolled about aimlessly in the mist, and some few huddled underneath the caissons for shelter and shut-eye.

"Grierson, I see your men made it through the rest of the day," Captain Polk said as he gingerly sat down next to Michael. His leg was set in a splint and wrapped by a bloody bandage.

"That they did, Polk. That they did. We didn't see much of the rest of the goings on after that big surrender." Michael nodded toward Polk's leg and asked, "Shouldn't you go to an aid station?"

"I'm putting that off for as long as I can stand it, Grierson. We pressed 'em to the landing, as far as I could tell, but it was like the wind had been spent in the army, and the men couldn't press on with vigor as they had previously. We had them against the river but lacked the power to do anything else." Polk grimaced as he shifted his leg.

Michael stuffed his notebook into his jacket pocket. Polk's words were not welcome, for they meant what Michael sensed: failure of the whole enterprise to destroy the enemy army in Tennessee.

"Pickets say there's chopping and lots of traffic noise up ahead, and it's all local, not headed away. What happened?" asked Michael, motioning to Polk's bandage.

"Leg's broke. Spent shell fragment. Got some Yank whiskey fer the pain. Grant got help from Buell toward dusk. That and Johnston's dead," Polk said dryly.

"Dead?" Michael turned.

"Happened this afternoon, least that's what the word is and seems to be truth. Something happened as you sort of get this sense that someone's changed drivers mid-stream, and the horses ain't being steered at all. Like the hand that guided and directed this army suddenly fell limp and left it to its own devices."

Polk paused to stare at the wet grass and dirt at his feet. "I got this feeling somehow after Prentiss's division surrendered in that wood earlier today. We took an entire division of the enemy, and then some, in that wood. Eight thousand Yankees surrendered, or so I'm told. You know those moments of success where it would seem that one need only reach out and pluck that sweetest of plums from the tree limbs? Where one would swear there was nothing to stop you from those fruits of victory, and then you pause to wait for the other boot to drop?"

"It did seem like we'd slowed down a bit," Michael conceded. "Though I confess I didn't look for that other thing to happen to counter our successes, and what was done today was fairly won. You know how a victory can disorganize the victor as much as the defeated."

"We were there, Grierson." Polk's voice quivered in anger and disappointment. "We were there and could see the river bank through the trees teeming with disorganized Yankees and the gunboats and transports on the river, and nothing but a line of guns stood between us and shoving all them Yanks to drown in the water. That plum was never closer to our reach than it was before dusk."

"You think we've lost?" Michael asked, surprised.

"We command the field, but if we couldn't push a few thousand fugitives into the river because we lacked the energy and drive to do it, then we've lost the initiative at the least." Polk tried to stand, in response to the emotion he felt, but the pain in his leg made him gasp and sit hard. He took a swallow of whisky before he could continue. "Buell is adding his numbers to that of Grant now, and we knew we might be able to defeat Grant if we were bold enough. But we are a day too late to do that, I fear, and tomorrow we will be assailed by fresh battalions."

"The infantry is exhausted, as is our own battery, but they are flush with victory. Perhaps that will mean the difference on the morrow," Michael said.

"Indeed, the morale is high, and perhaps that will carry us to the river in the end, despite the reinforcements we'll face soon. But you should have seen it, Grierson." He grabbed Michael's arm and stared into his eyes. "All was confusion in the enemy's rear, and we were on the brink of it all."

Polk's frankness was unnerving, and Michael had never seen him so open and disconcerted. "We're still on it, Polk. We own his camps, and we need but one more push to own his point of supply at the river. We take the landing, and Grant and Buell will have the swampy lowlands in their rear and our army in their front. They'll have to surrender."

"I'm not one for gloom, but I don't see what good will come of tomorrow," Polk said.

"You're not ever wrong. You've kept the battery from a world of hurt following that intuition of yours. I just hope you are wrong on this one count," Michael said.

"Well, Grierson, a commanding officer is never wrong as far as his men are concerned. He's always right even when he consigns them to their sure death. Only you and I can be wrong to the other. Between you and me, I do hope I'm wrong, or a lot of men were killed today for no result." Again, Polk struggled to stand, swinging his splinted leg around until he was steadied. Without further word he limped out into the dark.

Michael felt uneasy. Had his own eyes deceived him? He'd seen the columns of enemy prisoners filing to the rear in dejection. He'd seen the infantry of General Polk's corps advancing and beating the enemy back. Could so much have been changed in so few hours? Johnston's death was another blow—and one that would not be kept silent for long. If an army did one thing for sure, it took on the imprint of its commander. Whether they loved or hated him, the army rose or fell with its commander. If Johnston was gone, so was his drive and plan.

While the eastern armies had tasted a seemingly endless run of victories over their numerically superior enemies, the western armies had not been so fortunate. Fort Henry was taken with ease, and Fort Donelson was an embarrassment for Western arms. General Pillow surrendered the ten thousand-man garrison after a break-out nearly succeeded. With access to the Tennessee River denied to him, Johnston was forced to abandon Tennessee. Kentucky was also lost. Yet only a few days ago, as they marched out of Corinth to meet Grant at Pittsburg Landing, all seemed to have changed in their fortunes. Michael longed for some great success of arms to justify the expense of men and material. It had seemed within grasp that morning, though Captain Polk wasn't so optimistic.

Michael got up from his spot under the tree, overtaken by the need to calm his fears. He ventured into the drizzle to see for himself the state of affairs. Despite the rain, many men were going about their business. Michael gathered the gum blanket about his shoulders and walked in the direction he guessed the front lines might be. The battery had drawn up beside a captured enemy camp before dark and settled down, but other than the wounded infantry taking shelter in the tents, he saw nothing of the infantry brigades that were supposed to be in front of them.

The misty rain made the night that much darker and limited visibility to only a few feet. Michael knew he was in danger of blundering into some enemy vedette or picket line and falling into enemy hands. Many a hapless man had wandered blindly into the enemy and was captured, spending months whiling away the time in a prison compound. The danger of being shot at by his own side was also very real. But the enemy line had to be close.

"Where you headed?" a voice called out so close that Michael jumped.

"What?" Michael asked.

"Nuthin' but enemy out that way," the man said. He stepped out from behind a tree. Michael had walked right by the man without seeing him.

Michael looked over the man, trying to recognize him. "Whose picket line is this?"

"No one's. Provost guard posted me here to keep fellers like you from heading too far up this way."

"You mean there ain't no picket line here?" That was a surprise.

"Not that I seen. Could be up ahead, but I hain't gonna go that far ta find out, neither."

They both faced ahead into the dark rain, though there was nothing to see. Michael let out a sigh.

"Thank you, then. I suppose I'll go no farther."

"Hain't seed none of the enemy, neither, so they could be nuthin' up ahead. Prudence seems ta me to be had stayin' put right here." The man gave Michael a knowing look. "Although, if ya' listen real close, ya' can hear movement up ahead. Enemy's using axes in the forests. They meanin' ta stay, I think."

"Would seem that way," Michael replied.

"I thinks we might be able to finish it at light. I think we good to finish the job at first light."

"Let's hope the enemy don't know they's nothing between them and their camp. My guns aren't even unlimbered. We need to get some infantry to picket this area."

"That would be mighty prudent and no mind to me. Some Federal cavalry came snoopin' around here a bit ago, but I suppose 'cause of the darkness they din't see me fer they's enemy. I was able to turn them back by actin' friendly like." The man looked down and kicked a toe into the ground. "I'd shore feel better if I had some company."

"Indeed. I won't promise nothin'. Things seem pretty confused everywhere, but I'll see what can be done," Michael said.

The man nodded and leaned back against the tree. Michael started off a few steps and looked back. Already, the man was invisible to him, the blackness of the trees and the night hiding him completely. Michael quickened his pace, fearing getting lost and wandering into another vedette. When the surroundings began to take on a familiar edge, he relaxed.

"Mahoney, First Sergeant, where are you?" Michael called.

"Sir," Mahoney called back.

"Form a gun line right here and get the pieces primed. They ain't nothin' in front of us but the enemy. They ain't close that I can tell, but I don't like being exposed."

"What? They's supposed to be a picket line out there," said the haggard first sergeant.

"Well, they ain't. It's just us and one lone soul standing by a tree."

"Should I take one section as skirmishers?" Mahoney asked.

Michael chewed his bottom lip for a moment, then shrugged. "You kin try. Don't think the boys would know skirmish drill from Quinine Call, but yer welcome ta give it a go. I'm going to find some infantry to do it for real."

Michael turned and walked into the blackness. He chuckled to himself as he heard Mahoney get a section roused and armed. It wasn't for an artilleryman to perform such duties. The boys knew how to load and shoot a two-band musket if they had to, but most of their weapons rarely saw useful employment other than taking pot shots at live game.

Walking through the abandoned camp, Michael heard the normal murmur of quiet conversations within the tents and pitiable moaning. Michael was looking for a fire and any large gathering of men, but the camp was dark. Curious, Michael stepped up to a Sibley tent. He opened the flap, peeked in, and immediately gagged. Excrement, blood, and stale air assaulted his nose. Jerking his head back out, he drew a breath to settle his stomach and to purge his nostrils of the awful stench. Michael poked his head in once more after drawing a deep breath.

It was dark inside, and the walls of the tent had been pierced by minié balls—the canvas was ripped and sagging. A writhing mass of humanity covered the floor. Confederate and Federal wounded occupied this tent, and most still seemed to be alive and delirious.

"Water," a thick, raspy voice called.

Michael looked into the face of a young boy whose head lay directly below. Michael did not have his canteen.

"Water," the call was taken up by a few others in the tent.

Michael cursed himself for being curious as he had neither a way to succor these poor souls nor the stomach for such work.

"Hold on. I'll find a canteen."

Michael ducked out again and drew in clean air. He looked about for a canteen. Shattered rifles, blankets, caps, hats, coats, belts, cartridge boxes, torn haversacks, and camp equipage lay underfoot, but no canteens. He could outfit several men from the cast-off items lying upon the ground, and yet for the want of a single canteen he would give his rank. He pressed on through the camp and eventually stumbled upon a pile of discarded canteens lying around a corpse propped up against a tree. He was a Confederate colonel by his rank, and a darkened spot in his abdomen showed his death wound. The canteens had no doubt been gathered by someone to give the poor man some comfort before he passed on. Gathering the canteens, Michael hurried back to the tent.

"Water, boys. I got water," Michael said.

Several shaky hands reached out. Michael handed over several of the canteens.

"They's more layin' around if any of you can walk," Michael said and left them without further ado.

The next tent over was in similar straits, and the men therein also desired water. Former enemies of a few hours before lay side by side and tried to tend to each other's wounds as they were able. Michael was sure that in the annals of war, nothing quite like this had ever been witnessed by enemies so alike. It did not take long for Michael to distribute the water and move on.

When he reached the edge of the camp, Michael spied a series of fires and lanterns in an adjacent camp and headed for it. Where there's fire, there's headquarters, Michael thought. He stepped into a bustle of activity and a general liveliness not seen in the other campsite.

"Private, what HQ is this?" Michael asked a man who appeared to be standing guard.

"Polk's HQ. Polk's Corps HQ," was the disinterested reply.

"May I enter?" asked Michael, expecting the normal guard mount challenge and response.

"I ain't stoppin' ya'," was the reply.

Michael brushed passed the useless sentry and walked up to a tired-looking lieutenant. The man was sitting at a table, scribbling upon sheets of paper by the light of a lantern.

"Is General Polk about?" Michael asked.

The lieutenant didn't look up from his pages. "No. Bragg's HQ." Michael leaned over and saw that the lieutenant was copying orders upon a sheet of paper from another he positioned in front of him. He would write a word, look at the other sheet, then write another word. Either he was not too bright or he was very careful. Michael started to get irritated by the man's demeanor.

"Who can I speak to about positioning an infantry regiment in our front?"

"Major Pigeon over there, an aid de camp of Polk's." The lieutenant pointed over to a man leaning against another table and napping upon one arm.

Michael didn't bother thanking him. He walked over to the napping officer and cleared his throat. Major Pigeon didn't stir.

"Sir," Michael said.

"Yes?" Major Pigeon jerked his head up.

"Sir, Captain Grierson of Polk's battery," Michael said.

"Yes, Captain?" the major said, still in the daze of fitful sleep.

"Sir, I know it for certain that there is nothing between my section of Polk's battery and the enemy beyond but a single vedette, and a mighty lonely one at that."

"Oh?" the major yawned.

"Yes, he's already bluffed a Yankee cavalry patrol, and I'd feel a might better if my guns weren't so exposed. Not to mention the security of the division."

"Where?" The major blinked and rubbed his eyes.

"Two camps over to the south," Michael said curtly. His frustration was beginning to show.

The major eyed him thoughtfully. "If you can find an infantry company, you could have it. We're still trying to ascertain where the other divisions are, Captain. I'm sure the general would be right pleased you're so concerned for our front, but the fact is I don't have anything to order up to you. The brigades are scattered about, and few have sent in their returns or reports. I'd suggest finding your own brigade first since I'm assuming someone placed you where you're at now."

"Sir." Michael saluted and turned on his heel. The reproof had been unnecessary and unwelcome. Captain Polk was nowhere to be found and would be Michael's first and probably only step into the chain of command. Polk's battery was attached to B. R. Johnson's brigade, but Michael hadn't seen Johnson since mid-afternoon.

Michael began to understand what Polk had tried to explain earlier. Hopelessness was evident in the HQ, and if Captain Polk had been around it for any length of time, it was no wonder he was in a desperate mind. But, like a caisson under the control of a spooked team of horses, the battle was out of the control of any human hand, and the army was trying to cope as best as it could.

Back in familiar territory and the position of the battery, Michael walked up to Mahoney.

"We're not going to see any infantry tonight. We'll have to make do with our own preparations and hope the Yankees don't decide to press us at first light. Corps HQ doesn't know what's going on, and I couldn't find Captain Polk or even the brigade HQ. We're on our own for the time." Michael kicked at the dirt and looked back in the direction he had come.

"I see," Mahoney said and sniffled. "We kin rotate the sections every hour and a half. The boys is pretty tired."

"That'll work, Michael said. "I'll put Lieutenant Ford in charge of the pickets as officer of the guard. You seen 'im?"

"He's over by gun three with the other lieutenant."

"It's going to be a long night, and no one's gonna get any real sleep, but you try anyway, First Sergeant. The boys'll need you to be sharp tomorrow."

"I suppose it would be fruitless of me to suggest the same to you?" Mahoney gave him a wry look.

"Probably so. If we get settled right proper, I might steal a wink or two, but with this drizzle, I don't know if it will be possible."

"Well, I got one a.m. by my time piece, so we got another six hours afore first light." Mahoney winked at him. "I'll expect to catch you napping."

Michael groaned. "I'm going to make one last try to find Captain Polk and inform him of our situation. At least we can assume the enemy is just as disorganized and won't move until light."

"Hope so," Mahoney replied. "Don't you go and get lost."

"I'll try, Mother," Michael said and grinned.

Michael turned on his heel and walked back into the inky, drizzly blackness, leaving Mahoney standing alone.

"Section commanders," Mahoney shouted, "on me."

*****

Ten rods to the west, through intervening trees and blackness, the 36th Indiana was settling in for a long, uncomfortable night sleeping on their arms, which was to say in battle formation with muskets at their sides. Not a man among them was aware of the prize in cannon waiting to be claimed in front of them. Those who had feared missing the grand ball were satiated, and any who had feared his own cowardice was prepared to stand far more. The Indiana men had faced the elephant and lived to tell of it. Despite the rainfall, the Indiana men were chatty and restless. Every version of the late battle, both real and imagined, was told and retold, and changed and re-changed, until one could wonder whether the men had witnessed the same engagement.

Ahead of the regiment, the men of Company K were spread out the length of the line in picket posts of comrades in arms, huddled closely together for company and warmth. Though the rest of the regiment was equally uncomfortable upon the cold and wet grass, those on picket duty did not have the luxury of relaxing and participating in the tall tales of battle. It also meant little to no sleep for each post, as one man had to remain awake at all times. The Missouri men were spread out in four posts, in hailing distance of each other and struggling to not let their exhaustion win over their vigilance.

"Comrades, *Schläfrig bin Ich. Ich* need company," Huebner whined.

"That defeat purpose, Huebner, of you on watch. *Ve're* all tired," Piper said.

"Can't stay wake alone," Huebner said. He raised his arm over his mouth to cover a wide yawn.

"Hube, with you making noise, none of us can sleep," Robert said. He tried to roll his gum blanket around himself to keep the rain out.

Huebner shook Robert. "*Du kannst nicht.*"

"Hube," Robert pleaded.

"*Du* must."

"Hube, let us be!" Piper snapped at him.

"*Nein*, can't fall asleep. Comrades must help."

Robert sighed and rolled out of his gum blanket. "Piper, I'll stay up with Hube, so you sleep and take next watch."

"*Danke*, Robert." Huebner said and yawned again.

Huebner sat cross-legged with his poncho draped down over his legs and his rifle underneath the covering. The barrel protruded off to the side. Moments slipped by. Huebner seemed content to stare off into the blackness and let the rain water drip off his nose.

Robert had spent his days watching over Huebner like an older brother but had not had to keep him company or spend any time conversing with the misfit. With most men, conversation would be about the state of the rations or the officers or fatigue duty or the rebellion. Unpracticed at talking to him, Robert didn't know where to go.

Robert sat and tried to think of something to say or some topic that Huebner would be able to participate in. It suddenly occurred to him that Huebner had never spoken his mind on anything before that afternoon. He had always been in the background, always on the verge of causing some great camp calamity. He was a man who always acted on his first impulse.

Huebner broke the silence between them. "Hildebrande *und* Gustavson *sind getötet*, Robert. They're gone, *fällt sich*."

"Yes, Hube, *fällt sich. Sie schläft*. They sleep. "

"I miss them."

"They were our pards and mess mates," Robert added. To his ears, his words sounded eulogistic.

"They are *mit Gott*," Huebner said.

"Sounds better than sitting here in the rain," Robert replied.

Huebner turned toward Robert. "No, they with God and not because it sound better."

"I'd hope so," Robert said. He turned away under the pressure of Huebner's stare. It was there again, that look of conviction from such an unlikely source. Robert still could not reconcile the misfit with the man of forceful will. Huebner resumed his empty gaze into the night and lowered his voice. "Gustav Hildebrande was pious Lutheran. *Mein Vater und* Gustav's *Vater* serve *der* Regent of Saxony in fighting *der* Catholics in their war *mit* Prussia, serve in *der* special guard and all men followers of Luther. *Vater* deacon in *der* church *mit Herr Hildebrande als ich jung war*. I knew Gustav then. I knew Gustav's *Mutter. Frau* Hildebrande will be sad now. You think we see her again?"

"Hope so, though I'm not sure we will, if ever. If today was any indication of how we are doing in this war, it will be a long while,"

"I want to tell her...tell her about Gustav *der Soldat*."

"Someday, maybe," Robert said. As if life were not complicated enough, he now must contend with the oddities of relationships and comrades taken away. Huebner owed his presence here to Robert if for no other reason than avoiding capture. Yet this boy of simple thoughts and actions was putting Robert's own thoughts to shame.

"I hope I don't have to meet your *Mutter* with telling of Robert *der Soldat*," Huebner said. He wiped his nose on his soaked sleeve.

Robert froze and felt the uncomfortable notion that Huebner was about to get into territory best left unspoken.

"I'm happy you not *getötet*, too," Huebner said. "Who would look out for Hube then?" Robert tried to smile but stopped when he saw the serious look on Huebner's face.

Robert nodded and pursed his lips. How does one reply to something like that? One stood side by side with one's comrades in arms, day by day in fatigue detail and in drill. They slept in the same tent or under the same stars in the dry and in the wet and occasionally under fire. Everything in the army finally came down to the living and the dead. They had lost other comrades to sickness and disease, but they held onto their mess mates as if family. It was unspoken; one just felt it. To hear Huebner speak of it now made Robert uncomfortable, and he had no reply.

"We fight more tomorrow?" Huebner asked.

Robert welcomed the change of topic. "Probably. We aren't finished here yet. But will we be finished or do the finishing?"

"I'm sorry we have to fight more. More chances to lose more comrades."

"As long as the enemy holds our camp, we'll have to."

Huebner made a choking sound, and his voice was pleading. "But I got Gustavson dead. It was my idea go back."

"It was the right thing to do. You said so yourself. We followed because we knew it to be true. Gustavson knew it also. Not your fault Gus fell, Hube." They had returned to the line to fight for honor and cause, but Huebner was right. It was his leading that had brought them all back into harm's way.

"We still be by river bank and alive," Huebner said.

"Maybe, or maybe we'd have been rounded up by some provost guard and all thrown into the stockade for desertion. That's why we went back. You said it yourself earlier that you felt like a deserter. Now, not any more." Robert didn't think what he said had any effect, and he wasn't sure he really believed it himself.

"*Fahnenflüchtiger* Gustavson be alive *und* not *Soldat Gustavson kaput*," Huebner mumbled.

"Gustavson *gestorben mit* honor not alive *mit shamt. Komradschaft du Soldat,* Huebner, *und Soldat* Mitchell, *verstehst du*? We are all alive and together in honor, Hube." Huebner's face brightened somewhat.

Robert fished for his time piece and asked, "You think you can stay awake for another hour?"

"*Ja,*" Huebner answered.

"Be a good *Soldat*, Huebner, *und* wake Piper in an hour and then get some sleep. *Verstehst du*?" Robert asked.

"*Ja,* be good *Soldat* Hube for comrades." His voice held no cheer, but it was good enough that he agreed.

"Have Piper wake me after his stand," Robert said. Robert rolled himself up into the gum blanket. Though everything they owned in the world was left back in camp, there wasn't a want for blankets or other necessities that could not have been picked up from the ground.

"*Ja. Gute Nacht*, Robert," Huebner said and stared out into the blackness of early morning.

Chapter Thirteen

Mule started at the sudden crack from Johnny's rifle. "What'd you do that for?"

"Rebel pickets is pushin' forward," Johnny explained.

A loud report in front of them accompanied a minié ball zipping over their heads. The morning had been quiet save for the sudden disruption of solitude and the returning bark of an enemy musket.

"Fools!" came a shout from their left. "Whataya' think yer doin'?" shouted someone to the right.

The vedettes of the 24th Ohio were spread out at five-pace intervals in skirmish formation. Bright sparks of yellow lit up closer to the picket line than anyone had expected. Soon, fire begged counter-fire, and the picket lines livened with activity. The slumbering regiments farther back of the picket line began to waken.

"Ready!" Philip shouted to the man to his left. He needed his Comrade in Arms to be loaded and ready before he fired his own weapon. A crack and flash in front of him, no more than fifty paces he figured, was followed by the zing of lead the ball made as it passed. Philip knew the Rebel was out there and probably lying prone to reload. He jerked the hammer down and winced as the flash from the cap snapped into his right thumb. Not wasting any time to see if his round accomplished its goal, he rolled over on his back and dug into the cartridge box. On a skirmish line, it was safer to load while lying prone, but more powder poured down his chest than in the barrel.

"Ready!" Philip shouted to his partner, and it was his turn to wait and watch. He rolled over and onto his knees and waited. The flicker of fire dotted along the undulating ground for as far as Philip could see. Save for the bursts of musketry, little else announced the presence of either side. Brief flashes illuminated figures in split-second repose, silhouetting forms against the landscape as if they were posed mid-stride. It was impossible to tell how far away the enemy was or what he was really up to. Each man simply fired in the general direction of the other if for no other reason than to participate in the charade. If the enemy were pushing forward, they would be on top of Philip and the others before anyone could do anything about it.

The company commander jogged up behind Philip and peered over his shoulder.

"Too dark to see much, sir," Philip said.

Another flash from in front lit a line of Rebel skirmishers and nothing else.

"They jus' feelin' us out," the commander said and moved on.

"Ready!" shouted Philip's partner.

They had no target, just the vague impression of a shape created by the flash of a discharge. The glimpses were so brief that they might have been shooting at trees and stumps. The fire was coming from the enemy, but where was he? Philip took his best guess and fired, then repeated the business of reloading.

Philip hated skirmish detail. Skirmish detail was risky and personal. They faced their enemy in the clear, and they fought one man against another, not in the scatter spray of lead with which opposing lines showered one another. A skirmisher saw the man he was trying to hit, and was seen in return. In line of battle, they faced a greater barrage of flying lead, but it was impersonal. It was company against company, a collective effort to destroy as many of the enemy as one could. He saw men fall or stagger to the rear of the line, and it meant one less enemy to harm his pards. Here, on the skirmish line, it was vengeful. It took less personal courage than standing shoulder to shoulder to receive the enemy's first fire; it was a moral courage to willingly harm a man from a close distance.

"Ready!" Philip shouted. *Dear Lord, carry mine enemy into Your eternal rest should I take a life this morning,* Philip prayed. It felt odd to pray, but it felt worse not to. Philip didn't struggle with moral questions of life and death and sanctity. It was war. It was killing sanctioned by those higher than him. Had not the Israelites been commanded by God to take the lives of the Canaanites? Still, he was troubled by the thought of taking lives with no conscience. *Bear my pards upon wings of Your angels should any fall this morning, Lord. Bear Your servants on heavenly wings should they be counted among Your children.*

Skirmishers from other regiments began to fire upon enemy close enough to pose a danger. Farther to the left of the line, all was still.

*****

Robert sat up and rubbed his eyes. "What's happening?"

"Skirmishing down the right," Piper replied.

"What? How long?" Robert grabbed for his musket.

"Not long. Just began. Nothing happening in our front, though," Piper said.

"Ok, I'll wake Hube," Robert said. He nudged the snoring Huebner.

"Hube, wake up," Robert whispered.

"Huebner sleep through more racket before. Have to do better than that," Piper said with a chuckle.

Robert prodded a little harder. "Hube, wake up. C'mon, Hube, time to wake up."

"Remember when we found him asleep during skirmish drill? Fool slept through mock attack like nothing happening all around him. He's *kaput* to *der vorld*," Piper said.

"Well, I don't want him sleepin' if we get pushed," Robert answered. "Hube, wake up,"

"Let him be. You never wake him," Piper said and turned back to his front. The flashes of musketry to the left resembled a candlelight procession as the random rifle fire created a lane between the combatants.

"Oh yeah? Watch this." He reached for the mucket tied to his haversack. "Who's got the coffee up?" He tapped his spoon against the tin cup blackened from many a camp fire.

"*Kaffe?*" Huebner said and he sat up and looked around.

"*Mein Gott!*" Piper exclaimed.

"You gotta know what is important to a man to get him out of bed," Robert said, laughing. "Sorry, Hube, no coffee to kick over, just needed to get you up."

"What's that noise?" Huebner asked, rubbing his eyes over and over again.

"That, *mein Freund*, is the sound of skirmishing over that way *und* Lord willing will stay that way," Piper replied.

"Battle?" Huebner asked, surprised.

"*Ja*, Hube," Piper answered, "a battle, but it's still dark, and *die* skirmishers are nervous. Nothing to worry about, *mein* Jonah."

Huebner cocked his head to the side and looked at Piper. "Why you always call me Jonah? *Ich* Fredrich Huebner."

"Because, like in the Good Book, Jonah vas always in wrong place at right time," Piper said with a smile.

"*Nich namen* Jonah. *Ich* Friedrich Huebner," Huebner protested.

"*Ja*, Friedrich Huebner, *die* Jonah," Piper said, and he laughed when he saw the serious look on Huebner's face. He just wasn't getting it.

"It stop raining," Huebner said to change the subject.

"Some time ago," Piper replied. "If *die* enemy is in front, they is keepin' to they's selves. Between *die* jittery pickets *und* those gunboats firing all night, *Es überrascht mich* – surprises me -- you slept."

"*Kanonenboote, wo?*" Huebner asked.

"On *die* river, Hube," Piper said and rolled his eyes. "*Zwei Kanonenbootes.*"

"Oh, *das* booming, *ja?*" Huebner asked.

"*Ja*, Hube, *das* boom," Robert said with a laugh.

"It's Sunday, *ja?*" Huebner asked.

"*Ja*, it's Sunday, Hube, *der Tag des Herrn*. The Lord's Day. Why?" Piper asked.

"More fighting today, *ja?*" Huebner asked.

"Probably, Hube," Robert said.

Huebner hung his head and shook it. "No good to kill on *der Tag des Herrn.*"

"They say *die* Rebel Jackson prefers to fight on *der Tag des Herrn.* He thinks he's doing the Lord's work," Piper said.

"Jackson here?" Huebner looked up and asked.

"No, Hube, least not that I know of," Robert said.

"It's just another day, Hube," Piper replied.

"*Nein!* Remember *die* Sabbath *Tag und* keep it holy," retorted Huebner.

"I don't see how it can be helped, Hube. They attacked us, and now we have to drive them back or be forced back into the river and drowned," Robert said.

Huebner nodded. They each looked in the direction of the river and then toward the enemy.

"Well," Piper said, "it be light soon."

*****

Stephen Murdock gingerly stepped his way over the rows of wounded men, using a kerosene lamp he had borrowed from the church to see his path. He moved through trees that, with the lack of light and clouded sky, were not discernible. Hours of scrutinizing rigid or contorted faces slipped by. The church was a magnet for wounded men who could drag themselves there or who were helped by comrades. The Federal wounded lay near their enemy, and all received equal attention from the surgeon's saw. A wound equalized friend and foe.

Stephen's water can was long emptied. The sips he doled out were received with thankfulness, but he knew they were not enough to do any good. In their delirium or mumbled prayers, men called for water and mothers, and occasionally a father. He met familiar faces from the 6th Mississippi who had taken their wounds on the same hill as Stephen's pard, Willie. Stephen attended two in their death throes. Their deaths were painful to watch, as both men grabbed for him in one last effort to make contact with one last human being. He knew them by name only. One saw the men of other companies during drill, parade, or about camp, but generally one did not socialize outside of his own company.

Stephen supposed it did not matter to them that he was a stranger; he was still a familiar face with whom to share the last moments of life. The surgeons and hospital stewards kept a round-the-clock schedule to dispense what comfort they could. Opium, recovered from the Federal camps, was plentiful, and few sufferers had to endure the pain. Stephen knew he could leave whenever he wanted, but surgeons had to stay until the supply of wounded dried up, something that was unlikely to happen soon. Weary stewards tried several times to enlist his aid in the church, but he managed to stay away from the church building. He wasn't unsympathetic to the suffering; he wanted to find his pard.

The faces of the men he saw were tired. Their eyes were either fevered or closed forever. Some had died without having been attended at all. Farther from the makeshift hospital, he found blood-soaked clothing and entrails bursting from ruptured bowels in increasing frequency. For no fault but being out of arm's reach, these poor wretches died with no one but their fellow sufferers to comfort them. Thousands lay where they crawled or were dumped by stretcher bearers. Suffering alone was no way to spend the last moments on earth.

Willie could be one of them, and Stephen was compelled to roll over each corpse. Finding one man in the middle of such a host was daunting. Perhaps Willie had already been sent to the rear hospitals and was now jostling painfully in some ambulance on its way back to Corinth, Mississippi. Perhaps he was dead and awaiting burial, though, from the looks of the line of corpses stretched end on end and row after row, Stephen figured that not much had been planned for the burial of so many.

It was maddening to see face after face but not find Willie. No one was keeping records of who was treated or who had been sent rearward earlier in the day. No one knew of a William Hawkins, though he was directed to a host of wounded from the 6th Mississippi. Though the reunions were sweet, they were not the ones he wanted.

Sudden picket firing startled the wounded, and many tried to crawl away from the sound. Stephen froze in place and looked in its direction. It wasn't nearby, but it was close enough to agitate the fear of further wounds. As quickly as it started, the firing ended. He moved on in increasing frustration. Finally, Stephen was as far away from the church building as he cared to wander, and the supply of wounded and corpses thinned to nothing. It had taken hours to comb the grounds. He either missed Willie or Willie was just not there. There was very little to do but hope to stumble upon his pard on his way back to the regiment. Crestfallen, Stephen started back through the wounded and double-checked the faces he passed. There were other farm houses and outbuildings scattered all over the region, and they most assuredly were being used to house the wounded and medical staffs. He didn't have time or strength to visit even one.

The going was slow in the darkness. He had passed this way in the daylight; now everything seemed unfamiliar. He knew the church wasn't far from where they did battle upon the hill that morning because the 6th had marched past it sometime afterward before counter-marching to the rear by afternoon. There were Sibley tents all over the area, and in the dim light of pre-dawn, they all looked the same. The clouds kept the moon hidden but for a little sliver that glowed through the shroud. Half-naked corpses dotted the ground, victims of scavengers looking for booty or replacement clothing. Stephen stopped to decide which set of tents to head toward when he realized he was standing near the ground he had trod after the fight for the hill.

Walking quickly to the edge of the camp, he scrutinized every fold of ground to see if Willie might yet be lying upon the slope. Amid the usual cast off of broken equipment and head gear, nothing on the hill resembled his pard. He walked over to several bushes along the slope but found nothing. It was eerily quiet with none of the sounds that should be associated with this place. Nothing stirred. The top of the slope was littered with paper cartridges and more headgear and uniform parts. A few Federal corpses remained where they fell. Their stomachs protruded from drawers and trousers that now looked too small. They might have looked comical had Stephen not recognized them for distended corpses filling with gas.

Stephen avoided the grisly freak show and wandered into the camp proper where he and his fellow survivors had shouted in elation at the breaking of the enemy and his precipitous flight rearward. There was noise in this ghost camp filled with the dead. Faint whispers, moans, and gurgled breathing came from a few tents.

Stepping up to one large Sibley tent, Stephen pulled the flaps aside and, on a lark, called out, "Willie? Willie Hawkins, 6th Mississippi?"

"Who?" a muffled voice replied.

"William Hawkins, 6th Mississippi," Stephen repeated. The voice was unfamiliar, but in the dark and with the floor crowded with supine figures, Stephen would not have recognized his own father.

"Hammel, 25th Missoura. I think that man over there is from the 6th Mississippi," the voice croaked. "You got any water?"

"No, no I don't. You loyal regiment, or with us?" Stephen asked, though he didn't know why it might make any difference.

"25th Missouri loyal," the voice replied.

"Who else is still alive?" Stephen asked.

"Not sure. Most got quiet some time ago. Your Mississippi man o'er there hasn't moved in hours," Hammel said.

Stephen stepped into the tent. The air was stuffy and smelled like a sink. To get to the man Hammel had pointed to, Stephen was forced to step into the mass of figures and hope that solid ground met his toes. Stepping upon a living form and having to offer apologies for the inconvenience was bad enough. Stepping on a corpse was more than a little unsettling. His skin crawled when he made a misstep and the form under his feet made no noise.

It was easy to tell the man he sought was a Confederate from the lightness of his uniform, compared to the Kersey blue trousers and dark blue sack coats of the Union men. Stephen crouched down to get closer. The man's back was to Stephen, and his front faced the tent wall. Stephen hesitated to touch him.

"Willie, that you?" Stephen asked, hoping the man would respond. "Willie, that you?" he repeated. No response coming, Stephen reached out and grasped the man's shoulder and shook it. Still no response. Stephen tugged harder, but the form would not budge, the reason quickly apparent. The body was cold and stiff.

"He's dead, right?" Hammel asked.

Stephen sat back on his heels and stared at the corpse. "Yes, cold and stiff."

"He your man?" Hammel asked.

"I can't tell in the dark, and I don't want to move him more. Whoever he is, he's gone to meet his maker," Stephen said. He hung his head, eyes closed, and sighed. Stephen could not convince himself to disturb the corpse any further to satisfy curiosity. He would check back at first light or just move on to another tent. It was a large camp, and if all of the tents were full, he would need time to check.

Hammel's breath wheezed out, and he made a hacking sound. "Many done just that today, Reb."

"I don't think it is Willie anyhow," Stephen whispered.

"At leas' you hope it ain't."

Stephen stood up and backed away from the corpse.

"It ain't goin' to do nuthin' to you," Hammel said between fits of coughing.

"Don't matter. It still don't seem right to disturb him."

"Burial detail gonna do worse to it when they come 'round," Hammel replied.

"Why do you care anyhow?"

"Don't."

"Fer someone who don't care, you sure usin' lots of breath."

"Suit yerself, Reb." Hammel said after a pause. "Do me a favor, Reb?"

"What?" Stephen looked at the wounded man.

"Carry me out of this death tent? I want to die at least away from the rest of these departed souls and in some fresher air."

"I ain't gonna carry you far, Yank."

Hammel tried to sit up, but only got as far as supporting himself on his elbows. "No matter. Jus' get me outta here."

Stephen stepped over the corpses and offered his hand. Hammel weakly batted it away.

"I can't get up on my own, Reb. Done tried that." Hammel stared up into Stephen's eyes. Up close now, Stephen could see that he was covered in dried blood from a wound to his head that creased his scalp and ran down both cheeks.

Stephen knelt down, grabbed Hammel by the armpits, and hoisted the dead weight upward. Hammel groaned, and his head flopped down to his chest.

"No wonder I didn't get very far. I'm too dizzy and weak to even sit up."

"C'mon, I've got to get you up farther," Stephen said, and then grunted as he tried to lift the man. "Almost there."

Stephen made another effort to bring Hammel all the way up to his shoulder level. Hammel wasn't helping any. Despite Hammel's suffering, Stephen suddenly felt annoyed at this helpless Yank.

"Oh God, if dyin' outside's going to bring this much . . . ."

"Too late to change yer mind now, Reb." Straining everything he could, Stephen got Hammel up to his chest and swung the man's right arm over his shoulders to steady him. Hammel's head flopped against Stephen's shoulder, his eyes clenched in pain.

"Damn Yank, I better not find stones in those pockets!"

"Just fer you, Reb," Hammel said between breaths.

"I'll make you pay," Stephen grunted as he attempted to take a step. His foot got tangled in a corpse's arm. He nearly lost his balance and sent both of them careening into the tent wall.

"You already have," Hammel returned.

"Good, Yank. I'd say we're even, then," Stephen shook his foot loose and continued on.

"That's Corp'ral Patterson yer kickin, Reb," Hammel muttered. He tried to lift his head to look in Stephen's eyes but couldn't quite complete the motion.

"Sorry," Stephen said and completed his step over the man.

"He was always a laggard."

"Can you take a step?" Stephen asked, half of his body straddling the unfortunate corporal.

"I can try."

Already, Stephen was breathing heavily in the close atmosphere. "You gotta step over the body, or this ain't gonna work. C'mon, I got ya', one foot at a time."

For a moment, both men were silent, other than their labored breathing, and Hammel struggled to take a step forward.

"The deacon would be proud. I'd say this counts as my daily good deed."

"Don't think this gonna do you any good," Hammel said through clenched teeth. "Hell, coulda' been you what shot me."

"Keep not helpin' and there's still time ta shoot you." Hammel brought his last leg over the corpse, kicking it heavily.

"You know, I always did want to kick Paddy ever time I seed him lagging," Hammel said. He managed a laugh amid fits of coughing, "God fergive me the insult and Paddy the thought."

"Save that energy fer the next step, Yank."

"Gettin' through the tent opening's gonna be a trick."

"How 'bout I jus' roll you out?" Stephen grinned at the wounded man. "You'd prolly like to, Reb."

"I'm gonna have to duck down under the flap and drag you along. Ok?"

"Yeah."

Stephen tried to duck down as low as he could go and still hold on to Hammel. The lower he went, the heavier Hammel's weight pressed down. Stephen succeeded in getting his head through the flaps. He couldn't stand upright until he got Hammel's head out, too, and Hammel began to slip off of Stephen's shoulder.

"Hold on!" Stephen barked.

One last effort brought Hammel's head out of the flaps. Stephen straightened, and both men breathed in the cool air.

"Oh, thank God!" Hammel said. "I couldn't take another hour in that tent with that smell of death."

Dawn had broken, and the sun's light painted the eastern clouds orange. The morning was muggy. In the light, Hammel looked worse than Stephen expected. A fresh blood trail moistened his left leg from a reopened wound.

"Well, yer out. Where you want to go?" Stephen asked.

"Home," Hammel said and broke a weak smile.

"I ain't draggin' you to Missouri."

"Then drag me over to them trees." Hammel motioned with his head toward a copse of elms on the outskirts of the camp. It was some distance and would take a while.

"How 'bout I just drag you over to them boxes over there?" Stephen asked.

"All right. Just get me where I can get some shade when it gets hot," Hammel said and closed his eyes.

"Someone'll find you soon enough and take you to a field hospital."

"A good shot of laudanum or quinine with whisky would be nice." His breath grew more ragged.

"You could prolly get some Yankee medicinal from all the captured stores we done got." He laid Hammel by several boxes of smoothbore .69 caliber rounds. The boxes were emptied, and sawdust packing was piled up. Stephen laid Hammel's head on the saw dust.

"Should make a good enough pillow fer a Yank," Stephen said and smiled.

"I'm outta' that damned tent. Anything else is better." He closed his eyes. "God, my head hurts. Who was this deacon you was talkin' about?"

"My pa. He prolly woulda' quoted me lots of the Good Book to show me why I shoulda' he'p'd ya'."

"Well, he weren't here, but I thank you kindly fer the deed, nonetheless."

"No honor in tormenting a wounded enemy. Yer fight's done with anyhow."

They appraised each other for a moment. "I suppose," Hammel said, "I should thank you fer creasing my pate with a musket ball. Saved me havin' to run like a rabbit like the rest of the regiment did."

"You prolly wouldn't think that if you had escaped or been captured. You fellers put up a good fight."

"So, it coulda' been yer musket ball that give me a good scalpin'," Hammel returned.

"Coulda' been. Could also been your round that sent Willie to the ground," Stephen said.

"What would yer deacon pa have to say about that? What wisdom would the Good Book be fer this?"

"Vengeance is mine. If yer enemy strikes you, offer him the other cheek, steals from you, offer him your cloak. Do not sin in your anger." Stephen was pretty sure his father would have more to offer. There really was not much to compare with the oddity of the situation. Two enemies, stripped of their accoutrements and their units, were separated only by their uniforms.

"You fergot love yer neighbor and the Good Samaritan," Hammel said.

"Sure, them, too," Stephen said. He knew those parts of the Good Book, but he had a hard time believing they were relevant here. When did this man become his neighbor? The moment he dropped to the ground from his head wound or when Stephen stumbled upon him? What would the good deacon have to say about that? And did it make any difference? Stephen had no idea.

Chapter Fourteen

"It is a grievous evil, is what it is," John Murdoch said, dropping his fork on the table.

"But, Pa, it has been done. The senate drew up the articles of secession yesterday. It is all but for the vote," Stephen replied.

"That will not make it right, Son. It may have the support of the whole legislature; won't make it right." John sighed and stared silently at Stephen.

Sarah Murdoch spread the table with a smorgasbord of beans, bread, sausage, and a fresh pie, which, for the moment, sat pristine in the center of the table. There was no one to debate with tonight, and no stranger to entertain later with more talk around the fireplace. It was a rare dinner with just family. The strict rules of debate were still in force. Tonight, John seemed preoccupied. Stephen, enjoying his coming of age at the dinner table, was becoming more relaxed in his topic. Not long since first being allowed to participate as a man and adult in the table discussions, he was finding himself on the opposite side of his father tonight. Being a man in the house meant he could take the opposite side now without much fear of reprisal or anger, although tonight might prove to be a different matter.

"Ain't it right if our elected representatives support it by the people's will? Is not this matter one of respect for our chosen authorities?" Stephen countered. It was a question of to whom one should submit allegiance and which authorities were under God's grace. "Is the government in Washington not like Saul, Pa? God withdrew his spirit from Saul and gave it unto David as his chosen leader for Israel. Would it not be just to oppose that which is no longer under God's grace?"

His father answered in a tired and strained voice. "You may indeed be correct in making that comparison, Son. Yet, did not Saul remain king of Israel until he was killed in battle? David had the anointing of Samuel and was by all rights king of Israel, yet he did not raise his hand to even defend himself from his king's treachery. He hid and obeyed the command to respect the authority given unto him, even that of Saul. That man in Washington may not have our support, but he is no less our president, even if he makes war upon us. It is not for us to challenge anyone given authority by God, even if he be an enemy."

"Father, it was they who called up volunteers firstly to respond to the firing on Ft. Sumter. Why, even Virginia is talking secession now. The Old Dominion, Pa, that birthplace of our founding fathers, is going to sever itself from this Union. What other proof is there that this is naught but the will of God for our states?" Stephen felt the flush of unaccustomed victory washing over him. His father was not fighting very hard, but he didn't care; he was of age, and his opinion mattered for something now.

Stephen's father thought a moment before replying. "It matters little what the Old Dominion does or does not do. It matters what Mississippi will do. The firebrands in the capital have inflamed many a clear head toward this detestable goal. It can only lead to war, a war I fear that will not be just or needed."

"But, Pa, if the federal government chooses to oppose the right to sever the Union, then it will lead to conflict. But will it not be a just conflict? Did not God command the Israelites to conquer Canaan? Did they not defend their lands from the Philistine? If we secede, then we will have to defend ourselves."

"Yes, we will defend ourselves, and a war will erupt. The hot heads in South Carolina who not only seceded but also fired upon Ft. Sumter have doomed us to this state of affairs. South Carolina should be left to fend for itself now that it has its independence. We should not follow suit because our passions are inflamed," his father replied.

Elizabeth Murdoch touched John's hand gently, interrupting him. "Dear? It is time for the dessert, and the little ones are getting restless."

"Yes, indeed it is," John replied. Esther, Sarah, and Paul perked up in anticipation of the object of their long-suffering. John portioned out pie slices, which were never large enough to satisfy the smaller children. The discipline of today, he often lectured his children, would produce men and women of tomorrow, and they would know their places in society.

The children served, Stephen took up the discussion again. "The militia is forming in anticipation of a positive vote of secession. They are calling all men up."

"And it will be your duty to respond," John replied, "and mine as well."

"You?" Stephen asked, then regretted.

"I am of serving age in the militia. If it is called out, I will go." John replied. He took a bite of pie.

"Why call out the militia?" Elizabeth exclaimed. "From where would there be any danger?"

"To be prepared for war, Mother." Stephen explained.

"To give the hot heads something to do," John added. "Perhaps if they cool down in the cold and damp, their passions will be dimmed enough for cooler heads to prevail."

Stephen looked his father full in the face. "What if it does come to war?

Better to be prepared for it than not."

"And if it does come to war, it will be in opposition to the authority installed by God over this land. We will be in opposition to God's will for us, and I fear that it will cost us dearly."

"But what if that authority is no longer legitimate? Would we not be better to move from it and not suffer the fate of Israel to the Assyrians? Judah was split from Israel because of a pretender to the throne. What if we are Judah and the holders of the proper anointing of God?"

"But we are under a new covenant, Son. Jesus opposed the Sadducees and Pharisees because they knew the law but did not know Him. All authority is given by God and Christ. Steal a loaf of bread and you have broken not only the commandment but also the parish law. Why?" Steven had heard this refrain before, but he waited for his father to explain how it applied now.

"Because authority has been established," his father continued, "to define what is lawful and what is not. That authority deserves our respect if for no other reason than it is established by God. The federal government in Washington is that authority established and supported by God. It will be wrong to oppose it by force of arms and wrong to secede from it just because someone does not like a policy."

Stephen leaned in, sure that for once he would make a case to correct his father's confident explanation. "But are we not also under the authority of the governor and our representatives whom we send to the capitol?"

"Yes, and by that we will abide, by what our representatives vote on. It will not make it any more right if they choose to secede for all of the reasons stated. We will abide by our representation, but I will lament the decision should it go that way."

John's voice dropped on the last word, and Stephen knew this discussion was over. Stephen didn't know if he had won or lost, as his father had played both sides before growing weary of the discussion.

Last year, Stephen would not have been able to describe any feeling of ill will toward a far-off government. The election did not concern him because he neither owned property nor was of age to vote. He was not affected by the issues now under discussion. But then Lincoln was elected with support from northern free state votes with few southern votes. Suddenly, it was as if the country had experienced something of a renewal. Those who rarely discussed politics were caught up in the intrigue. Most of the folks Stephen knew were disgusted that the federal government might end slavery, something that it had not yet promised or threatened to do.

For Stephen, those were days of discovering his patriotism, mirrored by that of his fellow Mississippians, and finding something new: secession. He was caught up in it, despite his father's obvious disdain for the clamoring for separation. All the youth were mobilized by the thought of a separate entity where protections guaranteed by the constitution were paramount and the control of the federal government was curtailed or non-existent. He suddenly became an expert on constitutional law, as was anyone willing to listen at the post office or the church steps. Most agreed that the only answer was to secede to protect the right of the states to determine their own course. The Black Republicans, a derisive term given to the wing of the fledgling Republican Party, whose sole purpose was to emancipate every slave in the South, were in power for one purpose only, and they were put in power without a single Southern vote. Their goal was to rip away a century of culture and economics, even society itself, for the base purpose of satisfying their own decadent and misguided morality.

There he was, a year or so later, standing in the middle of a camp whose remaining tenants were either dead or nearly so, and all for the pursuit of the freedom to choose whether or not to own slaves. It was this freedom that drove him and his fellows into the ranks of an army of Americans who sought to make their own way apart from the constitutional authority of those in Washington, DC. They had their own constitution now, their own president, and their own army.

And now they were on the verge of their own victory, at least for the western army. While God may have smiled upon the eastern Confederates, God was apparently unaware of their western brethren. Albert S. Johnston was sent west to bring order and victory to Confederate arms in Tennessee. Finally, they would throw off the shroud of defeat for good.

Stephen looked across the tents he needed to scour to find his pard, but the breaking of daylight only meant the quickening of the hostilities. It was time to get moving lest some provost detail should come along and herd him back to his regiment as a skulker.

*****

Across the damp landscape, the opposing sides were shaking themselves out after a long, rainy night. Skirmishing along the line sputtered out as both sides tired of shooting at shadows. The skirmishers of the 24th Ohio braced themselves to begin the fight anew. Philip shivered as the blue of dawn revealed the surroundings in more detail. The stump that might have been a crouching Rebel skirmisher was now only a stump. He could see it several yards away, cut with holes. Philip shook his head at the many times in the dark he had fired into it, thinking it was a Rebel.

They had been on the skirmish line now for five hours, and he ached from the time spent lying prone in the damp. He was soaked. Despite the excitement several hours ago, Philip was groggy and fighting sleep. The enemy had been too close to pull normal picket duty. The skirmish line had been spread out with each man alert for any perceived enemy push. They were the early warning for the regiment and the screen that kept the enemy from finding out too much detail as to what lay behind. It was trying work.

The morning air was cold, and his breath billowed out in puffs. His blankets and gear lay in the rear with the regiment where he longed to hang his sack coat and trousers to dry while he wrapped himself in his wool blanket. But it was not to be. Not even the regiment had the luxury of drying itself out but was, instead, being roused to make coffee. This had been a singular experience for Philip and the rest of the brigade. Although the fighting and the repairing to encamp had always been near the enemy, never did they do so in such close proximity as during the last night. Picket details kept wary eyes on one another as the armies moved back and forth, dodged and parried one another, and attempted to bring their enemy to battle. Picket lines were often established a mile or two away, and they maintained contact with the main forces. Should the enemy suddenly advance, pickets could alert the army long before the enemy was able to attack. Word had it that Grant's army placed the picket line too close to the main force and had suffered for that oversight.

But the skirmishing through the night was something new. Even on picket one could rest as long as someone from the detail was awake. The men on the skirmish line could not rest.

The enemy's skirmishers were still invisible. Philip wondered if they had actually been out this close. Fire begets fire, he knew, and nervousness often produces phantom assailants. If the enemy was out there, they would soon start firing again.

"Now would be a good time to get relief," Sammy said. "If they don't do it soon, we won't be able to move without being fired upon."

"Smell that?" Mule asked.

"Smell what?" Philip replied.

"Coffee. They makin' coffee."

They smelled the air. It was coffee.

"They pull us off soon," Johnny assured him.

"Not soon enough," Mule said. "I just want a mug of something warm. I'm chilled to the bone."

"If you weren't almost six foot, Mule, I'd suspect you was a delicate city boy," Sammy said and laughed.

Mule shot him a pleading look. "Ain't nuthin' wrong with a little comfort!"

"Why we still here?" Johnny asked. "We shoulda' been pulled off hours ago! Skirmishin' is hot work." They nodded in agreement. "Captain must be all nice and comfy in a tent back there as I ain't seed him since we were thrown out here."

"I saw him go down the line during the firing a couple hours ago," Philip said and looked over his shoulder. "See, he's there behind us."

Johnny spit on the ground and grimaced. "If they keep tarrying, we'll be on this line fer sure once full light hits."

"I don't know about you," Mule said, "but I can't stop shiverin', and my teeth is chatterin' awful."

"They'll fetch us back," Philip reassured them, though without conviction. He didn't place much faith in military thoroughness or fairness. There was always a sense that some fatigue detail was too long and that some companies were favored when details and dirty work were assigned. Perhaps someone did forget to call them in, or perhaps the major was punishing their captain for some personal slight. Whatever the reason, they had been on the skirmish line far too long and would be useless in the coming fight if not allowed to rest.

Before frustration and fatigue could turn to despair, they heard their captain's call. "Company, prepare to fall in on the regiment!"

Behind them, another company spread out in skirmish formation and advanced on their position. Philip stood and almost fell over. After lying prone for so many hours, his legs were stiff and weak. He made his way on unsteady legs to where the regiment gathered in formation. It was the relief they had sought, but it looked to be short lived. The other companies had fallen in line and were shaking themselves out in front of the rifle stacks. This could only mean they were preparing to break those stacks and move out.

Their own company formed up at the end of the regimental line and dressed down. Then, much to Philip's surprise, their captain gave the order to stack muskets. He heard a collective sigh of relief as the men eagerly created the teepee-like rifle stacks with intertwined bayonets. Everyone knew the next command, an order that no soldier was reluctant to obey.

"Rest!"

Fatigued and drenched, the company broke in a collective stagger toward their knapsacks in the rear of the regimental line. Bedrolls were unfurled and dry undershirts unpacked. Someone started a company cook fire, and men were quick to find their tin cups. Mule was beside himself.

*****

Across the dead space separating the foes, a messenger charged up to Captain Michael Grierson with messages concerning the day's hostilities. Michael suddenly found himself in command of the whole battery. Captain Polk had succumbed to the wound in his leg and relinquished command to Michael. Frustration over being a subordinate evaporated, but the change in position came with responsibility. Michael had to determine where the other sections of guns were located and their deportment. Orders from General Polk and Major Bankhead, Polk's chief of artillery for the corps, followed in quick succession.

The enemy was making a fresh start upon their lines and would soon be in front of the battery. Was the infantry still out there? The morning fog from the late evening rain hung thick upon the ground, limiting visibility to a few tens of yards. Should the enemy appear out of the thick, the battery would be in dire straits. Through the fog, Michael heard firing begin to the right and roll in their direction.

"Lieutenant," Michael yelled to Lieutenant Young, "take command of the section and prepare the guns for action! Captain Polk has been carried from the field, and I must find his section."

"Sir," the young man replied and hurried off, barking orders as he went.

Mahoney gave Michael a look of concern and a quick tip of his hat in recognition of the gravity of Michael's sudden elevation in command. It was one thing to handle a section well in battle, but another to command the whole battery and have the eyes of the generals upon you. Captain Polk's orders were to bring the battery into action on the front of Cheatham's division, somewhere off to the right of where the other section stood in battery. Sounds of battle rumbled in that direction. Michael noted the brigades of marching men shaking themselves out in battle lines and the bustle of couriers ferrying orders to and fro from the headquarters. The men still had a tired look to them, but they moved with purpose. The rumble off to the left only added animation to their movements.

Yards away and separated by a wood, the lines were engaged in hot fighting. Scattered wounded and dead lay where they fell. Michael wished he could re-unite the battery, but by the sounds of it, they were committed where they stood. The familiar flags of the 2nd Divisional HQ of Polk's Corps fluttered into sight, and officers and cavalry clustered nearby. Passing the gaggle of braided sleeves and star-studded collars, Michael rode cautiously through the wood toward the booming of cannon. He nearly lost his hat to low-hanging branches and soon reached the cacophony of shouts and whizzing lead.

Two batteries were playing upon the advancing lines of blue but were being pounded in return by enemy guns unlimbered defiantly ahead of their own infantry. Enemy gunners worked their pieces like men possessed. Report after report shook the ground in succession of delivery and receipt. The enemy's columns filled the open space, and his skirmishers pushed forward. It didn't take Michael long to see that this side of the line needed help.

Heedless of the lead hissing by his ear, Michael spurred toward the other section of Polk's battery where men worked their guns with equal fury. Michael spied Lieutenant Parker, hatless, sporting a gash along his scalp and a trickle of blood running down his cheek.

"Parker!" Michael shouted as he ran up to his subordinate, "We're about to be taken enfilade. The enemy's brought up another battery on the left to that rise over there!"

"Sir, we're playing with all we have. We won't be able to hold for long," shouted Parker.

"Detail the leftmost piece to respond to that battery as soon as it unlimbers! Reinforcements are coming, but you're right, we're about to be overrun. How are your limbers? We're far away from our supplies."

"Limbers are full, but if the enemy pushes us, we'll have to leave some. We've lost ten horses in the last minutes, and I won't have much to retrieve the battery with if we have to leave quickly."

The fire of the enemy batteries concentrated on them. Bankhead's battery opened from a position one hundred yards to their right. Solid shot bounded through the caissons and took off the tops of nearby trees.

Over the noise, Parker shouted, "How is the other section?"

"In good spirits and unengaged when I left them, but the fight is moving their way. They are posted near that church."

Parker shouted to a harried-looking non-commissioned officer working the number one piece. "Sergeant Smith! Turn Number Three toward that enemy battery on the left and open on them with solid shot," Turning back to Michael, he asked, "How is Captain Polk?"

"I don't know. I saw him last night after dark. He was getting around and refusing to go to the aid station."

A cheer heralded the arrival of another brigade, and the infantry moved forward to meet those of the enemy, who had come even with his batteries and had begun to advance past them.

Michael pointed at the battery in the center of the enemy forces. "Now's the time to hit that battery there with explosive while they can't fire over their own lines."

The Union regiments, marching in front of his own batteries, masked their fire, giving Michael's section some breathing room.

"Battery!" Parker shouted as he ran from gun to gun. "Three-second fuses, counter-battery fire, fire for effect at the center battery!"

Loaders hustled forward with cone-shaped charges. Gun commanders measured and cut the fuses. The guns were loaded and fired as if nothing had interrupted their work. Puffs of smoke burst above the enemy guns. Everything below the explosions was showered with shrapnel.

"Adjust your elevation, Number Two!" Parker shouted.

Just as quickly, rounds began to crash around them from the enemy battery on the right. The number three gun responded in kind, but it was to be an unequal contest. The enemy's center battery was helpless to respond, with the Federal infantry blundering too close to their line of fire. It was their turn to suffer fire they could not return. Muskets from opposing lines of infantry cut loose upon one another. The situation looked as if it might turn to the better. Bankhead's battery was free to play upon the rightmost enemy battery, relieved of the pressure from the meddlesome center battery, which was now diving for cover.

Wounded and otherwise healthy-looking men filed by the battery in ones and twos from the infantry line fifty yards ahead. Without warning, a flood of panic-stricken men ran past the battery's left, followed by their colors and several screaming officers. Whether by hint of disaster or premonition of defeat, the regiments next in line also began to disintegrate. A roaring cheer echoed from the enemy lines, and a general advance began.

"Load canister! Load for canister!" Parker shouted.

Now it was their turn to sit helpless while their front was masked by their own fleeing infantry. Staff officers darted among the fugitives and saber whipped several groups to form a line. Those out of reach turned tail and continued the retreat. On the right, the lines were still exchanging fire. As each successive regiment had its left uncovered and open to the oblique fire of the enemy, the Confederate line dissolved.

"We need to slow them down!" Michael shouted to Parker, "but get the caissons ready to move!"

The enemy infantry marched triumphantly forward, freed to have a go at Michael's unprotected section of guns. The last of the retreating regiments cleared their front, and the guns began firing toward the approaching lines of the enemy. They were still out of musket range, but only barely. A volley of canister thrown into the enemy slowed their advance but did little more. The Confederate regiments to the right had begun to pull back slowly, fighting as they moved.

"We need to hold them a little longer, Lieutenant!" Michael shouted. "When they get into range, charge with double canister and let them have it!"

At best, canister range was slightly greater than musket range; double charge shortened that distance. The enemy would need to be close for full effect. Cheering, the enemy regiments pushed forward and entered that arc of deadly space where foes meet one another on equal footing. It would be five hundred muskets against double canister-loaded cannon, an equality that would last only for a single volley. Michael had to make it count if the guns were to be saved.

Chapter Fifteen

The church steeple Robert could see through the mist reminded him that this place was once peaceful farm land.

"Guide is left. Left!" shouted the captain as the 36th Indiana's line undulated in a serpentine manner.

Robert was already sweating. Steam rose off the shoulders of the man next to him, moisture from his damp wool sack coat evaporating in the morning sunlight. Fog was lifting along the trees and dissipating in the light. Booming cannon and musket fire thundered ahead. The men were excited but anxious. These Indianans were still green, despite having caught some small glimpse of the elephant the evening before. The hungry maw of the beast was ahead. Robert marched again into the face of battle but without his comrades at his side. Huebner was several paces away, as were the other men of his beloved 25th Missouri. That was home. They were family. The Indiana men around him exuded a naïve desire to pitch into the battle. They had something to prove, mainly that they were soldiers worthy of their calling.

Deafening musketry volleys and singing lead informed them of the struggle beyond the pall of smoke. He heard a Rebel yell over the cannon fire, sounding more like the shrill yipping of crazed animals than the voices of men. The yell reminded him that the enemy was in earnest and in good spirits. The sound turned his blood cold. The enemy was winning on this field.

The regiment broke through the curtain of smoke to face a field full of butternut and gray. Ahead of them, a brigade was advancing into the storm. Rebel batteries fired into the masses of blue-coated soldiers. When one brigade was unable to stand the tempest's pounding, another brigade took its pace. Flags fluttered in the centers of the regiments. The number of standards suggested to Robert the number of brigades and divisions arrayed against one another.

The regiment marked time nervously. Their glee at seeing battle once more melted in the face of horrible combat. The brigade in their front advanced steadily and bled a string of casualties. Men writhed or were stilled as they fell. Robert knew they would either charge and break the enemy or halt and be broken. Shots of grape and canister tore gaps in the double line formations, laying dozens low. Bravely, the men would cover down until the gap closed. Piles formed of broken bodies that were once healthy and stalwart humanity. If this brigade succeeded, they would be spared the chore of advancing into that cauldron.

The brigade advancing on its right halted and delivered a volley. The colors rose and fell to rise and fall again. The best men in the regiments, whose honor it was to carry the colors, stood to their duty, knowing full well they were the target of hundreds of muskets. Each fall meant that a brave man died, and each rise meant another brave man took his place. The brigade in front kept up their advance alone. Each step carried those regiments closer to delivering a volley into the ranks of the enemy.

The men in the Indiana ranks cheered from relief and from admiration for the men facing the sheets of flame and lead. The brigade covering its flank turned and marched back from where it came, leaving the other brigade of some hundreds of Union men alone to the work. Naked and drawing flank fire from the left, the lone brigade, too, stopped and delivered a volley, hoping to accomplish something, anything, for the price it paid in blood to get there. The *hurrahs* ceased. The unequal contest could have but one result.

The man next to Robert shouted "Look!" and pointed left.

Prodded by its officers, the brigade had regrouped. It marched forward once again to aid its sister brigade alone on the field.

Tired and gravelly throats shouted encouragement, and many uttered prayers. The regiments advanced as if into a strong wind. The men leaned toward their enemy. It was too late. The brigade disintegrated into a mob of fleeing blue. They had had enough. The second brigade halted but a few moments before slowly back-pedaling to cover the retreat. Exhausted and demoralized men galloped back toward and through the Indianans. The war was just ahead, and it was their turn to fight.

Robert had done this before. One stood in formation with every muscle tingling and the stomach in knots. When they received the order to advance, every man had to decide to go forward despite the danger. One did it because the fellow next to him did it, and so on down the line. These green Indiana men had an even greater reason. Not a man among them wanted to show the white feather of cowardice. They would march to the gates of Hades without the prodding of file closers. But even they, in their eagerness to prove themselves, had to take a moment to view the scene and wonder whether valor required a foolhardy charge into destruction.

Robert searched the faces of his pards to know their state of mind. Hildebrande and Gustavson were gone, the two old fighters and soldiers whom everyone in the company looked to in times of fear. They were the real veterans. They always stood to their posts in a way that caused Robert to admire their stalwart and stern countenance. He and the others from the 25th

Missouri were townsmen and patriotic to the core, but they were not professional soldiers. Piper looked worried, and Huebner looked scared and mouthed words that Robert did not follow. The other men were downcast. They knew that nothing would prevent their own march into the fire. How many would fall? How many would make it to the enemy's line? How many would never leave this field again?

They were a strong brigade, both in numbers and attitude. They would prove themselves or die trying. The big bugs, those with the shoulder straps who rode the horses in the rear of any line, would have their own superiors watching from glasses even farther to the rear. On it would go, down to the privates praying for deliverance from the pain of a minié ball wound.

Battle meant death, and death meant a departure from the pain of an earthly existence. Had each man made his peace with his maker? Would the cannon fire rend flesh from bone, or would a bullet crush the bone of an arm or leg, rendering it useless? Robert preferred to not think at all. Hildebrande always told them to follow orders and do what needed to be done. He realized that his small band of survivors might be broken up even smaller after this attack played out. Who would survive to collect his pards for final burial? Was he ready for the final reward?

The field quieted, save for the playing of the batteries on both sides. The space between the foes was torn and bleeding. Reinforcements were sorted out, and the regiments of the brigade shifted to form one long line of blue. The enemy stood to their weapons a hundred yards away. Another brigade emerged from the woods behind Robert and formed front—the next wave should this effort fail. The advance had to be made and the enemy well met.

War was fought in no other way but to close with the enemy and try his mettle. It mattered little that each man was a part of some other family in cities and communities all across the North and West. It mattered nothing that each man felt within his heart trepidation at taking that first step forward. They were no longer just men. They were soldiers, volunteers to a cause to reunite a sundered country. They were now 36th Indiana or 25th Missouri or some other designation. They would march and deliver their fire, standing the test until ordered to fall back or to charge forward.

Robert drew a deep breath, and the silence became oppressive. The church steeple, a simple cross that had survived the first day of conflict, now showed clearly above the tree tops. Ahead, the enemy looked at him and silently watched and waited. No one jeered; no one taunted or sullied the test of courage wrought upon this field. They would each to his own soon yell, shout, curse, and fire or swing the butt of a rifle in anger and desperation. For the moment, though, they gave each other a grudging respect.

The brigade color guard trooped forward twenty paces and halted. The moments ticked by. With the colors in front and in the most immediate harm, what man of them would deign to hang back now? The 36th Indiana's own color guard was trooped forward, and all was ready for the general advance in grand style. Robert's stomach tightened. There could be only one command remaining. Then they would tread this field of valor.

*****

"Drag it away! We've not enough mounts!" Lieutenant Parker shouted as the caissons were limbered up to the remaining horses in the battery. The enemy regiments were advancing cautiously, checked by the fire of canister into their ranks. But the guns were lost if a moment longer elapsed in the work of firing them. With trained precision, the battery moved from action stations to limbering for a hurried movement to the rear. The horses were brought from the picket line. With the injuries sustained along the picket line, four horses, rather than the typical six, were hooked to each cannon. None were available to pull the final cannon.

"We can't save it, and we've got no infantry left to help haul it off," Michael shouted in reply. "Spike it!"

As the last gun they could save was discharged and the caisson rolled up to retrieve it, Lieutenant Parker shouted, "They're going to make a go for us!" They fired the gun they could not save, and the enemy line surged forward with a shout.

Sergeant Hughes, the gun commander, grabbed the iron spike and jammed it into the touch hole. Sergeant Phipps prepared to hammer it down. The rest of the gun crew ran for the rear, leaving Parker, Michael, and Hughes looking aghast as Sergeant Phipps suddenly tumbled to the ground.

To leave a gun on the field was like leaving one's colors in the hands of the enemy. Although cannon sometimes had to be left behind when the fighting was hard and horses were not available, leaving a gun whole and un-spiked was something that could not happen. The enemy ran to capture the gun that seemed in easy reach. Sergeant Hughes hopped over the gun tail and retrieved the sledge hammer. Lieutenant Parker ran forward with revolver and sword drawn. The race was on. Michael wanted to tell them to hurry, to forget about the gun and save themselves, but knew he would be doing the same thing. The gun could still be successfully spiked if Sergeant Hughes could just have a few more seconds to wield the hammer.

A Federal captain raced ahead of his men and demanded that Lieutenant Parker surrender his sword. To shoot the captain would buy some time but would be tantamount to murder when surrender was offered. Michael was helpless to reach the gun in time to prevent or alter the outcome. He knew that Parker was a chivalrous officer who would do what was right. As Hughes swung the hammer to let it fall upon the spike, Parker dropped his revolver and handed his sword to the captain, raising his hands in ascension to the demand. The Union men, distracted by their new prisoner, gave Hughes time to drive the spike into the touch hole.

Michael knew there was nothing more he could do. He raced to his mount several yards beyond the lost gun and swung into the saddle. With a last look behind him, he saw the enemy swarming the gun and capturing Sergeant Hughes. But they had spiked it, making it useless to the enemy, and that was enough to salvage the battery's honor.

Michael raced Charger through the tree line. His hope to make it back to his old battery evaporated when Lieutenant Parker was captured. The field where Michael had encountered Cheatham's divisional HQ was now bustling with regiments. Screaming officers tried to rally their charges into another defensive line. The battery was shaking itself loose between two brigades of infantry, and Michael cleared the trees, hurrying to take station.

A new defensive line was forming three hundred yards past the trees atop a slope. Michael reined up behind the new gun line and leapt off Charger. His race across the field was the only reconnaissance they would get. The ground undulated like a series of frozen waves. The ground was not ideal; the undulations would provide cover for the enemy's approach and offer only quick glimpses of him as he crested each small hill. The guns would need short fuses to explode above the approaching lines.

"Lieutenant Gibbs," Michael shouted to the second lieutenant overseeing the placement of the caissons, "you are in command. Parker has been captured."

The nervous lieutenant swallowed. "Sir?"

Each officer and non-com knew he might be faced with the sudden ascension to command, but attrition among the officers had not treated this section well.

The men moved listlessly, as if mired in mud. They were exhausted and looked as if they had been on the receiving end of hours of pounding by enemy guns. They were fit only for the rear, but Bankhead's battery on their left did not appear to be in any better shape.

"That ground is going to give us trouble. Use explosive with short fuses. Try four-second fuses as they are forming, thirty degree elevation, and start from there!"

His orders completed, Michael remounted. He wanted to find General Cheatham and another battery to either relieve or augment what they had. Cheatham was not hard to find. Riders coming and going belied the location of the new divisional HQ. To Michael's surprise, Major Bankhead was also there.

"Grierson, how is Polk's battery faring?" Bankhead asked.

Michael offered a tentative salute. "Sir, Section One here needs relief and now. They are moving like they're knee deep in water. We lost one gun to the enemy and two men. The gun was successfully spiked. Sir, I respectfully request permission to pull them from the line."

"Denied, Captain. No fresh batteries anywhere on this end of the field. They will have to make do."

"Sir, this is horrible ground. The guns won't be able to play upon the enemy due to all that low ground. They will be upon us before we can respond effectively and that only if the men are alert."

"I understand your protest, Captain," Bankhead said levelly, "but there isn't anything to replace them with. They are holding on the right of our line by the church. We have to hold here, or the whole field will be lost."

"Sir," Michael said with another salute. He remounted Charger and wheeled about.

Just when he made it back to the section, the enemy emerged from the trees and formed up across their front. An unending line of blue started forward in line of battle. Michael saw a second line of Union blue emerge from the trees and knew that this was going to be a temporary holding place before they would be forced to retreat once more. Though the gun crews stood to their pieces, they did so as if asleep on their feet. The fighting died down off to their right where Bankhead stated the line was holding firm.

A quiet descended upon this place of conflict and death, but it brought no comfort. Birds began to sing again, perhaps convinced that the fuss below them was over. Except for the enemy line's approach, Michael could nearly convince himself it truly was a peaceful Monday morning.

The flags dotting the dark blue told of the enemy's numbers. Michael counted ten stands of colors, and that was just the first line. The enemy's colors were separated by a frightful distance, the intervening space, Michael knew, filled with enemy and fresh regiments to oppose the fatigued and whittled-down regiments of Cheatham's command.

The ground had been won the day before when the enemy had retired from it. To be forced to vacate it now when victory was in grasp was more than any man would concede easily, even one haggard by lack of sleep and constant marching into danger. To Michael's thinking, though, they had little to gain from pretending they might be able to hold the enemy at bay this time.

Michael dismounted slowly and handed the reins to one of the enlisted men detailed to care for the battery's horses in the rear. The loaders were lounging on their caissons and did not stir as he strode past them. Their job would have them run from gun to caisson and back again shortly. If the enemy was to be stopped, each opportunity to shoot into the crowded formations had to have effect.

Michael surveyed the broken men around him and sighed. "Gibbs, make sure the gun commanders pick their targets well. That field isn't going to allow for massing our fire. Make sure they understand it is up to them."

"Sir, they know their business," the young subaltern replied. "I'll tell them they are on their own for targets and fire."

Michael's work done, he had nothing to do but stand and watch. He learned the art well from Mahoney. Mahoney didn't seem to mind taking a back seat to his less-educated upstart. But Mahoney's direction and training in the regulars made the battery an efficient instrument of war and Michael an expert commander with an eye for terrain and logistics. Now, his eye for terrain told him this was not the place to make a stand.

Artillery was a curious weapon. Impersonal, it delivered fire safely out of reach of the mass of enemy musketry, but at the same time was only able to lob shells at the general direction of the enemy. Solid shot was good for disabling enemy cannon or bowling down a section of his line. Explosives showered him with shrapnel, and the bursts from above played upon his psyche. A cannon's greatest effect was in close quarters fighting. Though the gunners were in range of muskets, they could deliver deadly blasts of canister and grape shot into the masses, taking down entire formations with one blast. The other effect was to demoralize the enemy with long-range fire. It produced few casualties, but the mental strain created by the explosions and watching the twirling and sputtering cannon balls come at them was as potent as laying scores low. To demoralize an enemy before he could even respond with his own fire was the hallmark of artillery. Michael could not see how this was going to be achieved here.

"They are goin' to roll over us, ain't they?" Gibbs asked as he watched the enemy advance.

Michael nodded in reply. "I don't think we can stop 'em."

The section tensed as each gun commander watched and waited for the right moment to order the lanyard to be pulled. Each gun was at the ready, and the crews stood alert at their stations. The commanders stood frozen with arms raised, ready to give the signal.

Parts of the enemy's line disappeared for moments at a time as his regiments moved over rise and into valley. Bankhead's battery spoke first, farther down the line. All else was still. Cheatham's regiments waited for the enemy to come within musket range. Horses neighed and absently pawed the pitiful remnants of the oats scattered about. Here a man coughed, or there a tin cup banged against a bayonet in a hollow clink. Conversation halted. Michael scratched at his chin and felt the days of stubble upon his cheeks and chin. They were all a little worse for wear, and it was about to get worse still.

Chapter Sixteen

"Philip, we're marching off." A voice interrupted Philip's sleep.

"Uh? What?" Philip mumbled. He forced himself to sit up, the blanket rolling into his lap.

"We're going back to rejoin the regiment," Sammy said with a motion toward the company forming line.

Philip groaned. "That weren't near enough time to rest."

"No time fer vespers, Rev," Sergeant Harper said and sneered.

"Pity there's no time to save what soul you got left, Harper," Philip snapped back.

The fog of drowsy, dreamless sleep hung heavy upon Philip's eyes. It was time to gather his traps and prepare to march, but his body was not yet ready to move.

"C'mon, pard, we got to get moving," Johnny said. He started to pack Philip's knapsack.

"Ok, I'm moving, I'm moving." Philip rose and shooed Johnny away from his knapsack. "I got an order that stuff goes into this."

"Knew that would get you off your butt."

"Any coffee brewed?"

"Ha! Mule done downed it all."

Philip began straightening his spare shirt and socks into the proper compartment. All that he claimed as his own was in this small, sometimes burdensome, bundle. It contained his Testament and prayer book, his changes of drawers and dry socks, candles, foot and crotch powder, and any spare food that would not fit well into his haversack. As many men did when winter gave way to spring, he had sent his overcoat home. An enlisted man was given no baggage but what he could carry upon his back, and Philip was glad not to have to carry the heavy coat.

Mule looked at Philip and shrugged. "Didn't want it to go to waste."

"Here," Johnny said, reaching out with his cup. "I've still got some in my cup. It's cold but still got some of the good stuff in it fer a wake-up."

Philip took the cup and looked inside. The liquid in its bottom was oily and black, but for a more civilized existence would have been tossed out the nearest window. But a soldier relied upon only a few things: his morning cracker, salt pork or beef, and his coffee. Philip quickly tilted the cup and allowed the cold bitter liquid to wash his tongue and slide down his throat. It was not the satisfying sip of a steamy cup where the edges of the tin were still too hot to press against tender lips, but it was a jolt, nonetheless.

Grimacing, Philip handed the cup back to Johnny with a nod of appreciation.

Philip finished ordering his knapsack. He rolled up his gum and wool blanket and tied it to the top, for the blanket had to be put back into line with the rest of the company gear. His clothes were still damp, and he shivered as he donned the rest of his gear from the rifle stack and went to stand in line. The company was soon ready to resume its rightful place with the rest of its regiment. They were men who were used to marching and making temporary homes wherever they stopped. Hardened by privation, marching, and hours of mind-numbing drill, the men were disciplined to react and to wear army regulation and decorum like an ill-fitted but comfortable suit.

The company commander, Captain George Bacon, ordered the men to fall in, and with a few moments of rustling, the company coalesced into a rigid formation of two ranks.

"I trust the good Private Pearson will say a few words for us to the Lord on our behalf as we rejoin our regiment and face the enemy. Um, let's rejoin the colors," Captain Bacon said somewhat sheepishly before ordering the company to count twos.

Bacon was new to command. Commissioned only two months before, the man tried to hide the fact that command was as uncomfortable as the gloves he wore. The gauntlets were gangly upon his wrists, and his former pards knew it. He kept trying to hide his hands behind his back, being too proud of the special gauntlets his wife had made for him. Unfortunately for Bacon, he had bragged for weeks that his wife was making him the articles. Philip supposed he was too stubborn and ashamed to admit they were an unsightly nuisance.

"God save us from the Rev's prayers," Harper said quietly from the rear rank to muffled titters from several men.

"Quiet in the ranks!" Bacon ordered. "Right face!"

Marching columns formed of four-man ranks. The company peeled off and left the token guard behind to sit and do nothing but make sure scavengers would not disturb the company knapsack line. It was time to leave yet another temporary way-point and move out. This march would lead them directly into harm's way, though avoiding a toilsome day of trudging along and trying to ignore the pain from carrying their gear.

The irregular tromp of sixty feet upon the grass and the explosion of cannon fire ahead kept them company as they left behind the litter on the old skirmish line and marched off into the unknown. Though they were no longer so green, they were not seasoned veterans either, as one comes to measure the quality and steadfastness of a regiment in the line. The men carried themselves as if they had survived numerous engagements, especially compared to the greenhorn 36th Indiana. Cheat Mountain, Greenbrier River in West Virginia, Nashville, and now this place in Tennessee had introduced them to serious peril. Being the more experienced, the Ohio men loved to treat their Indiana comrades to exaggerated tales of fear and heroism.

The company neared the unseen point of contact between the opposing armies. Thunderous volleys barked, accompanied by hoarse cheering. Though they couldn't yet see it, they knew the battle had been joined.

"Them Indiana boys is gettin' a taste of it, fer shore," Sammy muttered

"They learnin' what fools they were," Johnny replied, "and what that elephant can do to a man."

Philip shook his head at Johnny. "They do fine. Them Indiana men is good stock. Westerners from farm country like us."

"Not all of us," Sergeant Harper spoke out.

"Every company gotta have its black sheep and brother of that black sheep," Philip retorted.

Harper sneered back at Philip and said, "You gonna enjoy bein' worm food with me in Hell, fer that's all that is gonna come of you. You forgetting that you is to love your neighbor lest you anger your God."

"God will damn you, Harper," Philip said with such anger that spittle flew from his mouth. "He'll damn you to the depths of Hades, you and all your parents' evil brood! Would that your bloodline could be ended on this field. No one would shed a tear at the passing of the Harper line."

Philip clenched the rifle sling on his right shoulder. The anger and shame at that one act all those years ago was still bearing its bitter fruit. Philip knew he had been right. Was he to lie? Was he to ignore the life lived in depravity and just give platitudes to the grieved? Should not they learn from a wicked man's life and give up their evil ways?

"Philip! You can't mean that," Mule said with a horrified expression. He quickly crossed himself.

"Even the detestable papist here knows better than to do that!" Harper said gleefully.

Mule took Philip by the arm. "Philip, go make absolution to God fer that insolence. Not even the Pope dares to curse someone to Hell."

"Oh, but see there, my good Pope follower," Harper said. "The good Reverend is better than the Pope, and anyone else in Rome, fer that matter. He must have some special dispensation with the Almighty that even your Pope doesn't have."

"I didn't lie to your mother when I said her no-good son was destined to rot in Hell for eternity. I won't shrink back from telling you that what my father said is surely true. There never was, never will be, a Harper worth but a damn!"

Mule pulled at his arm. "Philip, I . . . ."

"Quiet in the ranks!" First Sergeant Brooks ordered.

Each man within ear shot had been listening to the exchange. Now they had only the sound of their feet and the growing growl of battle ahead to occupy their thoughts. Philip brooded fiercely. That Harper incident had cost him his pulpit. It had been pride and self-righteous anger that had prevented him from saying what everyone wanted to hear, and it kept his mouth shut now. As a man of God, he was not allowed that pride, but it wormed its way into his thoughts and actions nonetheless.

Of all of the things that reminded Philip of his mistakes and misdeeds from his youth, Harper was the most constant reminder that Philip was indeed human and fallible. But being human and fallible was not enough for a man of God, or at least he thought.

Sammy leaned in his direction and whispered, "Ignore that dog."

"That's just it. I've ignored it too long, and neither of us is content to let the other be."

"Right now ain't the time to go un-ignoring it. That man is going to find some way to get satisfaction from the insult, and battle is going to be the time he chooses."

"If he wants to shoot me from behind, he's going to have to do it for the whole company to see," Philip replied.

"Just don't go and lose heart and make fer the rear. Then Harper won't need an excuse to cut you down," Sammy said.

"I wouldn't give him the satisfaction! Besides, he's not stupid. The penalty for murder is death, and he's not about to cut his own life short. He'd leave me to die in a heartbeat but he won't pull the trigger."

"You might also square things up with Mule," Sammy said. "You threw him fer a loop, I think."

"What do you mean?" Philip asked.

"He may be a papist and all, but you're still the closest link to God he's got, and he didn't get mass the other day."

"You're joking, right?" Philip looked incredulous and shook his head. "Mule knows we's all goin' to Hell if we ain't Catholic. That's why he won't attend Sunday vespers with the Protestants in the brigade. That's why that priest has to come from Division so's the Catholics can get absolution. He can't put much stock in me, a defrocked Methodist minister."

"Don't know much about all that, but Mule sure looks up to you in some strange way." Sammy looked away and took a deep breath. "Fact is, all of us from the county in this regiment do, aside from that brigand, Harper."

"Well, most of you were under my father. He's the real guiding light of the conclave."

"Your father ain't here right now. You is."

"Well, then everybody knows I'm just a man like I was before, no special calling and no special gift," Philip protested. "I'm just Private Pearson and a man susceptible to sin like everyone."

"That may be so, but you're still the vicar from the conclave most of us hail from. You can't escape that."

Philip fell silent. He had wanted to be just a regular man back when he did wear the cloth. But he knew he'd never escaped it, as everyone still treated him as if he were one of the regimental clergy, charged with seeing to their spiritual well-being. It was in his quiet demeanor and in his knowledge of applying holy writ to everyday problems. Philip tried to keep his mouth shut about things that he no longer felt a need to oversee, but his former parishioners would not let him off the hook. It was all he could do to keep some from electing him captain of the company when it formed. He was through with being in charge.

"So, how long you gonna keep playin' Jonah?" Sammy asked.

Philip gave him a wry look in return. "God didn't give me any word to spread to any Nineveh, and I'm not planning on taking a sea voyage any time soon."

"Maybe not, but they's not a man in the company that don't believe that a parson be called by God to preach the Word and see to us simple farmers."

"It was a mistake agreeing with father to go to school for divinity. Father wanted someone to follow along and keep what he had started going, and I dutifully listened and obeyed. But I wasn't a man cut from his cloth, and all of you knew it."

"We knew it, but his time had come to rest and pass his work on to someone else, and you were that someone else everyone accepted."

Philip frowned at him. "Don't you see? That is exactly the problem. Only because of father was I even acceptable. Not because I was as good a preacher as he was or because I brought something else to the pulpits, but because everyone loved father so much. You don't think people were satisfied to let me go after that ugliness with the Harpers?"

"You told that gathering exactly what was the truth about that man."

"Hah! People don't want to know the truth. They only want to hear something that won't upset their view of life, death, and mortality. That's why I was foolish to think I could fill father's collar. People only want to feel good and go home and expect that the good parson will visit now and again if they skip too many Sunday mornings. Father did that, and the farmers loved him for it." Philip shrugged and massaged his neck for a moment. "I couldn't do that, and people saw that I wasn't my father after all."

"You didn't give many people a chance to get used to you before you up and quit."

"It was for everyone's good that I did when I did." Philip pursed his lips and adjusted the strap of his musket higher upon his shoulder, knowing it would slip back down again in a few steps.

"God didn't let Jonah off the hook, as I recall." Sammy broke into a grin. "What makes you think He's gonna let you off the hook so easily?"

Philip shrugged again. "God told Jonah to go to Nineveh. I wasn't called into the collar."

"Jonah didn't think he was called to go to Nineveh neither, but he ended up there anyway," Sammy said.

Sammy's attempt at humor couldn't help but make Philip smile in response. Philip could almost love the man for the way he could bring cheer to a difficult topic. "I won't end up in a pulpit again anytime soon, and I don't think God's going to swallow me up in some fish. It's already been done."

"Well, anyway, about Mule. Papist or not, Mule thinks you walk on water, so you'd better go and straighten him out, if any of us walk away from what's up ahead, that is."

"Right, if any."

Philip wondered at the propensity for people to revere the title of minister. Just like Jonah, he had been unable to escape the command of God. But Jonah was God's chosen prophet. Who was he that God should call him anyway? The men of the company were just accustomed to a certain demeanor and carriage in a minister, and Philip felt he was never able to live up to that expectation. He wasn't given to coarseness, or drink, or carousing, but he'd not been able to pastor the flocks his father left him. They wanted too much of him. Being the son of someone privileged in the community was one thing. When he was expected to be that same pillar of virtue and moral leadership, he just couldn't do it.

Army life, though far from the comforts of home, was still more relaxing than the pulpit. He was not responsible for anyone, or at least he liked to think. And that was just the way he wanted it. Hearing that his comrades thought differently unsettled him. He'd done nothing to gather such respect, nor would he attempt to fit their definition of *spiritual*, whatever that was. Men like Harper only reinforced why he was glad to leave the pulpit to a stranger.

The company column wound its way through the wood line and halted at the edge of a field in time to watch their brigade advance in line of battle. Another brigade, the first in their division, stood fifty paces away, waiting its turn to move forward. Their regiment was already trudging up the height toward the enemy. The whole of the division was present, and its banners fluttered listlessly in the paltry breeze. The guns spoke with concussive force.

The enemy's infantry stood still, waiting for the moment to loose its anger upon the impetuous blue line of battle slowly making its way up to them. Their own banners stood limp on the staves. Their colors were numerous but protected by too few weapons between them.

They had been witness to this several times in battle, the audience to other formations confronting the enemy. The firing line was up close, disturbing in its lack of control. Only the opposing muskets of the enemy and the puffs of gun powder could be seen. Philip knew what they were thinking. Load and fire, load and fire, and wait for the order to advance. Their hearts would be pounding with fear, each man anticipating the next whizzing sound to be followed by the pain of being shot. To a man, they hoped that those ahead would succeed in breaking the enemy's will before they heard the call to move forward. The moment was full of pageantry and anguish.

Captain Bacon gave the command to right face, and the company changed formation from column to line of two ranks. The bark of volleys rang out as the enemy's line opened fire by regiment. Battles were gauged by which side could drive the other from the field. In that grand strategy of forcing the enemy out of one position to another, regiments and brigades played out the drama. The stage was one ridgeline to the next, one defensive position to the next, over and over.

Philip watched the brigades square off and advance into the muzzles of the enemy. Soon, in twos and threes, men trickled back from the firing line carrying wounded. The dead were left in place.

"I hate standin' here and watchin'," Johnny murmured from behind Philip, his place in formation when company front was ordered. His musket would fire over Philip's right shoulder.

"You'd rather we was up there?" Mule asked.

"I'd rather not have to watch but jus' be up there and done with it."

"Or not up there or here at all," Sammy said from a few positions to Philip's right.

"We'll be up there soon with our pards," Johnny said. "That enemy line don't look like it's gonna break."

"Someone'll break soon," said a voice farther down the company line.

Their own artillery was busy on a small rise of ground. It was a dangerous position to be in with solid shot and shrapnel flying about. The crews kept up a hurried rhythm of crash, fire, and concussion.

"They've had enough," Johnny said.

"They look like they's . . . " Mule started. What had been a solid and steady blue battle line unraveled as the left-most regiment began to fall back by company.

"Curse that 6th Ohio," Johnny said and spat.

"Ain't that the 36th Indiana?" Sammy asked.

"It's the 6th," Johnny said. "They always on the left flank and always findin' some reason to save they hides. Them city boys from Cincinnati ain't cut from the same cloth as us farming boys."

Philip shouted over the din. "Ammen's got the 36th Indiana in the center. Jus' look at them full companies." They stared at the men to their front. "It ain't the 6th or our 24th fer sure." Philip stated.

Sammy shouted back. "I suppose we'll be rejoining them right quick."

*****

Across the field and over the Federal batteries, the 36th Indiana men were receiving their baptism of fire in earnest. The twilight fight the night before and skirmishing in the rain were nothing compared to the briskness of the fire pouring into the Indiana and Missouri men. Their wild-eyed excitement was soon replaced with terror. This time, the enemy held a strong position and wasn't attacking. Men fell to the ground or out of formation in every company. The greenhorns fumbled their cartridges with unsteady fingers.

Robert saw many of the men around him on the verge of breaking for the rear. The sound of minié balls flying past their ears and the sight of fallen comrades was too much for some. But they stayed their ground as if nailed there; only their eyes belied the fear they felt. Between loading and firing, he kept a watchful eye on his own comrades. So far, everyone was still on his feet. He wondered if they would have stayed had he not been there.

"Steady," Robert shouted for no reason other than to allay his own fears. "You men stay steady!"

A lieutenant shouted, "To the rear, march! To the rear, march!"

The regimental line reversed face and marched away from the enemy. Robert quickly discovered why. The men of the 6th Ohio were scampering back down the slope in disarray, their backs to the enemy.

"Halt! About face! About face!" The order was parroted from company officer to company officer down the line, followed by the order to load. They delivered one more volley, and Robert found himself marching once again with his back to the enemy. Despite the obvious failure to break the enemy, men sighed with relief. Robert took a quick count of the men around him. Everyone was still with him.

A sudden blur caught his attention, something that crashed obliquely into the Indiana line, tearing into several men. Blood and brains scattered over anyone unlucky enough to be nearby. Robert winced as spatter flew into his face, coating his clothes. He'd seen this happen before but never this close. Those not rent in two lay writhing on the ground, clutching at stumps of missing appendages. In his horror and shock, he didn't hear the enemy cheering or cannon belching fire. The faces of the Indiana men, familiar from their brief time together, were now memories to be forever etched in his mind.

Each step drew him farther from the scene. The attack, as it ended, brought the regiments out and away from the destructive proximity of their enemy. New faces took the places of those left behind on the field. Robert shook himself free from the nightmarish images.

He looked around to count noses once again. Piper was missing, as was Georg Primble, the most unassuming and un-German of the noisy and bombastic former 13th Missouri ranks. Huebner was alive, but Adolf Goerdeler was not where he was supposed to be. Huebner caught his gaze and shrugged as if understanding the question Robert's glance asked. Robert knew where Piper was, now part of that tangle of blood and entrails left by that solid shot tearing through yielding flesh and bone.

The Indiana men were rattled and panting. Only a few forms lay still upon the slopes of the hill. There was hope yet that Georg and Adolf were still alive with the wounded. They retreated in good order. Robert knew what this meant—a slight respite before they would move forward again. The jittery greenhorns jabbered about their first real test of courage and eagerly stepped forward when the time came. Robert and his pards stepped off with less enthusiasm.

Another battery of artillery drove obliquely across their front, quickly unlimbering. The gunners were just out of reach of the enemy muskets but not from his artillery. The advancing infantry gave the gunners a cheer as they leapt from their caissons and quickly loosed several rounds upon the enemy infantry. The gunners themselves became the target of each enemy battery, and the ground around them was soon torn from solid shot and explosive discharges. Despite the punishment, the crews serviced each cannon with precision until the Indiana line came abreast the guns, and they finally fell silent. It was their turn to cheer on the advancing infantry brigades then limber up and escape further harm. Their dead and maimed had to be left behind. The enemy zeroed in on the spot vacated by the guns, punishing helpless infantry in their place. High explosive shot rained shrapnel from above, and solid case shot tore gaps in the companies.

Each puff of smoke revealed another enemy gun discharging, and at each puff, Robert expected to be sent to his Maker. They had only been in that space enough time to make two or three paces, but it was sufficient time for large numbers of men to fall. The whole division advanced to confront the enemy stubbornly holding on to that slope. Another few paces and the enemy riflemen would join in delivering the punishment. The bodies began to pile up. The blue line stepped over them and trudged on.

Chapter Seventeen

The firing line was hot, aside from the sweltering heat of noon tide. Rifles bobbed up and down as the process of loading times nine was rehearsed with automatic precision. Up and level, jerk in response, and then back down once again to load. One fired into the mass of enemy forms in the murky distance and repeated the steps until the barrels were too hot to hold or touch. Somewhere among the objects of this wrathful behavior, delivered with neither anger nor malice but out of duty, someone was maimed or killed with each round. Thousands of men in blue pressed the thin but stalwart enemy line, hoping to make some impression upon it.

Philip gritted his teeth and asked God to forgive him at each round he fired. He knew it was war, and war meant death and destruction. Perhaps each round sent down range meant safety for one of his pards. Perhaps each one meant more destruction than he cared to dwell upon. Fire and reload, fire and reload, until he emptied his upper tin in his ammunition box. Twenty rounds sent into the enemy. Rapid and automatic did the firing proceed. He struggled with the paper cartridge packages from the lower compartment of his tins. His grimy fingers dug into the paper packages, fumbling with the cartridges and feeding them into the upper container while keeping his musket steady and holding open the heavy leather flap of his cartridge box.

The brigade advanced, retreated, advanced, and retreated once again. Now they confronted their enemy too closely for either side to suffer for long. Already, many of the company were stumbling back down the gentle slope of the hill to get away from the dangerous ground separating the combatants. Other men suffered from his fire or by slow death, life escaping out of grievous wounds. Fire and reload. His tins full once again, he returned to the duty of any soldier in the line. Whereas he once labored to secure the souls of his flock and instruct them in the ways of righteousness, the job of firing minié balls into the enemy with neither passion nor hate struck him as absurd. But the whizzing by his ears of the enemy fire as it flew too high brought a sense of equilibrium. Kill or be killed. Fire and reload.

Twenty minutes of fighting is an eternity to the rifleman in the line where time is measured by the growing emptiness of one's cartridge box and the thinning of the line of pards. The enemy fire sailed harmlessly above their heads, given the odd luck of their being on lower ground. Someone would have to give—someone always gave. Roaring sound and the ringing discharges of his own musket engulfed Philip, insulating him from anything else. He saw others around him, but it was just him and his need to load and fire. Standing impervious to the destruction, he ignored it. God protected him. Why else, he reasoned, can I stand here moment after moment and not receive my just due?

The enemy infantry regiment in front of them suddenly vanished from view. Equally unexpected was the surge forward that dragged Philip along, like a strong river current. Hoarse *huzzahs* growled out of parched throats, and the regiment marched forward in triumph. The charge was short-lived as a line of determined but tired-looking Confederates marched up and delivered a blistering volley into their faces. But the momentum was not to be checked. The Ohioans weathered the blast unfazed. Cries of anguish and surprise mingled with the noise of battle.

They didn't receive an expected order to halt, and others down the line kept up their pace. Those who had been in Philip's immediate vicinity were missing, melted away, or swallowed up by the ground. Philip loosed his own yell, and it steadied his nerves. He didn't think about the battle, or the enemy, or his pards, only his job as a soldier, and as a soldier, he had to fight his enemy regardless of his qualms or past calling.

Others suddenly surrounded him, and he ran with them. The whole regiment was surging forward, chasing the retreating enemy in their front. Cresting the top of the hill, the Ohioans found themselves in command of the enemy's former line and the enemy in full flight. Soon, the whole position was covered in glorious blue, and the fighting abated into silence once more.

*****

Farther west from where Philip and the 24th Ohio stood panting, Robert and the Indianans collapsed from the strain of the mornings exertions. Instinctively, his Missourian pards sought each other out. Like their Indiana comrades, their numbers were fewer once again. Quiet conversations replaced the sounds of battle echoing among the hill and grass. The pause was welcome, though cruelly short-lived. War has little regard for flesh and will. Huebner sat slumped over as if weighted down with a heavy load, shoulders drooping and head hanging low.

No one asked where their missing comrades were, for their absence was evidence enough. A profound heaviness hung around the group. Even the greenhorns from Indiana seemed to have aged several years since the prior day. Gone were their cries for action and animated tales of bravery. They had earned their battle flag today. A name would adorn their colors to commemorate their first battle. If the standard for the 25th Missouri was not in the hands of the enemy as a trophy, it, too, might yet sport such a name for this place.

The colors of the 36th Indiana fluttered in a cool breeze. Robert found himself drawn to it as if it were his own. Perhaps it was as much theirs as it was the Indianans.

"We fought fer that standard," a familiar voice said. Robert didn't turn to see, for the voice was like that of his own flesh and blood. "Mebbe the 25th's escaped somehow."

"Maybe," Robert sighed and replied. "Might be a long time before we see another one flutter."

"We can't be too far from the camp," a voice piped up.

"Possible, we might be able to retake it before evening if'n the Rebels keep runnin'," Robert replied.

"You think we be punished for runnin'?" Huebner asked.

"Punish half th' army then," someone responded.

"True. Lots ran yesterday morning," replied another.

The Missouri men lay on the grass, out of sight of the putrefying dead and the wailing wounded. The enormity of what happened across the Tennessee farmland was inescapable. Eventually, they would be called to account for it. They took advantage of the calm to find the peace of a moment's rest.

*****

Michael reined up next to General Cleburne's staff and returned the adjutant's salute. What was left of the battery was drawn up a few yards distant, one gun short.

"Polk's battery is unlimbered and ready to support the line," Michael stated. "We need to replenish our caissons. We're low on grape and canister."

"Can't help you, Captain," the weary man replied. "Division supplies are way back in the rear and moving toward Corinth. You'll have to forage."

Michael was surprised. "Back to Corinth?"

"Beauregard's ordered the army to retreat. We're going to hold a line till the wounded and prisoners make it along, but don't expect too much standin' around."

"If the other section of Polk's battery turns up, point them my way. They was by that church this morning," Michael said and pointed.

The days of marching and fighting produced not a victory but a defeat. Surely the army was made of sterner stuff than this, Michael thought as he slowly made his way back to the new defense line. Enough stragglers to form several regiments had formed near the Corinth Road. The infantry, drawn up and waiting for the enemy to burst upon them, were a pitiful sight. The roads leading south were clogged with wagons, broken men, and thousands of skulkers seeking safety. From where they formed, Michael did not see the steeple of the church and wondered at the fate of his own Texans. With no caissons about or on the roads, Michael knew there wouldn't be any scavenging for munitions. The paltry supply he still possessed would have to do.

The men from Polk's section were strangers, though he knew their faces. He knew little of their personalities and less of their abilities. They were well-drilled. Save for the unfamiliar air about them, they performed no worse than his own Texans did. He still felt like an unwanted step-child in their presence, however. They just were not his own men. The bond of common upbringing and months of togetherness was not erased by the sudden elevation to command and responsibility. He did not know if any of them felt as he did. He only saw them respond to him as a superior officer.

One lieutenant and several sergeants remained to command the two-gun section. The privates did what privates do when left unmolested by their sergeants; they lounged and slept around their pieces. The acting first sergeant, a Sergeant Miller, looked up as he approached and walked over to meet him.

"Sir, we got five case of shot and six canister to our name," Miller said grimly, a darkness shading his expression.

"We're retreating, Sergeant, so we won't be firing that much, anyway," Michael replied.

"Any news of the other section?"

"None. They may be on their way back to Corinth by now," Michael said with a sigh as he dismounted. Clutching the reins of the horse, he led it up to the caisson line. Two of the loaders were leaning against the wheels, fast asleep.

"Sir, here's the roster as it stands right now for this section," Miller said. He handed Michael a crumpled piece of paper.

Michael read it quickly and folded it into his pocket. "Thank you, Sergeant. Have the crews stand down." He looked at the loaders and said, "They need the rest."

The sergeant saluted half-heartedly, but Michael ignored the gesture. The man's eyes said his mind was halfway to his pillow. His own weariness beginning to tell upon his legs, Michael walked his horse over to one of the caissons, tied the reins to a wheel, and settled in next to a snoring private. Little separated officer from enlisted man in this moment, as both were of flesh and bone and in need of quiet. He hoped the enemy would make a show of pursuit so he'd not be rudely awakened mid-stupor.

He watched the columns of wagon teams and soldiers move by. In the distance, he spied a familiar landmark, the hill they topped yesterday before being drawn away to bombard the sunken road. Many of the dead from the day before rested in shallow graves dotting the field. Only the stripped enemy dead lay where they had fallen. All the signs of victory were to be had yesterday evening. Upon the hill, in silhouette, the dismounted gun carriage still stood.

There was little to recount of the failure, save for the deplorable cohesion he witnessed last evening in his own army. Was it the rain? Was it the delays leaving Corinth? Was it General Johnston's death? Was it the arrival of Buell? Something went wrong, and someone was to blame for sacrificing men and material and then leaving the field to the beaten enemy. Someone was responsible. He grew angry thinking about it. His crews, both sections, did their part as well as any man could under fire. They did not run or shirk. What was it that Mahoney said? *"God's will"?* Was not God on the side of the rightness of their cause? Who shouldered the blame for such a catastrophe as this? Michael shifted uneasily.

"Captain?" a voice called through the fog Michael felt behind his eyes.

"Uh?" Michael looked up into the face of his lone subaltern. The lieutenant's uniform was open at the collar, and his vest open to the air showed a calico undershirt. His sword, the symbol of command, hung loosely upon the straps and trailed a step behind him. His unshaven and grimy face told Michael this man needed sleep more than he.

"Sir, there's movement out in front. Looks like Federal reconnaissance in brigade strength."

Without looking away, Michael blew out a long breath. "Rouse the crews," Michael ordered listlessly, hoisting himself to his feet. The infantry regiments on station around the battery were rousing themselves sluggishly, as well. Behind their thin screen, the retreat moved slowly down the Corinth-Pittsburg Road as if unconcerned with the imminent danger.

The crews to the two remaining guns stood to station and watched as the Federal brigade advanced with skirmishers out front. Michael hadn't noticed them before, but their own skirmish line was waiting.

"Parker," Michael called, "mind our skirmishers out there."

The lieutenant nodded in acknowledgement and motioned to each of his section crews. Soon the *pop, pop, pop* of skirmish fire filled the air.

A peppering of fire spoke from the opposing lines, and puffs of smoke appeared from the barely visible skirmishers who went to ground at the first fire. The enemy skirmishers advanced in spurts, firing, then standing to walk forward. Their own skirmishers merely seemed an annoyance to the enemy, who marched forward as if on a parade ground. They needed a miracle to save the ordinance train slowly creaking down the road.

In an instant, their skirmish line stood upright and bolted for the safety of the firing line. The Federal skirmishers barely trotted along, however, showing an uncharacteristic lack of urgency. A few walked as if on a leisurely stroll. Michael cast a glance behind him and toward the road the enemy was advancing obliquely to cut. The enemy banners fluttered some two hundred yards beyond the road, and, to the right, another defensive position was being prepared behind what looked like an abatis. They could use an abatis right now, as the only thing to prevent the fire storm of lead soon to be flying about was one's own body. If the fugitive trains did not hurry along, their retreat to the new position would be short. The enemy would gobble up the tired remnants with little effort. The infantry, bearing defeat as well as they could, readied themselves to resume the conflict.

"Parker, open on them with explosive. Watch your fuses," Michael ordered. Tired or not, the battery sprang to life. Fire belched forth from one cannon, then the other. Michael knew it was only for show. He hadn't the wherewithal to keep the enemy at bay or do any real damage. There only was the presence of a line of cannon to strike fear into the enemy's heart. Bluff was all they had left.

A few more shots and they would have to beat it to the rear, leaving the infantry to their own devices. All the same, Michael would put on a loud show. Shots flew down range and detonated airborne, though not near enough to the enemy to do anything but make them duck. The firing was sloppy at best and below their normal standards. Michael kept silent, knowing that each man knew this but was doing what he could.

The sixth shot arched toward the enemy, and Michael shouted to Parker to limber up. That was it; infantryman's best friend was cutting out. Michael gave a glance at the infantry line. The sudden movement of the guns toward the caissons drew men's eyes toward the battery with forlorn expressions. It was often the lot of the infantry to fight to defend the guns and retake them when lost. Gunners served a solitary weapon and alone were powerless to do much in a close-quarters duel between massed forces. Each man would fight to resist letting the cannon escape until he no longer had it in him. Should not the lowly infantry expect a little more loyalty in return?

The drilled precision of limbering up was executed quickly, and the battery was moving as fast as the remaining horses could effect. Michael galloped on ahead to the new line. He discovered a rich defensive position cluttered with felled trees and brush, a position that could not have been constructed any better had the army's engineers been put to the task. The fallen trees had been arranged hastily into crude breastworks. To his surprise, Michael found a familiar sight reclining on a cannon.

"Mahoney," Michael blurted out, oblivious to the military impropriety. Blushing a bit, Michael quickly dismounted and ran over to his old section of Texans looking tired but strangely exuberant.

"Captain, good ta see you hain't been captured," Mahoney replied and nodded in his peculiar frontier disregard for convention or etiquette.

"Tell me you have munitions," Michael said breathlessly. The rest of the section rattled across the open field and pulled around the infantry battalions to rest behind their barricade.

"A full complement, sir," Mahoney replied smugly.

"Good, this section is out." Michael nodded toward the arriving men and ran out to meet them. A spot was already cleared and prepped for the two guns, and they were soon in place next to their comrades. The Tennessee boys acquitted themselves well. But for the unfamiliar faces, Michael could have been with his fellow Texans. A sense of relief overcame him. Had the virtues of manhood not prevented it, he might have given each one there a hearty hug and handshake. He didn't feel naked now, as if the few piled-up tree logs and scrub brush were of any real military value for protection. Yet he saw the same expression on everyone's face. They were safe at last.

In their front, the regiments they had abandoned earlier were marching up to the position, unmolested by a cautiously following enemy. They, too, seemed energized by the position, as if they were marching into an impregnable fortress. A livelier step propelled the regiments forward, and the defensive line now appeared to have real force behind it. Yet the enemy approached with the brazenness of a predator closing on its wounded prey.

"I think the good captain will find this position a little more to his liking, no?" Mahoney said with a grin.

Michael grinned back. "Very, First Sergeant, very much to my liking. How did you come to have full caissons?"

"We had to pull back to replenish after you left. The fight went much better by the church than where you was at, I take it," Mahoney replied.

"Much better. We lost two guns and some crew. I think the left was under an ill star this day."

"They couldn't budge us. We had to move when the left collapsed."

"How are the men?"

"Tired, but we're all still here. A few minor scratches, but everyone stayed at his post," Mahoney answered.

Michael looked about at faces that told him he was home. Bandages adorned foreheads and arms, but it was good to see so many still on their feet. The pursuing Federals marched forward, undeterred by the strength of the position opposite them. An artillery unit raced across the field ahead of the Federal infantry and went into battery. With precision, the crews manhandled their pieces into position while loaders cradled shot in their arms, ready to be rammed home.

Michael, along with the rest of the battery, stood by, fascinated by the energy and work of their opposite numbers. Four guns were readied to fire in a matter of minutes, their first rounds crashing into the trees behind the Confederates. Perhaps it was the fatigue or perhaps just the admiration of a maneuver well executed, but the artillerymen watched agape. Four rounds of shot exploded before Michael nodded for Mahoney to prepare their own response. It was a dangerous game, this recognition of an enemy's prowess, and one measured in moments lost to the pageant. Once set in motion, the battery responded in kind. The air was soon filled with explosive rounds as the range was gained between the batteries and shot and shell began to fall uncomfortably close.

The approaching infantry pushed forward and passed the Federal battery, whose attentions were drawn to other parts of the Confederate line. Another Federal battery perched itself atop the rise of a hill, just behind the advance of their infantry brigades, and began lobbing solid shot at Michael's guns. They sat just out of range of Michael's smooth-bore napoleons, enjoying that rarest of opportunities to inflict damage while remaining untouchable themselves. The rifled guns of that battery gave them an edge.

"Get ready for grape shot!" Michael yelled. The Federal infantry closed to within musket range, and a peppering of lead flowed to and fro across the open space separating the combatants. Yet, the contest was uneven. The Federal brigades soon backed away to lick their wounds, all but that troublesome battery. It continued to plow the earth with solid shot all around them, seeking to knock out their guns and men with one well-placed shot. The Federal infantry gathered themselves once again to march forward and exchange blows. In moments, more of the field was covered with blue wounded and dead.

Again and again, the contest was renewed, and the firing was hot. A rousing cheer erupted from somewhere along the line that sounded strange to Michael's ears. It was from their own infantry, and it was of that kind of yell men give when achieving a victory or being relieved of a burden too heavy to bear. Horseman swept across the field toward the enemy infantry, which fell back after another attempt to break into the hasty redoubt.

"Cease fire, cease fire!" Michael shouted. He ran up to one of the guns and leaned upon the low breastwork thrown up.

The men of the battery raised their hats, waved their arms, and cheered as the cavalry cut into the now-fleeing enemy like demons bent upon scooping up the last remnant of the damned for Hades.

"Good ol' Forrest! God bless the man," Mahoney shouted.

Nathan Bedford Forrest's cavalry squadrons rode pell-mell into the fleeing enemy, cutting down as many as they could reach before running headlong into a charge of Federal cavalry themselves. The field, once covered with enemy infantry, was now an-every-man-for-himself clash of sabers and pistol shots. Even so, that meddlesome battery, undeterred by the success of Rebel arms and horseflesh, continued to prey upon Michael's guns.

"Damn that battery!" Michael cursed as another well-placed shot tore into the earth and shattered the hasty barricade in front of St. Paul. The shot furrowed the ground for a yard before bounding high into the air and over the surprised crews. No one was hurt but for splinters that showered all who were unlucky enough to be standing near the gun.

The Federal cavalry quickly enveloped Forrest's troopers, who were unaware of their approach until too late. Beating a hasty retreat back across the field, the horsemen galloped for the safety of the infantry and barricades, followed closely by a jubilant enemy.

"As soon as they clear, give 'em a face full of grape!" Michael shouted. The gunners regained their composure and readied their pieces. The Federal cavalry seemed hell-bent to ride over the abatis and engage in their own game of saber slash. As Forrest's men dashed toward safety, the Federal horseman nipped at their heels. The battery had them in oblique as the retreat took their own cavalry far to the left of the rest of the infantry and Michael's battery. Suddenly aware of the acute danger they had placed themselves in, the Federals reined to a halt too late.

The Confederate infantry let loose a volley at the instant Michael's battery fired by section, and the vainglorious pursuit melted away in a circus of spinning horses and flailing humanity. The dust and smoke settled to reveal a field empty once again but for hapless animals and men cut down from both sides. The Federals retreated to a safe distance to watch and wait. Many a man breathed a sigh of relief as they realized they and their pards were still standing. Still, that battery of Federal guns played upon the line. There was nothing to be done about it. The enemy was building barricades near the rise in front of that battery. Any attempt to silence those guns would lead to another engagement, and neither side really relished another clash. All they could do was wait for darkness to descend.

"Mahoney, get the sections to the rear for some coffee and rations. Leave a few by the guns for show. The men need to rest," Michael ordered as he felt his own exhaustion overtake his senses. A hot cup of coffee sounded heavenly. The infantry regiments were also settling down behind their protection and sorting themselves out for a rest. The remaining officers in the battery, all subalterns of lieutenant grade, gathered around a fire to absently poke sticks at the flames while waiting for the coffee to brew. Michael wearily walked up and took a seat upon a stump reserved for him by Mahoney. The Texans had little use for titles or formality, but even the seat of honor, such as it was, was surrendered to Michael in heed of his rank and command. Unable to refuse, Michael took his seat and stared into the dancing flames.

Though only a first sergeant, Mahoney's position as head enlisted man and his closeness to Michael granted him his place at the officers' mess. Officer's privilege also meant not having to cook for himself. That wasn't much of a boon today. The only food available was whatever they could find in the passing ration wagons, and that was paltry. A few of the enlisted men scurried around preparing the officers' mess. Usually, this gave them the chance to eat something other than poorly preserved meat. This evening, though, they would have to be content with the mean fare of boiled salt pork and captured Federal hard tack. Michael ignored the muckets filled with briny water and odd-looking meat and focused, instead, on the sweet aroma of coffee boiling.

"I'll bet you hain't had anythin' to eat since yesterday, Captain," Mahoney said. He made himself comfortable on the ground next to Michael and looked up with sallow eyes above sweat-streaked cheeks. His shell jacket was grimy, lying open.

"It ain't the food I want, First Sergeant. It's a good swig of what's brewin' on that fire," Michael said. Those around the fire all nodded in agreement.

"Don't worry, sir. Plenty for all," the enlisted man who was tending the muckets of boiling pork replied as he lifted the lid on the boiler holding the coffee. The water was steamy but not boiling yet.

"See that they get theirs first," Michael said and nodded at the other officers around the fire.

"Yes, sir," the man said and turned his attention back to slicing the few apples they had found. Another crash near the infantry line reminded them all that they were not on holiday.

"Bastards hang just out of range and shell us," one of the lieutenants groused.

"I believe it is called having the tactical advantage," another replied.

"It's un-gamely, cowardly, even." He was a stocky young fellow from Tennessee and someone with whom Michael was only barely familiar. His uniform, like everyone's, was wrinkled and unkempt. His beard and moustache were scraggly and showed lack of attentive grooming. Michael could tell he was fond of looking the part of the dandy in a polished uniform. His collar, still wrapped with a bow tie, was stained and dirty.

"I'd do it in a heartbeat," Michael replied. "Stand just out of reach and deliver blows with rifled cannon such that the enemy would think twice before advancing farther."

"Still, don't seem gentlemanly," grumped the chastened young man.

"No, it don't," Michael replied.

"Didn't think we'd be back here this soon," Mahoney said and suppressed a yawn.

"No, not back here holding the line."

"Any word on Captain Polk?" the young man from Tennessee asked.

"Nope, he's prolly back in Corinth by now."

"He was hit pretty bad in the leg. Might lose it, from the looks of it," the young man said. He didn't look away from the fire, where he pushed some coal pieces with a stick.

Mahoney made a grunting sound. "Shame. Good man."

"Better a leg than a life, eh?" another officer said.

"Suppose," Michael replied, the lone dissenter, "though I couldn't imagine a life with a wooden leg or on crutches."

"Better half a man in my estimation than a whole corpse," Mahoney added. "Not sure family and friends would disagree."

"What would a man do? Scuttle about and draw sympathy from every passerby? How would he make his way in life if he couldn't clear the scrub and brush from the land or make his way to the markets to sell his goods?" Michael asked. "Seems he'd be less of a man without the means to be a man."

"I seen men make they way with less," Mahoney said. "What makes a man isn't in his body but in his mind and heart."

"Not on the frontier where it's the hard work that separates a man of noble character from the town drunkard," Michael stated. He caught a waft of coffee aroma. "That done yet, Private?"

"Lemme check it. Yes, sir, boilin' good now," the man replied. Using a cloth wrapped around the handle, he lifted the coffee pot off the coals to a chorus of raised cups and expectant faces.

Mahoney shook his head and continued the discussion. "But it's the man of noble character that rises above the challenges of life and presses on. The drunkard may be whole but still a laggard while it's the half a man who sacrificed his freedom and limbs for a cause who has his life favored by the Almighty."

His cup filled and steaming, Michael lifted it to his nose, breathed in a deep taste of its aroma, and blew across its hot surface. The others cradled their cups as if they were valuable possessions. Just the aroma was enough to brighten the mood and lift the flagging will. Michael didn't really want to fall into this conversation as he quickly saw that he was outgunned and out-argued by his trusty subordinate and friend. He knew when he was out on a limb. But for the presence of the other subalterns, he would have ended it sooner.

"But what a high price," Michael answered Mahoney, "has been called upon by the Almighty this very day. How many men of noble character have been laid low and forfeited their lives for the Almighty?" Michael stated, instantly wishing he had kept his mouth shut.

"They did so willingly and knowing they were imperfect," Mahoney said. "They did so even as One who was without fault did so before them."

There it was again. Mahoney was not a man to be trifled with or matched for wisdom or wit. He certainly was not to be called upon to lose a theological debate. The others sat silently out of deference to their chief, unwilling to open themselves up to either Mahoney's or Michael's scrutiny.

"This they did," Michael conceded. "But how is one to add up such cost of what we have failed to achieve today? Was it to be God's own demand to throw us into conflict to lay waste to so many noble men?"

Mahoney looked hard at Michael and drew a long sip of coffee. "Don't know, Captain. Men have given themselves to lesser pursuits and for more sordid gain in the past. We give ourselves to a cause of freedom. What more noble cause can there be?"

"None," Michael answered, clearly troubled. "We do what our forefathers did against England. But had they lost, would not their sacrifice have been in vain and that of the Tory's been for gain?" He looked at the others gathered around the fire, seeing who nodded and who frowned. "Would not we today have been saying God upheld the rule of England over rebellion?" The coffee was now coursing down his throat and settling warmly in his belly. His senses brightened, and the drink sitting well emboldened him.

"No one dares speak of the possibility that we ourselves would wish for the reward of the Tory instead of the patriot. God's will is not clear in all of this." Mahoney gestured to encompass all the land about them, the carnage and the living. "What we all know is that we volunteered to free us from the dominion of a tyranny not unlike England's. We don't do this knowing the end, only knowing that what beats in our breast be freedom."

The realization that the outcome might be different than what they hoped and prayed for was an unwelcome guest in their conversation. To admit the desire that motivated hundreds of thousands of men serving in deprivation and hostility and also to acknowledge that the opposite desire might be true was, to Michael, a larger step than he was willing to take. He needed to believe that they were doing God's will. He could hold no other belief and yet continue. This time, he kept his mouth shut.

"That the Almighty could be on the side of tyranny and not on freedom is something we dare not think about," Mahoney continued. "But who of us knows the future from the past?"

To Michael's relief, another voice spoke up. "It was another failure born under a bad sign from the beginning. That we almost whooped them must have been more than we could have expected."

The question that had most been troubling Michael finally came clear. "How can we both act upon the Almighty's will? Either we or they are in the right, or, from what I can see, despite the punishment we gave him yesterday, the enemy is successful when he should have been thrown into the river." How absurd, he thought, to call upon God when he had little hope of expecting God's aide. "How can anyone call upon God to give special dispensation for anything when even in the rightness of our own cause, we find and taste bitterest defeat?"

"That's the thing, Captain. No one can ask but through faith. Perhaps in faith we are destined to lose. God certainly did not always give his own people victory." Mahoney fingered the lip of his cup.

"But their defeats came from sin," the young man from Tennessee spoke up. "We have no direct command from Heaven to do this or that or observe some special commandment. I won't believe that we are not on the side of righteousness."

"I won't pretend to know," Mahoney said. "I only know what I can understand and follow. He also raised up the nation of Israel to be a beacon to the world of his grace. That lasted only a short while, but He was in no less control over her, even in subjugation."

"Well, I'm not sure I'll put much into all of that. We win or lose based upon the fortunes of this war and the things that no one can control. We had the opportunity to keep the field and throw Grant's army into the Tennessee, but we were more disorganized in victory than the enemy was in defeat," Michael surmised.

"Who's to say the things that did happen were not supposed to happen?" Mahoney countered. "General Johnston dying was something that caused that confusion. I can't discount anything. Just because I can figure it all out doesn't mean that the hand of the Divine was not present."

"I suppose I won't ever have that understanding," Michael admitted. "It's all stuff that happens out of our control." He took a deep breath and looked at Mahoney, almost pleading to be convinced that God was in charge. "Perhaps more of that happened to us this time and not the enemy. We seem to barely have gotten away with our army more or less intact. For that I suppose we were lucky."

"I won't go about attributing every victory to God and every loss to sin or some disobedience," Mahoney said. His shoulders slumped a little as the discussion turned back to more tangible affairs. "We did not win this day, and the enemy got his reinforcements. We'll retreat back to Corinth and hunker down there for a time."

Michael thought about Mahoney's last statement. How easy it is to think one is safe when one is winning and all is right with the world and God. But once troubles happen and plans go awry, was it God's lack of support or active opposition? It made little sense to think that way, for Michael was sure he could never know, that no man could ever know, where he was in that mystical connection with God. Good today but wrong tomorrow; the harness breaks, and the field cannot be plowed; the rope breaks on the well because one didn't pray long enough that morning. There had to be more to it than just that.

The man sitting next to Mahoney said, "Maybe General Beauregard's not a prayin' man like Johnston was. He fergot to put in a good word this morning."

The group fell silent for a time, and the meal of fresh apples and boiled salt pork was ready. It smelled good to Michael. Anything would have smelled good to him after not having eaten anything hot for several days. The private doing the cooking had drained the pork from the water and fried it, with the apple slices and chunks of sodden hard tack making the pork edible.

Michael ate absently. With the thoughts in his head, he didn't notice the food he ate. Was the fate of thousands of men merely a product of chance and of little account? His side was not victorious, and the honored dead were not vindicated by clash of arms. Dead or maimed were left unburied and unattended upon the fields and thickets. That God would ordain one side to win and another to lose was not the question. That God would ordain one cause to be defeated and another to be victorious was the issue. How could freedom lose to tyranny?

Michael finished his plate and took his tin cup, now only half filled with cooling liquid, and stood up. The blood ran back into his legs, and he was unsteady for a moment. The lethargy of inactivity after a long spell of being on his feet made them feel strange. After taking one last swig of coffee, he walked back to the gun line. A few of the men were ducked down behind the barricades, chatting and eating as if they were back at camp and unconcerned about their proximity to an enemy. For their part, the enemy was unseen, other than his own hastily constructed abatis across the field. The skirmishers were silent and comfortable in rifle pits hurriedly dug into the ground. If one did not notice that battery upon the hill, one could nearly believe this to be a peaceful part of the line.

A report from those guns sent a shot hurling and arching over Michael's head. He could feel the rush of wind and ducked, and he heard a crash and alarmed cry. He looked in the direction the shot had taken. A cloud of dust hung over the officers' mess, and the fire was out. A few men were running to the scene, but Michael could see a jumble of arms, legs, and torsos where there used to be living men. In moments, the air was filled with shouts and calls for aid. Even knowing there was nothing he could do to help those men, Michael rushed forward.

Chapter Eighteen

After taking the hill, Philip's brigade found itself marching to the right where the battle was not going so well. Hardly allowed time to gain breath, the whole division marched toward the sounds of battle like insects drawn to light. The enemy stubbornly contested every inch of ground gained, though their flank was in the air with the collapse of Cheatham's line. Around the church, the ground was thick with wounded and dead. The maimed were finding comfort in each others' presence, regardless of affiliation. Hours later, the fighting on this part of the field was also silenced. The brigade had pushed the Rebels from their defensive line in front of their field hospital and through it. Now, they rested in line with arms stacked.

Where their line once stood, the enemy dead were especially numerous. The rows upon rows of silent fallen caused Philip to shiver. They were in every attitude of disquiet one could imagine, faces upturned in terror, bodies distended from the previous day or freshly ripped open by shell and minié ball in the aftermath of the recent fighting.

Philip and his pards lounged on the ground, the anxiety of the day melting away into exhaustion and unease. So many dead were about that he could not look in any direction without seeing a corpse. Where a battery had been, the rear of that line was littered with horses that had been cut from the traces, dying while still haltered to the caissons. The stench was beginning to tell in the heat. Some of the men were souvenir hunting among the dead, and others were combing the field of suffering around the church, giving aid.

"Them boys put up a fight, didn't they?" Johnny asked.

"When you think rations'll get up to us?" Mule asked and rubbed his sweat-stained undershirt. His sack coat was open, save for the last button at the collar, exposing his homespun flowered shirt. It was soaked, and his belly showed though the wet fabric.

"Plenty of haversacks out there," Sammy said and motioned toward the field.

"Yeah, but they's Johnny rations, and, well, them's dead men's possessions," Mule protested.

"They won't be needin' them vittles where they's going."

"Well, I can't go about doin' that."

Sammy made a snort. "What difference does it make ta the dead?"

"It not the dead I'm worried about," Mule protested. "It's the robbing that I'm against. They may be dead, but it's still they's food."

Johnny slapped Mule on the back and grinned. "Well, we all know how to protect our ration now."

"Not funny," Mule said, his face screwed into a grimace. "Looting is a sin, and looting the dead is worse!"

"So, the papist has a conscience," Johnny said.

"Enough to know right from wrong, heathen!"

"Let's ask our pard here," Johnny said with a smirk. "Let our former man of the cloth his'self answer to who's a heathen or not."

Philip shook his head wearily and answered, "You two can leave me out of it."

Relaxed for the first time since their hurried wake-up and departure from Savannah yesterday morning, Philip wasn't about to interrupt this peace and quiet by feeding Johnny's fire. That fire didn't need much to stoke it, and Mule always played into Johnny's hands. Johnny never passed an opportunity to needle their Catholic pard. For the most part, Mule put up with it, though Philip could tell Mule wished to be left alone with his faith, as did Philip. Though he felt no qualms about rummaging a haversack when hungry, he opted to let the hunger settle. What separated lifting some food from lifting other unneeded valuables that the poor souls couldn't take into the next life? A ring taken here, a gold filling there, a pocket watch or other valuables—they were the same as the food a corpse no longer needed. Rationalize one act, Philip thought, and soon they would be no different from the skulkers. Thievery was thievery, no matter what the object.

The afternoon was still hot and sultry, making their bodies feel wilted. There was little to separate this moment from the thousands of moments Philip had experienced in the war thus far. He had experienced endless days of fatigue duty or sitting around a mess fire, talking politics and army life. That this particular moment resulted from a battle's aftermath rather than other more routine experiences made no difference to him. It was enough just to enjoy the moment they had. Philip and his pards had found a patch of ground to call their own for the brief time they would be allowed to rest, and that patch of ground was cool and lush despite the heat. The silence, however temporary it might be, was divine.

Roll was called after the enemy retreat, and the vacancies in the company were noted for the casualty report soon to be tabulated at the various headquarters. Those numbers would create emotionless columns of killed, wounded, and missing, and those answering roll for each regiment of the brigade, numbers that could not communicate the human suffering and loss. One name stood out: Harper. The fifth sergeant did not answer to his name, and, for a moment, Philip's heart leapt. Johnny looked over at Philip and winked. It bothered him now, that moment of elation. Had he heard of the death of Jefferson Davis or some other personage in the enemy ranks, would he have been any more justified in feeling glad? No one saw Harper fall, and no one could confirm his death or wounding. He might yet be living. That his tormenter should be taken away from him was more than Philip dared hope.

The company was decimated after the last push past the church yard and to the spot where they lay. As the roll continued, name after name went unanswered. Many were lying wounded in the field hospital around the churchyard, joined with the enemy in suffering under the cross of Christ atop the steeple. Some died where they had stood. His pards were still here, but many familiar names were unanswered. Philip felt but the smallest pang of remorse at the winnowing of his former flock at the hand of the gods of battle.

Disease had claimed many before a shot was fired. The empty bedroll and a missing spot in the formation was a familiar condition. The funeral for the first victims of disease had been a somber affair that sobered all of them to the realities of service, but after the fifteenth funeral procession, the sadness was spent.

West Virginia showed Philip the reality of the war. The engagements they had fought and the prostrate forms of men he once knew as loyal parishioners left Philip with little reason to rejoice. Even so, the slopes covered with human and animal wreckage made those who survived a fraternity of veterans, men hardened by service and privation and the shared experience of combat. All boasting ceased on that day at Pine Mountain, West Virginia. No longer did they feel pressure to display prowess in courage and manliness. Meeting the enemy wasn't along a picket post or skirmish line but in a toe-to-toe delivery of fire into the face and body. Fear took on new meaning, braggarts discovered their own frailty, and those most afraid found expression to their fears. Still, all stood as there was nothing else to do but stand and load. It was up close and personal engagement with the sights and sounds of battle. It was the cannonade and rifle shot, wounded and dead, cowardly skulking, and heroic death. It was here where Philip renewed his longing for the pulpit.

Another battle fought and another battle survived for his little flock. Was it enough to just survive? Was the fire delivered in calculated steps for the sake of seeing the enemy cut down? The pulpit was a battle no less intense, but his true enemies were falsehoods and demons, not their unwitting servants. What purpose did this latest skirmish serve, if it could be called that? It was just another clash in a string of battles since Charleston fired upon Ft. Sumter. The ardor of patriotism faded with the first rainy night spent huddled over a fire to keep warm. The enthusiasm washed away with the first winter night spent on the picket line keeping watch for an enemy advance. The first long roll of the drums calling a man to stand with his fellows and advance upon an enemy line cured him of his eagerness for battle forever.

Anticipation of a peace and final defeat replaced motivations now long absent and forgotten. Israel, Philip mused, did not conquer the land given them in a day, and the union army under Grant and Buell had not yet won the war. Philip recalled with sadness the faces he only saw within his memory.

Philip took hold of Sammy's arm and said, "We should go find our pards."

"Huh?" Sammy replied.

"Our pards, find those who fell and see to their deportment."

"Yeah," agreed Johnny. "We should go find our wounded and see that they made it to the aid stations."

"Not just them. The dead, too." Philip's voice didn't betray what he was really thinking. Harper needed to be found, the man to whom the most harm could be forgiven if wished. Philip needed to know the truth about his state.

Mule eyed the dead bodies nearby with their full haversacks. "Yes, we need to bury our pards."

"Let's go retrace our steps," Philip said, rising to his feet, "and see that they are taken care of by our own." The peacefulness of the moment seemed incongruous with the human carnage not more than a few feet away. The birds returned to their songs, and a breeze blew over sweaty brows.

The group secured a pass, gathered their gear, and walked through crowds of soldiers relaxing upon the ground. They approached the church but found it impassable with every square inch of ground covered by some prostrate form. The bodies were Confederate and in pitiable condition. To avoid the pleas for water and aid, they gave the grounds a wide berth. Some of their number could be there, but the task of finding someone in that throng was more than any of the group cared to undertake. Finally, they reached the last line of battle. A few forlorn forms lay where they had fallen, and still more were in rear of where they had fought, having collapsed before finding succor.

"Here's ol' Parker," Johnny called out. At his feet lay a still form, face down. The group gathered round the body. His name had gone unanswered at roll call, but the first of their number to be found dead, where hope was to the contrary, came as a shock.

Philip remembered the old man, old even by most of their company whose ages ranged from twenty-five to fifty-five. Though the older men did not stand the rigors of army life well, Parker had stood with the youngest of them without complaint. Worse still, Philip knew Parker's brothers, wife and children. The man's brothers were in other Ohio regiments, and his own son was possibly somewhere on this field. Father Parker, they called him. Though he was quiet and unassuming, his presence in camp was always a welcomed sight.

"Sarah's going to be heartbroken," Sammy said, speaking of Parker's wife.

"Someone's already robbed him of his shoes!" Mule exclaimed in disgust. The body was stripped of cartridge box and belt. "Detestable thieves!"

"C'mon, let's gather him up over there by that tree," Philip directed. "Cover 'im with his sack coat." With as much care as they could, they carried the bodies of Parker and the others to a shady spot and laid them to rest side by side, six in all from the regiment. Some they recognized only by sight, and others, such as Parker, they knew from their own company. Moving on, the group found a few recognizable faces that had made it to a low spot in the field and were under the care of several divisional surgeons. They gave the wounded water and some food before leaving to see if anyone had made it farther to the rear.

"We'd look forever back that way. Let's go back to that hill where we caught up with the regiment earlier," Johnny said as the group started to range far apart. The bodies of both days' fighting were numerous. One poor man, his jaw and front teeth missing, was especially desperate for something, though no one could understand his gesticulations.

"I think we came along this way," Philip said as he pointed toward a heavy copse of woods. Here the dead were numerous and of no particular army. Some were leaning against trees with their coats and shirts ripped open to expose stomach and chest wounds. They lay still with heads hung low as if in deep sleep. Many were stiffened and starting to distend from mortification, making them appear to be fatter in the midsection. Hands reached up in claw-like grasps, and mouths puckered. Philip became increasingly disturbed at the number of bodies and the obvious pain in which they had died.

Ahead was a clearing and the most disturbing sight, equal to the ninth level of Hell. An open space in the trees, roughly twenty yards in length and ten in width, revealed a low-lying pond. The gently sloping ground around the water writhed with wounded from both armies lying side by side on muddy banks relieving their thirst. Many were still, but an equal number of sufferers had life in them. Stepping around the pond was impossible without kicking some poor soul.

"God have mercy," Philip whispered. Hospitals and aid stations on a battlefield were sights of suffering, but the sufferers knew help was on the way. This pitiful mass of bodies was a collection of all the desperately wounded on this side of the battlefield who had one desire in mind: water. They lay on top of each other, and those who did not have the strength or life left to draw their heads out of the water were pushed into the soft banks by those coming after. In their fight to relieve their thirst, man desecrated man to lap a few mouthfuls of bloody water.

"Have you ever seen the likes?" muttered Sammy.

The pond was tinged muddy red, and a few corpses were visible floating on the surface.

They gazed in silent disgust and horror. Mule asked, "You think any of our pards made it this far?"

"Don't know," Johnny said quietly, "and I don't think I can look."

"Don't we got to try?" Mule insisted.

"We din't come here to help all them," Johnny retorted. "We go down there, and they're all gonna want our help."

Philip couldn't look away from the sight, but he shook his head, rejecting Johnny's argument. "But what if some of the company made it back this far? We formed up not far from here, so we have to look." He stepped out from the trees into the small clearing. There were a few live men who'd had their fill of putrid water and cleared the way for others. The living huddled in groups and looked at the whole beings walking among them with feverish eyes. Philip stepped by the forms carefully, looking at each face. A few men with only superficial wounds crouched by supine forms, offering what care they could.

"Yank, got any water?" a man in Confederate uniform asked Philip.

"No, sorry, Reb. Emptied it awhile back for some of our wounded. I might have some hardtack left." He opened his haversack.

"Be obliged. My pard here is in a bad way," the man said and smiled weakly. At his side was another young Confederate soldier with a bad shoulder wound. The bones of the man's shattered arm were visible, and the man had done what he could to bandage it.

"You don't look wounded," Philip stated.

"Came back lookin' fer him," the man said and motioned to the wounded man.

"That's what we're doing."

"I suppose I'll be a prisoner since you'uns is walking about freely."

"Suppose so, but not by us." Philip handed the man two crackers. "Here's what I got left."

"Thanks." The man put the hardtack in his coat pocket. The man at his feet was still but breathing in shallow drafts.

Johnny looked from around Philip's side, his face tight. "He ain't gonna make it, huh?"

"Don't know," the man said. "I came lookin' fer him and finally found him here. He's been feverish but don't seem to be in much pain no more."

"Smoke?" Sammy asked as he and Mule joined the group.

"Been out fer days," the man said.

"Mule, give 'em some of that tobacco you carryin'," Sammy ordered. Mule hesitated. "Just do it, ok?"

"Uh, ok." Mule fumbled around in his haversack and pulled out his tobacco.

"He's gonna lose that arm, fer sure," Johnny stated.

"If that's all, he'll be lucky," Sammy said. "What's yer name, Reb?"

"Murdock, Stephen Murdock, and this is Willie Hawkins from Mississippi."

"Ohio, Samuel Henderson, and this is Theo Mueller, John Henson, and Reverend Philip Pearson." Sammy looked at Philip and blushed. "Sorry. Philip Pearson."

"Reverend?" Stephen perked up.

"Used to be," Philip said, glaring at Sammy. "Just a soldier now."

"Would you do the last rites fer my pard here?" Stephen asked. "He's a Catholic and I don't know the Mass."

"I only know the Methodist extreme unction, not really the last rites."

"C'mon, Philip," Sammy urged. "Man of the cloth or not, you're the closest thing to the Almighty His'self we got at the moment."

"We don't give last rites. Mule here'd be more qualified to give last rites than I," Philip protested. "I can pray fer him, but it's up to God and his soul to work out the rest. Nothin' I can say or do's going to change his eternal reward."

"Well, I s'pose anything would give him comfort," Stephen said. He looked straight into Philip's eyes.

"All right, faith or no, every man deserves a good prayer." Philip knelt next to the wounded man and removed his forage cap. As if directed, the others removed their headgear and bowed. Mule crossed himself. "Father God, we seek Thee with humbled hearts and distress at the end of this battle. Many a man has lain here on this field and met his eternal reward, and we ask that if this man's soul be prepared that You welcome it, and him, into Your rest. If his soul be not prepared, Father, allow him breath to confess his trespasses to You with earnest repentance. Receive this brother in arms into Your grace and all who bore the battle this day and have passed from this life. We beseech Thee, O Lord, in the name of the Christ. Amen."

"Thank you, Yank," Stephen said while looking into the peaceful expression of his sleeping pard.

Philip stood, feeling awkward. This was the first time in over two years he had practiced anything remotely spiritual. Silently, Philip returned the forage cap to his head and walked away from the group, stepping his way around the banks of the pond.

"Take care of yourself, Reb," Sammy said and followed Philip's footsteps. One by one, the group left the two Confederates.

The bodies surrounding the pond ceased to be individual humans and looked, instead, like so much fallen timber. So numerous were they that Philip found himself unable to feel anything for each individual face he encountered.

Those who were able to move about tried to care for those whose strength had left them. All were in a terrible state of filthiness from the muddy banks and blood. Stepping over each form took concentration, lest a wrong step plant the foot square upon the hapless wounded. The dead gave neither complaint nor moan, only an unsettling feeling of having disturbed their eternal slumber. The wounded pleaded with feverish eyes. Philip quickened his pace to escape the labyrinth, and his last careless steps sent two men into spasms of pain and cursing. Making the tree line and away from the clearing, Philip caught his balance against a tree trunk, hugging it as if he needed it to maintain his balance. Breathing heavily, he closed his eyes tightly to remove the visions of suffering.

"You're not well," Johnny said matter-of-factly.

"I'm fine," Philip puffed. "Just needed to get out of there."

"In all my days, I never want to see something akin to it again," Johnny said when the others caught up. The pond of suffering lay behind them with its bloody banks and its writhing forms.

"We goin' ahead?" Mule asked, his face paled by the effort and the scene.

"Yeah, we got to get to that hill we attacked earlier," Sammy said.

"I'll be fine. I just need to catch my breath," Philip said and exhaled slowly. "Let's find a different way back."

"Never heard the priests give such a prayer," Mule said, his eyes full of wonder.

"That's 'cause you papists don't pray at all," smirked Johnny. "You too busy talkin' to Christ's mother."

"Don't start with that, Johnny," Mule glowered. "I don't see you on yer knees much prayin' ta anyone."

"I left that far behind before," Philip said. "Don't any of you get any ideas about me performing your last rites, neither."

The trees were dense and used in typical southern farming fashion of allowing stock to run wild in the woods. The group stumbled upon a pack of pigs feasting upon the remains of a soldier. Squealing and grunting in anger at the interruption, they disappeared into the thickets, leaving their supper behind.

"Oh Lord, that is abominable," Johnny froze, his mouth agape and his hands listless against his thighs.

The body was opened in the chest cavity, and the swine had been feasting upon the entrails that were scattered about the corpse. The poor soul was missing his fingers and toes. The body had been stripped of socks and shoes by human scavengers. He was a Union man, and his Kersey blue trousers were open at the crotch. As if the pond hadn't been enough of a sight, to behold this beastly feast was enough to cure any man of the desire to find glory at the end of a bayonet. The group gave the scene a wide berth and hurried to leave the forest. Emerging from the trees, they stood to the right of their previous attack upon the hill. The ground was cut and furrowed by shot and littered with dead and wounded men. Several men were carting off the stricken as best as they could, to the discomfort of their charges.

Silently, they made their way to the crest of the hill amid the corpses of the enemy infantry and horses, walking down the gentle rise to the firing line marked by wads of paper cartridges and bodies. A few faces caught their attention, but they were of men only seen in the other regiments of their brigade. Finding their own firing line mostly void of casualties, they made their way straight down the hill, following the path of their own advance a few hours earlier. A few forms littered the direct path. They found a few men matching the names missing from the roll. They had been struck down as they marched and were forgotten by those marching next to them.

There was a melancholy wafting about the former field of flame and death. Examining the bodies of once life-filled comrades was vexing, for they had neither means nor tools to bury them. Each was left where he was discovered and noted. Far to the rear by the tree-line, more wounded gathered. Having found a few of their missing, the group presumed they would find more with the wounded. The gathering was larger than it had looked from a distance, for as the group drew closer, the whole field for a distance of several hundred yards was covered with the prostrated from both sides.

Philip was disturbed by not having found the one corpse he most sought. When he came across the bodies of men who had enriched his life, both in and out of uniform, he offered a short prayer. The condition of their souls had been decided long before he found their lifeless forms. The most he could do was hope their souls were written in the annals of God's kingdom.

They were greeted with something akin to the pond, only less disturbing. But the suffering was no less disagreeable. One by one, the group found a man from their regiment or company and stayed to comfort them until Philip was the only one still wandering from form to form. The search was strangely less emotional now, as if the brief exposure to so many wounded men was enough to harden his heart to the pleas from those obviously near death. The entire area stank of blood and excrement, and the flies buzzed over opened wounds like carrion beasts waiting for the desperate struggle for life to cease. Philip was helpless to improve their fate, and he was little inclined to try. He wondered what good came from his former life of ministry that he should be here right now, with nothing remotely godly to encourage a man. It was of little use to him, so why should it be of use to anyone else?

A Confederate lay near his feet, holding in his bowels, with protruding intestines crudely bandaged up with dirty rags. He suffered more from the sunlight burning his eyes than he did from the ghastly wound in his stomach. Try as he might, he could not avoid the bright rays of the sun nor spare a hand to block the light lest his bandage fall apart. Philip watched the man turn his head from side to side, squinting until his eyes were but slits. Something struck Philip's heel, and he swung around quickly.

"I'll be damned. It would be you," a voice croaked.

"Harper," Philip muttered, more to himself than to the man clutching his pant leg.

"Water, Parson?" Sergeant Harper said weakly. "Do you have any water?"

"No," Philip replied and knelt down next to the man and removed his canteen. Harper was gut shot. Of all the wounds that left a man alive and in great pain, this was a sure date with the grave digger. His face was pale, and his whiskers looked strange upon his cheeks, like that of a porcupine whose quills were flared in defense. There was little more than a drop left in Philip's canteen and little source for more save for that pond. Blood caked around Harper's undershirt. A pool of fresh blood rose and fell from the apex of the hole in his stomach. Philip let Harper sip the last of his water from the canteen.

"I'll bet you've waited fer this day, eh?" Harper said when he had drunk what was available.

"No," Philip lied. "I rather expected it would be the other way around with me being at your mercy."

Harper smiled and then grimaced as pain shot through him. When the spasm of pain subsided, he said, "I certainly would not have given you a second look."

"I know. I expected to find a corpse and not you alive; rather wanted a corpse."

"You'll get yer wish soon enough."

"I don't want that," Philip said and looked at his nemesis. He could not ignore the compassion that he felt. For all the other suffering beings about him, this one man elicited what should not have been possible.

"It don't matter what you want, Parson. It's gonna happen, though I'd be grateful if you could find me some more water."

"I'll see what I can find," Philip said. He looked around him for any canteen on the field.

"It wasn't easy hating you, you know," Harper wheezed. His stomach wound oozed blood and bile out of the hole. "I had to work ... work at it." Harper made a soft chuckle, and then a labored breath.

"I'm surprised I made it hard for you. I didn't give you much to like. You want any food?" With the wound in Harper's gut, Philip immediately realized the foolishness of his offer.

"Just water. Water is all I want. Will you get me some, Parson?" Harper sighed deeply and closed his eyes.

Philip stood and looked around. Most likely, not a drop of water was to be had among the prostrate forms. The only possible source lay up toward the hill in the canteens of the dead. The walk did not take him far before he encountered his first corpse. The young man had expired from a wound to his groin and his once-Kersey blue pants were stained with blood. His face looked peaceful as if he had merely fallen asleep. With luck, his canteen still held some water. Philip shook the canteen and felt the swish of water. As gently as he could, he removed the sling from the man's shoulder. One down.

Soon, Philip had several canteens draped over his shoulder. In spite of his feelings about robbing the dead, he was able to apply Sammy's logic of relieving the dead of essentials he, and not they, required. That done, he wandered looking for where Harper lay.

"Sergeant?" He nudged Harper's shoulder, and Harper opened his eyes. "Lee? Here, drink." Philip lifted Harper's head and held a canteen to his lips. Harper woke and drank in gulps. Each swallow sent paroxysms of pain rippling through his torso, but he took the next gulp greedily all the same. Philip moved the canteen away from Harper's mouth.

"More . . . please," Harper whispered.

"There's more, but let it wait. What good is more water if it kills you?"

"I'm dead anyway. Since when are you worried about my life?" Harper's face contorted in another spasm of pain.

"Then I wouldn't get the pleasure of watching you die," Philip replied with a smile.

"I see." Harper bit his lower lip and tried to smile in return. "We Harpers never forgave you Pearsons fer what you did to Henry."

"We Pearsons regretted it, for sure. It did little good to insult the living for the sins of the dead," Philip confessed.

"Damn right," Harper said and coughed. "Henry was a damned fool, and we swallowed what he done, but he was family." He eyed the canteen and motioned with his head. "More."

"Ok, but only a little more," Philip said as he lifted the canteen to Harper's lips. "You know, that's why I left the pulpit."

"You a terrible liar; it was my complaint to the bishop what did it. Can't say I's disappointed. You never should have taken it from yer Pa," Harper sputtered.

"That we can both agree to," Philip replied.

"Ma and Pa always defended you to us, even after Henry's funeral. They couldn't bring they'selves to break with what they saw as the church," Harper said. "They knew all too well you were right."

"I see," Philip replied, unsettled by the candor. This was not the attitude Philip had expected, and he was surprised, perhaps as surprised as Harper, at the civility of the conversation. "They never came back for services, and I assumed the obvious."

"That hurt Ma the most. She needed a word from the Good Book the way your Pa used to preach it. She liked your preaching just as well, but Pa wouldn't have nothing to do with the shame he felt," Harper said breathily. *Shame?* Philip thought. He had figured their behavior for anger. Everything he thought about the whole unpleasant affair, including his part in it, was wrong.

"If it's worth anything," Philip admitted, "that's why I was glad to give up the collar. It was either that or suffer a public defrocking by the bishop after your family demanded my collar. I wasn't my father."

"I was personally gratified when you did, and so was Pa, but Ma never got over the line being broke like that and some other preacher comin' in from Columbus to take yer place. She always said it should be kept in the community. Ma died of a broken heart. Pa never went to meetin' again."

"You want hardtack?" Philip asked to break the line of conversation. He reached into his sack.

"No. Stomach's too painful to put nothin' else in it." Philip just nodded and looked over the field. "Parson, will you present Communion fer me?" Harper asked after the minute of silence.

"What? Communion? I've got neither wine nor other sacrament," Philip said, shocked at the request.

"What do that matter, Parson? Just wine and bread served from some pewter plate and cup. Ain't it what it represents that matters?"

"Yes." Philip looked away, shamed by the obvious.

"Who's givin' the Eucharist?" another voice from behind Philip asked.

Philip turned to see a wounded Confederate. His arm was bloody, and he had a gash across his forehead crusted with filth.

"What? No, I'm Methodist." Philip protested. He felt himself dragged into actions that he felt nothing for and had no wish to repeat.

"I'm Methodist," another voice farther down the row of wounded called out.

"Lutheran," another said.

Harper grinned. "Ma would want her son ta partake before death and ta seek absolution fer his misdeeds. Yer the only preacher I knows of here." In a moment of pain, he grimaced, clutching his bandages, as if to emphasize the need to be timely.

"You realize that there's nothing sacred about the bread and cup that'll absolve you of your sins? All of you realize that?" Philip said louder, hoping to yet escape. "It's a reminder only and not a salvation."

"That don't matter, and shut up about it," Harper said gruffly. "We need comfort in our last hours. Do what ya' shoulda' done fer my family. Make up fer that, and I'll let my brother rest in peace."

Philip bowed his head, speechless, and nodded. Surrounding him were men rousing from their death throes, looking upon him with expectant eyes. A Federal soldier attending to one of the wounded walked up to Philip and enquired of his spiritual services.

"What's your name?" Philip asked him.

"John, sir."

"Okay, John. See if the surgeons have any wine they can spare. Quickly, man."

John looked and spotted the surgeons moving in the distance. He began to run.

Philip took off his haversack, fished out his tin plate, and untied his blackened cup. The crumbs of hardtack from the bottom of his haversack would be the bread, and any wine found would be the cup. As a Methodist, he didn't believe they became the actual flesh and blood of Christ, so his unorthodox supplies would serve just as well as the bread and wine he once served in services. These were not parishioners. They had not gathered under his auspices but were here because men preparing to die needed company. After spreading the crumbs out on his plate, he also fished from his coat pocket a beat-up Testament.

Harper lay at Philip's feet in agony. Others rose on elbows or shaky arms to bear witness of the ritual as they had been accustomed to in their own upbringing.

Seeing the men's behavior and knowing something unusual was happening, Mule walked over and asked Philip what was going on.

"I suppose I'm giving communion to these men," Philip said and shrugged.

"The Eucharist?"

"Yes, I suppose that it is, with much less ceremony as I've been taught it."

"Bully!" Mule exclaimed and slapped Philip excitedly upon the shoulder. "What can I do?"

"Give this to the men around us. Pitch in some of your hard tack."

Mule hesitated only a moment before he dug into his own haversack. Looking at the thick cracker he fished out, studying it briefly as if it were to be his last, he broke off the ends, adding them to the plate and began handing the plate around.

John, the man Philip sent for wine returned with an outstretched up. "Here's what I could get. Ain't much."

"Take it around to the men when I say so," Philip said.

Philip stood for a moment with the Testament clutched in his hand. His stomach trembled. His mind went blank. Opening his Testament, he scanned a few pages, hoping to find something to trigger what he was to say. There was the normal liturgy for passing around the bread and the cup, but it seemed inappropriate in this place and with this variety of beliefs. He looked into their faces, and the words came to him.

"Some believe the cup of wine to be the blood of Christ and the bread to be made into His body. Some believe it is just a remembrance, as the Jews of old were to observe the Passover in remembrance of their deliverance from Egypt. You may call it the Lord's Supper or Communion or whatever. It is our partaking of the death of Christ and remembrance of what was done before us. What is common among our beliefs is that Christ came to shed blood and offer Himself as a sacrifice. The Jews of old sacrificed in a temple to cover their sins. Christ, at the last supper, broke the Passover bread and handed it to his disciples, saying, 'Take and eat, for this is my body broken for thee.' "

Mule bowed before each supine man to offer him a chunk of hard tack. Those able-bodied enough to move on their own gathered around as Philip's pards began to distribute their remaining hard tack crumbs. Watching them, Philip felt a chill creep over him. He closed his eyes a moment before continuing.

"The gathering of disciples did not fully understand what it was that Christ was doing as He washed their feet as a lowly servant would. Then He said of the cup, 'This is my blood shed for thee. Take it and drink,' " He nodded to John that he should begin distributing the wine. John went from man to man and helped those who needed help to sip of its contents. Some crossed themselves, and others bowed their heads in silent contemplation. A few refused the cup for it contained spirits. He sent a questioning look to Philip, who simply pointed at a canteen. Those who would not drink wine accepted a drink from a canteen with the same reverence.

"I have not blessed this bread or this cup," Philip continued, "for I do not believe that they represent more than what they are. You may believe otherwise or have been raised in a different assembly. What matters is that we believe in a Lord who gave His life as a ransom for us. If partaking of this eases your mind as you face death, remember that our Lord has prepared a place for those who are to come after Him. If you call Him Lord, then partake of His sacrifice in remembrance of Him."

Philip looked down at his Testament and realized he had forgotten to read from it. He closed his eyes and bowed his head to pray.

Chapter Nineteen

"You still with me, Hube?" Robert asked over his shoulder. A sudden stumbling behind him gave an answer.

"I'm here."

Robert and Huebner, along with the few others from the regiment who had remained standing after the fighting ceased, slowly made their way back to their original camp. The Indiana Company was left where the regiment halted, and the Missouri boys bade them farewell and shook hands with the new veteran soldiers. Having ended the day in an unfamiliar area, the group meandered until Robert finally got his bearings. The way back was strewn with wreckage. Haversacks, knapsacks, canteens, horses, caissons, and the dead littered the way. The path to and from the main headquarters was now indistinguishable from the trampled grass. The campsites were mostly silent, but for the wounded.

Following the road they had taken when running for their lives, Robert and Huebner came into view of their encampment. Although the tents and layout were familiar, the emptiness was not. A few forms moved among the tents. Wounded men lay about in the company streets, and the tents were overflowing with the dead. A few Confederates moved about, caring for their wounded and, likewise, the Federals within arm's reach. Robert felt a little out of place.

"Mitchell," a voice called out.

Robert turned and recognized a familiar face.

"Tom? Thomas Stossel?" Robert said with surprise as he hurried to meet his boyhood playmate.

"Hube and Steiner? You both made it!" Stossel pumped Robert's hand and gave him a hearty hug.

Soon, others from the regiment gathered to welcome the prodigal sons who had arrived. A modest gathering of thirty men, none of whom were officers, stood in the parade field to catch up with each other. Many had scattered when the regiment broke and found themselves swallowed up in other commands. Some had finally been driven from the river bank and back to camp. None condemned those who'd sat the fight out. Instead, all were glad to see more of their pards still alive. Stossel belonged to another company, and he and Robert only connected when fatigue duty did not take either of them away. But now, with no command structure or duty to be performed, the survivors were able to finally catch up.

"I was taking Corporal Mueller to the rear," Stossel explained, "when the regiment disappeared! I turned around and only saw this line of Rebs coming through our camp. Me and Mueller made the best time we could, but I was certain not to be captured if I could help it. I left Mueller at the church, and I ran fer the river."

"We down at river, too!" Huebner exclaimed.

"I thought we was done fer. I didn't see no one I recognized the whole time I's there. I saw some fellers drown tryin' to get to them boats what came later," Stossel said as he kicked at the dirt. "I wished I'd found you. Was pretty lonely down there."

Huebner look down at his shoes. "We bury Hildebrande by river."

"Hilde fell?" Stossel asked, surprised. "Didn't think that old warhorse could ever die."

"Hube shamed the rest of us into getting back into the fight," Robert said and nudged Huebner. "We fell in with some Indiana regiment the rest of the time."

"Hube, you do that?" Stossel asked and smiled.

"Robert exaggerates." Huebner blushed slightly.

"Who else fell?" Stossel asked.

"Whole company, for all we know. Hammel fell early in the morning along with Gustavson and a few others. We had twenty of us when we met down at the river. Five of us made it this far. The others fell out this morning, but none of us knows where," Robert recounted.

Stossel mopped his brow and said, "Maybe some of them is at the aid posts. We can go look for them."

"Piper fell in last battle," Huebner said.

"Damn, not going to be anyone left from our synod," Stossel said and pursed his lips.

Robert shook his head at Huebner and said, "We don't know that."

"I know."

"I lost sight of most of them when we took that hill. They could have all been injured and fallen out of the line." Robert felt a little guilty for lying. He'd seen Piper and Keppler, along with several Indiana men, get eviscerated by a solid shot.

"I want to find him," Huebner said and turned to leave.

"Hube," Robert called after him. "Wait! We'll all go."

"That's odd," Stossel exclaimed and nudged Robert's arm.

A lone Confederate was approaching a large tree set off from the parade ground. He dragged something heavy behind him. The man stopped when he looked up and spied the crowd of federal soldiers. After giving them a steady look, he resumed his chore. At the tree line, the man sat down heavily and took off his hat. Huebner made for the Confederate.

"I'll go see what Hube is up to," Robert said and began walking away from the group, "and then we'll go comb the wounded for some of our men."

As Robert approached, Huebner said, "We need a shovel. He wants to bury his pard. He says they's a pond back there with lots of wounded and dead."

"This yer camp?" the Confederate soldier asked.

"Yes, 25th Missouri, Peabody's command," Robert replied.

"I see. My pard died of his wounds a while ago by that pond, wanted to give him a peaceful place for a grave and away from that hellhole, pardon my language."

"I know the place, Robert said. "We used to water our horses at it before the battle."

"My pard, Willie's his name, Willie Hawkins. He was my friend. He was wounded when we took your camp," the man said embarrassed.

"You fellas the ones that charged up at us over and over?" Robert asked.

Huebner looked from man to man. "I go get shovel." He left Robert to make time with the Rebel.

"Yes, Willie fell after the second charge up the hill. You punished us fer the privilege," the man said.

"Did you take lots of prisoners?" Robert asked. "We're looking for the rest of our regiment." Robert pointed with his thumb to the men gathered in the parade ground. "That's all that's left."

"Some. They was taken to the rear right away."

"What's your name?" Robert asked.

"Stephen Murdock, 6th Mississippi. We was marched to the rear after the attack on your camp, but I came back lookin' fer my pard Willie here."

"I suppose you'll be a prisoner then," Robert replied.

"Yes, s'pose so. After I bury Willie, you can march me off," Stephen said.

"I reckon the provost guard will do that shortly."

"I combed your camp lookin' fer Willie. Lots of men died over night in the tents. I s'pose most of them is from yer regiment."

"I saw a few of them tents. It will be a long while before any of them tents is used to sleep in again."

"See that grave?" Stephen said and pointed to the fresh mound of earth and crude cross on the other side of the tree. "I buried one of your men there. He helped me look fer Willie. He said his name was Hammel."

"Hammel? A first sergeant?" Robert asked surprised.

"Don't know. He didn't have on a coat."

"You did that fer him?" Robert asked again. He thought for sure Hammel died right there in the rear of the firing line.

"Was the least I could do for the man. He kept me company while I looked for Willie."

Huebner stepped up with a shovel and thrust it at Stephen. "Here. Shovel."

Stephen reached for the shovel in Huebner's hand, but Robert took it first.

"No. Hube and I'll do it."

"Let Reb do it," Huebner said.

"See that grave?" Robert said to Huebner and pointed. "That's First Sergeant Hammel. This Reb buried him this morning."

"You do that?"

"Yes, this morning. He helped me search for my friend."

"This looks like a good a spot as any," Stephen said, pointing a few feet from him.

"Ok, Hube, let's dig us another grave."

Robert walked to the spot and drove the shovel deep into the soft earth. The spectacle soon drew a crowd. They couldn't have imagined a less likely sight than two Federal soldiers digging a grave for one Confederate soldier while another sat idly by. Robert simply pointed to Hammel's grave and told them who had dug it. It was enough to set several men after shovels. Soon, they made a deep hole and laid the body of Willie Hawkins to rest. Sweating from their labors, the Federal soldiers paid their last respects, despite knowing that this man possibly was responsible for any number of deaths within their regiment. One by one, each man returned to the camp, and soon only Robert and Huebner remained with Stephen.

"I reckon you'd find a provost guard by headin' toward the river," Robert said at length. "C'mon, Hube, let's leave him alone with his pard."

"I know what it like to lose friend," Huebner said with a last look at Stephen before he turned away.

Robert led Huebner away from the camp and along the road.

"We go look for Piper?" Huebner asked.

"Go look for more wounded," Robert replied. "That Reb's regiment was the one that attacked us yesterday morning."

"But he bury Hammel," said Huebner, confused.

"He did. Peculiar."

"We go to that pond?" Huebner asked.

"No, not someplace I want to go to if the Reb's description is correct."

"Then where we go?"

"To that hill, I guess. You won't leave it be until you've found Piper, huh?"

"No, I want find Piper. I want find all *meine Freundin*."

Robert had no answer and kept moving forward. His face was grim.

Organization was returning to the armies as marching columns, accompanied by music, moved down the Corinth–Shiloh Road. With that reorganization came the return to military discipline and a cessation of errands, such as the one Robert and Huebner were on. But order had not yet visited the 25th Missouri, and Robert felt obliged to take advantage. Nearby camps returned to life with the sounds of men talking and wood chopping. But for the acrid smoke hanging in the air, the scene looked entirely ordinary.

Robert worried about Huebner. His other pards were now gone, leaving only himself as Huebner's sole mess mate and friend. Though he'd been less than friendly with the waif, the battle and the sudden maturity evinced in the man was heartening. Yet he was still an innocent youth whose approach to life was childlike. What would he do now that everyone he trusted and liked was gone?

"You think they still alive?" Huebner asked.

"I'd like to think so."

"I'll be sad if they gone."

"Me, too," Robert said, running his hands through his hair under his cap. "Did you grab any of that hardtack back at camp?"

"No. I'm *hungern*."

"Lucky for you I grabbed some extra," Robert said and winked. Huebner's normal youthful expression was absent, as it had been for most of the battle. "Here, have a few. The rest are for anyone we find wounded."

"*Ja, danke*." Huebner took the handful of crackers offered him. "No *Kaffe*?"

"Nope. That's back at camp," Robert replied, wishing he had stopped to fill his cup when he had smelled the brew.

"Went to tent, full of wounded. All knapsacks are gone."

"Oh? We skedaddled quick like, so that doesn't surprise me."

"My prayer book was with knapsack," Huebner said and pursed his lips.

"Sorry about that. I suppose I'll not be seeing my nice shirt again, either, the one my wife made."

"Belong *mein Vater*. It belonged to his *Vater*." His expression was distracted and distant. Most personal items were easily replaced, but not all.

Robert had personally discarded more than one keepsake item sent with him on his trip to St. Louis when the regiment was mustered into service. He was loaded down with useless minutia before he was further encumbered with the thirty pounds of uniform issue. All of the things that would not fit into his knapsack were sent home, save for the few trinkets squirreled away into its crevices: a pocket image of his wife that broke not too soon after their first march, a pistol sold to someone else in the regiment who sold it to a sutler soon after, and a Testament that was far too large to be carried about in the field.

"The whole camp was stripped clean," Robert blurted out for no reason but to break the silence.

"*Ja.*"

Robert stopped a moment and looked at the rise looming over them. "I think that's the other side of the hill we charged earlier."

Upon the crest, highlighted by the skyline, were the discernible forms of men and horses lying about. The litter of equipment ran all the way up the slope where the Confederates were forced to retreat. A few wounded enemies lay across the path.

"Water," whispered one man whose chest sucked in and out in sickening, slurping exhalations. He lay listless with hands cupped across his chest as if laid out upon his death bed for all to view. His hands were bloodied, and his face was pale.

Robert leaned down and let the man drink from his canteen. His mouth was reddened with blood, and he smacked his lips repeatedly as if something distasteful lit upon his tongue.

"Thank you," the man said and resumed his labored breathing.

"I'd move you to an aid station, but I don't think you'd make the trip," Robert said.

"Not without a litter," the man rasped.

"Who knows? Maybe someone will happen by with an ambulance," Robert said, knowing the chances to be slim.

"I thought ambulances were for generals to sleep in," the man said with a thin smile.

"Lucky for us they ain't that many generals around," Robert grinned before moving on with Huebner in tow.

"Them Rebs not bad when not tryin' to kill you," Huebner said.

"Not much different than you or me," Robert replied.

"They stand for wrong."

"Well, they stand for it pretty good."

The two reached the crest, and, after a few steps, started down the other side. In the distance was a patchwork of blue and butternut homespun.

"Aid station," Huebner said and pointed.

"Right." Robert scanned the area for a moment. "There. I think that was where we stood." Robert pointed to a spot amid a row of torn forms.

"*Ja.*"

The whole regiment had stood and traded blows with the Confederates on the crest long enough to mark the line at their furthest point of penetration. They surveyed faces familiar and not, cold stares, and eyes clenched shut as they walked along the old firing line. Many of the Indiana men from their adopted company had fallen on the slope. Robert looked at one particular lad who was boasting not hours before how he'd survived his first fire fight the night before and how the fear was over. A minié ball had torn through his temple and lodged in his forehead, now visible as a huge lump between the dead man's open eyes.

"They no here," Huebner said.

"No, I think they might be farther down there." Robert motioned toward another clump of dead to the rear of where they stood.

Huebner looked at Robert with sad, questioning eyes. Robert nodded. Huebner walked down the slope to the pile of remains. Robert knew who was there and how many were among the fallen. Robert headed down and immediately ran across Adolf Goedeler with a hole where his Adam's apple used to be. A few more paces and he was beside Huebner, who stood above Piper, or what was left of him. The solid shot had bowled through his chest, dissecting him messily. His shoulders and head were separated from his waist and legs, which were mingled with the remains of three others. Georg Primble was nearby, having been hit by the same shot, taking his arm off, along with a nasty gash into his neck.

Huebner stood for a while looking down into the faces and seemed to be transfixed by something that Robert failed to grasp.

"*Getötet, ganz getötet,*" Huebner spoke finally.

"Yes, all killed," Robert repeated.

"Gustavon, Hildebrande, Piper, Goedeler, Primble—*ganz getötet,*" Huebner said and wiped away a tear.

"They will be missed." The words seemed so shallow. Robert felt foolish even as he spoke them.

"*Ja,* missed."

Huebner dropped to his knees by the bodies. His shoulders sank low to match the expression upon his face. A soldier approached looking weary and carrying a book. Robert watched him walk up the hill and stop suddenly as he realized he was being watched. Hesitating, the man continued on toward them.

"Hube, someone's coming," Robert said softly.

Huebner didn't stir but stared into the pile of corpses. The blood in places was still fresh but was mostly matted on the grass and drying upon the rent uniforms of the lifeless.

"You men don't happen to have some food on you? The wounded down there are pretty hungry, and I'm collecting canteens and hard tack for a communion of sorts," the man said as he approached.

"We have a little of both," Robert replied.

"Pards of yours?" They saw he was ashamed to ask.

"Were," Robert replied.

"Communion?" Huebner asked.

"Yes, some of the mortally wounded insisted I give them something of a last hope," the man replied.

"I'm Robert Mitchell, 25th Missouri, and this is my pard, Josef Huebner. We came looking for some of our missing." Robert extended his hand, and the man took it.

"Philip Pearson, 24th Ohio," the man replied. "I don't mean to be ghoulish, but those men down there are dying for water. Can I have those canteens?" Philip motioned to the deceased. The expression on his face combined pain and expectation.

"I don't think anything is still useable from them after that solid shot did its work. But you can have mine," Robert said as he un-slung his canteen and handed it to Philip.

"You give last rites?" Huebner asked.

"No, I'm not a minister any longer. Nothing I can say is any more meaningful than what you yourself can say to the Almighty."

"So you won't do it?" Huebner pressed.

"I . . . I can't."

Huebner looked from Robert to Philip and then back to the bodies. His downcast face said what he refused to.

"All right, I'll do my best, but I'm going to do the Protestant version as I don't know the Catholic," Philip stated. He knelt down beside the torn bodies. "What are their names?"

"Georg Primble *und* Johan Piper," Huebner replied. "They Lutheran."

"Oh," Philip started. "Well, they are dead anyhow, so I suppose it don't matter much."

"We don't know these other men from the Indiana regiment," Robert added.

"Indiana, you say?" Philip asked.

"*Ja*, 36th Indiana. We join them yesterday," Huebner answered.

Philip muddled through an unconvincing prayer for the dead and their families. He apologized sheepishly for his unprepared delivery, but Huebner seemed relieved.

"It's over. They rest now."

"Yes, Hube. They rest now," Robert agreed.

"Over for this life," Philip added.

"*Ja*, this life."

"What other life is there?" Robert asked, knowing full well the reply he could expect from the former preacher.

"Would that it was only that," Philip replied, "to live and then to die and fade into nothing. No, it is not that easy."

"Heaven or Hell, do they really exist, or is it just something we came up with because we want the one to avoid the other?" Robert sighed. "I'm no blasphemer, but this day brings me to question that there is anything good or waiting for me should I draw my last breath."

"If it were not so," Philip explained, "then many of us are deceived and to be pitied." Philip pursed his lips and shook his head. "We all believe in something and know something else exists beyond the corporeal existence we know now. Every society encountered around the world believes in something of the afterlife. Either they are all deceived, or there is something of the truth in it. I believe there is the truth in it and a God who communicates with us about it."

"It's what to live for," Huebner said. "No life after, no life now."

"Did Piper and Primble believe in Heaven? Who's to say they are there now?" Robert said.

Questions of life and death always disturbed him. It meant admitting that he did not really believe in what he'd grown up hearing from the pulpits of the Lutheran church. It all sounded like convenient, wishful thinking. The hope that *something* was there that one could neither see nor know for certain always challenged his beliefs. It was always good to hope for the good and avoid the bad, but who was to say who was to go where and why?

"Don't matter," Philip said. "We see the Moon in the sky, but we don't know that it is not made of cheese. We believe that it is not by intuition and fact. We believe there is a Heaven and a Hell out of intuition and fact from the Good Book itself. One day, someone might journey to the Moon to discover what it is exactly and why. No one will venture back from Heaven or Hell to confirm them, but we believe that they are there and earnestly hope for the one while despising the other."

"So, in the long run, no one knows where they will end up, do they?" Robert asked and looked hard at his companion.

"No, not true, Robert!" Huebner protested. "I know."

"Hube, how can you know? What rules did you break or how many confessions did you give before you broke some more rules? To know is impossible, for sure." He was feeling uncomfortable, given the ghastly tumble of bodies in front of them.

"Not true!"

Philip cleared his throat. "There is a way, but I think you are inferring that it is impossible to know empirically, in which you would be correct. Faith must know when the mind cannot. It is faith that saves us from Hell and faith that instructs us to know where we go when we depart this earth. Huebner here believes where he is bound and, if I may be so bold, you do not."

"No, I guess right now, I don't know for sure what is going to happen to me, or them, or you, for that matter," Robert said, chaffing and uncomfortable at the turn of the conversation.

"Well," Philip said, standing, "I got men of my regiment dying for this water. I thank you for allowing me to take it. Enjoy the life you have right now, for days like this one show us how short life can be."

Philip walked slowly down the hill to the throng of wounded. Robert brooded to himself and tried not to provoke Huebner into more needling over issues of faith and the afterlife. He believed what he believed and wanted to keep it that way.

At last Huebner whispered, "Not know if Piper *und* Primble *mit Gott*, only hope they are."

"Sorry, Hube. I didn't mean to put that all in doubt, just wondering as to the reality of it all," Robert replied stiffly.

"*Du* believe what want. I believe Primble *mit* Gott. Piper only hope," Huebner said and stood up.

"Why Primble?" Robert asked and stood as well, dusting the grass off of his Kerseys.

"Because Primble believed in *Gott und Jesus*," Huebner replied with an air of fact and conviction.

"How did he know? How do you know?" Robert asked.

"Because *Jesus mit* inside," Huebner said and motioned to his chest. "Primble, too."

"We heard the same stories and sermons from the same ministers growing up, Hube, yet I do not believe, nor am I any more convinced now. I suppose it is not my time yet."

"Suppose," Huebner said sadly.

"We'd better get back before dark," Robert said and stepped away from the corpses of their friends.

"*Ja*, get back."

It was getting dark, and the sun was dipping in the western skyline behind the trees beyond the river. All was at peace, and the birds returned to their evening song. But for the distant booming of cannon, all seemed right with the world. Burial parties moved about and started a grisly work that would take many days to complete with clumps of earth and crude head boards growing out of the reddened soil like weeds. It was not work Robert relished.

Huebner was quiet the rest of the walk back to their camp. Fires danced in company fire pits, and something of the normality of army life crept back into the Union tents. Coffee boiled. Cook fires heated evening meals of scrounged hard tack and greasy salt pork that had not been hauled away by a jubilant enemy.

More of their pards had found their way back to the regimental camp with tales similar to Robert's. Some stood quietly, trying to hide their shame in cowering under the bluffs of the landing all day and night. Robert was surprised that so many made their way back, even some who had been prisoners until they managed to escape. It was still a pitiful few, but Robert felt good about seeing so many familiar faces rejoin the company. The dead had to be moved out of the tents, and the parade ground quickly turned into a grave yard as the work to inter the corpses went into the night. Those who had died from Robert's company joined ranks next to the grave of First Sergeant Hammel. The others, Confederates and a mingling of union men no one recognized, were buried in mass graves. It was pitch dark by the time the last grave was dug.

By the firelight, Robert sat as he always did before taps, watching the flames dance. Huebner sat nearby with the others who had survived the day, and no one spoke. Nothing needed to be said. Huebner hadn't stumbled, bumbled, or caused his usual mayhem. No one teased or joked, and Robert felt queer about the change. He'd lost his simpleton friend. Had it not been a victory? Robert wondered. But he was to weary too give the question much thought.

Chapter Twenty

Stephen Murdock sat among a sullen group of his compatriots under the watchful eye of several Federal soldiers. The silence was more from exhaustion than from defeat, but both weighed heavily upon each man. No longer soldiers but prisoners of war, they felt naked without their weapons and traps. Only the uniform and the guards reminded them of their former avocation. They were all enlisted men, with a smattering of non-commissioned officers, but no one felt compelled to take charge. They just sat and brooded. Stephen was scooped up by a roving provost marshal's patrol soon after sundown and made the lonely trek to Pittsburg Landing with a collection of other sad-looking and disheveled Confederates. They exchanged names and unit affiliations, but that was the total of the conversation. Stephen might as well have been alone. He knew the questions on everyone's minds. Would they be paroled, or would they be marched off to some prison camp? And which would be worse? To be paroled and face his father as a defeated warrior or to suffer some other fate in a vermin-infested stockade like the one at Johnson's Island in Ohio? Starvation or ignominy, it was a tough call. His mother would be relieved to see him still alive, but what of father? Would Stephen be welcomed to the table? The elder Murdoch opposed secession, but when it came, he had little choice but to become a patriot. The paddle steamers took turns disgorging supplies and troops from the landing, and a constant parade of people marched up the slope through a fire-lit path. The Union army they had once defeated in battle was looking very alive and ready for more. Some of the prisoners were wounded in the extremities and tried to find some comfort on the hard ground. Others were being cared for by a motley collection of Federal and Confederate medical personnel. Stephen sat cross-legged and watched another column wind its way down the road and out of sight. After constant activity, the inaction was unnerving.

Stephen remembered the young Dutchman and his American pard he'd met after burying Willie. He wondered at the Yankees' surprise that he had interred their company first sergeant. Would not they have done the same for him? Hammel had suffered so all through the night, and his last vigil with Stephen as he searched the tents had been a comfort. There were so many to bury, so many whose last moments were filled with pain or hallucinations of home. Stephen had ended his search of the camp in sorrow. Without understanding why, Stephen was compelled to bury this man whose company had calmed and steadied his nerves. That Dutch boy and the older soldier made small talk with him as strangers often do. They were both from Missouri and had stood their ground on that very hill earlier the other morning. There was a familiarity born of common tragedy and respect, nonetheless, when combatant enemies met in truce. Stephen hitherto had never been in close proximity to an enemy upon such terms. He was now beholden to these people, and he could hope in nothing more than their sense of decency and lenient treatment. The few guards that stood about with bored expressions were not even needed as many in their group had wandered up and surrendered earlier in the day. These enemy guards gave freely of their water to the wounded, and, but for the loaded weapons at shoulder arms, the assembled mass of men could have been mistaken for a friendly gathering. Stephen appreciated the graciousness in victory these men exhibited. Perhaps they were just as tired as their prisoners, but even the officers spoke with quietude to them. The orderlies gingerly began carting over the more seriously wounded prisoners from the aid stations, swelling their numbers. In the dark, Stephen recognized no one. A companion at this moment, even that Yankee first sergeant, would have greatly raised his spirits.

*****

Michael slumped in the saddle with a weak hold on the reins and his head nodding jarringly with each downward clop of the horse's hooves. It was three a.m. the last time he had looked at his time piece. Michie's Crossroads stood once again in a tumultuous sea of moving bodies. Despite the need, the men moved lazily like a slow stream down the road and past the crossroads tavern. The windows were all still lit, and men lounged on its steps. Polk's Battery lumbered noisily down the road, and its crews tried both to maintain balance and to drift off to sleep, doing neither for more than a few precious minutes at a time. Three days before, Michael was a subordinate, but at this early hour moving back to Corinth in defeat, he was in command of the whole battery. They were down a few guns and minus about as many in crews from injury, capture, and death. Comrades and friends were missing, some never to return. He felt the absence of so many comrades, but the absence of Mahoney was the hardest to bear. The next man in line would fulfill Mahoney's role in the command structure, but he could not fill the hole in the relationship with Michael. The battle all over but the final retreat and rearguard, an unlucky shot had snuffed out this man of piety. Michael, grieving, had been forced to appoint another to his place almost immediately.

"Sergeant Wilson, assume the post of first sergeant and get the guns limbered up," Michael had said to the man.

"Sir," Wilson had replied in a voice broken by dryness and fatigue.

"It'll be official when we get back to Corinth."

"Yes, sir. Are we really going all the way back?"

" 'Fraid so. It's back to our starting point for us."

"Yes, sir."

The command structure was built to make every man replaceable. But only the functions were duplicated. There could be no other Albert S. Johnston in command of the army, and P.G.T. Beauregard proved unable to do anything but occupy his place of command. Wilson was a good soldier and sergeant, but he was no Charles Mahoney. Almost fifteen years Michael's senior, Mahoney had been more than a friend. He had been a comrade and mentor. Michael would work closely with Wilson as he had with Mahoney, but would it be as before? No, it didn't seem likely. The burial had been quick and brief behind the barricades of fallen timbers. Three other officers perished in that bounding shot that had found the officers' mess. Michael remembered standing by the grave site and doing something unexpected. He had crossed himself.

Now, amid the voiceless clamor of men on a dreary march, Michael wondered what caused the involuntary movement. Mother's catechism and the days spent avoiding the parish priest as a lad in Natchez, Mississippi, were so far removed from the present that Michael was forced to reconcile the incongruence. Something of those times, when he was brought into the presence of the crucifix behind the pulpit, must have stuck. Michael smiled to himself as he thought about Mahoney's possible reaction to his Catholic gesture over the grave of a Protestant. Yet it was never that simple. Did not charity say that the lost were the ones to be found? But for some reason, Mahoney was equally concerned for Michael's spiritual state. His father's descriptions of the sectarian strife in the old country were foreign to him, with Protestants and Catholics fighting one another. Perhaps it was a strictly Irish affair. Perhaps he didn't think enough about what the differences were to even care that Mahoney was of a different faith than he. His father would have cared. Indeed, until Michael entered into life as a man, he'd never had a close friend of the Protestant faith. It just never happened in the circles his family kept. The Catholics in Texas were different from those in Mississippi and Arkansas. The faith of the Mexicans and natives he played and worshipped with had a mystical quality. They took their religion much more seriously than even his Irish Catholic father. Mahoney had been a different animal. His faith was neither mystical nor serious.

"What's so wrong with the faith of St. Peter and the true church of their Catholic fathers?" Michael had asked one evening after a long day of drill, although it stretched his own shallow understanding of the origins of the Protestant movement and Catholicism.

"Oh, something about St. Peter's Basilica needing a renovation, and the dispensing of indulgences to keep out of Hell for a price would about do it,"

Mahoney replied with a chuckle.

"But then why aren't you a Lutheran instead of a Methodist? Why was Wesley better than Luther?" Michael asked.

"Honestly? Because my mother was a Methodist," Mahoney admitted. "That and it just happened to be the faith passed down to me."

"But is there any real difference? Why the separation? Why not be some other Protestant sect?" Michael said. Mahoney shrugged. "Just not the way it is. Would you say that some of those Catholics fighting for the Federals are wrong or just of a different mind than those fighting for us?"

"Don't really know. It ain't a question of faith, just of politics and loyalty, I suppose."

"So, if they sin no more than you sin just by wearing a different uniform, then might the same be said of anyone of a different faith? We have different ways of expressing faith, despite the designations, but serve the same God. No matter what faith you grew up in, there is a need for Christ to cover all."

Those words still rattled around in Michael's mind as the road wound past Michie's and down the long way to Corinth. The Eucharist was something Mahoney did not partake of, one of the things that separated a Catholic from anyone else. Same wine, same bread, same prayers said in all reverence, but yet not the same. In the priest's hands, the bread and wine became something else in accordance with Christ's words to eat of His flesh and drink His blood or be found to have no part in Him. Not a big difference, perhaps. They still prayed to the same God the Father. Not like the savages roaming the Texas western plains who worshiped trees and birds and the elements. There was a difference there: many gods versus one God. Those were differences he could understand.

But now Mahoney had gone to whatever reward he most believed in. Heaven or Hell was waiting for his soul, and everyone's soul, once the last breath was breathed. There was another difference between the two men. Mahoney said he knew for sure where he was going, not just wishful thinking or vain hoping but knowing. Not even the parish priest would make such a declaration of himself. Was not there a balance to life with the good and the bad, sin and righteousness being held in account? Michael puzzled over this whenever he felt the most vulnerable or tired. His friend and the man whom he would gladly have called a brother was gone. He said he was clean as if the sacrament held by the priest in the chalice had done something permanent for him though he had never partaken of it. There was a difference that was hard to place with the man. Perhaps his own faith was the difference. Not the upbringing, but the faith. If faith was it, then was there more that he didn't understand about what makes a man accept death without feeling remorse for what lay ahead? Michael lowered his head and allowed the movements of his horse to lull him into a fitful nap.

Chapter Twenty-one

Philip stood vigil over Harper's corpse until he couldn't feel his feet. The passing had not been quiet or peaceful, but wracked with violent spasms of breath tingled with blood. Mule, trying to make Harper comfortable, had joined Philip in his ministrations. But there was nothing to be done to relieve the man of his torment. His last moments were filled with invective and cries for absolution from his sins. In the end, Harper pleaded with Philip to prevent his soul from experiencing the torments of Beelzebub. Philip replied that he needed not to seek it from him but from the Christ. Only Jesus could do such a thing, he said. Philip prayed aloud, stumbling over his words in frustration and exhaustion. The man was silent now, but Harper's passing was as trying to Philip's soul as the man's life had been.

"I don't want to go to Hell. Don't leave my father with more grief. See to it," Harper whispered.

"I cannot do anything for your soul."

"See to it!" Harper wheezed and weakly grabbed Philip's arm.

"Do you renounce the ways of this world?" Philip asked.

Harper mumbled something, closing his eyes tightly.

"Do you receive the Son as the only answer for your sin?"

Harper shuddered again and took in a deep, labored breath.

"Pray this to God and by faith accept the forgiveness and the spirit of life."

Harper did nothing, nor did he seem even to have heard Philip. A weakened hand gripped Philip's arm.

Philip, confused, tried to jerk it free.

"Say . . . say it," Harper struggled.

It was Philip's turn to squirm. Whether Harper was going to burn in Hell or live in Heaven was forgotten as the memory of the serious breach of his trust confronted him again. Harper was using his last breaths to drag out of him something that could easily be given but not easily felt. He had done his duty and even pressed it to Harper in as plain a language as he could. Harper's soul waited in limbo, and the only thing Harper could do in return was extract a last moment of retribution.

"I'm sorry," Philip said weakly. "I'm sorry I did not comfort you and your family in your loss at the funeral. Will you forgive me?" Philip cringed inwardly as he waited for what must be the last words to be spoken between them. So many in the intervening years had been wasted in hateful speech.

Harper forced a wry smile, or something akin to a smile. He blinked several times and looked at Philip, and his mouth moved in silent words.

Philip gripped Harper's shoulders. "What?"

"Momma for . . . forgave y . . . you. I d . . . do not." Harper drew in a shallow breath, threw his head back, exhaled slowly, and finally fell still.

Philip and Mule sat looking at the still form without a word. It was over for Philip. After so many arguments, so many harsh words, he didn't know what to do. His nemesis was removed, and his greatest, most secret, prayer answered. The torment of those memories might finally be put to rest now that the reminder of that day so long ago no longer needed to be suffered.

"You think he did it?" Mule broke the silence.

"Did what?"

"Gave it to God."

"Only God can know. I hope he did, or he wasted his last moments for an apology."

"And what about you?" Mule said.

"What? What about me?"

"It's something you should have done long ago."

"Apologized?" Philip stared at Mule, and then looked down at Harper's corpse. "Yes, I should have."

"He gone?" Sammy asked as he knelt down beside Philip.

"A time ago," Mule replied.

Sammy just nodded and said, "We've done all we can fer our wounded. We ought to head back to the regiment."

A lesson in humility from a crass and unrighteous man, from a crass and unrighteous family, was not something Philip could easily swallow. But how could he not? Forgiveness should have been sought from the parents years ago, the day after, even. But he was too proud. Who were they to question his pronouncement of truth? Pride for pride, was it not? That was the day his ministry died, as did his desire for it. But for a simple phrase, a simple question, he might have avoided years of strife.

"Harper didn't die in his sins," Mule whispered to Sammy.

"We don't know that," Philip shot back. "But he did accept my apology."

"You apologized?" Sammy asked, surprised.

Mule shrugged, looking at Philip. "I think he did."

"He stayed alive long enough to hear me say it," Philip said with bitterness. "I needed to say it and knew I needed to when I found him. He was dying, and instead of spending that time in confession to God, he wanted to see me squirm."

"I think he did you a favor," Sammy said.

Philip swallowed hard and was loathe to admit it. He already felt better and free.

"Let's go collect Johnny and make our way back," Sammy said and stood with a grunt.

Philip raised his hand, "I can't feel my feet at the moment." Raised upright and unsteady, Philip brushed his Kerseys off and straightened his empty canteen on his shoulder. He breathed an easier breath and stepped a lighter step, free from an unseen burden. Taking one last look back at the body as they walked away, Philip grudgingly thanked Harper for forcing him to make his own confession of sin.

Normality, if it could be called that upon the battle-scarred landscape, returned to Grant's army, but the cleaning up after the battle took weeks. The stench of rotting horse flesh hung heavily in the air as the thousands of carcasses festered where the beasts fell. The carnage was worse near artillery positions, marked by disabled gun carriages and caissons and horses felled in their traces. The carcasses were burned where they fell in great bonfires that burned the day and night. The dead humanity that littered the open fields and recesses of the forests were also collected or buried where they fell, Confederates in trenches and Union men wherever space allowed. Burial parties worked in shifts, and no one was exempt from the disagreeable work.

Reunited with many more of their comrades, the 25th Missouri regained their command structure and were again falling into the routine of drill, though much time was spent cleaning up their former parade ground. Robert and Huebner sat idly by their company cook fire with the remains of their company. There was no revelry such as they enjoyed before the battle. It was a forlorn affair spent mostly in the remembrance of fallen pards. It was April 11th, and both men were tired, as was everyone who took a place about the fire.

"I hear Halleck replaced Grant in command," a sergeant said absently.

"Some say he was drunk during the battle."

"Some say we killed twenty thousand of them Rebels."

"We must've lost many more."

"Newspapers sayin' we lose eight thousand killed and wounded."

"We lose too many *Kameraden*." That was from Huebner.

"*Ja*, Hube," Robert replied.

"Adjutant tol' me our returns was fifteen killed, three hundred wounded and missing," the sergeant added.

Robert picked absently at a blister on his palm from hours digging burial trenches. In the heat the bodies were an awful sight and grotesquely warped. They could do nothing more than dig and toss the bodies in like cordwood. It became an act of rote movement after a day. No longer did the humanity register upon his mind. Their tents had been used to house the wounded, making a hospital compound immediately after the firing ceased. New stores were soon appropriated, as were replacement equipment. The men of the company crowded into new Sibley tents.

New uniforms and tents did not replace the missing men. Standing above the parade ground as the sun was setting earlier in the evening, Robert had looked out upon the wrecked tree line below the encampment and the hill the Rebel host had charged. Now, everything was quiet. No longer did he need to fear the whip of minié balls past his ears or the barking of cannon. The fading sunlight cast shadows that hung long upon the matted grass. Spare and cast-off equipment still littered the gentle slope leading down to the uneven parade ground. No shot was fired in anger, but his nerves were tense. A finality escaped him.

Looking out to where it all began, Robert heaved a sigh and exhaled it slowly. Faces he would no longer see flashed through memory in sad procession. Gustavson growling at Huebner, Hildebrande chiding Gustavson about his age and experience, Piper worrying about making corporal, and he, Robert, fussing over Huebner like a mother hen. Huebner was alive and well but no longer the Jonah of old. He still looked to Robert with boyish affection, but he had also grown. He made it to formations on time, and though he still loved his *Kaffe*, Robert's own coffee was now safe.

It was a few minutes before Robert realized that Huebner was standing next to him in silence. Robert nodded at him.

"I miss Gus, too," Huebner said.

"*Ja*, me, too."

"Robert?" Huebner put his hand on Robert's shoulder.

Robert turned and looked into the eyes of an adult, set softly in sallow sockets, showing depth of insight and personality. "*Ja*, Hube?"

"*Danke*, Robert, *für Sein mein Freund, meine Kamerad.*"

Robert stared at his companion, dumbstruck. He was being thanked for something that he could barely call himself, friend and comrade? A few days before, he would consider himself a long-suffering acquaintance, not a friend.

"*Ja, ich bin dein Freund*, Hube." Robert let that hang in the air without reply from Huebner. The shadows grew long upon the field, and the light turned a cyan hue. Birds tittered among the leafless tree branches and fluttered about, jostling for position.

Earlier, he and Huebner, along with a few others, said goodbye to Hilde, Gus, and Piper, standing beside the freshly dug graves by the landing. When they first signed up to fight, the war had seemed an adventure. That fantasy, like Huebner's innocence, was gone. No longer playing soldier but becoming one had altered Robert's view of himself. He had run for his life and, but for Huebner, would have stayed at the landing. His view of himself as a responsible soldier for the Union had also been left upon the field of battle. He couldn't bring himself to call his actions cowardly. Certainly, no one else would. Neither could he call himself heroic.

As the rays of the sun sunk below the western horizon, Robert bade farewell to his self-misconceptions. He was neither a hero nor a skulker. He was but an average man put through horrific experiences.

Sitting now before the fire, Robert watched the dance of the flames and listened to the fire talk. Robert loved these tired and sometimes vulgar men. He was thankful for those around him and those he had lost, for they made him the soldier he was. He would stand with these men should the long roll sound and call them to arms again. He met the enemy in the field at daybreak and stood beside his friends to receive their fire. He feared and fought and carried the grief of loss.

He wasn't the soldier he once thought he wanted to be. He was the soldier Shiloh made him to be. They met at Shiloh, and Shiloh made them comrades.

Made in the USA
San Bernardino, CA
24 February 2015